FROM VALOR, TRIUMPH

FROM VALOR, TRIUMPH

Ray Mayer

Deeds | Atlanta

Published by Deeds Publishing in Athens, GA
www. deedspublishing. com

Printed in The United States of America

Cover design by Mark Babcock

ISBN 978-1-947309-31-9

Books are available in quantity for promotional or premium use. For information, email info@deedspublishing. com.

First Edition, 2018

10 9 8 7 6 5 4 3 2 1

PREFACE

This is a novel celebrating the valiant American warriors whose courage and sacrifice enable the American Dream. This book is humbly dedicated to the soldiers, Marines, airmen, sailors, and so many others of the great United States of America whose sacrifices beyond measure keep us safe in our beds at night and enable the American Dream to be a reality. God bless them one and all.

This is a work of fiction. All the characters herein, excepting the national figures, are completely fictional and none are fashioned after any one person. The national figures did not do or say anything portrayed in this book, although what is attributed to them is consistent with what they could have said or done. While the book is molded into historical events, there are exceptions, most notably rewriting the modern history of the South Carolina 2nd Congressional District and that the 15th SOG is entirely fictional. Otherwise, for the reader's benefit things such as military jargon, abbreviations, and radio call signs have been simplified. Still, they are unavoidable and therefore a Glossary appears in the following pages.

What was my goal in writing this book? "All good books are alike in that they are truer than if they had really happened and after you are finished reading one you will feel that all that happened to you and afterwards it all belongs to you; the good and the bad, the ecstasy, the remorse and sorrow, the people and the places and how the weather was."— Ernest Hemingway

It is my hope and prayer that you the reader finds that here.

—Ray Mayer

GLOSSARY

3: The number denoting an operations officer, S-3 (battalion, brigade and regiment), G-3 (division and corps) or J-3 (higher HQ).

5: The number denoting an executive officer, XO.

6: The number denoting a commander or leader; or directionally the area behind.

15th SOG (Abn): The 15th Special Operations Group, Airborne, a fictitious organization comprised of U.S. Army Reserve and national guard Special Forces (Green Berets) and Special Operations Forces (Rangers and attachments); and consisting under various headquarters over the years of a Group Headquarters rotating between three company installations: Company A at Camp Marion, South Carolina (woodlands and swamp warfare), Company B, California (desert warfare), and Company C, North Carolina (mountain warfare).

60: Short for M-60 machine gun.

201: Military individual personnel file.

Abrams: The U.S. M1A1 main battle tank, armed with a 120mm cannon and three machine guns with advanced thermal and night vision systems, protected by advanced armor, and capable of highway speeds, since the early 1980's was and remains the most lethal tank in the world.

AC-47 Spooky: A DC-3 aircraft converted to military use as a gunship, it was armed with several miniguns and advanced targeting systems;

early versions were known as "Puff the Magic Dragon;" replaced by the AC-130.

AC-130 Spectre: A modified C-130 Hercules propeller driven transport airplane modified to a gunship role, in service since 1966, it has very sophisticated integrated sensors, navigation and fire control systems and its weapons, fired from the port side, include a 105mm howitzer, a 40mm Bofors cannon and a 25mm Gatling gun (early models had the Bofors and two 20mm Vulcan cannons).

ACAV: See **APC**.

AH-1: See **Cobra**.

AH-64: See **Apache**.

AK-47: The Avtomat Kalashnikova 47 (later the AKM, a designation often ignored), the Russian (and later copied by other Soviet bloc countries and China, the latter being the Type 56)) standard automatic rifle of about every nation and group unfriendly to the United States. It fires a 7.62x39mm round, shorter than the U.S. 7.62mm round.

Alpha: Phonetic for the letter A.

AN/PRC 25 or 77: See **PRC 25 or 77**.

AO: Area of operation.

Apache: The AH-64 Apache attack helicopter began in 1986 to replace the Cobra. Armed with a 30mm chain gun and AGM-114 Hellfire air-to-surface missiles with advanced targeting systems, it was, and continues to be the finest attack helicopter in the world.

APC: The M113 armored personnel carrier was a fully tracked vehicle designed to carry a full squad of infantry. Its aluminum alloy armor provided good protection against small arms fire and shrapnel, but was vulnerable to RPG's and mines. An APC usually mounted an M2 .50 caliber machine gun and often one or more M60's (in the ACAV mode, behind steel gun shields). There were variants with mortars, anti-tank missiles, automatic grenade launchers and air defense systems. Beginning in the early 1980's, the M113 was replaced by the Bradley Fighting Vehicle, which had similar survivability disadvantages, which by 2007 was replaced by up-armored Humvees and MRAPs (Mine-Resistant Ambush Protected vehicles).

ARCOM: Army Commendation medal, subordinate to the Bronze Star, awarded for merit or valor.

ARVN: Army of the Republic of Vietnam, soldiers of South Vietnam; friendly forces.

BAR: The M1918 Browning Automatic Rifle designed by John Browning, firing .30-06 cartridges from a 20 round detachable box magazine and weighing a hefty 24 pounds, saw limited service in WWI, extensive service in WWII in Korea and some service in Vietnam until replaced by the M60 machine gun.

Barrett: See **Sniper rifles**.

Battalion: An Army organization usually consisting of three rifle companies, a weapons company and a staff for administration (S-1), intelligence (S-2), operations (S-3) and supply (S-4); commanded by an 0-5 Lieutenant Colonel with the highest-ranking NCO being an E-9 Sergeant Major.

Beehive: The name given to anti-personnel rounds fired primarily by artillery and tanks, each round containing thousands of finned metal darts called "flechettes."

Bird: Aircraft.

Black Hawk: The UH-60 Army utility helicopter that began replacing the UH1D Huey in 1979.

Body armor: A vest designed with advanced fabrics and ballistic plates to protect the wearer from shrapnel and small arms bullets; it replaced the flak jacket.

Bradley: The U.S. armored and tracked fighting vehicle that replaced the M113 Armored Personnel Carrier. It was armed with a 25mm chain gun, an M240 machine gun and often a TOW anti-tank missile system. The M2 series were Infantry Fighting Vehicles while the M3 was a Cavalry Fighting Vehicle.

Bravo: Phonetic for the letter B.

Bronze Star: A U.S. decoration awarded for valor (with "V" device) or merit in a combat zone.

Bunker: A fighting position ranging from a reinforced foxhole to larger sandbagged and otherwise fortified structures.

Bush or field: Any area outside of a city or military installation.

C rations or C's: The usual food of the infantryman, containing in a cardboard box canned meat concoctions of various palatability and depending upon the size of that can, cans of fruit in heavy syrup (the most desired); a can of cake; a can of cheese or peanut butter and crackers; packets of sugar, cream, and salt; more often than not a small pack of cigarettes; and sometimes a plastic spoon. The cans were opened with a P-38, acknowledged as one of the more brilliant inventions.

Captain: An O-3, CPT; a company commander, denoted in call signs by the number 6, or a staff officer.

CAS: Close air support.

CCP: Casualty collection point.

CH-47: See Chinook.

Charlie: Phonetic for the letter C; and short for Victor Charlie, slang for Viet Cong, VC; sometimes more respectfully "Mister Charles."

Cherry: An inexperienced replacement.

Chinook: The CH-47 (MH-47 for the spec ops variant) twin rotor heavy lift helicopter since 1962 capable of transporting a full platoon and/or hauling considerable cargo inside and/or under. It handled better than smaller helicopters at high altitudes and its armament was beefed up considerably for the war in Afghanistan.

Chop: Verb of the acronym for "change of operations."

CIB: Combat Infantryman's Badge, a coveted Army badge awarded to combat experienced infantrymen.

Claymore: Short for the M18A1 claymore mine, a directional plastic coated mine implanted with affixed stakes which fired C-4 plastic explosive electrically via a clacker device attached to the mine by wire or mechanically that propelled some 700 steel ball bearings with a killing range of about 50 meters; grunts usually carried a couple of them, each weighing about 3.5 pounds. Communist forces had a similar, larger version.

Cluster fuck: Any poorly organized event.

CO: Commanding officer.

Cobra: The AH-1 attack helicopter, often called the "Snake," that began in 1967 to replace the Huey gunships (and later was replaced by the AH-64 Apache); an awesome weapons platform more resembling a shark, it was only about 36" wide with a pilot and a gunner in tandem and was armed with rockets fired from pods and a nose mounted 7.62mm minigun with six Gatling-style rotating barrels capable of firing 2,000-6,000 rounds/minute, a 20mm cannon of similar design, or a 40mm automatic grenade launcher firing 400 rounds/minute.

Company: An army or Marine organization, in the infantry usually consisting of three rifle platoons and a weapons platoon and a headquarters section; commanded by a captain with the highest-ranking NCO being an E-8 First Sergeant (or Top sergeant).

Company grade: The first three officer grades, Second Lieutenant (0-1), First Lieutenant (0-2) and Captain (0-3).

Concertina: Razor wire fencing, an improvement over barbed wire, used to form obstacles around military positions.

Conex: The "Container Express" container, a metal shipping and storage container, 8'6" long by 6'3" wide by 6'10" high with double doors; often acquired for efficient and effective use in the field as ready-made command posts, bunkers, dispensaries, etc.

Corpsman: A U.S. Navy medic assigned to a Marine Corps unit, the Marines not having their own.

CP: Command post; at higher levels known as a TOC, tactical operations center.

CSH: Combat Support Hospital.

CW: Chief Warrant Officer; see **Warrant Officer**.

Delta: Phonetic for the letter D.

Delta Force: The 1st Special Forces Operational Detachment—Delta, the most elite of the U.S. Army's special operations forces, on par with the U.S. Navy's SEALs and other top tier special operations forces such as the British Special Air Service ("SAS") (after whom it was modeled) and the Israeli Sayeret Matkal. While its roots go back to the late 1970's with legendary warrior Charlie Beckwith in the lead as a relatively small unit specializing in counter-terrorism, hostage rescue and direct action, it grew in size to 1,000 personnel, roughly one third of which being actual operators.

DEROS: Date of estimated return from overseas.

DShK: Pronounced "dishka," a Soviet heavy machine gun in 12.7mm [or .51 caliber (so slightly larger than the U.S. M2 .50 cal)]; used by enemy forces in Vietnam, Iraq, Afghanistan, etc.

Dust off: Medical evacuation via helicopter.

E: Phonetic for the letter E; also a letter denoting enlisted grades, e.g., E-3 for Army Private First Class or E-6 for Staff Sergeant.

Evac: Short for evacuation.

F4 Phantom: The supersonic fighter-bomber that was the mainstay of the U.S. air forces in Vietnam and continued in service until after the First Gulf War.

FAC: Forward air controller who in combat guides close air support aircraft.

FDC: The fire direction center of an artillery unit consisting of gunnery and communications personnel and equipment, usually conjoined with a TOC.

Field: See **Bush**.

Firebase: Short for a Fire Support Base (FSB).

Flak jacket: A heavy, bulky vest designed to protect the wearer from shrapnel while ordinarily inadequate to stop a bullet; later developed to body armor.

FNG: Fucking new guy; a replacement.

FO: Forward Observer for calling and directing artillery, usually at company level a field artillery lieutenant.

Foxtrot: Phonetic for the letter F; sometimes "fox" for short.

FSB: Fire Support Base; usually of a battalion or more, used as a base of operations for a prescribed period of time for combat and support units and offering buildings or bunkers, perimeter concertina wire, helicopter landing zones; artillery and/or mortars; long range communications; and decent if rudimentary living conditions.

Fuck: Prolifically employed in the U.S. military as a verb, adverb, adjective, noun, etc. for far beyond the original profanity for sexual intercourse.

Gook: Derogatory for an Asian.

Green: Inexperienced.

Green Beret: See **Special Forces.**

Green tab: A tab worn on the uniform epaulets by an army officer or NCO in a troop leadership position.

Grunt: Slang for an infantryman.

GSW: Gunshot wound.

Gunnery Sergeant: A Marine E-7 NCO, typically referred to as "Gunny" and serving in a line company as the operations and training sergeant or at battalion level as a recon platoon sergeant.

H&I: Harassment and interdiction artillery or mortar fires at suspected enemy positions or avenues of travel intended to disrupt enemy movements or rest.

Hand grenade: A hand thrown bomb; the U.S. versions armed by pulling a pin and releasing a spoon triggering a fuse of 3-5 seconds; variants being fragmentation ("frags") (the "pineapple" grenades of WWII and Korea, the M26 and M61 series of the Vietnam era and later the M67), concussion and incendiary (thermite).

Hotel: Phonetic for the letter H.

Huey: Taken from the designation of "UH" for "utility helicopter" and denoting the various models, the troop and supply transports being the UH-1D or "slicks" because while they often were armed with a manned M60 machine gun at each of the two crew doors, they carried no rocket pods or nose guns as did gunships (UH-1B or UH-IC). Pilots most often were warrant officers or company grade officers. While the Army began replacing the Huey gunships in 1967 (see Cobra above) and the UH-1D's in 1979 with the UH-60 Black Hawk, many Huey helicopters remained in service in the 21st century.

Humvee: The common name given to the High Mobility Multipurpose Wheeled Vehicle (HMMWV), which in 1984 began to replace the M151 ¼ ton "jeep" and other light duty vehicles. Humvees first saw combat in Operation Just Cause in 1989 and future combat operations prompted expanded usage in many variations.

IED: An improvised explosive device; a handcrafted mine or bomb; formerly referred to as "booby traps."

JDAM: "Joint Direct Attack Munition," smart bombs.

KIA: Killed in action.

Kilo: Phonetic for the letter K; also short for KIA.

Kilometer: 1,000 meters, .62 mile; called "klicks" or "clicks."

Klick: A kilometer.

Lieutenant: There are two grades of lieutenants in the Army, Marines or Air Force. A Second Lieutenant, a 2LT, an O-1, the basic officer grade, is ordinarily an Army platoon leader or a Marine platoon commander; familiarly referred to as "LT" (pronounced "L-T"). A First Lieutenant, a 1LT, an O-2, ordinarily is a company Executive Officer ("XO") or a staff officer.

Lieutenant Colonel: LTC, an 0-5, a battalion commander or senior staff officer.

LP: Listening post, a posting of usually a couple of men during night hours outside a unit lines for early warning purposes.

M2: The venerable Browning M2 heavy machine gun, firing .50 caliber rounds with a range of 1,800 meters (2,000 yards), in service from 1933 to present day; (compare DShK.)

M4: See **M16.**

M16: Short for the M16A1 and later modifications, the primary infantry weapon for U.S. armed forces; a rifle weighing 8 pounds loaded and firing 5.56mm (or .223 caliber) rounds fully or semi-automatically from a 20 (later 30) round magazine, the small bullet being propelled supersonically by a considerable powder charge having the effect of tremendous damage upon impact and exit. While early M16's were prone to malfunction due to design, grime, humidity, and/or faulty ammunition, by 1967 they were mostly reliable and ultimately praised as one of the finer weapons in the world. In the 1990's the rifle began to be replaced by the M-4 carbine and later modifications, a shortened and improved version.

M24A1: See **Sniper rifles**.

M60: The basic "light" machine gun. Weighing a hefty 22 pounds, it commonly was called "the pig." It fired belt-fed 7.62mm (.308 caliber) rounds at a cyclic rate of better than 500 rounds/minute. Mostly replaced by the M240 and M249.

M82/M107: See **Sniper rifles**.

M113: See **APC**.

M203: A 40mm grenade launcher attached under the barrel of an M16 or M4 rifle.

M240: The U.S. military designation for the Belgium/French (copied from the German) general purpose machine gun that began replacing the M60 in 1977. It weighs a hefty 27 pounds and can fire its 7.62mm ammunition at over 750 rounds per minute.

M249 SAW: The Squad Automatic Weapon, a "light" (22 pounds) machine gun, in service since 1984, fires the same ammunition as the M16 and M4 rifles, but from linked belts fed from a 200 round ammo box under the weapon.

M1911A: The basic U.S. pistol firing 230 grain .45 caliber rounds semi-automatically from a 7 round magazine. Originally issued in 1911, the A1 model in 1924, it remained a mainstay for over 60 years.

Ma Deuce: See **M2**.

Mike: Phonetic for the letter M; also short for minutes, meters, etc.

Mk 19: Pronounced "Mark 19," it is a crew served 40mm automatic grenade launcher.

MRE: "Meal ready to eat," replaced "C" rations.

Murphy's Law: "Anything that can go wrong will go wrong" and dozens of similar sayings based upon the same; the absolute truism regarding the essential "cussedness" of inanimate objects is attributed to aerospace engineer Edward Murphy and sometimes intervened by Air Force Captain John Stapp.

Napalm: Jellied gasoline.

National Liberation Front: See **Viet Cong.**

NCO: Noncommissioned officer, a corporal or grades of sergeant.

NVA: North Vietnamese Army; more correctly the People's Army of Vietnam (PAVN); sometimes short for individual North Vietnamese Army soldiers.

O: A letter denoting officer grade, as in O-3 for captain; or words beginning with that letter such as operational, observation, etc.; phonetically "Oscar."

OD: Olive drab.

OGA: "Other Governmental Agency," usually referring to the CIA or other intelligence agency.

OH-6: The OH-6 ("OH" being designation for light observation helicopters) Cayuse "Loach" was an incredibly maneuverable helicopter that later served as the model for the MH-6 "Little Bird" flown by the 160th Aviation "Night Stalkers" for special operations.

OH-58 Kiowa: The light observation helicopters that began to be replace the OH-6 in 1969, which remains in service.

OP: Observation post, a posting of usually a couple of men during daylight hours outside a unit lines for early warning purposes.

OPFOR: Designated opposing forces in a training exercise.

P-38: A simple but ingenious tiny folding can opener for C ration cans.

PAVN: People's Army of Vietnam, also known as the North Vietnamese Army (NVA).

PFC: Private First Class (Army E-3 or Marine E-2); (also private fucking civilian).

Pig: See **M60**.

Platoon: A formation of three rifle squads consisting of 30-40 men and a weapons squad usually broken down into the rifle squads; led by a second lieutenant.

Platoon Sergeant: The highest-ranking NCO in a platoon, in the Army an E-7 Sergeant First Class (SFC), the Marines an E-6 Staff Sergeant.

Pogey bait: Marine slang for candy, sweets and the like. See "pogue" and "REMF."

Pogue: Marine slang for personnel in rear echelons; derived from the acronym for "people other than grunts" (or the Gaelic word for "arse?").

PRC 25 or 77: Short for AN/PRC, the standard radio carried at platoon and company levels; called the "prick" 25 or 77 for its acronym and hefty weight of 23.5 pounds plus spare batteries.

Purple Heart: Short for Purple Heart medal, a decoration for having suffered a combat wound serious enough to require treatment by a medical doctor.

REMF: Rear echelon motherfucker; anyone not a soldier serving in front line combat units.

RPD (later **RPK**): The standard Russian light machine gun firing the 7.62x39mm cartridge from a drum.

RPG: A shoulder fired rocket propelled grenade launcher designed by the Soviets and ultimately used in great numbers by every enemy of the United States. Designed for use as an anti-tank weapon, it was adapted to an anti-personnel weapon and occasionally effective as an antiaircraft weapon.

RPK: See **RPD**.

RTO: Radio/telephone operator; a radioman, the soldier who carries and operates the combat unit's radio.

Sapper: A combat engineer specially trained to covertly approach and breach fortifications, an extremely hazardous duty. In years gone by they were called pioneers. In 2004 the United States Army authorized the wearing of a red "Sapper" tab by combat engineers with that sub-specialty.

Satchel charge: A combat demolition device contained in a canvas bag, usually triggered by a pull igniter; the charges being dynamite in WWII and Korea and C-4 plastic explosives from Vietnam forward.

SEAL: Acronym for "Sea, Air and Land," the U.S. Navy's elite commandos on par with the U.S. Army's Delta Force and other top tier special operations forces such as the British Special Air Service ("SAS") and the Israeli Sayeret Matkal.

Sergeant Major: An E-9, the highest enlisted rank, assigned to battalion or higher headquarters, accorded considerable deference by all ranks below major and often by all ranks.

Sierra: Phonetic for the letter S.

Six: The number denoting a commander or leader; or directionally the area behind.

Skyraider: The A-1 Skyraider was an American built piston powered and propeller driven attack aircraft, nicknamed the "Spad." With extraordinary low speed maneuverability and survivability and capability of carrying 8,000 pounds of ordnance along with its four 20mm cannon, it was an excellent close air support airplane.

Slick: See **Huey.**

Smoke grenade: A hand thrown marking or masking grenade that released a cloud of colored smoke, usually yellow, violet (purple or grape), green or red; also white phosphorous, which also is an incendiary.

Sniper rifles: Military sniper rifles evolved over the years. Vietnam saw a variety, including modified M14 rifles to customized Remington Model 700's and others. The Gulf Wars brought the M24A1, a Remington 700 chambered either in the original .308 (7.62mm) or .300 Winchester Magnum, most often fitted with a Leupold 10x scope; and the M82/M107 Barrett, a whopping .50 caliber that could effectively engage targets more than a mile away.

Spec 4: An E-4 specialist, on par with a corporal.

Spectre/Spooky: See **AC-47** and **AC-130**.

Squad Leader: The leader of a squad, an Army E-6 Staff Sergeant (SSG) or a Marine E-5 buck Sergeant unless filled (often) by someone of lesser rank.

Starlight scope: A night vision scope that tremendously magnifies available light enabling the viewer to see a grainy, greenish image in what otherwise would be blackness.

Tango: Phonetic for the letter T.

TDY: Temporary duty.

Thompson submachine gun: The M1928A1 submachine gun, or "Tommy gun," firing .45 caliber rounds from a stick (20 or 30 round) or drum (50 or 100 round) magazine; although invented by John Thompson in 1917 and became infamous in the 1920's "gangster era," it was not adopted by the military until 1938 and then saw service from WWII to Vietnam.

TOC: Tactical operations center, a command post usually of units larger than a company where it is called a CP, command post.

TO&E: Table of organization and equipment, the makeup of any military unit.

UH-60: See **Black Hawk.**

V or **V device:** The device affixed to decorations such as the Bronze Star or ARCOM signifying that the award was for valor.

VC: Viet Cong.

Viet Cong: Vietnamese communist soldiers, VC for short; more correctly soldiers of the National Liberation Front (NLF).

Warrant Officer: A specialty (technical or aviation) officer designated as such by warrant rather than commission; there are five grades, all but the first being Chief Warrant Officers; most come from enlisted ranks and must complete Warrant Officer Candidate School; they rank above NCO's, but below commissioned officers (although the higher grades are treated with the respect of their expertise and experience).

Whiskey: Phonetic for the letter W; also short for WIA.

Whiskey tango foxtrot: Phonetic for "WTF," standing for "What the fuck?"

White phosphorous: Commonly called "Willie Pete," an incendiary chemical used for marking rounds and smoke screens; deadly on humans, its burning embers difficult to extinguish.

WIA: Wounded in action.

Willie Pete: See **white phosphorous**.

Wire: Usually referring to various forms of barbed wire surrounding an established position; also referring to communications wire in proper context.

WO: See **Warrant Officer**.

World: For Vietnam veterans, the United States or anywhere other than there.

XO: Executive Officer, at company level a First Lieutenant (1LT) position.

"Valor is a gift. Those having it never know for sure whether they have it till the test comes. And those having it in one test never know for sure if they will have it when the next test comes."

—*attributed both to Carl Sandburg and Napoleon Bonaparte*

I

The warriors gathered, not in some smoky hall surrounded by trophies and instruments of battles past, not in a great room with portraits of famed predecessors, and not even in any martial place or setting. These warriors instead sat in an assortment of deck chairs on one side of a swimming pool, the pool a rare extravagance for Tom Howard. (It is indeed remarkable what becoming a grandfather will do.) The coastal South Carolina summer sun was brutally hot, but none of the men appeared to care or even notice, probably a consequence of just a few too many beers. They were celebrating and, as with all things these men did, they were doing it quite well.

The women, always smarter than the men, claimed the shade under the pavilion across the pool. They too were celebrating and with the children shepherded to the beach and a delightful and potent rum cooler concoction also were doing it quite well.

Eve came out of the house, drawing attention to herself by fumbling with the screen door. Tom Howard looked over and marveled at the figure that strikingly contrasted with her age. He turned to Don Kennedy, uniformly attired as he—in faded camo cutoffs, equally faded t-shirts emblazoned with the image of a yellow on black Ranger tab, cheap flip-flops and expensive sunglasses (the only real difference between their attire being Don's shiny new titanium alloy leg)—and in salute clinked his beer bottle with his own like they were still college boys or young lieutenants.

They looked back over at E, as Eve was called (her single syllable name abbreviated as only southerners would). She was looking back at them, smiling, the telltale smile of one who very well may have imbibed just a bit too much. The smile morphed into a giggle, a cute, girlish giggle that quickly evolved to an eye-watering, shoulder-shaking, loss of control thing.

Don was the first to speak. "I think she looked up your shorts, Tom."

Without missing a beat, Tom replied, "I hope not. I only like to disappoint one woman at a time." Seeing that the giggling was unabated, he said, "Looks like you oughta go tend to your woman before she pees in her pants or falls into the pool."

Don snorted and then said, "If she does the one, she needs to do the other."

Tom fired back, "Spoken like the true romantic and distinguished West Point gentleman I know you to be." That brought a chuckle to Don's fellow West Pointer, Craig Clark, sitting to his other side.

By this time, Tom's Katie and Isaac Jefferson's Sarah had come to Eve's aid. Eve appeared to gain control, lost it again, and with a couple deep breaths somewhat regained it.

"What in the world, child?" asked Sarah, a big mistake that set Eve off again. Eve stifled her giggles and only then realized that she had the undivided attention of everyone around the pool. She composed herself well enough to address the men.

"I am sorry, *really* sorry. I know y'all are famous heroes and all, and I love you, you know I really do, but seeing you out there, all I could think was one thing," adding after a pause, "'battered and fried."

A momentary hush was followed by a man's laugh, another, and then a full round of laughter. Tom Howard was the first to respond. Draping a towel over the jagged scar on his forearm, one of several serving as daily reminders of Vietnam, he said, "Dutifully concealed, young lady; more than I can say about these others." He tossed another towel to Craig Clark, signaling him with mock sternness to cover his scarred lower legs. Craig used the towel to feign concealing a one finger salute before making a dramatic show of pseudo compliance.

Amidst the laughter from both sides of the pool, Don Kennedy, no stranger to crossing the line, diverted attention back to his best friend. "Tom never could wander into the forest without attracting metal."

Responding with neither shock nor offense, Tom fired back, "Now there's the proverbial pot calling the kettle black…," and seeking to divert attention away from himself, added,…, "and speaking of black,…"

Taking the cue, Tom's other closest friend, Isaac Jefferson, joined in, "At least these scars look good on me, in a most manly way, I might add."

As the bantering continued, Tom's son Jonathan, always one to be unobtrusive, leaned over to his younger brother Bo and quietly said, "Show 'em your scar, Forrest, show 'em your scar," aptly alluding to the White House Oval Office scene from the iconic Tom Hanks blockbuster movie from 1994, *Forrest Gump*. Correctly sensing that Bo would not be so circumspect, Jon added, "No, on the second thought, that would not be very presidential."

Bo retorted, "I don't know what in hell you're talking about, *general*." Bo was tempted to join the banter about the pool, heedless to the fact that his recent national prominence would not shield him from this merciless group. His grandmother, however, saved him.

Beatrice Howard, known to all for much of her life as "Miss Bea" (pronounced simply "B") and more recently as "Gramm'um," was the matriarch of the extended Howard clan. When she stepped outside, a respectful hush came over the crowd. Miss Bea had been working hard in the kitchen while watching and listening. With a voice clear and strong for a woman of her age, and with the rich low country southern drawl she liked to occasionally affect for effect, she proclaimed, "Battered and fried. Battered and fried. Ain't that the damned truth. You boys get your silly selves inside before that sun gets you to cryin' like little girls."

Before she could get back inside and anyone could begin to comply with her command, Tom, the only one who would dare to test his mother, responded in feigned sotto voice loud enough for all to hear, "Isaac, man, she just called you 'boy.' You gonna whip her butt?"

Isaac Jefferson ignored both that Miss Bea's full attention was directed at him and his wife's warning look and adroitly answered for all to hear, "Now, Tom, you know I amended my ways long ago. Besides, I fear, no, I truly believe, that it would be the other way around,… and in front of all these witnesses."

Even Miss Bea joined in the laughter at that, but then it was back to business. "All right, enough foolishness. Time to get to work if y'all want to eat before it gets dark." With that she headed back into the kitchen, the women dutifully filing in after her while the men dutifully headed either to the pickup truck that had pulled up to the gate, its bed full of iced down oysters and shrimp, or to the grills where Uncle Bob's signature barbecue was competing with Don's racks of ribs.

Tom Howard alone hesitated. He had enjoyed the fun, but suddenly he needed a moment to himself. The banter actually had cut him deeply. It was one thing to have been banged up pretty good in war, as he had in his first tour in Vietnam and as had both his father in World War II, and his grandfather in World War I, but it was quite another thing to have suffered through it happening to his son Bo over in the sandbox of Iraq. Tom's melancholy was interrupted by the children exploding through the gate, eager to show off the day's treasures from the beach. As Bo's two headed straight for him, Tom offered up a silent prayer, *"Not them, Lord, please not them too."*

* * *

The story, however, does not begin with any of these men. The Howard legacy began with Carl Howard, Tom's grandfather. In the early part of the second decade of the 20th century, Carl, an immigrant not quite in his teens, soon ventured from, indeed fled, the teeming metropolis of New York City. Some would say fate led him to the improbable destination of South Carolina. Had he heard such, Carl would have been quick to object for in his heart he truly believed, he *knew*, it was providence, not fate.

For several grueling years, young Carl Howard steadfastly eked out a living in the equally improbable vocation as a logger in the piney woods and swamps of the South Carolina low country. He got on with a crew under Jimbo Thompson, a big, coarse man, but one who paid fair wages and was willing to teach those willing to learn. Carl was one of those few.

Carl found that he was suited to the grueling work in the oppressive heat and humidity or bitter cold and most often the miserable wetness in either event. He also found to his liking the profane comradery with the rough men with whom he crewed, although he more enjoyed the solitude on days it was just too wet to take to the woods when he alone spent his hours sharpening the saw teeth and axe blades, maintaining the equipment, or working on the finicky steam engines used to power the winch and lifts. (He, however, did not much care for tending to the ornery mules utilized to pull the log skidders to the loader.) While Carl aspired to a better life, he understood that to gain his betterment he had to start somewhere, work hard, learn a trade, earn respect, and be smart with his money.

That is not to say that all Carl did was work. There were a few young ladies, but nothing as formal and serious as courting. What the young man really enjoyed was venturing to the woods, swamps, and marshes with a gun in his hands. Carl had learned to shoot as a boy and was able to pick up for ten dollars an old 12 gauge Winchester Model 1897 (known familiarly as the Model 97) pump shotgun (designed by the legendary firearms designer John Browning). Carl was pleased that after an afternoon of stripping the shotgun and patiently cleaning all its parts with brass wool and solvent and then oiling it with a fine cloth, the gun operated as good as new, if not better.

Carl used every opportunity to take advantage of working in the wilds and thereby learning where and when game could be found. It was not unusual for him to supplement the table fare of the boarding house where he was lodging with ducks, rabbits, and an occasional deer or wild hog. He learned that he could trade diamondback rattler skins or alligator hides for shells for the shotgun.

All the while, Carl paid scant attention to news of the war raging in Europe, the French and British apparently being steadily pummeled by the Germans since 1914. That was not his affair. He had trees to cut and pennies to save.

But then the war became America's affair. While the 1915 German sinking of the British liner RMS Lusitania with 128 Americans on board often is considered the spark that drove America to the war, almost two years would elapse before that happened, intervened by German submarines sinking a number of U.S. merchant ships and Germany being caught outrageously soliciting Mexico as an ally against the United States. There was the call to arms, a call many young men clamored to answer.

Carl Howard did not want to go to war. Unlike so many young men, Carl had no visions of glory, he had no desire to kill Germans, and getting killed or maimed did not factor into his plans. What soon placed Carl in the line at the recruiting office was a sense of obligation to this country, *his* country.

Carl had gone to his boss, Jimbo Thompson, with his decision. The reaction was unexpected. "Damn, son, not you too. *Damn!* Well, I figured you for it. Come to the house at first light. I'll have the wife scare up some breakfast and I'll drive you up to Charleston myself."

The hour or so drive from Beaufort was a quiet one. When they arrived and got out of the truck, Jimbo said, "Carl, you're a fine young man and a good worker. I hate to lose you and you understand that I can't promise you a job when you get back, but look me up when you do." Handing Carl some folded bills, he added, "Here, you owe me a week's wages." When Carl struggled to reply, the man cut him off, saying, "Best be on your way, son. God go with you." They shook hands and parted.

* * *

The United States Army was pleased to accept Carl Howard. He was healthy and fit. He could read and write. He knew which end of a gun the bullet came out of.

Carl fared well in training. He distinguished himself on the rifle range, having easily meshed with the Springfield M1903. Known as the '03 (either "oh-three' or sometimes "aught-three") it was a bolt action rifle with a five-round clip of .30-06 caliber cartridges. It was a wonderful weapon, light, comfortable, and accurate.

Carl was so convinced that he was destined for the infantry that the opportunity to test for training and assignment as a mechanic was a great surprise. Being a mechanic sounded a whole lot better than charging across some enormous barren field while being pounded by artillery and swept by machine guns, and it would give him a useful trade for after the war.

The candidates went through rudimentary testing, first to confirm they indeed could read and write and had at least fundamental mathematical abilities, and then on to practical testing for mechanical aptitude. One test involved a crude drawing and pile of gears, belts, and spindles with the simple instruction, "Make it work." Carl did so and was surprised to see several candidates being ushered out, having failed such a simple test. Another was a large log, too heavy to lift, near a wagon containing beams and a pile of ropes, chains, and pulleys with the simple instruction, "Put the log in the wagon." More candidates failed, but not Carl. The last test was being taken to a truck and told to drive it through a marked course around the building, with the trick being that a simple mechanical repair was needed to make the motor run. Once again, Carl was not among the forlorn group ushered away.

Carl was selected for the specialty, trained and put on a ship to France as part of the AEF, the American Expeditionary Forces, under the command of General John J. "Blackjack" Pershing. There he was given more training, this on the tanks the Americans would be using, courtesy of the French and British. Bizarrely, the United States entered the war with no tanks of their own. None. Not one.

It was not that America had missed the parade, so to speak, though. Tanks were a relatively new phenomenon, having been created by the French and British as a response to the stalemate of trench warfare and the slaughter largely attributable to massed artillery and machine guns. Tank designs featured caterpillar tracks allowing for traversing terrain unpassable to wheeled vehicles; the tanks could cross shell torn, muddy (if not too muddy) terrain and roll over barbed wire obstacles, but only sometimes cross trenches. The tanks further offered armor protection against bullets and shrapnel. While a direct hit from an artillery shell could obliterate a tank, the odds of that happening were remote. Similarly, while bombs dropped from aircraft could destroy or disable a tank, there again was little chance of a direct hit.

The British favored heavy tanks, the Mark series, while the French preferred light tanks. The offensive capabilities of the tanks of either nation were nothing of the sort the world would see in World War II. Mostly platforms for machine guns, the British Mark IV was the exception with a six-pounder gun and the Mark VI a 57mm gun along with machine guns. While the British provided the Americans with some two hundred heavy tanks, it was the French who provided the Americans with most of the tanks they would use, predominantly Renault light tanks. The Renault FT, for instance, weighed only about seven tons fully loaded, and was crewed by only two men, a driver and a gunner who had at his disposal either a 37mm gun or a Hotchkiss 8mm machine gun. Training in France for the American tankers was conducted at the school created and commanded by one George S. Patton, then a lieutenant colonel.

It seemed strange to Carl Howard that the Americans were there, obviously a lot of them; but while the French and British were battling the Huns, the Americans mostly stayed safely in the rear areas organizing and training. He shrugged it off, figuring the generals knew what they were doing. *Who am I, just a grease monkey, to question?*

Carl learned most ways the tanks could and likely would break down. He learned their weaknesses. Despite their appearance as metal behemoths, they were underpowered and their caterpillar treads were too narrow to cope with the deep mud of the pocked, battered, churned up fields. The tankers themselves woefully could add to the list. The tanks were under-armored, under-armed, difficult to see out of, and were very, very uncomfortable. All agreed that the brainy engineers should devise some sort of device so that the tanks could at least communicate with each other. (Although radios were in use at the time, technology had not yet advanced to allow for their use in mobile vehicles, especially with the beating they would take in tanks on rough terrain.)

*　*　*

"Call for you, Sarge."

Sergeant Kelly stepped away from his latest experiment and wiped the grime off his hands as he crossed the shop floor to where the telephone hung on the wall. He still was not used to the newfangled things, as he referred to them despite that there were millions in service, including for quite a few years military service. He lifted the ear piece off its cradle and simply said into the voice tube, "Kelly here." The voice on the other end was familiar, one from even before the Mexican bandit chasing days.

"I know I owe you a favor..."

"You don't owe me a favor; you owe me money."

"Be that as it may, one old, broken down cavalryman to another I call bearing gifts, or rather a gift, another guy for you."

"I'm listening."

"Decent mechanic. Good head on his shoulders. Strong. Redneck like you."

"How many times I gotta tell you, I may be a shit kicker from way back, but I ain't no redneck."

"Yeah, right, so you want to take a look at the kid or trust me when I tell you he'd fit in fine in your sorry outfit?"

"Lord help me, but I trust you."

"And I you, old compadre. I'll put him on the next truck headed your way. If he's okay, that'll square what I owe you?"

"You taking up bounty huntin' since they took your horse away?"

"Nah, just thought I'd give it a shot. I'm good for what I owe you, you know that. Maybe though you could kindly bring a bottle to the next game we can get up?"

"Corn liquor's scarce in these parts, but I'll see what I can conjure up."

"Good enough. I gotta go. More papers to shuffle."

"Right. And thanks for lookin' after me. Won't be long before we have to start earning our keep. Wait! What's the guy's name?"

"Oh, yeah, sorry. Howard, Carl Howard."

The call concluded, a satisfied Sergeant Kelly headed back over to "the Beast." She was an ugly thing, a Mack AC heavy duty truck, although so modified she was hardly recognizable as one. The Beast was massive, a six-ton monstrosity almost as heavy as a Renault light tank. Kelly and his crew of two had removed the metal truck bed and replaced it with heavy wooden planks. Bolted through them to the frame was a fabricated pivoting A-frame jib crane with a cable winch driven by a salvaged Ford motor and transmission mounted on the boards. Also mounted on boards were sturdy boxes for the storage of tools, equipment, and all manner of things.

Kelly's latest experiment was to mount a fabricated pedestal in the truck bed near the cab on which to mount a Lewis gun recovered from a crashed British airplane. He and his crew had been sent out to extricate the body of the pilot, a grisly task, and while Kelly dutifully had delivered the body of the airman and his recovered personal effects to the designated British aerodrome, he had taken the machine gun and spare ammunition drums "in payment." He really had no confidence that either he or his guys could hit anything with the weapon, but he felt better having it on board since none of them could hit the broad side of a barn with the M1911 Colt .45 caliber semi-automatic pistols they had been issued and the single Springfield rifle on board was not much compensation.

Carl Howard suffered a rough ride over rutted roads, cramped in a truck whose springs were shot. As they bounced along, heading closer to the front, signs of war increased — damaged or destroyed buildings, abandoned vehicles and equipment, dead horses left to rot, and many, many men with guns. Carl was not told his destination, but he expected it to be a motor pool or forward maintenance depot. He was right and he was wrong.

Carl and two others were dropped off at a makeshift motor pool surrounding a confiscated warehouse and large sheds, all showing recent repair. The detail corporal got out of the truck cab to stretch and handed a sheet of paper to a sergeant who had walked up.

The sergeant pronounced to the other two men their assignments and told them that he would take them where they needed to go. As for Carl Howard though, the sergeant turned to a grizzled, older sergeant Carl had not noticed, who stepped closer and asked, "Howard?" When Carl nodded, all he said was, "Good. You're with me." He headed toward one of the outbuildings. Carl understood to follow. He lifted his heavy bag and struggled to catch up and keep up.

They entered the far shed, which apparently had been recently sided rather crudely with obviously salvaged wood. When Carl's eyes adjusted to the dimmer interior, he saw that the structure had been set up so that there were working bays on one side in which there were several odd-looking trucks in various stages of dismemberment; and on the other side about a dozen cots with crude furnishings fashioned from scrap wood as well. Carl was directed to put "his shit" on the one bare cot as the sergeant continued to lead him toward the back corner where there were wooden crates, barrels, and mismatched chairs clustered around a stove.

"Gather up, girls, our newest recruit made it in one piece." The men put down whatever they were working on and ambled over, pleased to get a break, especially one with the prospect of some entertainment. Carl, his attention on the sergeant, failed to take notice of the almost gleeful looks of anticipation on the faces of the other men.

"Howard," the sergeant began, "my name is Kelly, Sergeant Kelly. You belong to me. You now are a member of this den of misfits and thieves of mine. We call ourselves 'the Labs,' short for 'Labradors.' Why? Because we're retrievers. We are the brigade's tank recovery guys. What that means is we're to go in behind the tanks and retrieve them's that're lost; get 'em unstuck if they're stuck, fixed if they're busted; and back in the fight if possible.

"As you know, the Brits and the Frenchies have been kind enough to provide the good ol' AEF with tanks, mostly the light Renaults. They're all shit, as I expect you know too, but nobody back home thought to design and build our own, so we're stuck with them. 'Beggars can't be choosers,' as they say.

"A few rules: One, do as I say, when I say, without question, unless you got a better idea and there's time for it. You'd better be right. Two, don't ever let the tankers tell you to help dig 'em out. That's their damn job. And three, we only do the possible,…" here Carl failing to observe that to a man his new teammates began mouthing the last part, "but ain't nothing impossible except maybe any of these ugly, smelly bastards getting in some mademoiselle's knickers."

Sergeant Kelly then took Carl and introduced him to their vehicles. There were five, an armored, tracked recovery vehicle fashioned from a tracked British Mark IV heavy tank chassis, and three trucks, two Liberties and a Dodge. Liberty Standard B trucks were a mainstay of the AEF. Weighing 3-5 tons, the cargo trucks had a strong (for its day) 52 horsepower engine and rolled on steel wheels with solid rubber tires.

Two years before, Dodge had won acclaim when during "Blackjack" Pershing's expedition into Mexico pursuing the revolutionary/bandit known as Pancho Villa, a young lieutenant named George S. Patton boldly and for the first time by anyone led about a dozen soldiers in three Dodge touring cars on a successful raid.

Each of the three trucks presented to Carl Howard was heavily modified and stacked with tools, implements, gear, and spare parts. At the end of the line was another truck, an even more heavily modified one identified to him as a Mack. "That," said the sergeant, "is affectionately known as 'the Beast.' She's mine, now yours too, with Swannie and Mo."

To Carl the sergeant said, "I'll take you over to HQ to make sure you're set and we'll round up some gear and supplies for you and then I'll bring you back to get settled in and get to know the guys." To the other Labs he said, "You know what to do. Do it."

The next couple of weeks were a frenzy of activity. Carl first had to learn the Beast and his role on the crew. Carl would be riding in the back on a fabricated seat bolted to the truck bed against the cab on the passenger side and if need be operating the "requisitioned" Lewis gun mounted on a pedestal right next to his seat. "Mo" Moreno, the other mechanic, was an Italian kid from Pittsburgh, good with his hands, and after a time more or less understandable. He rode in the back with Carl. "Swannie" Swanson, the driver, was from somewhere out west and had been a truck driver before the war. He was big and strong and could handle the Beast well.

Sergeant Kelly, or just "Sarge" when it was just the Labs, was exactly what one would expect of an army sergeant and a former cavalryman. He was stern, obviously cared deeply about his men and his vehicles, but would punish both to no end to get the job done.

The Labs spent long hours working on their vehicles and then in the adjacent motor park helping to ready the tanks for action. When the tanks went out for maneuvers, the Labs swarmed those that broke down or got stuck and afterward assisted in their repair.

And then the time came to put the training and preparation to use. The Americans would no longer augment and support the French and British divisions. They were given their own sector of the front lines. It was September, 1918, and the American army was to attack to push the Germans out of what was called the Saint-Mihiel salient southeast of Verdun with the goal of advancing to the city of Metz near the German border.

* * *

The tanks moved up to a staging area behind the front lines, the Labs not far behind. The word came down to prepare for action and in the meantime the Labs busied themselves, readying their vehicles and helping to work on ailing tanks.

It was near first light when the horizon lit up as batteries of artillery pieces commenced the pre-assault bombardment, the flashes quickly followed by sounds, the reports of the guns, the roar of the big shells passing overhead, and then the distant *krump* and *whumpf* of the detonations in and around the German lines. The Germans countered with their own guns, a deadly mix of high explosive and gas shells, first at the American guns and then at the American trench lines. More than a few of the high explosive shells hit near the Labs, but fortunately none of the deadly gas.

The feeling of helplessness was almost overwhelming to Carl Howard as he sat in the back of the Beast with shells detonating all around, some much too close for comfort. Carl was glad when they moved out, even though it meant heading toward the enemy guns. He felt like he was escaping his doom.

That feeling evaporated immediately upon crossing the forward trench. There right below him was a trio of prone khaki clad soldiers. For all their weeks and months of exhausting training and hardships, all their hopes and prayers, these hapless men had made but a single step or two into no man's land before being cut down, snuffed out, and left behind in the bloody mud without so much as a glance.

The tanks fanned out and the Labs split to follow. Neither tasked nor equipped to fight, they ventured forward only so far to keep the tanks in their respective sectors in sight. As the Beast slowly crept forward, Carl was concerned with the gunfire and occasional stray round zipping, buzzing, or whining by, but he was dumbfounded at the utter devastation in no man's land. The ground was pocked and torn from shellfire and littered with abandoned equipment. And bodies. Bodies new and old. Bodies whole and rent. There were wounded men too, suffering men awaiting death or a litter team to remove them from the field and give them some chance of survival. There, too, were a few, a relatively very few, who overwhelmed by the slaughter around them could not muster the courage to go forward and do their duty. They instead cowardly huddled in shell craters awaiting a respite in the firing to then slink back to their units with concocted explanations for their absence.

The first stationary tank the Beast came upon was stuck nose down in an enormous water-filled shell hole. Sergeant Kelly had his two mechanics dismount while he assessed the situation. Determining that they could get the stricken vehicle out, Kelly explained how to his men and the tank crew. While he stood on the back deck of the tank to give instructions to the tank driver and Mo operated the winch and jib to hopefully provide enough lift to help break the suction of the mud, Carl's job was to hook up and keep an eye on the tow cables. Of course, that was *after* he and the tank commander shoveled from behind the tank what felt like a ton of mud. (So much for Sergeant Kelly's Rule No. 2!)

When all was ready, Kelly signaled the effort to begin. The tank's engine roared and its tracks spun while the cables creaked and popped, making Carl fearful that one would snap and whip back to take off his head. The Beast strained, slipped and then held. Carl stepped back, colliding with someone he ignored. Suddenly the tank broke free and crawled out of the hole with Sergeant Kelly managing to get it stopped a hair from colliding with the Beast.

Carl was amazed and elated. He turned and his broad smile vanished as he noticed the man whom he had bumped and ignored. There before him stood Lieutenant Colonel George Patton, already a fearsome legend, now commanding a tank brigade. To Carl's great relief, the light colonel took no offense. He clapped Carl on the shoulder, went over and shook the hand of Sergeant Kelly, and then directed the tank commander to follow him as he and his orderlies strode forward.

It was only then that Carl realized that they were not alone at the crater. There were bodies strewn about, recently killed Americans. Carl eased over to one, an officer. From the young man's bloodied khaki blouse, he obviously had been shot at least twice in the chest. Carl, not yet accustomed to seeing up close victims of violent death, was transfixed by the man's lifeless eyes staring at the sky.

The spell was broken when Sergeant Kelly came over to see what had caught Carl's rapt attention. Looking down, Kelly muttered, "Poor bastard." Carl then was utterly dismayed when his sergeant proceeded to strip the corpse of his map case, binoculars, and belt with holstered .45 automatic pistol. Kelly kept the map case and binoculars for himself, but the pistol, belt, and holster he handed to Carl, saying, "I ain't no fucking ghoul, Carl. He's got no further use for this stuff anymore. We do. Better us than the fucking Huns if this little foray fails."

Sergeant Kelly walked over to another body and gathered the man's rifle and helmet. He shoved the bayonet into the ground, tied a strip of whitish cloth around the trigger guard as a flag and placed the helmet on the rifle butt, all to mark the location of the American dead. Carl then followed his sergeant back to the Beast and heard him gruffly order Swannie to move out.

The day wore on and they were able to get only one other tank back in action. However, they were later gratified to learn that the Labs' total was an impressive six. Even more gratifying was that when three days of fighting were over, none of the Labs had been hurt and none of the vehicles had been seriously damaged.

The Labs were ordered, without explanation, back to the motor pool. There would be no rest. Tanks were repaired at a feverish pace, the Labs struggling to steal time to devote to their own vehicles.

Within days after the battle, they embarked on an arduous road march to the northwest, the other side of Verdun, an area of the Argonne Forest to the west and Meuse River to the east, an area called the Meuse-Argonne. Over a million Americans would be committed to the offensive, many of whom would not witness the end of its 47-day duration. Losses would be staggering with more than 26,000 Americans killed and nearly four times that wounded. Carl Howard would be one of those casualties. He, like George Patton, would not last even a full day of the great offensive. Both, though, would make that one day count.

* * *

The offensive commenced with a bombardment from 2,700 artillery pieces and the infantry advance. The Labs went forward behind the relatively few tanks deployed, a factor of that neither the weather nor the terrain favored tanks (and later that with Lieutenant Colonel Patton put out of action the very first day with a bullet through his thigh there simply was not an equal to take his place). The Labs again spread out with the now too familiar sights of death and destruction along the way. The tanks faltered and those that could withdrew.

Disgusted, Sergeant Kelly directed the Beast to a shattered grove of trees. There they found a makeshift casualty collection point with a number of grievously wounded men. Kelly dismounted and spoke to a medic. He returned to the vehicle and told the crew, "Listen, there ain't much in the way of tank recovery going on and some of these men'll likely die if they don't get to the rear soon, so I've decided that today we're in the people recovery business. Help these medics load up as many as we can fit. Dump some of our shit we don't need right away to make room."

They loaded more than a dozen wounded and followed by a string of walking wounded slowly headed back south toward American lines. Carl was pressed into service to help the medic who came along to tend to the wounded, a sobering, but somehow rewarding experience.

They made it back to where they could see the shattered remnants of the American outer wire when Sergeant Kelly ordered Swannie to stop the Beast. Carl thought they were picking up more wounded as they had done twice along the way. He, however, was wrong. Pointing, Sergeant Kelly said, "That Hun bastard has been giving us the evil eye."

Carl followed his sergeant's point and saw a lone biplane circling in the distance. Studying it through the binoculars Sergeant Kelly had handed him, he could see that it was mottled gray on the sides and light gray on the underside. It reminded him of the shark he had seen strung up at a Beaufort pier. Carl was about to ask his sergeant how he knew it was a German when the plane turned and he shuddered in seeing the telltale black crosses on its wings and fuselage. Not that it mattered to Carl, but it was a Fokker with twin machine guns mounted fore of the cockpit, synchronized to fire through the propeller arc. What did matter to Carl was that they quite literally were sitting ducks out there in the open, the only vehicle not spewing a column of smoke.

"*Shit*," Sergeant Kelly said, "he's coming around at us. Get the wounded off! Now. *Now*! Not you, Carl. You get on the gun." Carl knew he meant the Lewis gun, the machine gun he'd fired only once and then only to confirm that it worked. In fact, Carl had only fired a machine gun once before, in basic training, and that was limited to firing for familiarity a Browning water-cooled machine gun mounted on a tripod. Thus, to now learn to shoot a machine gun at a moving target bearing down on him with deadly intent was a daunting prospect, to say the least.

Carl readied the gun while ignoring the commotion about him, his full attention on the airplane descending to an altitude of only a few hundred feet and lining up at them. Carl knew he'd have to lead the plane, putting his sights below the plane and then sweeping upward as he fired to theoretically allow the plane to fly into the stream of bullets.

The German fired first, a burst that went high, but was frightening nonetheless. Carl responded with a short burst, also to no effect. If the German pilot was surprised to be taking machine gun fire from the truck in his sights he did not let it faze him. He continued bearing down on his prey. He dropped the biplane's nose a bit and fired again, a longer chattering burst.

Carl stood fast. It did not occur to him to do anything but. He saw bullets kicking up dirt in a line toward the Beast and then heard rounds pinging off her metal parts and thudding into and splintering the wooden bed. One of the wounded howled as a ricochet under the vehicle ripped more hot metal into his flesh. Carl grimaced and fired again, but still with no apparent effect, even though the plane was closing, looming.

Carl then somehow noticed that battlefield smoke was drifting toward the south. He applied "Kentucky windage," adjusting his aim to account for the effect of the laterally moving air on the bullets, and fired a longer burst as the German airman did the same. More rounds hammered the Beast, one snapping so closely by Carl's ear that he could feel its heat. Carl clenched his teeth, raised the muzzle of the Lewis gun a bit and held the trigger down, his last chance at survival.

The next thing Carl Howard knew was that he was laying on his back in the dirt next to the Beast and that he was in pain. He was beyond puzzled, totally bewildered. *What happened? How did I get here? Why do I hurt so bad?* Faces loomed over him, mouths moving without sound. Hands were on him that transformed the waves of pain into bolts of sheer agony searing his brain. And then Carl Howard faded into merciful darkness.

Carl awoke to more confusion. He was on a cot in a room, a room with horrible smells, chemical and otherwise foul; a room crowded with men moaning, crying, shrieking; a room in hell. No, not hell. As he lay there, trying to sort it out, a figure appeared beside him, a lovely, smiling lady. A cruel apparition? No, she was real and Carl cleared his head sufficiently to grasp that she was a nurse. That in turn allowed Carl to comprehend that he was in a field hospital. He, however, still was puzzled. He took stock of himself and realized that he was bandaged about the head, arm, and leg. He was in throbbing pain and he was dreadfully thirsty.

"Well, soldier," the smiling nurse said, "welcome back. I was getting concerned. No, don't talk now. Have some water. Let me change these dressings and give you something for the pain."

A day went by and Carl was no closer to understanding what had occurred. His head still throbbed, but he could tell that the bandage was much smaller, as was the one on his arm. He tried to raise himself up to see his leg, the most painful, but a wave of nausea and the room spinning forced his head back onto the pillow.

Carl next awoke to see none other than Sergeant Kelly standing at the foot of his bed. A bed, not a cot. A different room, a quieter room, but still with the awful chemical smells. Even more surreal was that the sergeant was smiling, actually smiling!

Carl spoke first, "Damn, it's good to see you, Sarge." Then noticing the man's new insignia, "I'm sorry, *First Sergeant* Kelly."

First Sergeant Kelly laughed, pulled up a chair and sat, saying, "Well, it's not yet official, not until the paymaster says so, but I was told to wear them. Same for you, *Corporal* Howard." Seeing that the young man was perplexed, he added, "It seems that the powers that be think we're a couple of heroes. Not like Alvin York over in the 82nd, mind you, but heroes still. You up for me filling you in?" Carl nodded his affirmative, gritting his teeth at the pain of the simple movement.

Kelly continued, "Well, after your little duel with that German plane, it flew right over us and then instead of coming back around to finish us off it broke off and turned back north, trailing smoke. You hit him hard. He came down right in the midst of our forwardmost troops. I hear he was none too happy about being shot down by a truck, the ugliest one on the planet to boot.

"Of course, that was after he hammered the shit out of the Beast, Swannie, and you. Swannie caught one in the gut, but it looks like he's gonna make it. Mo's okay. Got you in the calf and the arm, both flesh wounds. I expect they hurt some all the same. One round dinged off your helmet and either it or your taking a back dive off the Beast knocked you out. You were in and out the whole way back, babbling on and off. Nonsense really. Damned if at one point though it didn't sound like German.

"Anyway, we got to the aid station, without losing any of the wounded I might add, and the Beast just quit right there, gave up the ghost. No matter really. One of the Liberties broke down too and Jonesy got the other one so stuck it'll be summer before anyone can dig it out. Battalion took the Mark IV, saying they needed it more in the depot than we did. That left us one truck and battalion snatched it too. Me, too. I'm now the motor sergeant, taking care of the likes of you.

"You, by the way, are still mine, excepting that you're back to being a mechanic. I'll find you something useful for when you get home. That's if I can keep you. You're to be cited for bravery. Gets you a little bauble to go along with your wound stripe. Them and your scars ought to dazzle the little ladies back in Swampland, U.S.A. Oh, one more thing…"

With that, Kelly reached down and pulled from the canvas bag Carl had not noticed a dishpan U.S. helmet and handed it to Carl, saying, "Thought you'd might like a little souvenir." It had a deep dent in the crown. Kelly then leaned forward and showed Carl the remaining contents of the bag, some shell casings from the Lewis gun, a .45 automatic and bottles of liquor and wine. He then stood and quietly told Carl, "The booze is from the infantry. They're mighty grateful for their wounded getting back. Keep the helmet and casings to show off to the pretty nurses. I'll hold on to this other stuff 'til you get released, pretty soon, I expect."

It was not but a few days before Carl hobbled into the repair facility in his new uniform, sporting corporal's stripes. He asked a mechanic where he might find First Sergeant Kelly and the man hollered out, "Top, there's a banged-up corporal here to see ya."

Kelly appeared from behind a jacked-up truck, wiping his dirty hands on a filthy rag and frowning his usual frown. Seeing Howard though, he allowed himself a smile (*two in one week!*). He walked over and warmly welcomed Carl, turning heads as he did so and prompting some murmurs. He led Carl to what was being used as an office. After giving Carl a cup of steaming, chokingly strong coffee, the two chatted a bit. Just a bit and then it was down to work.

"Carl," he said, "I'm damn glad to have you. Half of these monkeys don't know which way to turn a nut. I got a good gig for you. You've worked on enough trucks and tanks so I'm gonna put you in the section responsible for maintaining staff cars. Actually, I'm putting you in charge over there, you being an NCO and all. You've got a couple of decent guys and another maybe you can do somethin' with. C'mon, I'll take you over there."

When they got there, Top Kelly, commanded, "Gather up, girls." They gathered around a work bench. "This is Corporal Carl Howard. He was with me at the front. He's the one who shot down the German plane and saved more than a dozen wounded men, not to mention Ma Kelly's pride and joy. He knows his stuff. Anything he says is just like I said it myself. Any questions? No? Good. Carry on."

Kelly took Carl aside and quietly said, "You let me know if any of those wounds get to bothering you. Otherwise, push these guys hard. They've had it easy back here, a lot damn easier than the trench rats up front. And, oh, by the way, I still have that bag for you. Come get it. Better make it soon as that one bottle has been calling out to me."

It was a perfect job for Carl, and in no time the section was working smoothly as a team. But things do not last. In just a few short weeks, on the 11th hour of the 11th day of the 11th month of 1918, the war ended. That, however, hardly meant that Carl was soon to board a ship home and in the meantime staff officers could not afford to be without their precious cars. Carl kept busy and the learning opportunities were invaluable.

There also were a few opportunities for short passes and Carl got to see Paris, something to boast about later. There were other distractions, too, formations, ceremonies, and the like, at one of which Carl's wound stripe was presented along with a citation for valor accompanied by a small silver star to go on the Victory Medal everyone was getting. The great surprise was the inclusion of sergeant's stripes. The greatest surprise would come later though, for unbeknownst to Carl, the Army soon was to be sending a press release to his hometown newspaper in Beaufort.

* * *

Carl Howard did not expect a hero's welcome when he returned to Beaufort. For one thing, he correctly figured that many of the local boys had beaten him home and the people were ready to put the war behind them and get on with their lives. For another, Carl did not feel like he was a hero.

Carl found a room in the same boarding house at which he had stayed before the war and sought out his former boss, Jimbo Thompson. Jimbo scoffed away Carl's reminder that he owed the man a week's wages and put him on a crew. When Carl commented to him that his equipment was in a horrid state, something he could remedy, Jimbo took him up on it and Carl began to work in a makeshift shop. When Carl got Jimbo's dilapidated Dodge truck running, Jimbo gave it to him to use.

On his daily drive to and from the shop, Carl kept noticing a vacant farmhouse and barn. He checked into it and found out that it had been owned by old man Simpson before he lost it after two years of failed crops. Carl was told he ought to go see Mr. Greer over at the bank about it. Carl did. When he told the teller that he'd like to see Mr. Greer, she replied, "Old or young?" Seeing that Carl did not understand, she asked, "Old Mr. Greer or young Mr. Greer?" Carl opted for young Mr. Greer and after getting Carl's name, the teller excused herself to see if he was available.

The man, obviously not more than a few years older than Carl, came out of his office, approached Carl and said, "I'm Bill Greer. Come on in." He seated Carl and asked, "What can I do for you?"

Carl told him he was interested in renting the Simpson farm. Bill Greer's response was totally unexpected, "Okay if I call you Carl?" When Carl nodded his assent, the young banker continued, "Good. I'm Bill. My Dad is *Mister* Greer. Are you the Carl Howard I read about in the paper?"

Carl hadn't the faintest idea of what he was talking about, so Bill Greer produced a copy from a stack of newspapers on his credenza. After Carl had the chance to read the article, he sheepishly responded, "Yes sir, I suppose that's me."

Bill Greer replied, "First, it's 'Bill,' not 'sir;' I'm not a lieutenant anymore; and, second, I am proud to meet you. My service was with the artillery and I never saw what, if anything, we ever hit. We sure made a lot of noise though."

The banker continued, "Back on point, you don't want to rent the Simpson place. It's in sad shape; the house has running water only in the kitchen, if it still works; the barn roof leaks; the fields, as you know, are overgrown; and, quite frankly, it's been a drain on the bank. If I could sell the idea to my Dad, how about you move into the place and fix it up? The bank'll pay for materials and assuming the value of your work meets or exceeds what we could get in rent, it wouldn't cost you anything out of pocket."

Carl pondered the unexpected offer for a minute or so and responded with, "Well, that sounds good, but my idea was, is, to convert the barn into a shop, buy some tools, equipment, and a decent truck and then see if I could make a living as a mechanic, the truck being to go out to farms and do repairs there."

Bill Greer considered what Carl said in the context of benefit to the bank and then excused himself, returning after ten minutes or more, obviously with his father. The older Mister Greer shook Carl's hand, told him he was pleased that they would be working together to their mutual benefit and departed.

When Bill Greer resumed talking, Carl's surprise turned to astonishment. The plan had bloomed remarkably. He was to put his meager savings from the army into the bank; move into the house at his earliest convenience, and assess and prioritize needed repairs and improvements, reporting the same to the bank; and the bank would provide him funds to commence work and then on an ongoing basis. Bill Greer assured Carl that once they were satisfied that the relationship was proceeding as intended, the bank would help him get his business venture up and running and when the time was right, the bank would sell him the property for ten percent over what the bank had in it (explaining that he needed to "show the bank auditors that while I may not be the best banker in the world, I am not an idiot") with a mortgage at their best rate. As he was walking Carl to the door, Bill told him, "Oh, and let me see if in the meantime I can talk Jimbo into letting you hold on to that ratty old truck for a while without asking for too much repair and maintenance work in return."

The relationship worked wonderfully, mainly due to that Carl worked prudently, skillfully, and tirelessly; but also due not only to that Bill Greer saw in it the profit potential, but that he and Carl had become friends.

That did not mean that Carl ever had money to burn though. As the business began to grow and thrive, what cash he earned mostly went back into things he needed. With times being hard for many in the post-war years, he often found himself working for trade in the form of labor at the farm, produce, livestock, and poultry and all manner of things.

Some of the trade was small parcels of land deemed for one reason or another as unproductive for farming or otherwise not valued by Carl's customers. The bank occasionally would buy the land, always candidly for less than it was worth, but always more than Carl felt like he was due. For the parcels the bank did not want, Bill arranged for the bank's lawyer to handle the deeds for a modest fee, sometimes in trade too.

One day Carl was taking a rare break at the shop when he saw a young lady, a very attractive young lady, walking up the path to the house. Wiping the sweat off his brow and grime off his hands, he walked over there. Introducing himself, she sweetly responded, "Pleasure to meet you, Carl. My name is Faith."

In a very few minutes, Carl learned that she was the granddaughter of old man Simpson, that she now lived in Beaufort and worked as a seamstress, that both her grandfather and her mother had passed away, and that she had come by, prompted by a feeling of nostalgia. She asked to see the inside and Carl, embarrassed at what she might think of his housekeeping, reluctantly agreed. Out of respect, he stayed on the front porch as she slowly went through the small house.

Coming out of the house, she sweetly said, "Thank you for that. You've done wonders with the old place. No offense though, but it could use a woman's touch."

As the saying goes, one thing led to another and a short but respectable courtship led to marriage with Bill Greer being Carl's best man. A son, Daniel, followed a year later, then later with a daughter, and then another son. Life was good. They were living the American Dream.

* * *

The American Dream, the term credited to having been later coined by James Truslow Adams, was stated by him in 1931 to be "that dream of a land in which life should be better and richer and fuller for everyone, with opportunity for each according to ability or achievement... It is not a dream of motor cars and high wages merely, but a dream of social order in which each man and each woman shall be able to attain to the fullest stature of which they are innately capable, and be recognized by others for what they are, regardless of fortuitous circumstances of birth or position." The American Dream also has been defined as "a national ethos of the United States, the set of ideals (Democracy, Rights, Liberty, Opportunity, and Equality) in which freedom includes the opportunity for prosperity and success, and an upward social mobility for the family and children, achieved through hard work in a society with few barriers."

However articulated, the American Dream was not a novel concept in 1931, or 1921, or even in 1886 when the Statue of Liberty graced New York Harbor, or even when the American colonies became the United States of America. To Carl Howard, the American Dream was not some lofty ideal, but an absolute truism. Carl believed in it. He embraced it. He lived it. He embodied it.

To Carl Howard, the American Dream was a thing of real substance. It was a cornerstone of his life, shared with God, country and family. In time, it became a dream fulfilled and in so doing Carl laid the solid foundation for the future of the Howard clan and, in a much broader sense, the Howard family.

Perhaps Carl's greatest flaw was that in his resolute pursuit of the American Dream, he failed to take into account that it was not the only dream. There were many other dreams, all too often dreams of more ambitious people, more powerful people, more ruthless people; foreboding, maleficent, sinister dreams of the few that would become nightmares for the many; ominous, foreboding dreams.

Carl Howard, having witnessed the horrors of war, its death, destruction, and its appalling waste, naively could not imagine that mankind would allow such an awful tragedy to recur. "The War to End All Wars" was supposed to be just that. Carl was sadly mistaken.

Antagonistic dreams once again would conflict and resoundingly clash with America's and defy and defeat statesmen. When the voice of reason fails, the call to arms all too often follows.

A century of Howards would answer the call.

2

ONE EVENING IN MAY, 1940, THE HOWARDS SHARED THEIR USUAL meal and afterward as usual Carl eased out to the back porch for his coffee and a smoke. Staring out across the broad expanse of the Coosaw River, Carl once again privately thanked the Lord for his many blessings, not in the least that He had led him to Bill Greer and Bill had made it possible for them to now be living in this glorious place.

Carl was mildly surprised to hear his older boy Daniel come out and take a seat. That was unusual. He glanced over at the boy who then broke the silence with, "Dad, can we talk?"

"Sure thing, son. What's on your mind?"

Dan took a deep breath and struggling to recall his carefully crafted and rehearsed lines he began, "Dad, I know that you're expecting me to take over the logging crew after I graduate and learn the business, but you know better than I do that we're going to war. Most folks say it'll be against the Germans, but Mr. Hadaway says it'll be against the Japs first."

Sensing the need to pause, Dan smartly did just that. Carl indeed needed a few moments as well. At the word "but," Carl's heart had sunk. With the world in turmoil he sensed that he was about to face the same thing that hundreds if not thousands of American fathers would be suffering. The mention of Hadaway's name distracted him further.

Carl was not surprised that his son would find credible what Dave

Hadaway had to say, and rightly so. Before Dave went to college and became a local high school teacher and coach he had gone overseas as a Marine and saw considerable action. He and Carl had shared many a story over the years at the Masonic Lodge.

Carl struggled to compose himself and return his attention to his son. When the two regained eye contact, Dan understood he had his cue and resumed, "Dad, I want to serve. I want to enlist right after graduation, before the war breaks out. I know you served in the army, but I am thinking of the Marine Corps. When it's over, I promise I'll come back and fit into any of the family businesses however you want me to."

It was Dan's turn to try to frame a response. He too took a deep breath, locked his eyes on his boy's and began, "Dan, I don't know that this country is going back to war. I pray not. There's nothing glorious about war. It's just a horrible waste, beyond imagination. But I know that there are men, prideful men, ambitious men, maybe evil men, who've already led their countries to war. I had hoped, prayed, that what we went through in the last war would convince our leaders to find a way to keep us out of it, both in Europe and the Pacific. But, I, too, am losing faith in their abilities, or even desire, to do that. As much as I hate, truly hate, even the thought of you going to war, I cannot fault your patriotism.

"I want you to do two things though. First, pray for guidance to know your true motivation. Is it truly for the right reasons or is it for adventure and glory? If, and only if you are satisfied that it's out of a sincere sense of duty, you'll have my blessing. Second, if that's the case, let me be the one to break it to your mother. Deal?"

Dan, uncertain whether his voice would betray his emotions, merely nodded his head in assent. He got up to leave, but was surprised when his father stopped him. Their eyes again met and Carl fiercely embraced his son before gently pushing him away and with a forced smile saying, "Go finish your chores and do your homework. You're not graduating until Dave Hadaway and his colleagues say you're graduating."

Dan went about his business while Carl stayed out on the porch, now mostly to avoid Faith until hopefully she'd forget about asking what her two men were talking about in the approaching darkness. "*Approaching darkness*," thought Carl, a man rare to cuss, "*how apt, how fucking apt.*"

* * *

For United States Marine Corps recruits (boots) from generally west of the Mississippi River, basic training, or boot camp, is conducted in San Diego, California. For recruits east of the Mississippi River, they go to the Marine Corps Recruit Depot Parris Island, known simply as "Parris Island." It is an island located in South Carolina, on the Atlantic coast between Beaufort and Hilton Head Island, where the Broad River and Beaufort River flow into Port Royal Sound; about five miles from where Dan Howard grew up. The Marine Corps was quite proud of the hell they put boots through for thirteen weeks, and the Corps' ability to, in that time, transform candy ass civilian pukes into the best killers in the world.

For Dan Howard, boot camp at Parris Island was not as hard as it was for many. For one thing, Dan was accustomed to the climate; for another, he was strong and accustomed to early hours, hard work, and exacting standards; and for yet another reason, he was properly motivated. Moreover, he had been given excellent advice from Dave Hadaway: "For the first two weeks, be invisible, lost in the crowd; and for the next two, show some promise. The key, though, is the range. Marines pride themselves on being the best marksmen in the world. Be one of the best of the best."

Dan heeded that advice. Dan, like his father, was no stranger to guns and when it came time for the range he immediately took to the standard issue rifle, the Springfield M1903, the '03, the same bolt action rifle his father had used in World War I over twenty years before. Dan paid rapt attention to the instructors and showed that he listened and was capable of learning. He was rewarded by extra attention in return, a recipe for success. Dan was the only boot in his platoon to qualify as expert with the '03. He, in fact, did so well that the colonel was invited to watch him shoot an extra round. Dan demonstrated that his score was not a fluke by matching it in that round as well.

The colonel was impressed, so much so that he summoned the senior instructor to break out one of the Army M-1 Garand rifles that had been provided to the Marine Corps. Dan at first was not as impressed with it. Although it fired semi-automatically and had an eight-round clip rather than a five, it was larger, less sleek and heavier. Inserting the clip without painfully smashing one's thumb as the bolt was tripped to slam forward and chamber the first round would take practice. Still, with the guidance of the senior instructor, Dan warmed to the rifle, zeroed it without much difficulty, and fired a good round, good enough to qualify as sharpshooter.

While that achievement was of no official importance since there was no distinction of rifle types on the marksmanship badge, and Dan's expert ranking on the '03 trumped the M-1 score, it served well by further impressing the drill instructors and officers. From that day forward, boot camp was considerably easier for Dan and those others who had performed well at the range.

Marine Corps tradition was that the honor graduate in each cycle was rewarded with a certificate as such in his official file, a promotion to private first class, and sometimes a choice assignment. Those honors were bestowed upon Dan Howard. His assignment was indeed choice, to the range cadre at Parris Island.

As the lowest ranking man there, Dan had to perform much of the scut work, but that did nothing to diminish the thrill of getting to shoot in the off hours with the instructors, experts one and all. Dan's ability to go home regularly certainly was a perk as well.

After a few months into the job, another life changing event occurred in Dan's life. He was attending to his duties, at the moment issuing and accounting for ammunition, while the instructors were conducting remedial training, dealing with those recruits who had failed to qualify, when one of the instructors suddenly bellowed, "Howard! Get your ass over here." Dan promptly complied and the sergeant continued, "Take these three knuckleheads down the end of the line and see if you can get them to shoot worth a shit before I shoot each one of them dead, graveyard dead, and send their worthless carcasses home to their mamas."

Dan dutifully complied. Not being trained to train, he had to devise a plan while the four men trooped down the line of firing positions. He decided to start with the basics. He reviewed with the recruits the proper firing position, proper seating of the rifle butt in the hollow of the shoulder with the chin firmly pressed against the stock, proper alignment of the front and rear sights, and the imperatives of breathing control and squeezing rather than pulling the trigger. He then had each of the three practice the same and then go through the firing drill, patiently observing and correcting faults as noted. Bar none, yanking on the trigger was the most common, a typical fault, guaranteeing that the bullet would miss its mark.

More or less satisfied, Dan then had each fire a clip at a 100-yard target while again patiently observing and correcting faults. Marines in the trench at the base of the target line displayed via white circular placards mounted on poles where each round had struck and Dan explained the cause of each errant one. Dan then repeated the process.

Dan was able to send one recruit back to the instructor after just a few such cycles. The second required several more. The third one seemed hopeless, and it was not until after everyone else had left the range and then before anyone else arrived the next morning that he finally caught on. That day, all three qualified, and Dan earned the respect of the cadre.

With each successive cycle, Dan found himself being tagged to assist with a "problem child" or two, or three or more. On one such occasion, he was spotted by the captain and after an inquiry was made, the senior sergeant was summoned to the colonel's office.

"Damn it to hell, Gunny, we can't be having a lowly PFC conducting training, even remedial training. If this Howard fella is as good as you must think he is, put corporal stripes on him and tell the adjutant's sergeant I said to make it official." The Gunny responded with the appropriate, "Aye, aye, sir," and made it happen. Dan Howard was about to become a non-commissioned officer in the United States Marine Corps.

Dan's fears that the sergeants, for most of whom it had taken years to get promoted to corporal, would take a dim view of his early promotion were soon allayed when he was invited to go with them to the NCO Club and there, after more than a few beers, they presented Dan with a plaque:

THE U.S. MARINE CORPS NCO CREED

I am an NCO, dedicated to training new Marines and influencing the old. I am forever conscious of each Marine under my charge, and by example will inspire him to the highest standards possible.

I will strive to be patient, understanding, just, and firm. I will commend the deserving and encourage the wayward.

I will never forget that I am responsible to my Commanding Officer for the morale, discipline, and efficiency of my men. Their performance will reflect an image of me.

Presented with earned respect to Corporal Daniel Howard, USMC, by his fellow range instructors at Parris Island, S.C., this 7th day of March, 1941.

Semper fidelis.

As the months clicked by, so did life at Parris Island. War loomed. There was not a soul in the Marine Corps who doubted it. The only thing surprising about December 7, 1941, was that the Japanese mounted their assault on Pearl Harbor without first declaring war and thus prompted an immediate patriotic fervor in the United States. The need to greatly and urgently expand the armed forces was suddenly realized and acted upon. Recruits flooded into Parris Island. The instructor staff worked feverishly to accommodate them and insure their training. The efforts were hampered, but not thwarted, by the constant reassignment of officers and instructors to line units.

Dan Howard was not one of them. Although he pestered the adjutant's office as much as a lowly corporal could, it was to no avail. From the safety of the shores of South Carolina, Dan chafed as he read and saw the news of one disaster after another, Pearl Harbor, Wake Island, the Philippines, and more.

After agonizing months of waiting, Dan was summoned to the adjutant's office where a sergeant informed him, "Congratulations, Howard. Your orders came through. You've been assigned to the First Marine Division. All your questions are answered in this packet. Any questions? No? Good. Good luck, son. Give 'em hell. Dismissed."

Dan Howard, his heart pounding and his head spinning, nearly floated from the headquarters building. After all these months, he was finally, *finally* in it. *He was going to war!*

First though, Dan had to be *sent* off to war. That was the responsibility of the senior range instructor. He dutifully convened the range instructors at the NCO Club. After a few rounds of beer created the appropriate mood, he cleared all but one chair from a table, placed Dan there, and solemnly began the ceremony.

"Corporal Howard, while we are sad to see you go, we take great pride in knowing we are sending a fine young Marine. As a token of our esteem, I present you with this heartfelt gift." He handed Dan a crudely wrapped elongated box. Dan, already suspecting that this event was not going to go well for him, held the curiously lightweight package as if it posed some grave threat.

"Well, open it, damn you. It ain't gonna bite."

When Dan reluctantly complied and discovered a box for a Camillus

Cutlery Ka-Bar knife, the picture on the lid showing a fighting knife with a heavy seven inch clip point blade and leather washer handle with "USMC" stamped into the blade and embossed on the leather sheath. Dan did not know that the knife then was only being considered by the Marine Corps and that knowledge would have made him wonder how the weapon got into his hands. Dan opened the box that he already knew from its weight was empty, the cue for the sergeant to loudly exclaim with mock outrage, "*Empty!* An *empty* box! Which one of you sorry ass bastards stole the friggin' knife?"

Turning to Dan he said, "Just kiddin' ya, Dan, here's your knife…," producing it in its sheath from somewhere behind him. Instead of giving it to Dan though, he continued, "… but it ain't ready for you. It needs to be suitably tempered."

The assembled NCO's closed in more tightly as the Gunny produced a jar, a vial, and a Zippo cigarette lighter and someone handed him a rusty World War One vintage dishpan helmet without the webbing, a bottle of bourbon, and a bottle of whiskey. Placing the helmet upended before Dan, the sergeant held up the bottle of bourbon, earnestly explaining, "This, my son, is fine Kentucky bourbon, the finest tasting elixir on planet Earth. It's to be enjoyed later. This," picking up and uncapping the other bottle and then pouring half of the contents into the helmet, "is rotgut Tennessee whiskey, which'll do for a desperate man, but is best used for…" and with the Zippo he lit the whiskey fumes (which had been boosted for effect with pure alcohol). He then unsheathed the knife, handed it butt first to Dan and instructed him to hold the blade over the flaming alcohol.

When the sergeant was satisfied that the knife was hot enough, he picked up the jar, unscrewed the lid and explained, "This, my brothers, is hog's blood, taken from a monster boar I personally shot right here on the island, at three hundred yards, mind you." Ignoring the guffaws from the assembled NCO's, the sergeant poured the blood over both sides of the hot blade, the blood hissing and smoking and the excess pouring into the flaming whiskey. The smell was revolting, but certainly fitting with the occasion.

Then uncapping and holding up the vial the sergeant explained, "This, brothers, is rattlesnake venom, taken from that big 'un Smitty got last week at the range." With equal flourish, he proceeded to drip the poison on the blade as well, the excess also dripping into the helmet and its flames.

On cue, the sergeant was handed a full glass of beer and a pair of empty whiskey glasses. After quickly downing half the beer and placing the now half-filled glass before Dan, the sergeant poured into each of the other glasses a healthy two inches of the bourbon and placed them in front of himself.

He sternly hushed the crowd and announced, "The process nears completion." With that, he picked up the helmet by its brim, blew out the dwindling flames, rather sloppily poured some of the contaminated contents in with the remaining beer, dropped the helmet noisily to the floor and took the Ka-Bar from Dan's hand.

Pausing for dramatic effect, the sergeant continued, "It needs only one more ingredient, a *vital* ingredient," and spitting on the still hot blade he added, "the spit of the meanest, toughest, shootinest NCO in the whole friggin' United States Marine Corps." The distinctly boisterous unkind reaction of the assembled NCO's was quite predictable.

"Quiet, damn you. *Quiet!* The prescribed ritual is not yet complete." The crowd dutifully hushed and the sergeant proceeded to stir the glass in front of Dan with the blade of the knife and set the glass on the table before Dan. He then wiped off the knife blade, sheathed it, and handed it to Dan. "Here," he said rather anticlimactically, "This is to you, from all of us."

The sergeant stared at Dan who sat there, uncertain of what to say or do. "Well, what the hell are you waiting for? Drink!" Dan naturally balked at that, but succumbing to peer pressure he grasped the glass with its foul contents sitting before him and slowly raised the glass to his lips.

The sergeant startled him by snatching the glass, sloshing its contents, and saying, "Not that poison, you fool! We ain't that damn stupid!" Now laughing along with his audience, no longer able to play out the farce, he set down the beer glass and handed Dan one of the glasses of bourbon. Clinking it against his own he proclaimed for all to hear, "So, farewell, fine Marine. Godspeed. Do us proud, as we know you will. *Semper fi.*"

The drinking resumed with gusto. Dan Howard survived the night, barely, just barely, only just barely.

* * *

Dan Howard was glad to arrive at his duty post after a mostly boring trip. Reporting in to division, the admin sergeant told him, "You're assigned to the 1/7, the 1st Battalion of the 7th Marines; Chesty Puller's outfit. Heaven help you." Dan was excited. Lieutenant Colonel Lewis Puller was a Marine Corps legend, having already earned two Navy Crosses, an award for valor second only to the Congressional Medal of Honor, in fighting against bandits and rebels in Nicaragua. (Puller ultimately would be awarded an unprecedented five Navy Crosses as well as the Army's equivalent, the Distinguished Service Cross, plus four other decorations for valor.) Puller was known as a hard taskmaster, which was fine with Dan.

Dan was directed to the battalion headquarters and his welcome there was less perfunctory. In fact, it was considerably better. Upon showing his papers to the clerk, the young man immediately went over to the sergeant major who beckoned Dan to follow him. Stopping at a door, the sergeant major said, "Colonel, Howard's arrived."

Directed to enter, Dan had his first look at the legend. Short, barrel chested, not what one could say good looking, Puller returned Dan's salute, shook his hand, and after rummaging around his desk for a bit, came up with a sheaf of papers.

With a Virginia accent, the first pleasing thing about him, Puller said, "Been waiting on you, son. Got a letter from your colonel at Parris Island. Seems like you impressed him, enough to write you a Letter of Commendation. Here's a copy. Good thing to have in your service record. He says you can shoot and, better yet, get others to shoot. I need that. I need *you*, old man. You'll be assigned to HQ here, but what I want is you to get right back to what you were doing. The sergeant major will get you set." Taking that as an obvious dismissal, Dan saluted and followed the sergeant major out.

Dan resumed what he had been doing at Parris Island, fortunately again under capable and decent sergeants. The resulting improvement in firearms proficiency in the battalion was satisfying. The unit shipped out in April, 1942, landing in Samoa. There Dan once again resumed those duties for more than a month, again with appreciated good results. Although Dan was proud of his accomplishments, he was not the least bit unhappy when he was informed that he was being assigned to "Recon," the 1/7's reconnaissance platoon.

Dan was first paired up with a scrawny fellow, Private First Class Stuart Markowitz. It took a few days before Dan allowed himself to ask, "Markowitz, how'd you come to Recon?"

The PFC smiled and said, "You mean, how'd a scrawny little Jew like me get through boot camp and then into such an elite outfit?" Dan's blushing was a dead giveaway. "No offense taken, corp. Well, every platoon in the Corps is supposed to have an Indian, but apparently we were running low on them and me being the only other tribe member on hand, I got the nod.

"Seriously, I may be the first and only Jew to ever get Florida swamp mud between his toes. I grew up in Miami, didn't want to work in the family clothing store, and took up surveying. Spent a lot of time in the woods and swamps. Lot of swamp down there getting drained so members of my tribe can flee the frozen, sooty north."

Dan soon realized that while Markowitz indeed was a character, there was no doubting that he was good in the woods and always had a good sense as to where he was. Having himself grown up in the woods and swamps, Dan was both surprised and pleased how much he was able to learn from him. The two were paired well and got to stay together when Dan was made a section leader.

The other section leader, a PFC named Jackson, also was good at his job. He could move through the thickest thickets like a cat, or a ghost, and Dan knew to learn to mimic his every move. Like Markowitz, Jackson also was a character and the three got along quite well. Their squad leader, a sergeant, was another matter, however.

The training ebbed and flowed during their time on Samoa with most of the men getting increasingly more eager to get into action, to kill those lousy Jap bastards. In September, the eager ones got their wish. The 1/7 shipped out, the destination being one of the chain of islands in the Solomons, the one called Guadalcanal.

* * *

Landing on Guadalcanal was anticlimactic. There was no opposition. The Japanese had opted to make their fight inland rather than massing on the beaches where naval gunfire and air strikes could more easily obliterate them.

The pounding from the Navy indeed had pulverized much of the landing beaches and Japanese fortifications there, but the Marines were amazed how little the shelling and bombs affected the island not far inland. The primary objective, the airfield, was taken and the Marines pushed inland at a snail's pace. Recon patrols produced not a single live Jap for days, just the misery of the heat and humidity, being sliced by sharp-edged grasses in the open fields, poked and torn by thorny vines in the thick stuff, and constantly besieged by clouds of mosquitoes.

It was Dan's fourth or fifth patrol. Jackson's section was in the lead, Jackson himself on point. Jackson was moving slowly and deliberately and frequently stopping despite urgings from the sergeant to pick up the pace. Jackson stopped again. Frustrated, the sergeant told Dan to go up front and see what the problem was. Thinking, *Why don't you do it, sergeant?*, Dan kept his mouth shut and eased forward.

Despite Dan's efforts to be stealthy, Jackson sensed his coming and without a word signaled that he heard something and then turning toward Dan signaled that he smelled something too. Dan joined him in scanning the jungle, so thick that visibility was limited to yards except for an occasional lane offering somewhat of a view out to twenty to thirty yards.

Suddenly, Dan sensed that Jackson tensed. He turned to view where Jackson was intently staring. An apparition appeared not ten yards away. It was like a man, a man covered in branches and leaves. Dan's mind was just beginning to comprehend that this was a Japanese soldier when Jackson's Thompson submachine gun shattered the stillness. The heavy .45 caliber slugs hammered the man and he fell back, his twitching body suspended on vines and branches.

There was commotion behind the scout and Jackson and Dan emptied their magazines toward the sounds. They waited a very long few minutes and then slowly moved forward, Jackson watching the front and right and Dan the front and left. The two inched to and past the Jap, clearly dead. Dan leaned against the trunk of a tree, staring into the dense jungle while fighting the urge to wipe away the sweat dripping down his face and the mosquitoes whining in his ears and bumping into his face.

Suddenly Dan caught some movement. He stared with an acuteness he had never before felt nor employed. Seeing another hint of movement, Dan slowly brought his rifle to his shoulder. This time he was not unnerved when a camouflaged Jap materialized. Dan aimed and fired. The soldier fell and did not move. More unseen commotion and then the jungle stillness returned.

The two Marines stayed put for several minutes. The lieutenant came forward and after a minute or so quietly asked for a report. Jackson answered, "Jap patrol, sir. I got the point man and the corporal nailed one more over to the left. Maybe killed or winged more, but we were firing blind. I figure the Nips beat feet, probably setting up an ambush a ways up the trail."

The lieutenant replied, "Well, I hate to disappoint them, but I think it's best we head back and report in."

Such was the life in recon for several more days, occasional brushes with the enemy without any clear indication of his strength or intentions. The highlight of the time was when Markowitz showed up at Dan's tent with a brand new M-1 rifle and several bandoliers of ammunition, saying, "Here ya go, corp, courtesy of the doggies from the American," before slipping away with whatever other loot he had relieved from the careless soldiers of the 164th Infantry Regiment of the U.S. Army's 23rd Infantry Division, brought to Guadalcanal to fight alongside the Marines.

Dan's sergeant continued to disappoint, but one day he was gone, just disappeared into the long tail of the fighting Marines, and Dan became the de facto squad leader. The lieutenant accompanied Dan's squad on their first patrol with him as leader. His reaction to Dan's new rifle was next to nothing.

They eased along the Matanikau River with Jackson, as usual, on point. When Jackson stopped, the lieutenant eased forward and after a few minutes summoned Dan to join them. When Dan reached the two, he realized that they were on a bluff over a wide stretch in the river and could see down it for two hundred yards or more. The lieutenant had his binoculars to his eyes, lowered them, and said to Dan, "We think we got something here. There's a double line of Japs standing in the river just this side of the far bend, just standing there." Handing the binoculars to Dan, he continued, "Do you think you can get a good shot off if some fat colonel comes traipsing through that line?"

Dan studied the line, first through the binoculars and then the naked eye, before concluding, "Maybe so, sir; kinda like threading the needle though."

"Okay, get set and we'll see what happens. May be a good opportunity, but no sense blowing the patrol with nothing to show for it. You're the expert, Dan. It'll be your call."

The waiting was not too long. A gaggle of troops appeared along the bank and began to traverse the river between the two lines of men still there. Through the binoculars, Dan could see that the central group was comprised of officers and that they clustered around a heavier set one in particular. He handed the binoculars back to the lieutenant and began tracking his target. He could not get a clear shot. When the group reached the middle, Dan knew that his opportunity was fading. He surprised the lieutenant and Jackson by uncharacteristically blurting out, "Fuck it. I'm going to clear a lane."

With that, Dan aimed and fired and a heartbeat later a Japanese soldier threw up his hands and collapsed into the water. Dan fired again and the target officer went down. That, however, created a great deal of turmoil below. Japanese soldiers scurried and splashed about while firing blindly in the general direction of the Americans as others clustered protectively around the stricken officer. Dan fired again, trying to hit his target, but instead struck another officer in the back. Men began dragging the target officer through the water, adding more motion and commotion to hamper Dan's aim. He rushed and wasted a shot and then dropped another officer. Now a Nambu machine gun joined the riflemen in lashing out, with rounds beginning to impact uncomfortably close. Dan fired until his rifle pinged empty, seeming to hit another soldier shielding the target and maybe again the target himself, who by then was practically out of sight. As Dan reloaded his rifle, he felt a hand on his arm and heard the lieutenant say, "Time to go, Dan."

Dan was dejected when the trio rejoined the patrol. When asked what he thought, Dan could only reply, "I'm pretty sure I hit the older, heavyset officer, but I can't say if good enough."

Jackson chimed in, "Shoot, yeah, you got the sumbitch. I saw the spray where your first bullet hit him in the side. More'n that, when they were carting the old guy off I counted four Japs left bobbin' in the water."

The lieutenant mulled it over for a few moments and then decided, "Okay, that'll be the report. Fine work, Dan, fine work. Now let's get the hell out of here before the Japs rain on our little parade."

The next day, Recon was ordered to accompany a large reconnaissance probe by elements of the 1/7 and of the 1st Raider Battalion deeper through the jungle in the Lunga River area near the slopes of Mount Austen. The operation was doomed from the start with faulty intelligence appreciation, a less than a cordial relationship between the combined Marine units, and that Chesty Puller was not the commander on the ground. The Japanese anticipated the action, attacked in force, and drove the 1/7 back to Point Cruz, spelling disaster, but for that Puller bravely came to their rescue.

A second effort fared no better and the 1/7 and Raiders settled into defensive positions protecting Henderson Field, both tasked with covering a front greatly exceeding what an infantry battalion could hope to effectively cover.

3

THE LIEUTENANT SPOTTED CORPORAL DAN HOWARD AND PFC JACK-son sitting together and walked over, nonchalantly asking, "Mornin', men, whatcha doing?"

Dan responded, "Mornin' to you too, sir; just admiring the Jackhammer's new toy."

Displaying his Thompson, Jackson chimed in, "Look at this here, sir, a drum magazine for my tommy gun. Traded some Jap stuff for it."

The lieutenant too admired the outfitted weapon and responded, "Well, now, Jackson, now you're a real Chicago gangster. Go ahead and load it up. I expect you'll have use for it soon. Dan, come with me, please."

The lieutenant led Dan to the headquarters tent bustling with activity and to the map board. Pointing to a spot on the map, the lieutenant told Dan, "We have a mission. There's a gap between these companies. The colonel wants us, *you*, to check it out and report back. I'll let both companies know you're coming, but be careful. They might be a bit jittery."

Dan returned to his squad area and found Jackson and his other section leader waiting for him. He got right to the point, "HQ wants us to check out a gap in the line. Gather 'em up. Full combat packs with entrenching tools, full canteens, plenty of ammo, in case we get stuck out there."

Thirty minutes later, satisfied after a cursory inspection of the men, Dan had the squad headed the short way to the line, conferred with the Gunny of the near company, and then continued on to and beyond their flank position. They followed the ridge until they hit the flank position of the neighboring company, a distance Dan figured to be more than a hundred yards. After instructing a corporal there to pass the word to his commander, Dan turned to Jackson and said, "Let's ease down a bit through this thick stuff to see what we can see below. You lead."

What Dan found was concerning. Although dense at each flank, not much more than fifty yards below the ridge the jungle thinned in the center with a sluggish creek at the bottom. It did not take Dan more than a couple of minutes to make a decision.

"Jackhammer, you and one of yours here; send the other two midway to the thicket on the right." Turning to his other section leader, he said, "You do the same on the left, but leave me Stu." Easing down behind a rotting log, Dan pulled out a small notebook and a pencil and pondered what to report. He was interrupted by a hushed report of movement below, beyond the creek, spotted, of course, by Jackson. Dan put down the pad and pencil, readied his rifle, and carefully surveyed all he could see.

The movement materialized into a well-camouflaged Japanese soldier moving expertly toward them. Another appeared and then others. Dan had no doubt that his Marines soon would be spotted. Still he waited for the optimum time and target. Dan discerned an officer, thought to take him first, but then decided on an apparent NCO nearer.

Dan waited until the Japanese point man crossed the creek, with the NCO mostly concealed behind a tree on the far side. He briefly took his eye off the NCO to confirm the officer's location and then put the M-1's sights on the NCO's tree. As soon as the man eased out from behind the tree, Dan tightened his aim and squeezed off a shot. As he was turning his attention to the officer, Dan was conscious of the NCO reaching to steady himself by the tree, failing and falling forward into the creek; Jackson's tommy gun firing and the Jap point man going down; and his other Marines firing as well. The officer lingered, exposed a moment too long, and Dan hit him in the chest and head. The firing quickly died out as the survivors of the Japanese patrol fled out of sight.

Taking a few moments for the adrenaline rush to fade and to determine that no Marine casualties had been sustained, Dan signaled Jackson to go down and check out the downed officer. Jackson stealthily moved down the hill, confirmed that the Japs at the creek were dead, crawled over to the officer, and moved back up the hill to Dan. He handed Dan some papers, including a hand drawn map, and showed him the pistol he had taken off the man. Dan took the papers, ignored the gun, and sent Jackson back to his position. Dan then began to write:

Subject gap more than 100 yds wide. Jungle opens up 50 yds below the ridge to a creek bottom parallel to our lines. Good corridor. Japs know. Jap patrol approached at 1140. Bearer has papers off officer. Some got away. No friendly casualties. To hold this pos would take min of 2 full squads with an MG, mortar support, and wire (comm and barbed). Will hold until relieved.

Howard, Cpl.

Thirty minutes later, PFC Markowitz delivered the message to the lieutenant, the lieutenant to the intel and ops officers, and they to Lieutenant Colonel Puller. After reading the message, Puller pulled the omnipresent pipe from his mouth and commented, "Hmmm. Good report. Succinct. Better than most." Turning to the recon lieutenant he said, "I trust Howard. I don't want to monkey with the reserve. Support'll have to be from you. I don't want to tell you your business, old man, but I'm thinking send half of each of your other squads up there. No machine gun though. Can't spare it. Make sure Howard gets another BAR instead. Extra grenades too. Scrounge up the wire. Any objections, tell 'em I said so. Clear?" The lieutenant nodded and left.

Two hours later, Dan was pleased to see Stu coming down off the ridge and leading a dozen men laden with supplies and the platoon gunnery sergeant. The Gunny scanned Howard's line, such as it was, and below, including the visible Jap bodies, and said, "Looking good, Dan. Brought up some wire, as much as could be carried. This wireman'll lay comm wire back to the CP. I'm afraid to tell ya, but you're staying put. It'll be your show at least 'til tomorrow. I'll leave you eight of these guys, one with a BAR. I'll come back up to see you in the morning, that is if the Japs don't push us back to the beach tonight and make us swim up to Florida Island."

Dan tried unsuccessfully to hide his disappointment. The Gunny shrugged and said, "You can handle it, Dan. Holler for the fire brigade if you need to." With that he left with the wiremen in tow.

Dan turned his attention to the reinforcements. He directed each one into position and told them all to dig in deep. He took the two lugging the barbed wire down to just above the creek and directed where to string it. It would be a pathetic single strand at knee height, not even spanning the detachment's front.

Dan took Stu and three of the new riflemen and the BAR man to the right. Deciding along the way, he dropped one man off with Jackson; another five yards beyond with one of Jackson's section; another and Stu ten yards past where Jackson had placed his other two; and the BAR man and a rifleman on the flank. Returning to his position where the remaining four riflemen waited, Dan similarly placed them on the left, the difference being that he had to place one of his former section members, a reliable man, in a hole alone.

Dan brought one of his guys back to share his hole and to help to monitor the field telephone. Surveying the line, Dan could not help but to frown. He said to himself, "*Not good, but the best I can do.*" He then joined his new companion in digging the hole.

By the time the holes had been dug and somewhat camouflaged, and some brush cleared for better fields of fire, daylight was beginning to fade. Dan ensured that the meager munitions were evenly distributed; he inspected the foxholes and directed a few improvements; he made sure that every man knew his sector of fire, to shoot low ("in their damn balls") and not to shoot except upon his signal; and finally he made it clear to each and every man that there would be no falling back. Once that was accomplished, Dan returned to his hole, made sure he still had communication with the CP, and laid out his ammunition and grenades.

As darkness enveloped them as it does quickly in the jungle, Dan munched on a ration while thinking over and over what he could have, should have done, and what, if anything, he could improve. Coming up with nothing, Dan settled down to wait on the Japs. He did not have to wait on the evening onslaught of mosquitoes, their incessant whining making it difficult to differentiate anything abnormal in the sounds out there in the dark.

The Japanese were not as timely. Hours passed without any indication that there even were Japs out there. Firing erupted somewhere down the line and a flare went up. Flares can illuminate the battlefield, but they also can cast shadows darker than the night. For Dan and his Marines, it was more the latter.

But the visual problem was not just isolated to the defenders. The first indication that the Japs were coming was a loud splash in the creek almost directly below Dan, as if a Jap soldier had blundered into it. Dan sensed the range, pulled the pin on a grenade and tossed it. The explosion instantly was followed by a cry of pain, confirming it was a human and not some errant jungle creature. Dan readied his rifle, but still could not spot a target. Jackson recklessly stood up in his hole, his Thompson at his shoulder and over and over said to himself, *"Come on, Dan. Come on!"*

After what seemed like an eternity, a flare drifted favorably their way, exposing a wave of Japanese soldiers on the near side of the creek. The flare drifted away and Dan fired three quick shots at the memory of one, the signal for the line to commence firing. The Marines let loose a volley, causing a number of Japs to fall, but it was Jackson and his Tommy gun with drum magazine that would never be forgotten.

Starting right of center, Jackson swept a long burst to his left and then from left of center, an equally long burst to the right. The effect of the automatic weapon and especially the enormous fireball erupting from the muzzle of the gun quite literally paused the fight. Some of the Japanese hunkered down and began firing their rifles, a cry of pain down the Marine line evincing that at least one of their bullets found its mark. Other Japanese soldiers sought the flanks to avoid the killing ground in the center, most only to be cut down by the BAR's.

A shouted command, followed by the scream of "Banzai! Banzai! *Banzai!*" got the Japanese soldiers to their feet. They came up the hill in a rush, yelling as they came. A flare, however, caught them in the open. Dan shot two, then another. He quickly reloaded and gasped to see a Jap a mere ten feet below him. Dan put three rounds into him.

Dan then caught movement in his peripheral vision and turned to see a Jap viciously thrust his long bayonet into a Marine in the hole to the left, yank it out, and thrust it in again before rifle fire killed him. Seeing that Japs were reaching the line, Dan looked to his right and in horror saw a Jap looming over Jackson and Jackson batting the bayonet away, only to be butt stroked in the side of the head. Dan emptied his clip into the man and the man collapsed on the front lip of Jackson's hole.

The assault ended as quickly as it had begun. Several Japanese lingered to fire from the perceived cover of the creek bank and trees, only to be met with concentrated fire from the Marines. Soon the remaining Japanese were either dead or opted to join their comrades in melting back into the darkness.

Dan waited for a few minutes to confirm that it was over, at least for a time, before getting on the field phone. He reported, "Recon hit by approximately company strength. Quiet now. Line thinned, but holding. Casualty report to follow. Request resupply of ammo and a corpsman and litter bearers standing by."

Dan knew that to leave his hole was tantamount to suicide, but he worried about his men, Jackson especially. Telling his foxhole mate to keep his eyes and ears open and to monitor the phone, Dan threw caution to the wind and slipped out of the hole.

As he crawled toward Jackson's hole, Dan softly called out. No answer. *Shit!* Dan continued to call out softly as he inched toward the hole. Reaching it, he found Jackson unconscious, his foxhole mate dead. With nothing to be done for Jackson at the moment, Dan continued his trek down the line. In the next hole, both men were wounded, but functioning; in the next, Stu was okay, but his hole mate was badly wounded; and in the flank position both the BAR man and the rifleman okay.

Dan returned to his hole after getting an ammo status at each hole and issuing what he hoped to be adequate admonishments and encouraging words. Dan continued past his hole and found the left much like the right. In the first hole, one dead and the other wounded but functioning; in the next the solo Marine was okay; in the next both wounded, but neither seriously; and at the flank the BAR man was out of the fight with a head wound, his weapon in the hands of his rifleman hole mate.

Dan returned to his hole with mixed emotions. While he was horrified that he had suffered more than half of his men as casualties, he was strangely elated under the circumstances that only two had been killed. He dutifully made the report to the CP and settled down to await the next Japanese assault. After no more than ten minutes though, he told his hole mate he was going to check on Jackson, ignoring that a professional NCO would never abandon his post for such a reason.

Dan was gladdened to find Jackson sitting upright in his hole, his Tommy gun within easy reach. He asked, "Well, howya doin', Jackhammer?"

Jackson groaned and muttered in reply, "My friggin' head hurts, corp."

"It's supposed to. That Jap was swinging for the fences when he connected with your hard head."

"Ya get him for me?"

"Yeah, he's right here at the front of the hole. You could piss on him if it'd make you feel better, but it'd be dangerous to stand."

"Well, it can wait. What happened to the Japs?"

"Don't know. Gone. At least those you didn't kill."

"Yeah, that sweet ol' Tommy gun was sure barkin' somethin' fierce."

"I gotta get back. I'll see what I can do for that head of yours when it gets light."

Dan returned to his hole, this time staying for the duration of the night, waiting for the Japs and as always feeding the mosquitoes. Dawn, however, blessedly came without any Jap resurgence. Dan forced himself to wait still for a short while and then went over to check on Jackson, the other Marines to the right, and then those to the left. When he returned to his hole, he decided to ease down the hill.

He passed a half dozen Jap bodies below his hole and could see that there were more than a dozen bodies below Jackson's, two of them officers; there was a row of Jap bodies on and around the pitiful excuse for a wire obstacle; the sluggish creek was stained red with the blood of a dozen more; and he could see more beyond the creek and to the left and right. Dan collected the officers' swords and brought them up to Jackson, telling him, "Here're some souvenirs off the Jap officers you mowed down. You already have a pistol, so I'm keeping the one I found."

Dan caught movement to their rear and whirled toward it, his rifle at the ready, only to realize that it was the Gunny leading down the rest of Recon, the lieutenant shadowing none other than Chesty Puller. The better part of a line platoon was following along with corpsmen and stretcher bearers. Dan approached the first group, accepted the Gunny's outstretched hand and then the lieutenant's, who then led him to his battalion commander in the middle group.

Dan spoke first. "Colonel, you shouldn't be out here. We don't know that the Japs are gone."

Puller, puffing on his pipe, scoffed at that and said, "Tell me about it, old man."

Dan, figuring that the colonel had been informed of his reports, gave but an abbreviated report of the short, but violent fight, adding, "Sir, what broke their back was PFC Jackson killing their leaders and a bunch more. Took the starch out of 'em."

Puller surveyed the carnage below Jackson's hole and then that below the next hole. Pointing there with the stub of his pipe, he asked, "Yours?" When Dan nodded in the affirmative, Puller said, "Well, it looks like Jackson had a little help from you." Looking around, he added further, "A company you reported. Looks like more than half of them are still here."

Looking Dan Howard in the eye, Lieutenant Colonel Puller said, "Good work, son, good work. Makes me proud. More than proud. Howard, consider yourself a sergeant as of right now. Clear?"

"Clear, sir. Thank you."

"Don't thank *me*, old man. You earned it, and more. Now, here's what we're going to do. We're going to tend to your casualties while this platoon with me sweeps your front and your Recon compadres check the officers for anything of intel value. The platoon is going to take over here and you're to lead your men back to the CP. I'm going to want a full report of this action, including recommendations for awards, in two days, that is, if the Japs stay quiet. Right now, I need to finish trooping the line."

* * *

The Japanese knew they were defeated on Guadalcanal, the only thing left to do was to die an honorable death and take as many American devils with them as they could. It took more than another month to root out and eliminate the remnants of the Japanese forces. The low point was when Chesty Puller was wounded, one of the high points being when he refused to leave his command. The 1/7 finally left around Christmas, 1942, the most common sentiment being *"Good riddance!"*

The 1/7 was given considerable time to rest and refit. Based largely on Dan Howard's report, considerably enhanced by his lieutenant, PFC Jackson was promoted to corporal. Although he made no mention of himself in the edited report, the lieutenant was duly credited, promoted to captain, and moved up to S-2. Chesty Puller went on to greater fame. The Recon Gunnery Sergeant was made First Sergeant of a line company and arranged to have Dan moved over to lead one of the squads. Dan was saddened to leave Recon, but his Guadalcanal experience gave him the confidence that he could be a good squad leader. His first order of business was to get them to the range and get them shooting like they should.

The 1st Division did not see combat again for nearly a year, then on New Britain, an island off New Guinea. Dan Howard, suffering a recurring bout of malaria, missed that battle. He, having been recently promoted to Staff Sergeant and moved back to the range as a staff NCO at Division, felt terrible about it.

Dan Howard would not see battle again until September, 1944, in the Palau Islands near the Philippines, a miserable chunk of coral and scrub called Peleliu. There, Howard, back in a line platoon by request and acquiescence, would reunite with Stu Markowitz, still a PFC, for what was to become a horrific bloodbath.

Unlike Guadalcanal, the Marines on Peleliu faced heavy, fanatical resistance from the very beginning. The Japanese, having anticipated the American attack, had laboriously and meticulously entrenched themselves in fortified caves with interlocking fields of fire supported by ample artillery and mortars. Learning to defeat them was by costly experiment. Marine casualties were staggering. Dan Howard's platoon was no exception. In a matter of days, Dan was commanding it, although by then attrition had reduced it to not much more than a squad.

Dan Howard and Stu Markowitz learned from attached combat engineers (every one of whom had been since killed or wounded) how to eliminate the cave fortresses and devised their own effective method: Stu, covered by Dan and the platoon and sometimes attached machine guns and/or tanks, would climb next to or above a cave opening and blast the Japs with explosives. The method was extremely hazardous, being ordered to accompany Markowitz considered the kiss of death. Markowitz himself did not expect to last many days at it unscathed, and prayed only to be wounded rather than killed.

The Marines fought their way southward, one coral ridge after another. Stu lost track of how many. It was just another miserable, terrifying day when Sergeant Howard was ordered to lead the assault on yet another steep ridge pocked with cave openings, an equally battered 3rd Platoon to follow. Dan cringed when he looked over at the 3rd's new platoon commander, a fresh second lieutenant experiencing his first combat.

The remnants of Dan's platoon bolstered with a handful of replacements edged forward under machine gun and rifle fire, past yet another smoldering tank and all too familiar clusters of dead Japs, and dead Marines. The following platoon lagged behind.

As they neared the base of the ridge, Dan pointed out to Stu the cave opening from which the machine gun fire was coming and already claimed two more casualties in the platoon. The two veterans figured the best approach, one that involved crossing rough ground, scaling a cliff, and then continuing to climb a slope of jagged coral, all the while subject to fire. Dan ordered two of his men to accompany Stu and positioned the rest of his men to suppress fire from a supporting enemy position almost certainly to be up to the left. He alone moved forward to where he best could keep the heads of the Japs in the target cave down as Stu and the two other Marines alternated slithering and darting up the slope from one bit of cover to the next. Dan glanced over his shoulder and frowned when he could not see 3rd Platoon, whose supporting fire could make the task at hand easier.

Despite Dan's expertly putting several clips into the cave opening, Stu alone made it to cover to the right of it. Exhausted mentally and physically from the climb and knowing that getting into position where he could swing the satchel charge he carried into the cave was going to be dicey, Stu laid his carbine across his knees and pulled out his canteen. Dan saw it and understood the need to pause and screw up one's courage for the death defying act he was requiring Stu to again perform.

The thought was punctuated by the sudden appearance of a Jap emerging from a crevice not twenty feet away from Stu, his rifle aimed at Stu's head. Stu too caught the movement, but with a canteen in his hand and his weapon on his lap he could only gape at the soldier, expecting imminent death. Instead, the Jap soldier's head exploded in a spray of blood and bone. Looking downhill and making eye contact with Dan, Stu raised his canteen in salute to the man who once again had saved his life.

Stu steeled himself for the final movement to the selected vantage point above the enemy position, primed the explosive, took a deep breath and launched himself as Dan resumed steady fire into the mouth of the cave. Stu heaved in the smoking satchel charge and barely had rolled away when the blast hurled rocks, shattered weapons, and body parts from the cave.

When the dust cleared, Dan signaled Stu to hold tight. Dan had another task to do. He slipped back down the slope to where he could see over the lip of the cliff. There below was 3rd Platoon, huddled in the cover. He furiously bellowed, "Get your sorry asses up here!"

The Marines moved. As the first few came to him, Dan directed them to the left, beyond his men. The next Marine was their green lieutenant, who looked sheepishly at Dan, knowing that the timid approach of his platoon had been due to his failure to effectively exhort his man. Dan allowed the officer to pass by without a word.

The same was not true when the platoon sergeant came upon him. Heedless of that he had no authority over the man and even may have been outranked by him, Dan roughly halted him and, punctuating his words with vicious jabs to the man's chest, savagely said, "Do your fucking job, Marine! Your lieutenant's green, but he'll lead if you'll push the men for him!" Shamed, the sergeant looked at Dan, meekly nodded, and moved on. Dan was satisfied in seeing what he perceived to be rekindled resolve in the man's eyes.

Dan returned to his men and when 3rd Platoon was set, the Marines resumed their assault up the ridge. They were soon met by withering fire and their advance slowed to a literal crawl. As Dan crawled forward, a Japanese soldier popped out of a hole not ten yards above him. Dan killed the man and resumed crawling, almost immediately shooting another Jap emerging from the same hole. Stu watched Dan creep up to the hole and then both men were startled to see the Jap soldier moving, an impossibility due to the fact that the back of his head was a gaping hole.

Dan realized that hands from below were pulling the body back into a cave or tunnel below, probably so more of them could emerge. Dan crawled the few more feet to the hole, pulled out a grenade, pulled the pin, and held the spoon down as he waited until just the enemy's arms were visible. Dan then released the spoon, letting the grenade "cook off" for a couple of seconds before he dropped it into the opening. As soon as the grenade exploded, Dan took out another grenade and dropped it into the now mostly cleared shaft. A more muffled explosion followed and smoke curled out of the hole.

Dan was debating whether to drop in another grenade when a round cracked closely by his head. He whirled to see a Japanese soldier twenty yards away working the bolt of his rifle. Dan snap fired twice, hitting the man once in the shoulder. He jerked with the impact, but still steadfastly tried to raise his rifle, a commendable effort terminated by Dan's next shot. Dan then resumed crawling up the hill, keeping his men abreast.

Unbeknownst to Dan, his actions were observed by a cluster of officers who had been watching for some time through their binoculars. The officers continued to watch as the Marines slowly but steadily advanced, clearing Japanese from the face of the ridge. The officers, of course, could not hear the voices of their Marines.

Dan Howard cringed as his sole remaining BAR man fell. Looking around, he spotted Markowitz and called him over to him. In a few moments, Stu crashed down next to him after a zig-zagging sprint. He let his friend catch his breath before telling him, "Ditch that peashooter of yours and grab that BAR up there. We're gonna need it when we get to the top." While Stu was not thrilled at the prospect of carrying a weapon triple the weight of his carbine, he understood that Dan was right, the BAR's killing power was far superior. The two of them rushed up to where the BAR man lay still.

Stu had just recovered the BAR and bandolier of twenty-round magazines when Dan banged out a full clip of ammo. Looking up, Stu saw a line of Japanese on the crest of the ridge, foolishly silhouetted from their vantage point below. He joined Dan and by then the other Marines in gunning them down. The surviving Japanese fell back and at the shouted command of the young lieutenant the Marines surged forward and upward to wrest control of the ridge crest.

The battalion CO observed the success and after a "Hot damn!" ordered the rest of the company forward to reinforce them. Thinking it through, he decided to commit his reserve company, did so, and ordered his S-3 to so inform regimental HQ of the same and that he was moving his own headquarters forward to just behind his new line. Satisfied that he had his forces in motion, he turned to his Sergeant Major and said, "I want the name of the lieutenant who led that assault and the name of the sergeant, I presume, on the right, the one who got things moving and who killed all those Japs."

Meanwhile, Dan surveyed the terrain to his front, the stunted trees and vegetation that had managed to grow in an otherwise moonscape of ancient coral mostly having been blasted away by shell fire and bombs. Dan positioned his men to defend against a counterattack, coordinating with the now more confident 3rd Platoon commander and sergeant. Dan was pleased to see that they both quickly had followed his lead in getting the men to gather anything they could to provide some cover, the ground being too hard to dig in to, and in sending details back down the slope to check on the casualties and to gather ammunition, grenades, water, and medical pouches.

The counterattack soon came as expected, preceded by a fierce mortar barrage. Dan and Stu, twenty yards apart, exchanged knowing looks with the first telltale *thunks* of the mortars. Dan then was on his feet, yelling first to the left and then to the right, "Mortars! Get down! Get down! Be ready to shoot as soon as the mortars quit!"

Perhaps Dan miscalculated the impact of the mortar rounds or perhaps he disregarded the danger to get the warnings out. In either event, Stu was shocked beyond belief as Dan, whom he was beginning to believe was impervious, suddenly was enveloped in a huge explosion that hurled him back down the slope, weaponless and helmetless, to land on a jagged coral outcropping with a sickening crunch. Stu wanted to rush down there, but explosions rocked the ridge and he knew the counterattack would follow.

There were a lot of Japanese, but owing to their communications by then were in shambles, the assault was poorly coordinated. It was quickly beaten back. Stu wasted no time rushing down to where his sergeant was lying motionlessly, blackened, and bloody with one leg obviously badly broken. Stu was astonished to find that Dan was even alive.

Stu was unchallenged when he began barking orders to the reinforcements making their way up the slope. He had Dan placed on a makeshift stretcher and again unchallenged when he detailed four men to carry Dan back to the casualty collection point with two others to provide protection along the way. He returned to the line, aware that he now was in charge of the few remnants of the platoon, and angrily shouted at them, "Well, whadya waiting for? Get off your sorry asses and kill more Japs. Kill every goddamned one of those sonsabitches, then kill 'em again."

* * *

Dan Howard's wounds were his ticket home, but not for a quick trip home. It took him weeks to reach the west coast and weeks to be released from the hospital. By then his hearing mostly had returned, and his powder burns and flesh wounds had long healed with minimal scarring. The leg bones had mostly mended too. He could walk with a cane.

Dan was able to stand tall at an ad hoc awards ceremony where he was presented his Purple Heart and a Bronze Star for valor, the latter a decoration that had been established the year before in recognition of the many heroic acts previously unrewarded because they were deemed not quite worthy of the greater Silver Star. Although he had sworn that he would never touch alcohol again, he allowed himself a taste of the bottle one of his fellow ambulatory produced for the occasion.

Upon release from the hospital, the administrative clerk explained the packet of papers she was giving him, among them being his travel pass to Charleston and then on to Beaufort, his orders for thirty days' convalescent leave, and his provisional duty assignment to none other than Parris Island. She explained that "provisional" meant that he first would have to pass a fitness examination at the Charleston Naval Hospital, failure of which would result in a medical discharge. Dan endured the trip home, finding that being a wounded war veteran and decorated Marine NCO had its perks.

After a joyous reunion and his favorite meal, Dan found himself on the back porch with his father, again gazing across the river. Carl

Howard recalled that this was where they had left off more than two years before. It then was Dan's turn.

"Dad, I know I told you that I'd be back, ready to get back to the logging crew, but I don't know that this leg is ever going to let me do that well."

Carl cut him off, saying, "That's no problem, Dan, no problem at all. The logging is handled okay. So is the saw mill. The new shop is doing well and I'm now selling cars, trucks, and tractors, too. What I need, what I was hoping to interest you in, is you working with me to get and manage state road contracts and to work with me and Bill Greer over at the bank to manage our properties. You can have the old home place for a while, but I have to tell you that Bill is interested in it, says we both should make good money off it after the war."

Dan could think of nothing more to say than, "Thanks, Dad. I'd be glad to."

The rest of Dan's leave was immensely enjoyable, with Carl mock scolding his wife to stop feeding the boy so much or he would not fit back into his uniform. A high point was a letter from Miami, addressed only to him in Beaufort, SC. How it had not been doomed to the grave of undeliverable mail was a mystery.

Dear Dan,

I guess this made it to you. I figured it might, you living in a podunk town and all. I hope it didn't take too long. I pray to God this finds you well. You weren't looking too good the last time I saw you, but you are one tough Marine.

I expect you know all about our little island paradise after you departed. You won't believe this, but they made me a sergeant! (Maybe the only Jew sergeant in the entire Corps?) But that's history. As you can see, I am home, having earned enough points trudging along with the 1/7. (Jackhammer too, also a Sgt.—he's in California.)

I am back to the shady business of trying to convince northern members of the tribe to buy dream property down here. It's looking good. Come see me. I will show you real beaches. Send me your address and let me know how life's treating you. I am sure that it beats where we were any day of the week.

Oh, by the way, if you're wondering what came of your Ka-Bar, I have it. Some other stuff too that got past the inspectors. I'll get it to you.

Semper fi, Stu

***

The time then came for Dan to go to Charleston for his medical examination. He arrived on time and was ushered into an examination room and told to strip down and put on a provided gown. Afterward a naval lieutenant nurse, a *very* attractive young lady, entered the room. Unfortunately, she not only was an officer, but all business as well.

She reviewed Dan's chart, examined first his healed puncture wounds and then his leg, followed by a long series of questions. Dan quickly tired of them and began to give rather flippant answers. When she asked if he could run, his answer was, "Listen, ma'am, I just want to spend the rest of the war down at Parris Island doing nothing but training boots how to shoot. I don't need to run anywhere."

The nurse very quickly grew tired of that nonsense and walked to the door. Dan's only thought was, "*Oh, shit, I royally fucked up this time. She's gonna go get the doctor and he's gonna send me packing.*"

Instead, the nurse closed the door, almost violently spun around and harshly scolded Dan, "Listen, *Mister* Marine. I am here to examine you because the good doctor is out playing golf or some such other foolishness. He'll sign whatever I put in front of him, so if you don't start cooperating nicely, I will put you on a bus back to Farmville or wherever."

Dan, embarrassed, stared at her for a moment and then the words that came out were, "Beaufort, ma'am, just down the coast from here by Parris Island. And I apologize. Ask away, please."

"Okay, can you run?"

"No."

"Listen to me, Marine, and *carefully* think it through. Can you run?"

"Ugh, yes?"

"Good, can you jump?"

"Ugh, yes, ma'am."

The farce continued for several more minutes, at which time she concluded with, "Well, Sergeant, it's up to the doctor, of course, but I see no reason here to deprive the Marine Corps of an enthusiastic and I assume qualified marksmanship instructor." She then handed him a card with her name and number, smiled and told him to call her with any questions, and left Dan alone in the room.

Dan thought about her often during his final days of leave. Those thoughts, however, fled his mind when he received a telephone call. It was a lady caller and she told him that his orders had been amended, that he was to report directly to the Commanding General at precisely the given date and time. Shocked, Dan's reply was, "Aye, aye, ma'am."

At the appointed time and place, Dan was standing before the general's secretary. He was announced and before too long ushered into the general's office. Dan came smartly to attention the prescribed distance from the desk, saluted smartly, and said, "Staff Sergeant Daniel Howard reporting as ordered, sir."

The general looked up and Dan expected a return salute. Instead the general roared, "You're in my presence out of uniform, Sergeant!"

Dan was aghast. His mind raced. His uniform was freshly cleaned and pressed. His ribbons and badges were properly in place. His shoes were immaculate. *What?* And then he had his "*oh, shit*" moment. "*My cane. I have the cane dad made for me, the <u>nonregulation</u> cane!*"

Dan stammered, "Begging the general's pardon,…," which was as far as he got before the general rose and began reading from a piece of paper in his hands.

"Attention to orders,…" at which time Dan heard people he had not seen slip into the room snap to attention, "Daniel Carl Howard is hereby this day promoted to the rank of Gunnery Sergeant… Sergeant major, sir, madam, if you will."

At that the Sergeant Major stepped up to Dan's left and Dan was greatly surprised to see his mother and father come around to his right. The general handed the orders to the adjutant and he handed them and a set of chevrons to Dan. Handshakes, photographs, and a proud loving hug from Dan's mother then followed. The general wrapped up the occasion with a short speech:

"Ladies and gentlemen. It was my great pleasure to officiate this little ceremony. This lad, Mrs. Howard, is a true American hero. Guadalcanal under no less than Chesty Puller. Peleliu, nasty business, even worse than Tarawa. A wounded warrior, decorated for valor. He's also one of the finest marksmen in the Marine Corps, with the Marines being the finest marksmen in the world. At least they ought to be. We still have a war to finish and we need superb instructors like Gunny Howard here to make sure that happens. I am glad to have him and proud to serve with him."

The general's speech certainly inspired Dan to perform to his utmost in sending shooters to upcoming battlefields like Iwo Jima and Okinawa. Dan liked to think that through his intensive training he saved many a Marine's life while helping send many a Jap soul to hell.

Dan was still training Marines, these bound for the invasion of Japan itself, when on September 2, 1945, the Japanese surrendered, ending the war. He pulled from his wallet the card the nurse had handed him months before, took a deep breath, and called the number. A female voice answered in military fashion, giving her rank and name. Dan took another deep breath and began, "Ma'am, this is Gunnery Sergeant Dan Howard. We met some months back and you gave me your card."

"Yes, Sergeant, I remember. How can I help you?"

"Well, it's like this, ma'am. I am soon to be *former* Sergeant Howard and I was wondering if you would care to go out with me, a private citizen, in Charleston, Beaufort, wherever; lunch, dinner, a walk in the park, on the beach, whatever, whenever."

After a long pause she replied, "Show me Beaufort. Saturday. Meet me at the hospital entrance at noon. And stop calling me ma'am. I'm soon to be out too. It's "Bea, b-e-a; pronounced 'b," as in the letter, or the bug; short for "Beatrice."

"Deal! I'll be there." Excited and without any forethought, he threw caution to the wind and added, "Oh, pack a bag if you think there might be a chance you'd like to stay over, respectably, at my Mom and Dad's."

Bea laughed and left it at, "Well, we'll see about that."

Saturday came and Dan pulled up in front of the hospital entrance in the 1941 Nash coupe his father loaned him. Bea was there, looking marvelous. And she'd packed a bag! They drove down to Beaufort, talking the whole way. Dan showed her the beach, the docks, downtown, the old home place, and they finally ended up at his Mom and Dad's. After visiting and enjoying a splendid meal, they retired to the back porch for coffee, pie, and a beautiful evening with the river changing each moment as the sun set. Bea agreed to stay and after Dan's mother left, pretending to need to prepare the bedroom, and his father making even more of a lame excuse for departing, Dan took Bea into his arms and they kissed, first tentatively then passionately.

Bea was in love. Dan was in love. The rest was history.

* * *

The year 1945 saw the end of World War Two, but the world was not at peace. Largely to blame were United States politicians and diplomats who bungled the peace as badly as had their predecessors after the First World War.

One such instance pertained to Korea. At the waning days of the war, after the United States had all but secured victory by the nuclear bombing of the Japanese cites Hiroshima and Nagasaki, the United States tossed a bone, so to speak, to the Soviet Union in myopic consideration for that they had borne the Nazi onslaught at horrendous cost while the United States amassed its juggernaut.

The bone was agreeing to the Russians unnecessarily liberating the northern half of Korea of Japanese forces no longer a viable threat. The Cold War then led in 1948 to a formal severance of Korea at the 38th parallel and installation of a communist government in the north lusting for the south while being beholden to both the Soviet Union and China.

On June 25, 1950, North Korea invaded South Korea, soundly defeated its armed forces and proceeded to all but drive out of the country the United States forces who were unprepared on every level and woefully unsupported. The Americans and remnants of the South Korean forces held on in a tiny perimeter at Pusan at the southern tip of the country. General MacArthur reversed the course with a brilliant invasion (including the 1st Marine Division) on the northwest coast at a place called Inchon (or Incheon) and drive through the captured capital of Seoul.

The North Koreans, already dangerously over-extended and now having their supply lines severed, were evicted from South Korea, but MacArthur and the United States leaders were not satiated with the victory. They decided to capitalize on their successes by pushing into North Korea, seizing the capital city of Pyongyang and driving the North Korean forces ultimately to the Yalu River border with China. It was both predictable and unforgivably unexpected that China intervened in a big way, with nearly 300,000 troops supported by armor and artillery (and soon Soviet air support), ratcheting the conflict up to a two-year major war.

Dan Howard struggled mightily with what to personally do. The patriot in him wanted to re-enlist while the family man in him favored his responsibilities to his family. Ultimately the decision was made easy for him. One day when patriotism edged out family, he had made an inquiry as to how he, a married man with a child and not 100% physically fit due to his war wounds, could serve. In due time, Marine Corps headquarters responded that he could reenlist for a one-year term with the assurance that he would go no farther than the rifle ranges at Parris Island.

To be sure, the Marine Corps needed the help of Dan Howard and his expertise as a marksmanship instructor. The Corps had dwindled from an all-time high at the end of World War Two of nearly 500,000 Marines to one sixth of that, about 75,000 men. That number would triple over the course of the Korean War, with most of them being re-servists in dire need of marksmanship training, be it basic or refresher. Dan would serve in that capacity for a year when sufficient numbers of qualified instructors rotated home from the combat zone.

***

Instead of Dan Howard, it would be his younger brother Bob who would serve in combat in Korea. Too young for the Second World War, Bob saw it as his duty to enlist as had his father and older brother. Like Dan, he chose the Marine Corps. He would be in boot camp during the Inchon landing, Pusan breakout, and Battle of Seoul and would not make it to Korea until the Chinese had intervened. He found himself at the Chosin Reservoir under the command of no less than Colonel Lewis "Chesty" Puller.

There Bob Howard met the legend. Bob, an infantryman, also was a skillful jeep driver. One day he was ordered to drive for the colonel. Puller truly loved his men and welcomed the chance to talk with them. True to form he asked his new driver, "So tell me, old man, what's your name and where do you hail from?"

"It's Howard, sir, Bob Howard, from South Carolina."

Colonel Puller chewed on that for a minute before remarking, "In the last war I served with a Howard from South Carolina, a mighty fine Marine he was."

"Sounds like my older brother Dan, sir."

"Dan Howard, Dan Howard. Yes, that's the one. He was with me at the 'canal and Peleliu. Last time I saw him he was pretty banged up. How is he?"

"He's fine, sir. He served out the rest of the war back at the range on PI [Parris Island], married his nurse, and settled down. He's back in, but sitting this one out back again at the PI range."

"Well, good. He's seen enough combat to last a lifetime and suffered plenty. Nobody, certainly not me, could fault him for 'sitting this one out' as you say. He was a mighty fine combat leader, but what he's doing is nothing short of essential, invaluable."

The Chinese had with 120,000 men encircled the 1st Marine Division and Tenth Corps at the Chosin Reservoir and Bob Howard's driving experience became one of running the gauntlet to bring desperately needed supplies to the beleaguered Marines and sometimes wounded men back on the return trip. It was not uncommon for him to be forced to halt and trade shots with enemy soldiers either at hastily formed road blocks or firing from the ridgelines.

To make matters exponentially worse, it was winter and the weather was beyond brutally cold with temperatures often below zero, sometimes as much as thirty degrees below zero. Most everything that could freeze froze. It was all Bob could do to keep the engine block from freezing to enable him another trip over rutted, icy roads, often enough under fire. For himself and any passengers he had blankets on the floorboard and seats and one or two for cover.

One night he lost that battle. That afternoon Bob Howard was in a column of trucks and jeeps led by a lone tank. Bob's jeep was fourth in line, behind the lone M46 Patton medium tank leading, a deuce-

and-a-half (2-1/2 ton 6x6 truck) outfitted with a .50 caliber and two .30 caliber machine guns, and the convoy commander's jeep. Bob was bringing a trio of replacement second lieutenants and trailer full of essential radio batteries and medical supplies. It was bitterly cold. Despite that Bob wore two pairs of wool socks inside his boots, had another two pair over his boots, and rubber overshoes over them covered with a wadded blanket, his feet were numb and despite that he had three pairs of mittens on his fingers were too. The lieutenants, being too new to scrounge extras, suffered more.

Bob's mind was on the warming tents at their destination while his focus was on his interval and keeping the jeep on what served as a road. The tank rounded a curve and Bob heard the crack of the 76.2mm gun of a Soviet T34 tank followed by the boom of the Patton's 90mm. Intense small arms fire joined in, punctuated by grenade explosions.

The deuce-and-a half proceeded to the curve with guns blazing and was promptly knocked out. The same fate awaited the convoy commander's jeep. While Bob did not follow suit, his jeep nevertheless was raked with machine gun fire that flattened three of the four tires and holed the radiator and water hoses. The replacement officer in the front seat next to Bob was hit in the face and one of the two in the back seat was shot through the heart and killed.

Bob slid the jeep to a stop against an embankment, pulled the wounded lieutenant clear, and dragged him to a relatively protected spot with a folded blanket under him and two over him. The wound was ugly, but not patently life threatening, and the cold already was slowing the bleeding. The other lieutenant ran back down the column, ostensibly to take command.

Bob crouched next to the jeep fender and reached up to pull his M1 and bandolier of ammunition from the sleeve strapped to the hood. It was fortunate that he learned early on to avoid normal oiling the weapon because even gun oil would freeze in these temperatures and thereby disable the weapon. The jeep was doomed, but he was determined to save the critical supplies. For the next two hours, Bob would trade shots with the Chinese on the ridges and coming around the curve, the latter dashing any hope he had that the tank would return and save him.

Bob alternatively thought that it was a miracle that the jeep was not set ablaze by what seemed like dozens of rounds striking it while on the other hand fantasizing that the fire sure would feel good. The Chinese fire diminished and then abruptly ended at sunset, Bob surmising that the cruel drop in temperature was just too much for the poorly clad soldiers. Bob turned the lieutenant virtually into a mummy by bundling him in more blankets and adding the trailer tarp. He wrapped himself in the remaining two blankets, slipped the dead officer's .45 pistol into his armpit, and he waited in the cold darkness for rescue or death.

It was to be rescue. Not long after daylight, American artillery crashed in the hills and beyond the curve and a trio of tanks with supporting infantry made their way past the destroyed or disabled vehicles further back in the column. They continued past Bob and broke through the road block. A line of trucks followed. An ambulance stopped and picked up Bob who by then could not even walk on his frozen feet. As he and the lieutenant were being loaded, Bob was gratified to see that his supply laden trailer was being hooked up to another jeep.

Bob was taken to the warming tent he had dreamed of all night long and then to an aid station crammed with men suffering the same fate. When he was evacuated, he had already lost to frostbite the tips of both pinky fingers and parts of several toes. Eventually he would lose the rest of two of the toes.

Bob Howard, however, did not complain. He had "seen the elephant," had done his duty and he, more or less was on his way home, a place that only rarely dropped below freezing and never below zero.

* * *

As he had with Dan, Carl Howard found a fit for Bob and it too was a perfect fit. He put Bob in the farm equipment business and the family soon learned that he not only loved it, but was very, very good at it. After a time, he was running that business and he expanded it to include heavy equipment, all the while helping in and then too running and expanding his father's small car dealership as well. They, Carl, Dan, and Bob were a mighty team.

Bob was the rowdy one though, although he never let his rowdiness interfere with his obligations. The mid-1950's was a time for fast cars and so was Bob. He soon learned though that the smarter way to go was in selling fast cars and the parts to make them faster and sexier. He settled down; married Jean, a wonderful young lady; they had a son, Tim; and Bob kiddingly lamented that he was becoming downright respectable.

It was more than that. The Howards were not only respectable, but highly respected in the Beaufort community.

4

Lieutenant Thomas Howard, standing behind his sand-bagged bunker as the sun was just starting to clear the trees at the far tree line, could already feel that the day was going to be yet another scorcher and thought, "… *another glorious day in the tropical paradise of South Vietnam.*" In fact, but for the oppressive heat and humidity, having to live in the mud, having to lug around more than fifty pounds of stuff whenever you moved, the billions of bugs, the snakes, the leeches… and people trying to kill you, many parts of Vietnam indeed would be a tropical paradise. Not so much the southernmost part of the country, the delta, the Mekong Delta, the AO (area of operation) of Tom Howard and many more who looked just like him and did not belong there.

Some six months earlier, Tom Howard had been among other FNG's (fucking new guys) flown from the massive Tan Son Nhut airport outside Saigon, the capitol, to the base camp called "Bear Cat." He was greeted by a sign of welcome bearing the insignia he recognized from division shoulder patches displayed at Fort Benning, Georgia, home of the U.S. Army Infantry School. An octofoil red over blue heraldic design referring to a ninth son, it was that of the 9th Infantry Division, the "Old Reliables," which had been among the first U.S. combat units to engage in offensive ground operations during World War II, theirs in North Africa and the others in the Pacific, and had been reactivated and deployed to Vietnam from Fort Riley, Kansas, not too many months before.

Tom's posting there was no more than a matter of chance, a slot that needed filling because some other second lieutenant had moved up or had gone home one way or another. He really knew nothing of the division. At IOBC, the Infantry Officers Basic Course at Benning, Tom had learned of the "Brown Water Navy" where Army soldiers conducted riverine operations. The thought of creeping along in a small boat through narrow waterways bordered by dense jungle providing a million vantage points for ambush following which for the grunts, the infantry, meant going into the forbidding tangle after the assailants, was not the least bit enticing.

The flight to Bear Cat revealed billiard table flat terrain comprised mostly of rice paddies, waterways, tree lines, and patches of jungle spanning the 15,000 square mile southern tip of the country from the South China Sea to the Gulf of Thailand beyond view. It did not take superior intellect to connect the dots. The Brown Water Navy and the 9th Infantry Division were one in the same. *Shit!*

Tom Howard, therefore, was greatly relieved when he was assigned to lead a line platoon in the brigade not directly involved in riverine ops. That he instead would spend the next six months slogging through rice paddies fertilized with human excrement or fighting his way through dense jungle full of thorny vines and creepy crawlers somehow seemed less dreadful. Either way, Tom Howard would lose pints, if not quarts, of blood to clouds of mosquitoes, disgusting leeches, and all manner of plentiful voracious organisms, more than he ever would from getting shot.

And Tom Howard would become a seasoned combat veteran, a warrior. He then would have loved a quote from a book forty years hence: "Bring it. We are the infantry. War's a bitch, wear a helmet."

Tom Howard went back to the business of cleaning his weapon. It had gotten grody over the last week out in the bush. There would have been hell to pay had he caught one of his men with such a foul weapon. He smiled as he thought, *"Ah, hypocrisy, where would we in the great green machine be without it?"*

Howard's musing was soon interrupted by the familiar sound of an approaching helicopter. He could tell by the sound that it was a Huey, probably the log (logistics) bird, the daily (weather permitting) resupply. Catching sight of the helicopter, he could tell that it was heading to the landing zone adjacent to the battalion TOC, the tactical operations center.

Satisfied that it would not fly overhead and blow grit all over his cleaned and still disassembled M-16 laying on a towel on the roof of his bunker, Howard looked down the bunker line to insure, needlessly as always, that his platoon sergeant had a detail hustling to collect the rations, ammo, and any other supplies the helicopter was delivering before those thieving bastards from third platoon got there. With any luck, his First Platoon would be the thieving bastards today. With even better luck there would be socks and bug juice, the Army's potent 100% DEET insect repellent potion.

Howard then went back to his business of assembling the weapon and cleaning and reloading the ammunition before attending to his personal hygiene and his plan of enjoying the early morning sun and a day not out in the bush. As with most positive plans in recent memory, however, that plan soon went awry.

No sooner had Howard settled down behind his bunker and closed his eyes when Staff Sergeant Milliken, his platoon sergeant, walked up and said, "CO wants you at the CP." Howard's thought, *What does the Captain want?* was cut off by, "Don't ask me what the Blade wants," using the logical if uninspired nickname given for their commanding officer, Captain Gillette; and adding, "Top didn't say." Again, Howard's thought, *What's the First Sergeant doing out here?* was cut off by, "The XO came in too" and, cutting off the anticipated question of why the company executive officer was out in the field, "I know, I know, Whiskey Tango Foxtrot."

"'What the fuck' is right," Howard said, ending the one-sided conversation. He groaned as his smiling sergeant extended a hand to help him to his feet. Howard grunted his thanks, grabbed his rifle and helmet, and headed toward the trio of bunkers that comprised the CP, the company command post. He went by way of his bunker line, careful to avoid looking too officer-like and thereby tempting some enterprising sniper who may be lurking in the tree line across the paddies with a dumbass lieutenant target.

The first couple of bunkers were unoccupied, not unusual for daytime. Behind the next bunker, Howard saw a cluster of his men, all white; and as he neared them he could hear the oft argument of best cars. As he approached the group one pimply PFC looked up and asked, "Hey, LT, so which is better, a Mustang or GTO?"

Feigning thoughtfulness, Tom came back with, "Go with the GTO, Gordo. Even you could get laid with one of them." He continued past the mocking group and blushing PFC Gordon, taking note that they all had their weapons and helmets handy.

Howard passed another vacant bunker and saw another cluster of his men, these all black, behind an M60 machine gun bunker. Again, one soldier, this a hulk of a man, looked up. He said, "Hey, LT, I heard you lying to Gordo. That dude couldn't get no pussy in a motherfuckin' Cadillac."

"That what you're getting when you get back to the world, Bull?"

"Oh, hell yeah, LT; and let the ladies beware," the Bull answered, then asking, "How 'bout you LT, a 'vette?"

Howard laughed and said, "That new '67 is sweet, but I'll take anything with air conditioning." The group laughed with him. He walked on, again noting and pleased that each of the soldiers had his weapon and helmet within arm's reach.

Seeing that the rest of the line looked good, Howard angled toward the CP, again wary of being out in the open. He spotted the XO, First Lieutenant Hank Parker, walking toward him, apparently not sharing his concern. Howard amused himself with the thought, *How soon they forget,* and was smiling and shaking his head as he shook the XO's extended hand. His smile faded though with the XO's greeting, "How the hell are you, Owie?"

Cringing a bit at that undesired moniker, Howard retorted, "What's a REMF like you doing out here in the bush? There are bad guys out here, you know."

Unfazed by being called a rear echelon motherfucker by a junior officer, Parker laughed and exclaimed, "My boy, back in the old days when men were men and the Fighting First of Chargin' Charlie was led by a mighty warrior, that would be yours truly, we humped the bad bush and all the little Victor Charlies trembled in fear!"

The two continued to banter until they reached the CP. Clustered there behind the sandbagged walls were the CO, his RTO's (radio-telephone operators, radiomen), the senior medic, the first sergeant, and off to the side an obvious FNG (obvious in that he not only was wearing spanking new jungle fatigues and un-scuffed jungle boots, but he had "the look" or, more appropriately, he failed to have the look of a combat seasoned grunt).

Captain Gillette was sitting on a wooden ammo crate, using other stacked crates as a makeshift desk. As he worked his way toward him through the gaggle of men, Howard nodded to the first sergeant and ignored the FNG.

Seeing that his senior platoon leader had arrived, Captain Gillette smiled, got up, offered his hand and asked him, "How goes it, Owie?"

This time Howard suppressed a reaction to the moniker and instead just smiled back, saying and asking, "Same ol,' same ol.' You wanted to see me, sir?"

Captain Gillette said, "Yeah, Tom, I've got good news and bad news." Speaking louder so the men clustered around him could hear, the captain ordered, "First, you all need to come to attention." When the group had done so, the captain solemnly stood in front of Second Lieutenant Howard, took from the first sergeant a proffered sheet of paper and formally read from it. The CO enjoyed the surprise on Howard's face as he realized that he was being promoted and then with obvious pleasure the CO pinned on Howard the black field bar of a first lieutenant, shook his hand, and offered his sincere congratulations. He handed the lieutenant a copy of the orders, another black bar for the camouflage cloth cover of his helmet, and a pair of the single silver bars denoting the new rank to be worn on his dress or khaki uniform.

After the others congratulated Howard, Parker with a painful but friendly slap to the back, the captain had his two senior lieutenants join him by sitting on the empty ammo crates collected for that purpose. The others went about their business while staying within earshot to eavesdrop on the conversation of the officers.

"Now for the bad news, Tom. I am sad to say that it's been deemed time for you to move on. You've done a helluva good job with first platoon and I am going to miss you, we're all going to miss you. No cushy staff job for you, though."

There was no surprise there. Tom was aware that both he and the captain had gained reputations as competent, intuitive, aggressive, and altogether solid combat leaders, while on the other hand aggravatingly never amenable to exposing their men to unnecessary danger. Both men were naturally proud of the former, but having no career aspirations, neither was bothered by the latter. In fact, a few weeks back, the battalion commander, Lieutenant Colonel Mike Nichols, had royally chewed Tom's ass out for having the audacity to over the open radio net question the S-3, the battalion operations officer, over the lack of sense in putting the lives of his men in jeopardy by lingering in a hot zone just to make a body count. The Blade had to intervene on that one. Still, expecting the captain to tell him that he was moving up to Charlie Company XO so that Hank could wind down his tour in a staff job, Tom was unprepared for what was next said.

"The XO over in Alpha rotated home early, Coach asked for you and the boss agreed."

Shit! That was solid proof to Tom how far he had fallen from grace with the battalion command and staff. "Coach" was Captain Al Fuller, the boisterous commander of Alpha Company; a former football player at Auburn University who treated his company like a football team, complete with near constant aggravating football jargon. Worse, he had his XO and first sergeant hump with the company rather than handle their duties in the rear like most did. Even worse, Howard knew that with Charlie returning to the battalion laager, Alpha would be going back out. *So much for a break from the bush. Shit!*

Answering Howard's questions before he could ask them, Captain Gillette told him the move would be later that day, after he had signed over the platoon to his replacement, Second Lieutenant Blake, indicating with a nod the new guy Howard thus far had ignored. Conceding defeat, Tom Howard turned to the new lieutenant, shook his hand, muttered some insincere welcome and then turned back to the CO, asking rather rudely since the new guy was right there, "Okay if I park him here while I tell the platoon what's what and have them get ready for the changeover?" The captain nodded his assent and Howard turned back to Blake, telling him he'd send somebody over for him in a bit. Howard then headed back to the platoon area with mixed feelings, the best of them not very good.

When Howard was out of earshot, the new lieutenant could not contain the question, "'Owie' Howard, sir, as in 'ouch' owie?"

The CO smiled and said, "Exactly," and recounted the story behind it. "It was a little less than a month after Tom had taken over first platoon that he got into his first big firefight. The point man had alerted to the presence of VC, Viet Cong guerillas, ahead, and Tom proceeded to deploy his men accordingly. In making signals with his left hand like he was taught at Fort Benning, he took a round through the palm of the hand and cried out "*Ow!*" Sergeant Milliken, his, now your, platoon sergeant, was crawling over to him at the time and exclaimed loudly enough for many to hear, "Ow. *Ow!* Godammit, LT, you don't say '*ow*' when you get shot!"

The captain then proceeded to tell his new lieutenant that Howard got his hand quickly bandaged and then proceeded to earn on top of his Purple Heart a Bronze Star medal with "V" for valor by leading his platoon against what turned out to be a VC company, routing them and killing a dozen or more in the process and then killing at least that many more by alternately calling in artillery and air support on the fleeing enemy and then their base camp; all with suffering only two other casualties and neither of them critical.

* * *

The full story is worthy of recounting. The mission of the day was a routine one, to check out a local village (or ville as they called it) where the inhabitants were suspected of aiding the enemy, whether voluntarily or involuntarily. In typical fashion, the grunts were to hump around the wide openness of the villagers' rice paddies while avoiding the likely boo-by-trapped trails and to swing around to approach the village from the other side. Just as typically, the travel route involved cutting trails through dense brush, in some places jungle, and crossing two fields of elephant grass before resuming in the brush. While to the S-3 safely ensconced at Bear Cat it was doable in a day, there was no way that could happen.

Tom Howard had his men stop early to set up and dig in for an NDP, night defensive position, early to give them ample time to do that as well as to tend to the myriad of cuts suffered from the razor-sharp edges of the grass and punctures and tears from the "wait a minute" thorny vines in the bush and to rid themselves via insect repellent or lighted ends of cigarettes of leeches they picked up in the thick stuff along the way. He as always directed LP's, listening posts, be sent out, as well as ambush teams near a canal ahead and on their back trail, relying on his sergeants to follow through and to set watch schedules on the perimeter. In the meantime, Tom sat with his FO, forward observer, to plot and coordinate artillery fire if needed.

In the morning, after an uneventful night, the platoon recovered the claymore mines they had put out the early evening before, repeated the ritual of ridding themselves of leeches who found them in the night, tended to their biological needs, wolfed down a C-ration meal, and moved out. They turned before the canal, paralleled it for an hour, and then turned back toward the village. It was on that leg of the patrol that they intercepted a VC squad and it was then that Tom Howard made his first mistake.

Believing he was out of sight of the enemy, Tom raised his left hand to signal to his left squad. One of the VC just happened to be at a spot where there was a lane in the brush through which he happened to catch the movement. The VC spun and fired a quick three shots from his SKS semiautomatic rifle before he was shot to pieces by the Americans. One of the 7.62mm rounds from the SKS bore through Tom's hand.

The platoon's return fire not only killed the one VC, but another, and wounded two more. Unfortunately, the VC squad was about to link up with two more and those men joined in the fray. An intense firefight ensued.

Tom Howard ordered his center squad to maintain a base of fire while he took the right squad around to the right while the left squad went around to the left. It was almost unheard of for a VC unit to stand and fight unless it had a significant advantage. Tom's second mistake was to expect that to happen there. It did not. The VC platoon not only held their ground, but they were reinforced by two more platoons who quickly added their firepower to the mix.

Tom Howard somehow managed to maintain his composure in the incredible noise of the unexpected battle and the enemy rounds clipping leaves and branches only feet, sometimes inches, away. Tom scooted over to the squad leader and issued orders to fall back ten meters and then resume sustained, but controlled fire. Tom then took a deep breath and dashed through the fire to get back to the center and his forward observer.

The FO already had plotted the fires and Tom told him to call them in and adjust them. The FO expertly walked the artillery rounds up and down the VC line. In the meantime, Tom called in helicopter gunships and requested fixed wing air support too.

Satisfied that the artillery regained them the advantage, Tom had his men in unison hose down the VC lines, reload as the FO checked the artillery fires, and attack. The combined effect of the artillery and the unexpected assault caused the VC to break and run, leaving their dead and a few of their wounded behind.

Tom continued to press the fleeing VC, knowing from studying his map that they soon would be funneled between rice paddies and the canal. He called the approaching helicopter gunships to cover both and had the FO shift the artillery to the funnel until they were on station.

The VC commander had no good options from which to choose, which mattered little because by that point his men no longer were under his control. That they scattered though was what saved many of them because as individuals and small groups they presented lesser targets. Still, a full third of the company was lost against having inflicted a mere three American casualties.

But Lieutenant Tom Howard was not yet done for the day.

In the lull of fighting for the ground troops, Tom went back to his map. He studied it for a few minutes and got on the radio to the pilot of the OH-6 scout helicopter (known as a Loach, for "light observation helicopter") accompanying the pair of UH-1C gunships.

"Sparrow hawk Two-zero, this is Charlie One-six, over."

"Go ahead, One-six."

"Sparrow hawk, the way I see it, the victor charlies ought to have cut and crossed the canal to the north before we brought in the arty [artillery] and had y'all on station. Instead, they stayed and blocked us from heading west, knowing the shit was going to hit the fan. Suggest you go out the canal and check out the woods south of the canal beyond the corner of the paddies."

"Wilco [will comply], One-six." With that the Loach dropped to the deck and zoomed west, barely above the surface of the canal. The warrant officer pilot was on his way to earn a Silver Star to top the two Distinguished Flying Crosses he already had been awarded. As he approached what he believed to be due north of the corner of the rice paddies he brought the bird up to visually confirm it, dropped back down, and slowly proceeded up the canal.

The pilot spotted a barely perceptible trail and turned to follow it slowly at tree top level. After a few hundred yards, his co-pilot spotted a structure through the trees. The pilot hovered and then eased the little helicopter back and forth until they spotted more structures. They were well-camouflaged and therefore a base camp rather than a village, non-combatants having no need to conceal their location from eyes above.

The audacity of the airman was too much for a VC sentry below who fired a long burst from his AK-47 automatic rifle at his first glimpse of the intruder overhead. The Loach shuddered with numerous hits to the air frame, tail boom, and rotor blades. With unbelievable courage, the pilot cooly jinked the helicopter to spoil the man's aim and resumed slowly overflying the base camp as his co-pilot dropped one smoke grenade after another to mark it, taking several more hits in the process, and only then scooted away.

By the time the smoke from the grenades reached the tree tops, the Loach was clear of the area and the pilot cleared the pair of F-4 Phantoms by then on station to attack. The jets made run after run until the base camp was all but obliterated, either by the bombs dropped or the ensuing fires. The Loach returned and went to work hunting squirters, fleeing enemy soldiers, prey for the helicopter gunships impatiently awaiting their turn.

The gathered group of Lieutenant Tom Howard, Staff Sergeant Milliken, the ever-present RTO's, and the medic could not see any of that. They, however, plainly could hear it and monitor parts of it over the radio. After a short time, it subsided but for the aviators "playing" by pouring fire at fleeting glimpses at VC by this time fleeing in ones or twos.

Tom's RTO on the company net passed him the handset, telling him he had a call from "Six," meaning Captain Gillette.

"Charlie Six, this is Charlie One-Six, over."

"One-Six, Six, report status and ability to sweep the field and conduct BDA [bomb damage assessment]."

Tom understood that "field" was used in the generic sense and was keenly aware that the terrain between them and the base camp was a real bitch, a quagmire which would take a long, miserable day to traverse. He did not even ask for Milliken's advice before he responded: "Six, One-Six. Status all but two effective, but, sir, the men are flat wore out and they're about bingo on bullets, beans, and water. Also, I'm a whiskey [WIA]."

"One-Six, Six, say again your last."

"Six, One-Six, I am a whiskey, golf sierra ["gs," gun shot], hand. Over."

"Roger, One-Six. Do you require dust off?"

Tom then looked over at his platoon sergeant, who nodded yes, and his medic, the latter responding, "I'd say yeah, LT, you ought to. Lots of stuff in the hand; bones, tendons, nerves, blood vessels; and your fingers are starting to look like fat little sausages."

Tom smirked at that and got back on the radio: "Six, One-Six. If you're pulling Charlie One out, I'd say that is affirmative. Over."

"One-Six, Six. Roger. Stand by."

It was five minutes or so before the captain got back to him. While inclined to agree with his experienced, trustworthy lieutenant he aggravatingly still had to first gain clearance from battalion to do so. In the meantime, the medic removed the hasty bandage he had put on

Tom Howard's hand, inspected, cleaned, and re-bandaged the wound and asked, "You want a shot, sir?" The lieutenant shook his head no.

The CO came back on the radio. "Charlie One-Six, Charlie Six. COM [change of mission] follows. Move your men to the ruins by the canal for extraction in three zero mikes. Copy?"

"Charlie Six, Charlie One-Six. Copy and wilco."

"One-Six, Six. Roger. Good work out there. Report personal status when you can. Six out."

Sergeant Milliken spoke for the first time. "Outfuckingstanding! LT, live it up, take the shot. You earned it. I can get us up there before it takes effect." Tom Howard relented.

The platoon made it to the ruins with time to spare, although Milliken was wrong about the effect of the morphine. They were not halfway there before the lieutenant was, as the platoon sergeant later would joke, "wandering around and bumping into things." The medevac was the first helicopter to arrive. As Milliken and the medic laughingly helped their doped-up lieutenant to the open bay, Milliken yelled into Tom's ear, "See ya in a few days, *Owie!*"

Tom was airborne for several minutes before his morphine-fogged brain made the connection. *Oh, dear Lord, I'm never going to live that down!*

***

Without even knowing that full story, it still was somewhat with a sense of awe that Second Lieutenant Blake later met up again with newly minted First Lieutenant Howard and more than a little trepidation when Howard and the XO walked off after signing the platoon over. Sensing those feelings, Staff Sergeant Milliken clapped his new lieutenant on the back and told him, "No sweat, LT. Owie was a rookie when he got here too and the Blade and I got him squared away in no time. Watch, listen, and learn and you'll be a living hero like him too."

While Lieutenant Howard was getting his gear together, members of the platoon had come by, usually in twos or threes, but a few on their own, to wish him well. Howard and Milliken then said their goodbyes. That took longer. For both it was too damn close to tearful for comfort. They had been through a helluva lot together in the six months Howard had led the platoon and they had grown close.

Sergeant Milliken had waited for the troops to make their way past Lieutenant Howard's bunker and then came over, Howard by then having packed and was just sitting and staring off into space. He offered his lieutenant a warm beer, saying, "I know a southern gentlemen like you would rather have some fine whiskey, but this is all I got."

Howard smiled and replied, "Now, Abe, you know that we Howards are just a bunch of swamp loggers."

They laughed. They drank their beers. They talked some about Alpha Company and some of the NCO's Milliken knew over there. After a time, Howard grudgingly got up to leave, the two warmly shook hands, told each other to keep safe, and Tom Howard walked off toward the Charlie CP on his way to his new home with Alpha Company.

It would be much more of a temporary home than expected.

* * *

Tom Howard's meeting with Captain Fuller was about as expected. The unexpected part was that despite all his bluster, Coach's sincerity was obviously genuine. It did not hurt that Coach introduced Howard to his platoon leaders and sergeants by saying, "Lieutenant Tom Howard here is our new XO. He comes to us from Charlie Company, where he was a jam up platoon leader." That was not news. Infantrymen, by nature, whether it be competitiveness, self-preservation, or idle gossip, paid attention to who in the battalion was exceptionally good or bad. Charlie One fit into the good category with a reputation of being a kick ass platoon. Coach continued, "He's a Citadel grad and a warrior."

The assembled leaders all were familiar with The Citadel, the Military College of South Carolina, which along with the United States Military Academy at West Point and VMI, the Virginia Military Institute, and a short list of other distinguished military schools, had a fine reputation for producing quality leaders. Coach then concluded with, "Whatever he says will be as if it was said by me."

Howard was pleased with the introduction. He then was pleasantly surprised that Coach showed in his briefing to the company leadership that despite his annoying football jargon he knew his stuff. *Maybe this won't be so bad after all*, he thought.

Using his map, Captain Fuller outlined the plan. The company was to combat assault (CA) into a field, secure that landing zone (LZ), patrol a couple of klicks (kilometers) or so of the valley [bearing in mind that in that part of the country what constituted hills, ridges, and valleys more often than not were but a mere few feet in change of elevation, rarely enough to rate a contour line on the topographical maps they used], work their way up a ridge to the north and then patrol it back, all the while looking for the VC they all knew were there. Three nights, tops. The captain succinctly detailed the radio frequencies, call signs, flight order, and other essential details. He straightforwardly answered a few questions, gave his signature pep talk, and released the leaders to prepare their men.

The Alpha platoon leaders were the usual mixed bag. Howard was particularly impressed with Second Lieutenant Craig Clark, the 2nd Platoon Leader, an Airborne Ranger West Pointer with four months' experience in the bush. His platoon sergeant was sharp too. The First Platoon Leader, Second Lieutenant Eddie Masters, a Texas A&M Aggie with a couple of months behind him, seemed okay while perhaps a bit too aggressive. His platoon sergeant was solid though. The potential weak link was the Third Platoon Leader, Second Lieutenant Doug Smith, with just a few weeks leading the platoon; and Howard could not get a good read on the platoon sergeant, an E-7 Sergeant First

Class named Ross. The bonus was Second Lieutenant Dave Martin, their assigned FO, artillery forward observer, who not only was sharp but also a likeable fellow.

The helicopters arrived on time the next morning and after a short flight, 2nd Platoon and the CO and his crew plus the FO team assaulted without incident, followed by 3rd Platoon, and then 1st Platoon with Tom Howard, his RTO and the first sergeant, the latter being a burly, no nonsense professional. Once the entire company was on the ground and the LZ was secured, Coach had them move out in column with flank security.

The command element initially was second in line. It was a gaggle consisting of the CO and his team of three RTO's (Spec 4 Mosley on the company net, PFC Cotton on the battalion net, and another whose name Howard did not catch for contact with air support), and two grunts Coach used respectively as runners and personal bodyguard; the FO and his RTO; Howard and his RTO; the senior medic; the formidable first sergeant; and a reserve M60 machine gun team. As Tom Howard viewed the command group, especially with all the radio antennae conspicuously sticking up as they moved through the tall grass, the displeasing thought came to mind that it had target written all over it.

The company moved well enough, skirted a large field of head high grass with edges like razors, and then cleared a stand of timber, all uneventfully. Beyond the trees was an enormous grass field with scattered scrub trees. After a short break, Captain Fuller put 2nd Platoon on the far right, 1st Platoon in the lead at the left edge, followed by the command element with 3rd Platoon trailing. He had Tom Howard and his RTO slide back to accompany the rear for a while.

Their goal was to reach, scout, and occupy a hummock or knoll, a small island in the sea of grass, a few hundred meters ahead. That was accomplished sooner than expected, but the island proved to be too small for a company NDP, so Captain Fuller had 1st Platoon scout the forested higher ground to the left while having 2nd Platoon hold at the far right two hundred odd yards away and 3rd Platoon move into the tree line about the same distance behind.

The command element occupied the island, or rather the first of what turned out to be two small knolls separated by a thick stand of bamboo. Fuller and Howard stood and watched 1st Platoon until they were out of sight in the brush and then the trees. They figured they had not much more than an hour to make a decision on an NDP, an hour to get everyone assembled and then an hour to get settled in before dark. Fuller sat down to study his map for options, including where to send out an ambush squad from one platoon, maybe two. The RTO's on the company and battalion nets sat nearby. The FO, Lieutenant Martin, was busy on the radio updating the artillery of the company's positions and beginning some preplanned fires.

Tom Howard, with nothing really to do at the moment, asked the first sergeant to check out the knoll they were on while he took the M60 team and one of Coach's guys to the other knoll to check it out. The bamboo in the center was so thick that they had to walk around.

After no more than twenty minutes, everyone on the island was alarmed by the sound of an M16 firing on full automatic and moments later the distinctive sound of AK-47 return fire. *What the fuck* was on every man's lips or mind as the firing increased and stray rounds passed overhead. Howard positioned the three troops he had with him on the northern knoll and hustled back to the CO. By the time he reached him, the firing had grown to a crescendo punctuated by grenade blasts.

After several tries by Fuller to get Lieutenant Masters on the horn, the platoon leader finally replied. He excitedly but succinctly explained that as his point man crested the ridge about a hundred yards into the trees he spotted and fired on a VC cresting the ridge from the west and that no sooner had he deployed the platoon when a platoon or more of VC took them under fire. Fuller asked if the VC were dug in and Masters replied no, they were on the move. Two minutes later, with no letup in the firing, Masters radioed that he had four men down, that the VC were more like two platoons and were maneuvering to his flanks.

Captain Fuller contemplated what to do for about a minute, which seemed like an eternity to everyone else, and made a decision. He got back on the radio, "Fox 6 [Masters with 1st Platoon], Alpha 6 [Fuller]. Make ready to break contact and fall back to me on my order. Break. Sierra 6 [Clark with 2nd Platoon] and Tango 6 [Smith with 3rd Platoon] stand fast and stand by for movement on my order." Fuller now regretted having separated his platoons, even if it was a common practice, but he did not want them moving until the situation was clarified. The platoon leaders each acknowledged and the CO concluded the call.

Turning to the FO, a raising of his eyebrows was all it took to get an "I'm on it" from him. Turning to the RTO in contact with the air support produced a thumbs up, reflecting he too was on it, first priority being to get a dustoff or medevac helicopter in the air and then to find out what Air Force and/or gunship support was available.

Turning then to his XO, Fuller asked, "Tom, how many will that other hill hold?" Howard told him a full squad plus the machinegun already there. Noting it, Fuller told him to grab a few men and direct them to clear an LZ on the shielded side of the island. He then told PFC Cotton on the battalion net to report and took Mosley with him as he walked out into the grass separating the island from the tree line.

It was a very long couple of minutes when Fuller heard the first 105mm artillery rounds coming in beyond 1st Platoon's reported location. Confident that Martin would effectively adjust the rounds, he took the radio mike and called, "Fox 6, Charlie 6. Move. I say again, move, *now!*"

Lieutenant Masters quickly rogered, but it was a tense five minutes before the first of his men emerged from the tree line. They were struggling to carry men on ponchos. The first sergeant went out to help while Tom Howard resisted the urge to join. The fight was not over. More bullets were coming in, the angle of fire now making them a threat.

After three men on ponchos, the third obviously dead from a round through the neck, the rest of the platoon began to appear. They were firing and falling back in good order. The artillery rounds now were hitting closer and Martin was starting to work them along the ridge. Captain Fuller directed the first approaching squad leader to the northern knoll and the others and finally Lieutenant Masters to the southern knoll and followed them in. By then rounds were zipping by and kicking up dirt.

No sooner did the platoon enter the island and begin to take up fighting positions when the VC emerged from the trees, firing as they came. Fuller and the first sergeant were both shocked. Neither one had ever seen or even heard of an attack like this in daylight hours. They joined in the furious fire aimed at the VC, as did Tom Howard with his little band on the other side of the bamboo cluster.

What 1st Platoon had collided with was the flank element of a VC company screening the southern flank of an NVA battalion en route to a base camp deeper in the dense woods and jungle. The VC company commander responded instantly. Under strict orders to protect the NVA, not only from being attacked, but being observed at all, these Americans were too close for comfort.

After sending a runner to the NVA commander with his report of the situation and his intentions, he personally led half of his men toward the Americans, the other half remaining strung out to maintain the screen. He wanted to drive the enemy back out into the open where they could be cut down and to do so swiftly before they could bring their dreaded artillery and air support to bear.

The Americans, however, fought back well and brought their artillery in much sooner than expected. Their assault was stopped cold. Leaving his dead and then scattered scouts and snipers, the VC commander withdrew his men back into the trees, back over the ridge and outside of the impact area of the American artillery.

The VC commander chided himself. Attacking into the open had been a costly mistake. It seemed that he had lost nearly a quarter of his men, dead, wounded, or missing, losses he could not afford to effectively carry out his screening mission.

As is common in combat though, he did not know that the missing men were not lost. In fact, seven of his men, led by a sergeant who happened to know the area, made it through the American fire to the island via a narrow dry creek bed hidden by the grass. Stranded when their comrades withdrew, they were hiding in the thick bamboo between the two hills.

The Americans suffered as well with one dead and five wounded, three of them seriously enough to be evacuated. Unlike the wounded VC, the American wounded were tended to by two highly trained and well-equipped medics and those needing it soon would be evacuated by helicopter to a hospital. Unlike the wounded VC, their chances of survival were remarkably high.

The survivability of the men left behind remained in doubt though. Captain Fuller got the men on the southern hill digging in and told his XO to do the same on the northern hill after he got the seriously wounded off on the approaching chopper. Fuller had the other two platoons hold tight while he continued to assess the situation.

The medevac bird, guided by the smoke grenade Tom Howard tossed, flared and hovered a few feet off the ground. The wounded were quickly loaded and the helicopter was just as quickly gone. Tom immediately headed around the back of the bamboo thicket toward the northern knoll.

***

Tom Howard was halfway there when he heard a flurry of shots close by and recognized them as AK's. *What the fuck* immediately came to mind once again and he took off running to the position and the sound of more firing, now M16's. That firing suddenly, curiously, stopped as he rounded the bamboo and climbed the short rise to that hill.

He crossed over to the squad leader and quickly learned what had transpired. A squad of VC had burst from the bamboo in the center, fired them up, and escaped over the machine gun position, taking the gun *and* the gunner with them and leaving the assistant gunner shot but alive. The Alpha troops had fired on the fleeing VC, but quit in fear of hitting their own man.

Tom Howard stared at the young man incredulously and then suddenly stood, dumped his web gear and helmet, and to the utter astonishment of the young sergeant and his fellow soldiers, took off running down the obvious recent path in the grass. He did so without a moment's thought to the rashness of what he was doing.

He had gone perhaps seventy-yards when rounding a bend in the trail he came upon a VC kneeling on the trail no more than twenty feet ahead. They fired at the same time. Howard felt a round impact his rifle and the rifle being torn from his grasp as the impact also spun him and sent him crashing into the grass. Dazed for a moment, he recovered and rolled back onto the trail to face what he feared to be an approaching enemy. The VC, however, was lying on his back with his knees drawn up.

Howard spotted his rifle on the other side of the trail and in retrieving it saw that the fore grip was shot off and the gas rod severed, rendering it a single shot weapon at best. He also saw that he had blood on his hand, but there was no time to worry about that. He quickly approached the fallen enemy while listening for the sound of any others coming back down the trail. The VC was staring up with pink, bubbly blood coming from his mouth and nose; his black shirt wet with blood. Hit in both lungs, he was clearly dying. Howard dropped his damaged rifle, pulled the dying man's AK from his hand and took off running again up the trail.

Thirty yards, another bend, and twenty yards ahead were two more VC with their captive at their feet. Howard shot the man on the right, but before he could shoot the one on the left the AK either jammed or ran dry. Howard let his momentum carry him forward, notwithstanding the panic he felt as the VC brought his rifle to bear.

Howard lived only because the captured gunner rendered a vicious kick to the back of the VC's knee, causing his AK burst to arc harmlessly through the sky. Howard was on him in another instant and he butt stroked the man into unconsciousness. Turning to the gunner, Howard said, "Thanks, buddy. Hurt?"

The man replied, "Yeah. The motherfuckers shot me in the ass."

"Can you walk?"

The gunner replied that he could, adding, "The gooks got my pig!"

Tom Howard thought for a moment and decided that he could not let the VC keep the M60, not if he could help it. He told the wounded gunner to grab the AK dropped by the shot VC, head back down the trail and to yell out as he got close to the island and toss the AK to avoid getting shot. Howard then tossed the first AK deep into the tall grass, grabbed the other fallen man's AK, and headed up the trail, leaving the dismayed gunner to fend for himself.

Howard was no longer running. As the grass became shorter, he crouched down as he moved, hoping that the last firing being limited to AK's would make him unexpected or at least cause them to pause long enough to improve his chances of living for a few more minutes. The trail now twisted and turned around scrub trees and thorny bushes. *Fuck it*, he thought, and resumed a quicker pace.

He hit a straightaway and saw another pair of VC. They too saw him, but hesitated. Tom Howard did not. As he continued to run toward them he let loose with an unaimed burst from the captured AK. He either inflicted minor wounds or missed altogether, the price of not aiming, and the VC took off, dropping something as they went. Howard continued on to where he had lost sight of them and was rewarded to see the M60 lying in the crushed grass of the trail. Breathing a sigh of relief, he grabbed it, and hauled ass back down the trail.

Tom slowed only when he got to the pair of VC downed where he had found the gunner. Catching his breath, he resumed running back down the trail, leaving the stricken VC to be captured later, recovered by their comrades after dark, or to succumb to their wounds. It was not in his character to execute wounded men.

He reached the first VC he had shot, now dead, and stopped to again catch his breath and listen for any sound of pursuit. As he did so, he stared down at the dead man. The man seemed somehow smaller in death and a sudden sadness came over Tom. He let out a sigh as he realized this was the first man he knew for sure he had personally killed.

Shaking off the feeling, he found and retrieved his battered M16, turned and hustled down the trail, now carrying three weapons. At about the hallway point, he slowed to a walk and started calling out to his men on the hill. Only when hearing an acknowledgment did he toss the AK deep into the grass and cautiously ease toward the hill with his hands held high, grasping the distinctive machine gun.

Tom Howard ignored the awestruck looks of the men as he made his way up the low hill. The squad leader came up and blurted out, "*Goddamn, sir!*" Tom all but ignored him, instead handing him the recovered machine gun and telling him to get it up. Tom then eased over behind a tree and slumped down, suddenly exhausted. He looked around for and spotted the gunner, who was all smiles now despite the extra hole in his now bare butt and the ribbing he was taking for it.

Tom's lower right arm and elbow reminded him that he was injured. As he was about to pull his shirt sleeve up to inspect the arm, the squad leader scooted over with the gear he had dropped. The sergeant's words stopped short anything to do with his arm, "Coach is down, sir. Sniper got him."

Tom just stared at the man as he thought, "*Could this fucking day get any fucking worse?*"

* * *

Tom Howard quickly recovered. He told the squad leader that he was going over to the other side, confirmed that the recovered M60 was up and told the young man to get his men dug in. He signaled the wounded men to come with him, but then stopped, thinking about the VC who had come from the interior of the position.

"Where'd those gooks come from?" he asked the sergeant, who in response pointed to an almost imperceptible opening in the bamboo. Howard told the sergeant to have a couple of men go in there and make sure there were no more VC lurking and to see what sort of trail might be in there. Howard then got to his feet, wobbling a bit, put on his helmet, strapped on his gear, and carried his useless rifle as he walked in a crouch toward the back of the hill with the wounded soldiers in tow.

Howard rounded the bamboo and saw that the CP was digging in on the backside of the hill and could hear the others digging in on the tree line side. He directed the wounded troops over to the one medic and then approached the senior medic who with the first sergeant was kneeling beside who he correctly supposed to be the CO. As he knelt too, the medic said, "GSW, abdomen. Liver, I think. Bird's on the way." The CO was out of it.

An RTO announced, "Dustoff called. Two mikes out."

The first sergeant said, "On it."

Indicating with a nod of his head, Tom Howard said, "I got two more to go from the other side."

Howard started when he saw a soldier and then another emerge from the bamboo before he grasped that they were the ones the squad leader on the other side had directed to clear the thicket. He motioned them over. One told him that there was a narrow winding trail through the thicket that made a T toward the west side. Spotting a machete strapped to a rucksack, Howard nodded toward it and told them to take it and widen the trail on their way back so that men could more easily and quickly traverse the two hills.

Tom then turned his attention to the approaching Lieutenant Masters. He did not notice that the two men from the other side had stopped to talk with the first sergeant.

Masters had just left to comply with Tom's order to shift four of his men to the other side when the first sergeant came over and gruffly directed Tom to sit before he got his fool head blown off. He followed suit, reached over, and less than tenderly grabbed the lieutenant's right hand and proceeded to examine his bloody forearm with more blood seeping through a hole in the crook of his elbow. He called a medic over and then said, "Jesus, sir, I heard about your little exploit over there. Real Audie Murphy shit. You going out?"

"What? Out? No. No! But I do need a new rifle."

The medic washed the blood off Tom's forearm, revealing a long, jagged tear pointing to the hole in the elbow. Seeing the wounds, they instantly started to hurt worse and Tom snorted at the obvious psychosomatic effect he could not will away. The medic gently manipulated the lower arm to satisfy himself that the joint was not shattered, but even the gentleness caused a wave of blinding pain. Too gruffly he said to the medic, "Quit that shit, Doc. Patch me up, but I gotta be able to move this arm."

"You're not going out, sir?"

"No!"

The medic shrugged and asked, "Want somethin' for the pain?"

The pain indeed was intense and Tom asked back, "Whatcha got?"

"Morphine and APC's."

Tom thought about the options. APC's, pills comprised of aspirin, phenacetin (an anti-inflammatory) and caffeine, were the military's ubiquitous remedy for most anything short of compound fractures or gushing wounds. Tom had too often seen the effects of morphine and knew he could not afford to be disabled by the narcotic. He opted for the APC's. The medic gave him a bottle, told him to take three, but go easy on them as too many would make him sick. The medic then went off into the gathering darkness to check on the wounded not qualifying for evacuation. Tom took three of the pills, having little faith (actually no faith) that they would do anything except maybe blunt the edge off the throbbing pain.

The first sergeant returned with an M-16 he had selected from the growing pile the dead and wounded left behind. Handing over the rifle, he sat down heavily. Tom correctly sensed that the top sergeant was awaiting orders. *Damn*, Tom thought, *I need to be thinking like a company commander.*

His training kicked in. Situation, options, action. Perhaps it was pride, but he as quickly rejected the notion of requesting that the company be pulled out as he had the thought of his own leaving. Turning to the sergeant and seeing his look of concern, Lieutenant Howard said, "Top, I think we're okay for now, but I don't think they're going away."

The first sergeant, pleased that his new CO had his head in the game (to borrow one of Coach's typical sayings), replied, "Roger that, sir. What about 2nd and 3rd Platoons? Also, you gotta report to Mike 6 [referring to the battalion commander]." Tom Howard did not directly respond. Instead he motioned Cotton and Mosley over.

Howard first took the handset from Mosley and called out on the company frequency, "Sierra 6 and Tango 6, Alpha 5, over," and after each answered he transmitted, "Sierra 6 and Tango 6, Alpha 5. I am now Alpha 6. I say again I am now Alpha 6. Sierra 6, dig in there for the night, *quietly*; LP's [listening posts] out; fifty percent alert, be prepared to move toward me on order. Tango 6, you do the same, no digging though, LP's close. Over." Both acknowledged and Howard concluded the call.

He passed the handset to the RTO and pulled his map out of the cargo pocket of his jungle fatigues. It was almost too dark to see. He managed to find their locations though and to determine the grid coordinates of each. He then took the handset from Cotton, paused for a few moments to collect his thoughts, and called battalion.

"Mike 6, this is Alpha 5, over." When the battalion commander's RTO answered, Howard called back and said, "Mike 6 Romeo, this is

Alpha 5, now Alpha 6. I need Mike 6 actual, over." The RTO told him to wait one and within a minute the battalion commander himself called back. Howard responded, "Mike 6, this is Alpha 5, now Alpha 6, with a sitrep. Are you prepared to copy same, over?" The CO immediately replied, telling him to go ahead and that the S-3 was monitoring.

Howard called back, "Mike 6, Alpha 6. Sitrep follows: Locations of Alpha elements are," and he gave the coordinates for each. "Alpha Foxtrot made contact with victor charlie at 1600 hours. Foxtrot and HQ elements then attacked by enemy, two platoon strength or more. Alpha sustained one kilo [killed], nine whiskies [wounded], including the 6 [commander], with six evac'd [evacuated], including the 6. Enemy losses unknown, but exceeding ours. Situation quiet now except for sporadic sniper fire. To commence H&I [harassment and interdiction] fires at full dark. Request resupply of ammo, meds, and water. Request an hour to put together a plan for if charlie does not break off."

Lieutenant Colonel Nichols, while wanting more information, was satisfied with the report and responded, "Roger, Alpha 6. Negative on the resupply tonight. Brief your plan to the 3 in six zero. Mike 6, over." Howard concluded the communication with, "Roger, Mike 6. Alpha 6 out."

Howard checked his watch. The image of the Battalion S-3, Major Waters, came to Howard's mind, a warrior and superb operations officer, even if they often clashed. Howard then exhaled hard, somewhat relieving the stress of having his first significant contact with the battalion CO. He turned to the first sergeant and the forward observer who had joined them, saying, "Give me a half hour to come up with a plan to run by you two. In the meantime, Dave, get those H&I fires started. I want those tubes on target in case the shit hits the fan."

Howard then settled into the hole his RTOs had dug for him, thanking them, and began to think. He was thankful that at least the enemy was quiet, giving him the needed time to do so. He tried not to think of his throbbing arm or of the cloud of mosquitoes drawn to the blood seeping through the bandages.

The thoughts at first were unorganized. The worst-case scenario was that the VC would not leave, but instead would reinforce and attack the island or one of the isolated Alpha platoons. There, however, was no indication that they even were aware of the other two. *Great, they think it's just us, a juicy target. They would hit us before dawn to take advantage of the dark and the sleepiness of the men. With nothing but open grass behind us, it would be a piecemeal slaughter if we abandoned the position. If they hit us hard and fast enough they'd have enough light for an orderly withdrawal before 2nd or 3rd could even come into play, <u>after we're all dead</u>. Or they could just zero mortars and rockets in on the field and hammer us when the slicks come in to get us or ambush us if we march out.*

Tom Howard was not one bit satisfied with that line of thinking. He compelled himself to think more effectively, coming to, "*Or <u>we</u> could be the ones on the offensive. Yes, better to hit the gooks first.*" With that tentative more satisfactory conclusion, Tom began to focus his thoughts, to formulate a plan.

By the time the first sergeant and FO joined him, Tom Howard had the makings of a plan. He briefed it to the two men, got some good feedback, and adjusted the plan accordingly. Precisely at an hour after his call with the battalion commander, Tom put in his call to the S-3. He succinctly outlined his plan and reasoning therefor. Major Waters listened, asked no questions, made no comment and said he would call back in a half hour. Lieutenant Tom Howard had no idea the flurry of activity that ensued at the battalion TOC in those thirty minutes.

Howard nervously awaited that call back, the nervousness increasing exponentially as the minutes ticked by beyond the thirty-minute mark. He tried to bide the time by chatting with the first sergeant while Lieutenant Martin busied himself coordinating artillery fires. Lieutenant Masters had joined them too, but he was mostly quiet.

Tom took notice of that the mosquitoes were out in full force and they were hungry (*or thirsty*). He liberally applied bug juice to his exposed skin, flinching as the chemical burned the many grass cuts and gasping as his sweat carried some of the potion under the bandage on his arm and into the wounds.

When the call finally came at closer to an hour, Howard was relieved that his plan largely had been approved, with the S-3 augmenting it by telling him that two Bravo Company platoons would CA in a klick to their north, followed by a platoon from Charlie Company to occupy the island; and that both he and the CO would be overhead at first light to coordinate. They would be fine tuning the plan during the night. When the call ended, Howard briefed the congregated leaders and they went about their business. Tom briefed the other two platoon leaders via radio calls. He then popped a handful of APC's and settled in to agonize over the plan and all that could go wrong to turn it into a catastrophe.

Tom Howard was startled when Mosley woke him at about 0430 hours, astonished that he had been sleeping at all. It took Howard a few moments and a few swallows of tepid water from his canteen to fully shake off the grogginess and to fully take in his surroundings. He could see that the command element was awake and each man was quietly doing what he was supposed to be doing.

When the RTO was confident that the lieutenant was fully awake, he told him that 1st Platoon was now at 100% alert, that the listening posts had gotten back in safely and that one of them reported movement as they were heading in. Howard was neither pleased nor surprised by the latter. Mosley waited for the lieutenant to acknowledge that report before finishing with that 2nd and 3rd Platoons were in position. Tom nodded his thanks.

Tom had ordered 2nd and 3rd Platoons to quietly move into positions on either side, north and south, of them; to dump their heavy packs there; and to be ready to attack with two up, one back, meaning two squads on line followed by the third squad twenty or so yards behind. Meanwhile they would then sit in the mostly open field with nothing but waist high grass and darkness to protect them.

Tom was advised that they could expect two F4's on time. "On time" was to be at 0515 hours, what ought to be about thirty minutes before the first gray of dawn and about the time he expected the VC to be moving into their final assault positions. Tom looked at the faintly luminous dial of his watch. Things were going to get hairy soon. In the meantime, there was really nothing to do except wait, worry, and pray.

5

At 0512, Lieutenant Howard was advised that the jets and a FAC, a forward air controller, were two minutes out and he confirmed that Lieutenant Masters had his machine gunners standing by. Lieutenant Martin had the artillery check their fire and confirmed the adjustments to be made and that they would be standing by to resume firing at 0520. Twenty seconds later the lead pilot radioed, "Light 'em up, Army," which was instantly relayed to Masters.

At a few seconds into 0515 the black sky lit up with tracer fire. Howard had directed Masters to line up three M60's in a line parallel to the tree line and on command for each to fire straight up a continuous burst of ten tracers (about fifty rounds total), standing by to repeat on order.

The two pilots saw the vertical lines of tracers from the three machine guns marking the front lines of the combatants on the ground and while they made their final minor flight adjustments the leader called, "Outstanding, Army, get your heads down." Seconds later the soldiers could hear the jets coming in and a moment later screaming out. Few saw in the gloom the two silver napalm canisters each of the two planes had released, but there was no mistaking their effect.

The first F4 was perfectly on line with the ridge and the second mere yards to his left, on line with the low ground on the west side of the ridge. Two of the napalm canisters ignited in the trees and the flaming jellied gasoline rained down for nearly a hundred yards. The other two canisters made it to the ground and were tumbling forward as they ignited, flinging their fiery death almost that far as well.

Depending on one's outlook, the effects were spectacular or horrendous. For the Americans, the napalm strike was amazing. Better yet, it was perfect! For the Viet Cong, it was nothing less than hell on earth. The air strike had caught them exposed in their attack positions, the assault waves just inside the tree line, the command group just behind the ridge and the reserves were moving in behind the next ridge.

The napalm injured few of the lead element too close to friendlies, but it all but annihilated the command element. Over thirty men were dead or dying in the flames or incapacitated by the superheated air from them. For the lead element survivors, the air strike was paralyzing and the screams of their comrades was nightmarish, but what was even more awful for them was the torrent of ground fire the Americans next unleashed.

Howard had directed that as soon as the air strike hit they were to fire a "mad minute," everyone was to light up the tree line; each rifleman to fire two full magazines on full automatic, grenadiers to pump as many rounds out as they could and machine gunners to rake their appointed sectors.

The tactic caught the VC as they raised up to see the aftermath of the air strike. Though few were killed outright by the ground fire, more than a dozen were wounded. The combined effect of the air strike and ground fire, not the least being the disruption of command, was that the attack was doomed.

The commander of the lead element realized that at once. Through shouted commands and runners, he ordered his men to quickly gather the wounded who appeared to have some chance of survival and what weapons, ammunition, and medical supplies they could find and also carry and to reassemble at the designated rally point.

The Americans were not far behind. Tom Howard had decided that if the air strike appeared to be effective, a counterattack immediately following the mad minute would have the best chance of spoiling the VC plans. His men were prepared for it and with a simple, "Go! Go! *Go!*" over the radio a line of six reinforced rifle squads followed by a line of three more and the command element hit the tree line, firing constantly and continued up the side of the ridge unhindered by enemy fire. In fact, but for a single RPG round that sailed past the island and exploded harmlessly somewhere behind them, there was no indication the enemy was even there. The smattering of rifle fire coming from the VC rear guard was unheard above the din of their own weapons and was ineffective.

By the time the Americans reached the ridgeline, the flames had mostly died out, but the air was thick with oily smoke and its heavy chemical smell comingled with the nauseating reek of roasted flesh. There was ammunition popping off from the fires and the ground was too hot to linger. As Howard climbed the slight hill toward the ridge line, he actually could smell the rubber soles of his jungle boots on the verge of melting and could not help but thinking, "*Should have thought of that, dumbass!*" and he gave the order to push on to the next ridge. He grabbed Lieutenant Martin and told him to shift fires out another two hundred meters.

Still in darkness, the Americans crested the first ridge, went down the opposite slope and into the ravine filled with even heavier smoke and the stench of death. As they emerged from the smoky bottom they suffered their first American casualties, one killed and several wounded, but they continued up the next slope, firing as they went, and drove the VC off that ridge and out into the dark beyond.

As soon as Howard settled on the near side of the crest of the second ridge, he ordered the platoon leaders to halt and position their men there with particular attention to the flanks, and then to report casualties and ammunition status. He told Martin to have the artillery check fire. Realizing that first light was starting to appear and chiding himself that he as the company commander had no business on the front lines, Howard headed back with his RTO's to the first ridge. On the way, he was reminded that his arm was throbbing in pain and that he was both light headed and nauseated from it. Angrily he told himself to "*suck it up and move on,*" and he did.

The disgusting smells of and from the napalm lingered, but now in the early light it was the sight of the effects that emptied more than a few stomachs. In the ravine between the two ridges was a tight cluster of maybe a dozen bodies, all burned to a crisp. A mostly melted radio and a pistol next to a blackened, shriveled form suggested that this had been the VC command group. The Americans now could see more bodies near the crests of the ridges where the artillery had taken its toll as well.

Howard ordered the platoon leaders to detail troops to sweep the slopes for any wounded VC and to report what they found. The platoon leaders reported the one friendly KIA and their WIA's, one needing to be evacuated and the others for the time being able to stay in the field. Howard radioed the status and instructions to the first sergeant back at the island with the earlier wounded and a few other men and the packs and extra gear. The first sergeant would handle the medevacs and resupply. Howard's next call was to the FAC to relay to the pilots, who still were orbiting overhead in case their guns could be of service, a "spot on target, job well done, body count to follow, many thanks." Howard next took the handset from PFC Cotton and reported to battalion HQ.

"Mike 6, Alpha 6, over."

"Mike 6 actual, go ahead Alpha 6, over." The reply was instantaneous. Lieutenant Colonel Nichols obviously had his handset in his hand awaiting the call.

"Mike 6, Alpha 6. Sitrep follows. NDP secure. Air strike and assault as planned and effective. Lead elements at" and he gave the grid coordinates. "Victor Charlie KIAs exceed twenty, could be twice that. Unknown size unit has broken contact. Friendly casualties, one kilo and three whiskies, one being dusted off. Alpha to chow down while we search for the Victor Charlie trail and wait on resupply en route.

Plan is to pursue. Request the follow-on unit do a full sweep here after we're gone. Over."

"Alpha 6, Mike 6. Good work, Alpha. Bravo elements en route, ETA one five mikes, one klick to your echo [east]. Charlie papa [Charlie Company platoon] element to follow to your NDP. Will sweep and mop up. Mike 3 [the battalion S-3 operations officer] will be overhead. Mike 6 out." While it was not his call to terminate, he after all was the battalion commander.

Howard handed the microphone back to Cotton, reached for Mosley's and called to the platoon leaders on the company net, "Fox 6, Sierra 6, Tango 6, this is Alpha 6. Have the men eat and clean weapons. Send details down when you hear the log bird inbound. I am coming back to the Fox pos. I need the best tracker we have and a squad to meet me there. Over." After they rogered the call, Howard concluded it and moved out, back around the gruesome remains of the VC command group. By the time he returned, the first platoon squad was assembled there.

The platoon leader, Lieutenant Smith, and a squad leader with a man in tow met Lieutenant Howard near the top. "Sir," the sergeant said, "this is Corndog. He's the best tracker in the battalion." Seeing the CO's inquisitive look, the sergeant answered the unasked question, "Yeah, sir, 'Corndog,' country as corn and the nose of a hound dog."

Tom smiled at that and gave the tracker a quick study. He was wiry, of an indeterminate age, and had that "West by God Virginia" look about him. The man's eyes, however, were constantly moving and piercing when they met his own.

Lieutenant Howard explained to Corndog that he wanted him to find the trail of the fleeing enemy. The man replied, "Figured that, suh. Can do. Already seen some blood trails and they'll come t'gethuh soon 'nuff." Howard was thankful that his South Carolina upbringing enabled him to more or less follow the speech of the man.

Corndog and the squad moved out. Having faith in the man,

Howard called the three platoon leaders to him to explain the plan he was in the process of conceiving. While he waited, Howard slumped down next to a tree and swallowed another handful of APCs for whatever good they would do to blunt the pain and to check the fever he now had to admit he had. As the four lieutenants gathered, the sound of the choppers bringing in the Bravo platoons could be heard off to the east.

* * *

Lieutenant Howard told the platoon leaders that assuming the VC trail could be found, they would follow and push the enemy hard. They would move in column, in order of 3rd (because the tracking element had come from that platoon), command element, 2nd and 1st. He told Lieutenant Martin that he wanted him to be with the lead squad and to keep the artillery firing a couple hundred meters ahead of them as they moved. With that he hoped to inflict more enemy casualties on rear guard elements and at least to interfere with and discourage their slowing to emplace booby traps.

The officers were just wrapping up their session when the 3rd Platoon squad leader reported that Corndog had found the trail and the dinks were heading northwest. Howard told the lieutenants, "Good. Brief your papa sierras [platoon sergeants]. Dave, get to work on that artillery. We move out in ten mikes." As they walked off, Howard reported the same and the plan to the S-3 somewhere overhead. PFC Cotton monitored on the battalion frequency the S-3 telling Bravo to take a parallel course and advised Howard of the same.

They were moving before the Charlie Company platoon arrived at the island. On them fell the unpleasant task of policing up the battlefield. They counted forty-six VC bodies and collected half as many weapons, leaving the destroyed ones. Upon reporting that to battalion, the battalion commander flew in to see for himself, it being the greatest success any unit in the battalion had achieved in some weeks. He left somewhat unnerved, not with the carnage, of which he had seen plenty in Korea and a previous tour in Vietnam, but that he, who prided himself in what he considered to be superior ability to assess men, may have underestimated young Tom Howard.

Alpha followed the trail for several hundred yards and then came upon a grisly sight. At what apparently had been the VC rally point there was discarded equipment, blood everywhere, and just off into the thicker jungle three bodies hastily covered with leaf litter. Two were horribly burned and the third was both burned and wounded by bullets or shrapnel. Howard reported the finding to battalion and ordered the pursuit to resume aggressively.

After just another couple hundred yards, Alpha hit the first blocking position. The point man (not Corndog, who had been relieved of that duty because the trail now was easy to follow), seeing, hearing or just sensing imminent danger, dove off the trail. His slack man, however, had hesitated and paid for it with a bullet to the face, shattering his cheek bone. The 3rd Platoon troops hit the ground and returned fire at what was soon estimated to be a squad-size VC detachment.

Hearing the firing and shouts for a medic, Howard quickly moved forward. He found Lieutenant Smith and SFC Ross crouched behind a fallen log and straining to see through the jungle. Howard flopped down between them, gasping out loud at the pain to his injured arm. He quickly forced himself to recover and to Ross he said, "You know the drill. Squad in contact lays down a base of fire; you take a squad around the right and I with Lieutenant Smith will take one around the left; when one fires, the other moves in quick and hot." SFC Ross rogered the order and acted on it.

Howard turned to PFC Cotton and told him to tell Clark to move up to that position and for Masters to secure the small clearing just recently passed for an LZ. He told the other RTO to get a medevac chopper in the air. Turning back to 2LT Smith, Howard said, "I'll show you how this is done, Doug. Follow me." They and their RTO's moved out, picking up the remaining squad as they went.

Howard quickly took the men about fifty yards off to the left, then as many to the right and then, on line with Howard in the lead, right again to the sound of the firing. Howard slowed when he could tell they were getting close to the VC, still obscured by the thick brush. As he carefully but steadily continued to move forward, Howard put his M16 to his shoulder and Smith and then his men followed suit.

Howard was within twenty yards of the near flank VC soldier when they simultaneously spotted each other. As the VC whirled toward him, Howard fired a short burst and the VC went down, blood spurting from his throat. Howard and Smith together gunned down a second VC and the rest of their men opened fire as well. On cue, SFC Ross led his squad from the other side, firing as they closed on the enemy. The base squad increased their firing to pin the VC at the center and then quit to avoid fratricide. The VC tried to break and run, but it was too late. In less than a minute, all ten of them were dead.

Howard yelled for a cease fire, an order immediately relayed by subordinates. Ross's squad swept through the VC position and took up position on the other side. Howard was among those who inspected the enemy dead, finding that every one of them had been earlier burned and/or otherwise wounded, one who amazingly had gotten that far with a splint on his leg. That renewed and enhanced the respect the Americans had for their adversaries.

After seeing to it that his wounded man was taken back to the LZ to be evacuated, Howard reported the contact and consequences. He then ordered the company to move out, rotating the squads to the lead, 1st Platoon to the middle, and 2nd Platoon the trail.

For the next hour, Alpha continued to follow the trail. All the while Martin kept the artillery firing, one tube at a time, ahead of them. Twice they were slowed by sniper fire and twice more to disable hastily placed booby traps that the alert point men had spotted, but Howard kept pushing his men on. He knew that if he could not run the VC to ground within the next few hours, they would get away. That their relentless pursuit was effective was borne out by two more bodies the VC left behind. Howard had Cotton report the same and that they were continuing the mission.

After about another hour, they came upon a sluggish stream and stopped to fill their depleted canteens, hazarding to rely on halazone tablets to kill harmful organisms. It was only by dumb luck that a soldier wandered dangerously far to the left for water not muddied by the soldiers ahead of him and there he found a puddle of fresh blood. Howard had Corndog investigate and the scout soon ascertained that the VC had switched direction at the stream. The VC now were heading west, having first futilely left another false trail to the north.

Howard had Cotton radio the change in direction to battalion. Cotton reported back the good news that he heard Bravo being ordered to turn and follow and the bad news that Mike 6 was choppering in for a face-to-face. *"Damn it to hell,"* Howard silently fumed, *"we don't need this delay!"*

The C&C bird (command and control helicopter) soon dropped in to a small clearing billowing the "goofy grape" smoke of a purple smoke grenade and then immediately took off as soon as the battalion commander, his sergeant major, and RTO were clear of the blades.

Lieutenant Howard dutifully reported to his superior and led the group into the shelter of the trees. As the helicopter climbed to orbit at a safer altitude and quiet returned to the jungle, he was taken aback by his CO's first words, "Tom, you look like shit!" It was the not the insult that got him, but that the man had for the first time called him by his first name. Noticing the filthy, bloody, smelly bandage on Tom's arm, LTC Nichols asked with sincere concern, "Did you get hit today?"

Tom Howard, still shaken, replied, "Uh, no, yesterday." Tom missed the momentary look of confusion on his superior's face, his mind wandering to the thought, *"Was it only yesterday?"*

The two officers knelt on the leaf litter of the jungle floor over an acetate covered map spread out. Soon satisfied, the battalion commander motioned his RTO to call the helicopter back in and the two officers, trailed by the sergeant major and RTO, headed back toward the clearing where Tom was dumfounded that the CO gently shook his hand and clapped him on the opposite shoulder before boarding the helicopter then landing.

One thing Tom Howard had no way of knowing was that back at the island, the sergeant major had taken the opportunity to talk with the Alpha first sergeant out of earshot of the battalion commander. The first sergeant professionally reported the shape of the men and then gave a report of the events of the day from the perspective of being on the ground. He then, with obvious awe and pride, gave an only slightly exaggerated rendition of Tom Howard's heroic rescue of the machine gunner and recovery of the weapon. That story was being relayed to LTC Nichols as Alpha Company resumed their pursuit of the fleeing Viet Cong.

It was more of the same for Alpha, except that for Tom Howard each time a thorn caught on and tugged his bandages and each time he bumped the arm on anything solid was more and more painful. The fever seemed to be worsening and Tom was concerned that he might have only a few more hours in him before prudence would dictate that he admit ineffectiveness.

Corndog kept on the trail despite the enemy's repeated efforts to conceal it or to draw them off it. Those efforts included false trails, one with not only another corpse but also two gravely wounded men who could not possibly survive the agonizing trek. Their final service was to hopefully buy their comrades desperately needed time and space. Understanding their ploy, Tom Howard marched his men past the VC wounded, leaving it up to the radio-alerted S-3 as to whether troops would be dispatched to capture them or just leave them to their fate.

Alpha had moved another hour or so, this stretch without contact, when the pilot of a scout helicopter flying outside the artillery flight path radioed that he had observed about thirty VC, some carrying stretchers, cutting across a large field. He gave the coordinates. Tom Howard studied his map and figured that they were about a klick, a kilometer, about two-thirds of a mile, behind them. He rotated platoons, putting the fresher 1st Platoon in the lead, and ordered them to advance as quickly as they dared.

The brutal sun was high overhead when the Alpha point reached the field. Howard quickly made his way to the front. He was dismayed to see that the reported field was a vast expanse of grass waist to chest high with scattered bushes and a few trees. It offered scant cover. There was a copse of trees and tall termite mounds roughly in the middle.

"If I was a gook, that's where I'd be," Howard thought. He ordered the FO to put some rounds on the copse of trees while the men took a break and then radioed the first sergeant to get a chopper to shuttle out to them resupplies of ammunition, rations, and water; warning him to avoid the flight path of the artillery.

Lieutenant Martin called in and adjusted the artillery fire, calling in repeats until enough rounds detonated in and around the trees to satisfy himself and Lieutenant Howard that any stay behind force was dead or gone. With convenient timing, Howard was informed that the resupply bird was inbound and he had Martin call the artillery to check their fire and prepare to fire on order the coordinates of the far tree line.

A Huey slick descended and hovered a few feet off the ground. Howard watched the crew chief and door gunner toss out supplies and then was surprised and pleased to see the first sergeant hop off. The helicopter quickly departed, taking with it one of Alpha's walking wounded, who by then was feeling poorly, and two new men on the verge of heat exhaustion. As the supplies were being distributed, Howard called the platoon leaders to come to his location and briefed the first sergeant on the situation and his tentative plans. The first sergeant then made his way through each of the platoons to conduct a personal assessment of the unit's fitness and morale and to make absolutely sure that he had a proper head count.

The tentative plan Tom Howard had in mind was to attack. The plan was built on the supposition that the VC had formed a hasty defense in the far tree line and would be vulnerable. Now, though, as Tom waited for the lieutenants to arrive, he was all but immobilized by doubt, a nearly overwhelming bout of uncertainty. For the first time, the enormity of his responsibility as company commander hit him like a ton of bricks. He had neither the experience nor even the training to confidently send over a hundred and fifty young men in a frontal assault over open ground against an enemy position. Tom's mind wandered to the thought, "*This sucks, big time. Crossing that field, even with arty prep, could be like Pickett's charge,*" referring to the ill-fated assault Robert E. Lee had ordered at Gettysburg.

Tom struggled to regain his focus, his composure. He pondered the right move, all the while a voice from IOBC, the Infantry Officers Basic Course, once again screaming in his brain, "*Make a decision, lieutenant, make a decision.*" He stalled by calling battalion with his status, speculation, and general plan, also asking the location of Bravo Company. He was disappointed with the response to the latter. They still were an hour or more away. He called the FAC orbiting overhead and was told it would be thirty minutes before any fast movers (Air Force close air support jet aircraft) would be available and on station. The only good news was when he got the call that a pair of Charlie model gunships from the venerable 48th Assault Helicopter Company, the Jokers, were coming on station with another pair trailing.

Tom's melancholy was broken by the first artillery rounds impacting the far tree line. He watched the explosions though his binoculars. He was pleased.

Tom made his decision. They could wait neither on the fast movers nor plodding Bravo, for every minute of delay was another minute of preparation for the enemy. He radioed the FAC that he would be needing the fast movers on the ridge line to his front where artillery continued to explode just as soon as they could get there, for them to come up on his company push (frequency) so he could guide them in. He radioed the army aviators to hold back until the artillery lifted and then to move up to the edge of the field and when they saw the infantry reach the middle to expect his order to blast the tree line to their front.

The platoon leaders had assembled and more or less had been privy to the radio calls from which they had begun to understand what was about to transpire. Tom turned to them and started by demanding a status report from each who in turn responded. Tom looked over at the first sergeant who had returned who nodded his concurrence. Tom then addressed the lieutenants.

"Okay, here's the deal. I figure that the VC have left a platoon or so in those trees we're blasting to hold us off until dark. We can do nothing, in which case they'll get away or we can kill them and maybe press on to get eyes on the main unit before it's dark and pound them.

"I didn't call you over for just that though. You have the right to know that factored into my decision to go with the killing them option is me. I am fading. I figure I'm done for after we hit those guys, however it turns out. That means that command will pass to you, Craig, or you, Eddie, or you, Doug. If the plan goes to shit, we'll need to either hunker down and wait for Bravo or fall back. If the plan succeeds in killing those guys, the decision will have to be made whether to drive on until contact or dark or hold tight. You have to be thinking about that. Understood?"

When he was satisfied that all three understood, Tom proceeded to detail the plan of attack. He then released them to their platoons after setting the jump off time to give them time to brief their sergeants and get their men staged. When they hustled off, Tom looked to the first sergeant who comprehended the unasked question and gave him a broad smile, just the encouragement he needed.

On Howard's order, the men moved out into the field in a line of platoons, each in column formation with the command element trailing the middle column. As they approached the copse of trees, they, now replenished with ammo, liberally fired it up. They and the command group reached and swept through the copse of trees without incident. Scattered body parts and blood trails reflected that the VC indeed had left another squad or so there to slow the advance of the Americans, a tactic as unproductive as it was costly.

Howard, sweating profusely in the sweltering heat and otherwise suffering more with each step, knew he and his men had to take another break. He called the FO over and said, "Dave, here's the plan. We're going on line. We're going to halt halfway this side. That'll be your cue to check the arty. Tell them to add two hundred and stand by. When the last rounds hit, the gunships will take over and we'll assault to the trees." Martin rogered and Howard called to platoon leaders to get their men on line, two up and one back, and to move out.

The infantrymen reached the midpoint without taking fire. There they hugged the ground as the artillery fire on the objective ceased and on order the first pair of gunships began their run. Green tracers erupted from the trees, confirming that the VC indeed were there, in force and willing to fight.

Disregarding the deadly fire, the Jokers bravely closed on the enemy and unleashed their rockets in pairs. It indeed was a sight to behold, trumped by that the gunship pilots then boldly flew forward over the huddled infantrymen so that their door gunners could rake the enemy position with machine gun fire as they broke to clear the way for the next pair.

Tom Howard was suitably impressed and confident with the aviators' control that he ordered the company to rush forward even as rockets were being launched. It was a risky gamble, but a good one. The soldiers made it to the tree line without a single casualty.

But that was only the beginning.

* * *

The first man to go down was Lieutenant Craig Clark. As soon as he entered the trees, an explosion of unknown origin blasted him back out into the field, his right leg shredded by shrapnel and his left calf muscle all but severed. He was writhing on the ground when a medic reached him seconds later.

The VC had taken refuge in a well-camouflaged trenched and bunkered position dating back to the war with the French. It and they had withstood the American artillery with few serious casualties; the helicopter rockets had inflicted more; and the fire from the approaching infantry had the desired suppressive effect, but all that had been expected and the VC swiftly recovered.

The explosion that felled Lieutenant Clark was their cue to open fire and they did so with a vengeance. While they still were hampered by the smoke from the explosions and a few resulting fires, they now had the Americans silhouetted against the brightness of the open field behind them. In that fusillade of fire, several soldiers went down, one of them being Lieutenant Masters with an ugly wound to his upper arm. In a matter of seconds, two of the three platoon leaders were out of the fight.

Alpha took cover in the trees and returned fire while the VC continued their high rate of fire. It was a cacophony of rifle and machine gun fire; of bullets zinging, cracking and whining, thudding into the ground, thwacking into trees and thwapping into men; of exploding grenades, shouted commands, and cries and screams of the wounded. Visually it was smoke, muzzle flashes, crisscrossing tracers, and explosions. The Americans tenaciously managed to achieve a parity of fire and then a superiority of fire, but they on the lower ground with the field behind them still were at a distinct disadvantage.

Howard exhorted his men to push up the semblance of a hill and maintain their rate of fire. Moving from tree to tree or from anything that offered some protection to the next thing offering some protection, they slowly made their way half way up the rise. There they were stopped by the fierce rifle, machine gun, and RPG fire, now augmented by thrown hand grenades; and mounting casualties. There they suffered their first KIA. While hundreds of enemy bullets missed their marks, one incongruously hit an unlucky soldier right between the eyes, killing him instantly.

Tom Howard and his RTOs took cover in what they incredulously realized was a trench line. They shared a section of the trench with the body of a VC who had been blown in half. Another VC body lay just outside the trench, riddled with holes. It was impossible to see through the dense smoke of the battlefield, but Tom knew that their momentum had been checked. *Almost time to play the hole card.*

The battalion commander, who could not discern the action in the smoke-filled trees from his lofty perch of his C&C bird high overhead, was demanding over the radio a situation report. Howard was annoyed, thinking, "*Why do highers always have to do that? Don't they fuckin' know that I'm pretty fuckin' busy down here?*"

Tom, however, was no fool. He relented, took the microphone from Cotton, and started to call in when a tossed stick grenade bouncing end over end down the hill was seen by Mosley. He yelled, "Grenade!" and hit the dirt, pulling Cotton down with him. Howard had no time to do anything but turtle his chin to his chest and close his eyes before the grenade detonated less than three yards away. Red hot fragments burned into his exposed left shoulder and shredded the camouflage cover on his helmet and the blast was deafening. He had to fight back tears and a wave of nausea as he could feel the hot metal sizzling in his skin and muscle.

When he opened his eyes and blinked away the tears, he was reminded that he had a radio microphone in his left hand, the cord stretched taught to the radio on Cotton's back. Tom forced himself to recover.

"Mike 6, Alpha 6, over." When the CO immediately responded, his tone expressing that he was miffed, Howard called back, "Mike 6, Alpha 6. Sitrep follows. Enemy in place two hundred meters inside the trees. Number unknown, but estimated at two platoon strength with RPD's and RPG's. No indirect fires." Without thinking of the consternation he would be causing by his next lines, he continued, "Friendly casualties light, but two papa limas down and I got dinged again. Enemy casualties unknown except for the two sharing the first trench line with me. Alpha charlie mikeing [continuing mission]. Over."

Tom Howard's situation report triggered a collective "*oh, shit*" feeling among the battalion and brigade command and staff officers monitoring the frequency. LTC Nichols and his sergeant major sitting next to him in the C&C bird exchanged alarmed looks. *Two platoon leaders down? Howard 'dinged' again? Trench line? What the fuck?!*

The sergeant major spoke first. "Mighty tough on green tabs [leaders] down there, boss."

Forcing a smile he did not feel, LTC Nichols asked his senior NCO, "You ready for a second star on your CIB?" He was referring to stars over the Combat Infantryman's Badge denoting infantry combat action in successive wars. The sergeant major did not hesitate in nodding his assent and the CO ordered the pilot to put them down at the tree line.

The battalion CO called, "Alpha 6 Romeo, this is Mike 6 actual. I am inbound. Acknowledge. Over." PFC Cotton failed to acknowledge because he was otherwise occupied firing his rifle and ducking return fire. Alpha did not know they were getting company. LTC Nichols did not know that they did not know. He had not paid attention for an acknowledgment. Instead, as the C&C bird descended to the Alpha Company rear he was on the radio most emphatically exhorting the Bravo Company commander to "get the lead out of his ass" and get up there to support Alpha.

Thus, when the C&C bird landed at the CCP (casualty collection point) the first sergeant was one startled individual. He hastened to greet the arrivals as their pilot hastened to depart. No sooner had the helicopter cleared the other end of the field when all at the CCP were literally stunned as Lieutenant Tom Howard played his hole card. Two F-4 Phantoms screamed in, each dropping a pair of bombs on the hidden enemy positions, then circled to drop canisters of napalm and then circled once more for a gun run.

Tom Howard, knowing that smoke grenades likely could not effectively compete with the smoke obscuring the battlefield, had opted to employ the trick that had worked so well earlier that morning, namely having his M-60 machine guns fire vertically so the pilots could orient by the tracers. The Air Force flight leader acknowledged and when Tom had the guns fire, the pilot radioed, "Got your tracers, Alpha. Commencing runs west to east, bombs, then nape, then guns; danger close, your call, Alpha 6; I say again danger close, your call. Get your heads down."

The bombs exploded deafeningly on target and it seemed like chunks of debris had just finished falling on and about the Alpha troops when the air was sucked from their lungs as the napalm erupted above them. When the Phantoms roared in for their gun run, Tom Howard gave the order, "Alpha, Alpha 6. Attack now! Attack now! Don't stop for anything!"

Alpha Company complied. They left whatever cover they could find and advanced up the rise, firing as they went. Tom Howard himself climbed out of the trench and advanced with his RTO's behind.

Despite the hell the Air Force had just unleashed, the surviving enemy incredibly still had fight left in them. The VC soldier who had wounded Tom with the grenade popped his head out of a spider hole and Tom blew it apart with a burst from his M-16. After a few more steps, Tom paused to shoot another VC becoming visible through the smoke ahead and above.

Tom Howard took further advantage of the pause to look around to confirm that his men indeed were progressing. Smiling, he swiftly reloaded his rifle and set out again. Tom, however, took only a few more steps before a mule kick to his upper left chest knocked him almost back down to the lip of the lower trench.

Mosley and Cotton, who both heard the *thwap* of the bullet striking and in horror saw the puff of dust and mist of blood as the bullet exited their CO's back, watched him cartwheel past them, his rifle flying out of his hands and his helmet taking its own course down the slope. They rushed to his aid and dragged him by his web gear suspenders down into the trench. Cotton put pressure on the entrance wound and screamed for the medic while Mosley cradled his commander's head and talked to him to try to keep him from going into shock.

Mosley had the presence of mind to call on the company net, "Alpha, Alpha, this is Alpha 6 Romeo," and without waiting for any acknowledgments, "Alpha 6 is down; I say again, Alpha 6 is down." He then audaciously took it upon himself to add, "Stand by for further from Sierra 6. Charlie mike [continue mission] in the meantime."

Few of Alpha Company were made aware of the awful event. They by then were fiercely seizing and clearing the upper trench line and bunkers. And killing.

Meanwhile the medic slid into the trench and after a quick assessment he bandaged the stricken commander's wounds and then told the RTO's to get him down to the CCP, admonishing them to tell the senior medic there that he had not given him morphine. The medic then was off, responding to other frantic calls for him.

It was the RTO's and Lieutenant Martin who carried and dragged Tom Howard to the CCP on a poncho in what was an astronomically painful trip for him. The first sergeant, battalion commander, and sergeant major were alerted by an RTO as to his coming. As he and the men struggling to tote him appeared, another announcement was made over the radio, ignored for the moment as the lieutenant was lowered to the ground as gently as the exhausted bearers could. The senior medic immediately went to work.

Understanding that his excruciating torture trip had finally ended,

Tom Howard looked up to see the familiar faces of his RTO's, the FO, and first sergeant, but was confused in seeing the faces of his battalion commander and the sergeant major. It was LTC Nichols who spoke first, "Rest easy, son. Your men have taken the position." It may have been that news or it may have been the morphine the senior medic injected taking effect, but Tom Howard just smiled as he drifted off.

As Lieutenant Colonel Nichols stood with his sergeant major in the now strangely quiet battle space watching the medevac chopper disappear, he remarked, "In the twenty-four hours that Tom Howard commanded this company, he was attacked, he was wounded, he rescued, he attacked, he pursued, and he attacked again. He killed maybe a hundred VC, maybe more; at a loss of what, five friendly dead? Amazing. Simply freakin' amazing! I am proud as I can possibly be. And I am ashamed that I underestimated that young man. We need to make it right with him."

6

ALL OF THAT, OF COURSE, WAS LOST TO TOM HOWARD. HE MIGHT
have taken comfort in what LTC Nichols had to say, but probably not.
Tom then was in a single focus existence, one of abject misery that
kind words could not assuage. The pilot of the medevac chopper had
raced to the relative safety of altitude and while at first the cooler air
was a welcome relief to the sweltering heat below, the combination of
the increasingly cooler air, blood loss, shock, morphine and the metal
floor of the helicopter on which he was lying made Tom Howard cold,
so cold that his teeth were chattering and he was violently shivering.
The brief respite as the helicopter landed on the hot tarmac next to
the evacuation hospital was just a tease as he almost immediately was
rolled on a gurney into a cold triage room where he laid shivering while
waiting his turn. His croaking request for a blanket was ignored by the
busy medical staff. Alpha Company had sent them plenty of business
that day and they were not the only show in town, so to speak.

First Lieutenant Dana Williamson, RN, was about to get a rude
surprise on this, her second full day in Vietnam. She in a fresh uniform
carefully pressed to make a good first impression was being given her
orientation tour of the facility when all available medical personnel
were ordered to the triage room. Her tour guide pulled her along in
that direction.

Whatever she had envisioned a triage room in an evac hospital in a war zone to be, this was not it. Immediately upon entry into the room she was greeted by bedlam, seemingly barely controlled chaos, but the smells that assaulted her were the most unnerving—blood, urine, excrement, and unwashed men topping the list. She was pushed over to a young, semi-conscious soldier on a gurney and told to prep him. Despite her medical training and clinical work, she had no idea what that meant.

A huge black orderly rudely shouldered her aside, produced a wicked looking knife with a curved blade and proceeded to cut off most of what was left of the man's uniform. Nurse Williamson, trying to be helpful, started untying the man's boots, but the orderly again rudely pushed her aside and using the blade quickly slit the bootlaces and tossed the boots onto a nearby pile.

Nurse Williamson stared down at the man. She first noted that his darkly tanned face and neck were starkly contrasted by the fish white of the rest of his body. She observed the fresh bandage on the man's upper left chest and a filthy one on his lower right arm. She noted untreated punctures to his left shoulder. The shoulder looked as if a big dog had chewed on it.

As the orderly pulled off the chest bandage, producing a slight groan from the patient, Nurse Williamson gazed at a small, perfectly round hole surrounded by a large, ugly, dark purple bruise. Her nurse training kicked in and she imagined the internal anatomy and mentally composed a checklist: Patient presents with likely gunshot wound to the upper left chest, about 9mm in diameter, bullet path undetermined; possible organs and structures affected, left lung, blood vessels, third rib, nerves, scapula. She doubted that the subclavian artery had been perforated because, well, because he was not dead. A compromised subclavian vein could not be ruled out though.

The orderly interrupted Nurse Williamson's thought process by telling her more than asking her to help him roll the guy over. They rolled the man onto his side, producing another moan of pain, and revealing yet another bandage on his back. The orderly pulled it up, revealing the bullet's jagged exit hole from which blood was oozing. Nurse Williamson again professionally assessed the diameter of the hole to be 16mm. She was imagining the bullet path when the orderly put the bandage back in place, let the man settle again onto his back and without so much as a word hustled over to another wounded soldier just brought in.

Left alone, Nurse Williamson surveyed the man before her. He was young, about her own age; fit, but dirty and smelly; she compassionately covered the man's nakedness with a cloth and in doing so noticed that his hands were crisscrossed with cuts and punctures of varying ages, many of them festering. (She later would learn that most of the grunts who came through would bear similar wounds from grass cuts and thorns compounded by the infinitude of bacteria thriving in the harsh climate.)

She also noted that he had curious scars on the top and palm of his left hand, each about 10mm in length, but she did not have time for idle curiosity. Her focus returned to the bandaged lower right arm. The bandage was loose, filthy, and bloody. She decided to remove it.

Removal of the bandage revealed a long, jagged, deep tear from the wrist to almost the elbow and then a hole in the crook of the elbow. The wounds were nasty and infected, angrily red and oozing blood and puss. Nurse Williamson shuddered when she detected that some of what she first supposed to be dirt actually were insects, some still alive.

She was about to clean the arm and wounds when the same orderly returned with an equally harried doctor. The doctor gave Nurse Williamson a cursory nod, listened to the orderly's clipped rendition of the wounds, gave the patient a perfunctory examination to confirm the same and barked orders for his care and treatment before moving on to other patients.

Tom Howard's torture session had not ended. Another doctor in another room gave him a more thorough, and more painful, examination, his findings duly noted on the chart. Howard's wounds were cleaned and redressed. He finally got his blanket, but he was able to enjoy the warmth it afforded only for a few minutes before a second dose of morphine sent him back to La-La Land. He never knew that he was wheeled to an x-ray room, x-rayed and parked in a hallway until the x-rays could be read and his treatment decided therefrom. In the meantime, Tom was given a much-needed sponge bath, of which he also was oblivious. He was not even aware of being wheeled out to a waiting medical transport plane.

Tom Howard missed the elation of leaving Vietnam.

* * *

Tom Howard awoke to find a doctor gently shaking his foot. "Well, good morning, Lieutenant. I am Doctor Jones. Don't worry, that's not an alias." When his little joke fell flat and the nurse accompanying him rolled her eyes because it *always* fell flat, the doctor continued. "I am your attending physician. I am here to answer your questions and fill you in on your situation and status.

"First question, 'Where am I?' You are in Japan. Second question, 'Why am I here?' Because you were shot and blown up. Third question, *'How am I?'* Let me take that in some sense of order.

"First, the nurses tell me that your man parts are okay. The gooey feeling you have down there is ointment to treat your raging crotch rot. For that matter, the gooey feeling on your feet is for raging foot rot too. I will assume that since you are an officer and a gentleman that the abysmal hygiene allowing the rot to thrive was beyond your control.

"Second, the cast. I will spare you the medical terms unless you just need to be impressed. A bullet fragment severed your biceps tendon. No big deal really. An orthopedic surgeon went in, pulled the tendon back down and reattached it. You'll have to keep the cast on for a month or so until you're sufficiently healed. You'll have about an eight centimeter, under three inches, zigzag scar from that in the crook of your elbow.

"Under the cast, you also have a bandage for a crooked, jagged tear, close to eight inches long, on the top of your forearm as it would appear when bent. We figure it was from a bullet ricochet that ended up in your elbow joint. That will leave a scar, hard to tell how bad. We don't think there is any nerve damage, but let us know if you feel numbness or tingling in your fingers.

"Third, the bandage on your left shoulder. You took some grenade fragments. We took most of them out. Should be no problem. Small scars. Again, let us know of any numbness or tingling that might suggest nerve damage we don't think you have. Here are some souvenirs," handing Howard a vial with small, jagged metal fragments.

"Fourth, the bandage on your chest. You were shot in the upper left chest, just missing but bruising the left lung and most fortunately missing the big blood vessels there. The bullet broke a rib going in and holed the shoulder blade before exiting the back. Scar in the front should be about an inch and a half and the scar in the back a bit longer. We expect you to heal well, but we're watching to make sure. Again, let us know of anything that might suggest nerve damage, which again we don't think you have.

"Lastly, unless you bring some other malady to our attention I can tell you that your prognosis is excellent and we're thinking we can get you on the big bird back to the States in a week or so; you'll then spend some days in an army hospital, usually as close to your home of record as feasible; and then I expect it will be just a matter of days before they will release you to a thirty-day convalescent leave with follow ups and the cast coming off somewhere in there. The cycle will end with an examination to determine your fitness for further military service and your decision whether to instead opt for, say, a less hazardous occupation. That's it in a nutshell. Any questions? No? Okay, let us know if you have anything that might signal nerve damage or really of anything that alarms you."

The doctor's projections were accurate. As Tom Howard made his way home, his life as a patient in the military hospital system was typical. There were daily checks by the nurses, daily sessions of physical therapy (although nothing like it would become in later years), and decreasing visits by doctors. Tom rightly took that as a good sign. Otherwise he occupied his time writing recommendations for awards for his men in Charlie and Alpha companies; reading whatever was available, letters being the most looked forward to; catching up on his letter writing; a lot of talking with his fellow "inmates," as they likened themselves; an occasional movie or recorded sporting event; playing a lot of cards; and more than catching up on his sleep.

One day a boxed Purple Heart medal with order of authorization caught up with him and was unceremoniously delivered to him. Tom was only briefly and mildly disappointed with that. "*At least,*" he mused, "*the first time someone bothered to pin the thing on me, but then maybe that was only because I was getting the Bronze Star too.*"

Then, with a packet of orders (hospital discharge orders, travel orders, an order authorizing convalescent leave, orders for medical follow ups, and an order saying that an order would be sent to his permanent residence directing him where and when to report once medically cleared), Tom Howard finally was on an Air Force flight to Charleston and awaiting parents to take him home.

***

The scene at Charleston Air Force Base was quite predictable. It, of course, was a joyous reunion of Tom and his parents, but the excited and nervous chatter during the drive south through the outskirts of Charleston on their way home was to Tom on the verge of overwhelming. The opportunity presented itself to break the tension and he seized it.

Seeing ahead a Krispy Kreme donuts store with its "HOT NOW" neon sign ablaze, Tom apologetically interrupted his mother to ask his father to pull in. Five minutes later, back in the car, everything was all right in Tom Howard's world as he savored the sweetness of the glazed donuts and cold chocolate milk.

Arriving at the family home place outside of Beaufort, Tom inwardly groaned though as he could see cars and pickups in the drive and spilling out into the yard and even the road and a couple dozen folks on the porches. It was another joyous reunion, together with a fine southern meal of fried chicken, homemade biscuits, fresh vegetables, and sweet iced tea. It also was exhausting for Tom and he was secretly glad when most of the people departed, leaving him on the back porch with his father and his father's brother, Uncle Bob, later joined by his grandfather Carl. Tom's mother made herself scarce when the liquor and cigars came out.

Tom dearly loved and admired his father, Daniel Howard, who at forty-six years of age still was an imposing man. The same was true of his Uncle Bob, eleven-years junior to Tom's father and thirteen years senior to Tom. And the same was true of his grandfather, seventy years old and still going strong. Each of these men had started in their early teens working in the logging business and years of grueling work in the pine forests and swamps of the South Carolina low country had made them tough as nails.

While Carl kept a hand in the logging business, the business he had built stemmed more from mechanical work and it had branched out from there. Tom's father and uncle learned the lessons their father had taught them well. By the time it was Tom's turn to tag along when he was a mere youngster, the Howard elders only occasionally physically worked in the timber end of the business. But they were hardly out of it. They had several crews cutting timber and hauling logs with machinery, equipment, and vehicles owned debt free. Most of those logs went to the big chipping plants, but the choice timber went to the Howard saw mill.

But business success told only a small part of these men. They were wonderful husbands and fathers, deeply rooted Christians without being sanctimonious; proud southerners without the bigotry prevalent of the day; and all three were combat veterans and firm patriots. But even those attributes fell short of defining the Howard men. Perhaps though, it was enough that the label "good man" was affixed to each of them by one and all. There never was any doubt in Tom Howard's mind that he, like his father and uncle, would follow in Grandad's footsteps.

And so the four Howard men, content in each other's company, talked for hours about anything and everything, that is, anything and everything except Vietnam. They probably would have continued late into the night, but at some point, the elder Howards realized they had lost Tom. He was sound asleep.

* * *

The next day, Tom was up surprisingly early. When his father asked why, Tom explained that he'd been doing hardly anything but sleeping for weeks. Tom's father laughed because he could relate. He too had come home battered from war a long time ago.

As father and son made their way to the back porch with steaming cups of strong coffee, Tom's mother made them an awesome breakfast of eggs, bacon, grits, biscuits, and lots and lots of butter. Afterward, Tom asked his father to come with him to his room. There Tom explained that he needed some help getting ready for a shower and he did not want to upset Mama in doing it.

Daniel Howard was no stranger to wounds. He still bore the scars of those he had suffered in the Pacific, and he had been witness to countless other wounds before, during and after. Still, he was taken aback when his son pulled off his shirt, revealing the scar where the bullet had struck. It did not take a medical degree to understand that an inch or two had been the only difference between life and death. Wordlessly and with surprising gentleness, he removed the cast which had been cut and taped back on. He gritted his teeth when he saw the scars there. He then left his son to enjoy a long, hot shower.

The shower indeed was wonderful, absolutely luxurious, and it was a while before Tom relented to ending it. He shaved, put on a pair of boxer shorts and stepped out in the hall to return to his room to get dressed. There, to his surprise, stood his mother holding a basket filled with bandages and medicines. When their eyes met, she could plainly see his embarrassment. She said, "Thomas Howard, do you think I turned into a delicate flower while you were gone, that I'd fall out with the vapors if I saw you'd gotten yourself a mite banged up? Now get yourself over here and I'll get you fixed up."

As Tom's mother proceeded to examine him with the studied eye of a career nurse, Tom noticed that she had made his bed, tidied up, and had laid out clothes for him to put on. She padded the blood and gook oozing from softened scabs in a few places, applied antibiotic cream, and redressed the wounds with practiced hands and tenderness. Tom balked when she pulled out a jelly jar containing some sort of viscous substance.

"Whoa, Mama. Tell me that's some FDA approved medicine you pilfered from the hospital or even some medicine you were taught to concoct rather than some low country Gullah voodoo thing."

"Oh, don't be such a baby. It's a salve that will fade those angry scars of yours."

"Didn't seem to do much good on Dad's leg."

"Well, smarty pants, just so you know, it did help and would've helped more if he wasn't even more stubborn than you."

"Well, the nut doesn't fall far from the tree."

"Nor the fruit. You are your father's son, no doubt about that, and I am as proud of you as I am of him. Now shut up and let me rub this stuff in. You'll need to do it yourself after every shower until it runs out."

Bea Howard proceeded, concealing the anguish she felt as her fingers worked the lotion into the scars, the irrefutable evidence of her boy's pain and suffering and of the fact that she very nearly had lost him. She composed herself, helped Tom get into his clothes and then his sling, only mildly scolding him for refusing the cast.

She then took Tom by the arms, gave him a mother's hug and with tears in her eyes told him how happy she was that he was safe back home. She stepped back, composed herself again, and said, "Now, finish up and be quick about it. Your Daddy is waiting."

Tom obeyed and found his father downstairs. His father smiled and invited him to come along with him while he checked on the logging crews and the shop. Tom followed him out to his old pickup, past a new one Tom had to assume also was his Dad's. Together they headed out to the locations the loggers were working.

At each stop, Tom was gladdened to see those rough men, many he had grown up around and later worked with; a couple of whom also had been to Vietnam. Tom felt a sense of pride when every man showed sincere respect for his Dad, whom without exception they referred to as "Mister Dan."

The highlight, though, was when they rolled up on Big Jake's crew, who were then taking a lunch break. Jake was "Big Jake" because he was big, like NFL lineman big. He loved Mister Dan whom he knew had scoffed at violating what many considered absolute norms by putting him in charge of the crew, over white men.

Jake met them with a broad smile as they were walking from the truck. He shook Dan's hand and succinctly related their progress for the day. Only then did he turn to Tom, smiled even more broadly, and gave him a hug while being careful of the young man's injuries. He said, "Praise the Lord you got home safe, Tom, even if busted up a bit."

Their joyous reunion, however, was interrupted when one of the crew, a big redneck probably close to thirty-five years old with the look of someone who enjoyed his beer too much, his toothbrush not enough, and favored wrestling and NASCAR over anything the least bit intellectual, came up to them. He obviously was agitated about something, but from a sideways glance Tom could tell that other than being annoyed his father was unconcerned. Without so much as a greeting, the man confronted Dan and loudly enough for all to hear said, "I ain't taking no more goddamn orders from your goddamned nigger."

Before anyone could say a word, without conscious thought, Tom pushed between his father and Jake and with one punch from his good arm knocked the loudmouth out. To say that the group, Dan, Jake, and the entire crew, was momentarily stunned would have been a gross understatement. Dan Howard surveyed the scene and then broke the silence, addressing the now closely gathered crew.

"Any of y'all got a problem with that?" No response. "Any of y'all got a problem with Tom?" No response. "Any of y'all got a problem with Jake?" No response. "Good. Now get out there and cut me some wood. Jake, put ol' Bubba here on the loader when he finishes his nap. I expect his head will be hurting a mite too much to be hopping around on the ground. Let me know if Tom's attitude adjustment didn't do the trick." With that he and Tom left.

As they were heading back to the house, Dan surprised Tom by pulling into a convenience store and then astonished him by coming out with a six-pack of beer. He got back into the truck and handed one to his son. "Coldest beer in town. You've earned it. But I have to say, Tom, that it's a damn good thing Bubba didn't get up. You're in no shape to fight and I'm too old to fight. I'da had to kill him and then spend a big chunk of your inheritance buying off the witnesses."

The next day changed Tom Howard's life forever.

* * *

It was a Friday. Tom again woke up early. He decided to shave and shower before going downstairs and he even managed to band-aid the few wounds still needing cover. Without any real forethought, he pulled from the drawer an Izod polo shirt and took from the closet khaki pants and dock shoes, looking quite the preppie. At the head of the stairs, he caught the wonderful aroma of coffee and bacon and hastened down the stairs. As Tom and his parents had breakfast, his father asked him to take some deposits to the bank in town, meaning Beaufort. Handing Tom the keys to his new Ford pickup sealed the deal.

The truck was reminiscent of Tom's last day with Charlie Company and his guys arguing over best rides. They all may not have agreed with him, but in his mind this one topped the list. It was a 1967 F-100 4x4 with a 390-cubic inch 8-cylinder engine, a twin I-beam independent suspension, automatic transmission, air conditioning, a good radio, and bright red paint. It took Tom close to an hour to make the ten-minute trip to the bank, but he nevertheless was there before lunch.

Walking into the bank, he naturally chose the line with the cutest teller. And she was cute, amazingly cute. When he reached the head of the line, he presented her with the packet his father had given him and she gave him a smile in return that literally made him weak in the knees. He managed to smile back, but was unable to form any cognizable words. He tried to think of something clever to say. He failed.

Seeing the sling on his right arm, the young lady politely asked him what on Earth had happened to him. For no reason he could give, then or ever after, Tom replied, "Bar fight."

She gave him a look that suggested suspicion and curiosity, looked down at the papers, looked back up and said just a little too loudly, "I know damn well who you are, Tom Howard. Don't you lie to me. I know you were shot."

That, of course, drew considerable unwanted attention and caused Tom to blush like a fool. He leaned closer to the girl and said, "Such language from a fine young southern lady, and the daughter of a Past Master of the Lodge!"

She cut him off by saying, "I could say the same about you, except the "fine young southern lady" and "daughter" parts.

Tom jumped right back in. "Well, no need to exclude them. I've been called words to that effect once or twice. And I know damn well who you are too, Miss Katie Greer." And then with uncharacteristic boldness he never would be able to explain he added, "Tell you what, let me make it up to you by buying you lunch. How 'bout it?"

After a painfully long pause that really was only seconds, Katie smiled that smile again and answered, "Well, okay. Twenty minutes?"

Katie Caroline Greer, 18, was the youngest daughter of Bill Greer, Jr., the owner of the bank with whom Tom's father had loyally banked for many years, his father having done the same with Bill Greer, Sr. Katie, Tom soon would learn, was headed back to the College of Charleston in the fall, meaning she was home for the summer.

It may not have been until their second date that Tom became aware that he was in love with Katie Greer. Katie much later admitted that it was the same for her. They saw each other as much as they could until Tom had to report to Fort Benning, the Infantry School, Office of the Director of Instruction.

* * *

A permissible couple days before Tom Howard was to report for duty, he drove across Georgia to Fort Benning, a sprawling reservation on the south side of the city of Columbus, on the Alabama line. He found that he needed every bit of those days to report in, get his required post sticker, get final clearance for duty, get uniforms altered or replaced, and patches sewn on them, get some food, get settled into his room in the BOQ (bachelor officer quarters), recon where he needed to be on day one, and make the obligatory trip to Ranger Joe's for the "cool stuff" he would not be getting from the Army.

On that first day, he dutifully, timely, and correctly reported to his new boss, the Director of Instruction, Colonel Kennedy. First impressions were lasting impressions and this was no exception. Tom's first impression was drawn from the dress green blouse hanging on a coat rack he could see from the secretary's office immediately outside the colonel's office. Rows of ribbons pushed a CIB with star, signifying combat as an infantryman in two wars, nearly to the uniform epaulet;

and below those ribbons were paratrooper's wings with the coveted bronze star signifying a combat jump. The colonel was just as impressive.

Colonel Kennedy explained to Tom what he would be doing and what was expected. For the first several days, however, the two spent considerable time just talking about things, Tom's training experience, and a great deal about Vietnam. Tom ultimately realizing that they weren't chatting, but working, the colonel picking his brain to assist him in assessing the Infantry School curriculum. Tom met the colonel's wife, a gracious lady. And he met the colonel's son.

It was in his second week when one afternoon Tom was called into the colonel's office and there he found a very fit captain sitting very much at ease on the colonel's couch. The captain was the colonel's son, Don, a spitting image of his father. Don was on the staff of the Ranger School. He was an Airborne Ranger with a MACV (Military Assistance Command, Vietnam) combat patch, a CIB over his left pocket, and Vietnamese paratrooper wings over the right. Tom also identified the school ring on Don's finger as that of the United States Military Academy at West Point on the Hudson River, New York (or, as Tom and his fellow graduates of The Citadel, the Military College of South Carolina, preferred to call it, the "Hudson High School for Troubled Boys").

The three men talked for a while and then Don asked Tom if he played racquetball. Tom said that he did and with an unspoken question by Don and an unspoken answer by his father, the two young officers were on their way to the gym.

Tom had not thought that through at all. With wounds still tender, and his arm out of the cast for only a few weeks (and he being otherwise occupied during that time), Tom had exercised little. He barely was able to do twenty-five pushups and he doubted he could do no more than a few good pullups. He had no business launching into a racquetball game against a very likely skilled and competitive opponent.

Tom made it through game one all right, losing but not humiliated, but he had to bow out of the second, his body hurting, his head spinning and his stomach tossing. Tom headed straight to the locker room, Don over to the free weights.

Don Kennedy found Tom sitting shirtless on a bench in the locker room, head between his knees. Don's thoughts that his Dad had a wimp on his hands were quickly erased when he saw the still pink telltale scars of a through and through gunshot wound to the chest in addition to the gnarly scars on the right arm he had seen earlier. Their friendship began right then. For the next several weeks the two of them played together, ran together, worked out together, and drank beer together. Tom had no idea that somewhere along the way Don had developed an ulterior motive with the physical regimen.

Tom learned that Don was just back from Vietnam where he had been an advisor to a company of Vietnamese Rangers. He had seen a fair share of action and had done well. He was at the Ranger School only temporarily while awaiting IOAC, the Infantry Officers Advanced Course, and was planning afterward to qualify for Special Forces, the Green Berets. Tom shared his experiences in the delta and one evening after a few too many beers confided that the only reason he did not go into the Marine Corps as his father had done was because he aspired to be a Green Beret too.

Tom continued with his job of reviewing Infantry School lesson plans in light of directives from TRADOC, the Training and Doctrine Command under whose jurisdiction Fort Benning fell. He met with Colonel Kennedy regularly, the meetings rarely limited to Infantry School issues. As Tom rose to leave from one such meeting, the Colonel said, "Oh, one last thing, Tom. I need you, spiffed up in your greens, ribbons and all, to meet me at the O Club [Officers Club] Friday at 1600." Thinking nothing of it, Tom left with a "Roger that, sir."

That Friday Tom arrived at the club a dutiful ten minutes early. He was looking good. One thing four years at The Citadel did was to teach him how to shine things. Entering the club, he was directed to one of the banquet rooms. Standing at the door was a first lieutenant with aide de camp insignia. The lieutenant read his name tag, extended his hand, introduced himself and told Tom to go on in. Tom found that mildly strange, but proceeded into the room without a second thought.

There he saw the post commander with a group of field grade officers, including Colonel Kennedy. Tom also saw Don Kennedy off to the side with a smaller group of company grade officers. When their eyes met, Tom gave Don an inquiring look and received in return a *"hell if I know"* look. Colonel Kennedy noticed Tom, said something to the general, and waved Tom over. Introductions were made and the general said, "Well, let's get to it," and headed toward a podium in front of the appropriate set of flags. Colonel Kennedy lightly touched Tom's arm and Tom understood that they were to watch whatever the event was from up front.

When Tom reached the front and happened to glance back at the doors in the rear, he was bewildered to see the general's aide escorting into the room none other than his parents and, even more astonishing, Katie and her parents. Eye contact with them was precluded though by someone positioning Tom and someone else calling the officers to attention. With *what the hell?* echoing in Tom's brain, the general began speaking:

"Thank you all for joining us here this afternoon. We are here to recognize the extraordinary conduct of one of our own, Lieutenant Tom Howard." It took every bit of control Tom could muster to maintain his proper position of attention. The general continued, "While ordinarily it would suffice to read the citation and move on to pictures, coffee, and cake," met with dutiful chuckles, "this instance calls for more. This young lieutenant came to us straight from Vietnam. Well, not straight from Vietnam, from Vietnam via a series of Army hospitals. We are gathered here to award his heroism, sacrifice, and service over there."

The adjutant handed the general a medal and with that commenced the ceremonies. Tom Howard, still befuddled, caught only few of the words, words that only compounded his confusion. "Attention to orders… Secretary of the Army… Army Commendation Medal for Valor… ground actions against hostile forces in the Republic of Vietnam… courageously… platoon leader… consistently performed his duty as an infantry platoon leader, company executive officer, and acting company commander outstandingly through his strong leadership skills, admirable calmness, bravery under fire, and inspirational acts of valor…"

Tom would have laughed had he heard how the award came about. Lieutenant Colonel Nichols' tour of duty as battalion commander was winding down and he wanted to make sure that his men who had distinguished themselves through meritorious or valorous service were duly awarded. He therefore sat with his adjutant and they went through the battalion roster, starting with his company commanders and principal staff officers. The adjutant asked, "What about Lieutenant Tom Howard? He is not coming back and therefore is due an end of tour award. BSM?" The Bronze Star medal, awarded either for heroism or meritorious service in a combat zone, typically was awarded to officers and senior NCOs completing their tours of duty. It became so commonplace that it was fairly disdained, held in no higher regard than the "I was there" ribbons everyone received.

Lieutenant Colonel Nichols knew that, thought about it, and decided, "No, he's already got a Bronze Star, and a real one for valor. I tell you what, write him up for an ARCOM with V. It's lesser, but it'll stand out on his chest and worded well it'll stand out in his 201 file too."

The general pinned the medal on Tom's chest, but then in Tom's mind oddly just stepped back. Tom heard the adjutant again call attention to orders and read that he, Tom, was receiving the Purple Heart medal. Tom was confused. It was a mistake. Tom's mind raced as to what, if anything, should he say or do about that he had already in the hospital gotten his Purple Heart as the purple ribbon with oak leaf cluster affixed on his chest attested.

Tom opted to do nothing when the general announced to the assemblage. "This punctuates the medal I just pinned on Tom's chest. This is Tom's third award of the Purple Heart. *Third!* Now I've known some grizzled old sergeants with that many, but very few officers. Now, not to make light of Tom's sacrifices, not at all, but if what I've been told is correct, the circumstances surrounding the first one generated a nickname for Lieutenant Howard, a nickname I will be gracious enough not to elaborate upon. Instead I leave to him to confirm and explain at the appropriate time and place."

"*Oh, God,*" Tom Howard silently whined.

It was wise for Tom to remain silent. Later, when he compared the new Purple Heart citation to the one he had received in the hospital, he realized that the dates were different. His wounds from day one were treated separately and distinctly from those of day two. He knew of instances where wounds suffered over the course of a battle had been lumped into one award, but could not appreciate how unusual it was not to treat them in such fashion.

While Tom had no way of knowing it, it was his battalion commander's last tribute and act of atonement to him when he ordered his adjutant, "To hell with policy and protocol. Tom Howard got wounded in battle number one and in battle number three and I'm not going to lump them together. Do two award recommendations, one for each date, word 'em differently, and space them apart. Make it happen."

Expecting conclusion to the ceremony and having to explain the nickname comment, Tom was so unprepared for what then transpired that once again his mind could only grasp some of the general's words: "... the Silver Star Medal... for conspicuous gallantry in combat action against hostile forces in the Republic of Vietnam ... as Commanding Officer of Alpha Company...," followed by a somewhat embellished account of the island fight, the morning fight and hill fight, and ending with "his extraordinary valor reflecting greatly upon himself, his unit, and the United States Army." As the general pinned on Tom's chest the medal with distinctive red, white and blue ribbon, he said with complete sincerity, "Lieutenant, you are a true hero and I am proud to honor you for your conduct."

There then were handshakes, congratulations, photographs, and Colonel Kennedy inviting all to stay for dinner in Tom's honor. Looking over at his mother and Katie, one thought suddenly came to Tom's mind, "*Oh, shit!* For his mother, it was because she now knew that he had downplayed the events to the point of actually lying about them; and, for Katie, "*What kind of a nut does she think I am?*

Tom excused himself from them to use the restroom and as he was washing his face, Katie's father came in. Tom blurted out to him, "I am so sorry, Mister Greer. Katie's got to be thinking I'm a nut case!"

Bill Greer studied the young man for a long moment, put his hands on his shoulders, looked him right in the eye, and said, "Son, I think y'all are going to be all right."

Dinner was a blur, as was the evening. The next afternoon, however, the parents left Katie and Tom to themselves. Tom took Katie to see his BOQ room and the rest was history, *private* history.

That night, Tom and Katie double-dated with Don and his current girlfriend. After steaks, beer, and wine they went to Don's BOQ room after stocking up on more beer and wine. It was a grandly fun time, until a pounding on the wall signaled that maybe they ought to hold it down. A few minutes later, Don punctuated the evening.

"People, I have a pronouncement. From my extraordinary powers of observation and my keen intellect honed to a razor's edge at the United States Military Academy at West Point, I am confident to report that Katie and Tom did it." The beer spewing from Tom's nostrils and Katie's blushing confirmed understanding of what "it" meant and that Don indeed was correct.

Later that evening, Katie walked her inebriated lover to his BOQ, sadly declined his invitation, and drove his truck to the motel. She greeted her parents who were reading in bed and said she was going to take a shower and go right to bed. When the sound of the shower could be heard, Mr. Greer took his wife's hand and quietly said, "It seems, my dear, that our little girl is all grown up" and, after a pause adding, "Could be worse" and then "I think Katie would appreciate it if we were asleep when she comes out." They were feigning sleep when Katie came into the room and quietly slipped under the covers in the adjacent bed. It was quite a while before she was able to drift off to sleep.

The next morning, the Howards and Greers met at the Officer's Club for brunch and when they parted in the parking lot, Tom and Katie's hug, held maybe a bit too long, prompted Tom's folks to also correctly conclude that their relationship had turned a corner.

* * *

For Tom, Monday was more abnormal than he had expected. An unusual number of officers came by the office delivering papers and packets that normally would have come through interoffice mail or even intraoffice mail. They were surreptitiously coming by to check out the young first lieutenant with three awards for valor, one of them being the Silver Star, and two oak leaf clusters on his Purple Heart. They were somewhat disappointed for Tom, as usual, adorned his uniform with nothing other than his CIB.

Don Kennedy's emotions concerning his friend's new prominence spanned on one hand happiness and pride and on the other outright dissatisfaction. To Don it was a travesty beyond measure that such accolades fell upon a leg, a straight-leg non-paratrooper, however courageous the conduct may have been. He therefore decided it was time to implement the devious plan he had in the making. He knew that Tom was about midway through his one-year interim assignment with the Directorate of Instruction while awaiting his slot in IOAC and even his minimal schooling in economics persuaded him that the law of diminishing returns would render Tom's benefits thereto declining.

Toward the end of the day, Colonel Kennedy called Tom into his office and told him that he had an assignment for him. Tom was completely unaware that a devious plot was about to come to fruition. The colonel told Tom that he wanted him to assess the Basic Airborne Course. Tom remained oblivious and Colonel Kennedy struggled to maintain a poker face.

When Tom asked when he wanted it done, the colonel smiled and said, "Well, the course starts in two weeks and it's a three-week course, so have the report on my desk three days after you finish." Maybe he was being obtuse, but it was not until then did Tom understand that he was to do the course. *So much for it being voluntary training.* The colonel added, "Another thing, I understand that you may want to work on your pull-ups before you go."

Suddenly it was all clear. It did not take a rocket scientist to realize that Don had a hand in this. Tom correctly imagined Don's thought process: *It's a freakin' shame that a hero like Tom is a damned leg.* Tom felt like a dolt. He struggled not to show it, but his "Roger that, sir," was not very convincing.

So, for the next two weeks, with Don Kennedy (who had been forgiven) as his coach when training cycles allowed, Tom ratcheted up his running and workouts, doing hundreds of pushups and improving his pull ups. Jump school turned out to be mostly fun and the jumps themselves were exhilarating. He reported the same to the colonel, applauded the course, and told him the only changes he would recommend would be to tone down the boot-campish bullshit (he had grown that comfortable with the colonel) and instead weed out the undeserving with a strict PT test and get the students on the jump towers earlier. Colonel Kennedy told Tom to draft a cover memo to the jump school leader *after* he got back from the weekend, meaning he was giving Tom a couple of days off.

That night Tom called Katie. She was pleased to say that her parents had plans to go out of town that weekend. Tom's thoughts on the matter were perhaps a bit more lustful. He pictured her wearing the t-shirt he had gotten for her adorned with paratrooper wings, that is, wearing nothing but the t-shirt adorned with paratrooper wings. And so, after a dutiful day at home, Tom clandestinely made his way over to the Greers for what he planned to be a marathon of love. Indeed it was, and it was a sad parting when he headed back to Georgia on Sunday.

Tom had his assignment to Colonel Kennedy that first day back and the colonel forwarded it with his endorsement to his counterpart (an old friend) at the Airborne School. Nothing would come of it, of course, but it was good to remind folks now and then that their way was not necessarily always the best way.

Three days later, a rather clandestine telephone call to the colonel presented an interesting suggestion. The colonel thought it over for a bit, liking it more and more, and then promptly acted on it. The next day he called Tom into his office.

"Tom, I've got an assignment for you." The *déjà vu* moment filled Tom with trepidation bordering on full dread. "I was pleased with your report on jump school. Good work. How about doing the same thing for Ranger School?"

It was all Tom could do to keep his jaw from dropping. *Ranger School! That'd be nine weeks of hell!* Tom swallowed, bucked up, and replied, not any more convincingly than before, "Certainly, sir. When?" That he again was to be given but two weeks to prepare hit Tom in the gut like a punch. He knew he'd again turn to Don, regardless of his complicity in the matter, to coach and push him.

* * *

Ranger School was every bit as hard as Howard had been told and a battered body on the mend did not help. Still, as Howard had been forewarned, the challenge was much more mental than physical. Long after he completed the course, two incidents would stand out in his mind.

The first was when he was having a particularly bad day and the idea of quitting was looking better by the moment. One of the instructors came up to him and said, "Listen to me, Howard, and listen to me good. You are an infantry officer and most of these other guys are private snuffies, maybe junior NCO's. And you are a hero. Don't you fuckin' let them down by showing weakness."

The second was similar, but funnier. After his group had all but miserably failed an exercise and were hanging their heads in exhaustion, shame, and self-pity, an instructor kicked the toe of Tom's boot. When he sullenly looked up, the instructor nodded to a fellow student mirroring Tom's mournful conduct and said, "See that guy over there. He's sitting there saying, 'Ow, ow, ow, my pussy hurts.'"

While Howard was never a frontrunner for top of the class, he was sufficiently inspired and motivated to successfully muddle through the course and receive the coveted yellow on black Ranger tab. Katie was there to see it and afterward she accompanied Tom to Ranger Joe's for him to buy her a "Ranger" t-shirt and then accompanied him back to his BOQ where she wore it, briefly.

Tom returned to work and Colonel Kennedy again gave him time for a long weekend off. Tom was in Beaufort before he remembered the envelope the colonel had given him as he was leaving. He opened it and found notification that he was to be promoted to captain, orders to attend IOAC, and a congratulatory note from Colonel Kennedy. It seemed that he and Katie would have plenty to talk about over the weekend.

Tom returned to his duties and dutifully wrote an assessment of the Ranger course, with which again the colonel was pleased and again he forwarded to the school leader with his endorsement. The only negative comment Tom made in his report was that while training to think and act while stressed and exhausted clearly had merit, the students could learn a lot more if their minds were clear and therefore a better balance might be achieved. The suggestion, of course, was rejected, but that never was the object of the exercise anyway.

Tom was duly promoted to captain and upon the conclusion of his assignment, he was surprised with the award of an Army Commendation Medal. He moved on to IOAC and found that while some of it could be written off as bullshit, it by and large was good instruction and training and he met a lot of good people. The course also afforded him time to go and see Katie and for Katie to come and see him.

Tom had orders for Germany following IOAC, manning the border against the Soviet Bloc hordes. While he and Katie had thus far only vaguely touched on the future and the subject of marriage was avoided, Germany was not in the picture. With the war still going on, Tom was not ready to contemplate leaving the Army, but Germany still was unattractive. But how to get out of it?

Don Kennedy was in Special Forces school at the time and there were a number of Green Berets in Tom's class. The idea of trying out was re-sparked, then rekindled, and then it grew. Tom posed it to Katie as objectively as he could. Katie was ambivalent at first, but warmed to the idea. After much deliberation, and with Katie's consent, Tom volunteered for the training. In due time and after the assessment and qualification process, he was accepted.

Special Forces training in many ways was easier than Ranger school, although much longer. Like both Airborne and Ranger schools, it had its fair share of bullshit, but Tom mostly enjoyed it, his fellow students, and most of the instructors. He learned a great deal, not the least of which being that Vietnam was but one of many very real threats to the United States and that a very real need existed for special forces to keep those threats at bay. Tom made it through the course and earned his green beret. Tom expected, and Katie feared, orders back to Vietnam. Instead, Tom found himself in limbo for a time at Fort Bragg.

7

WHILE CAPTAIN TOM HOWARD WAS UNDERGOING HIS SPECIAL FORC-es training, the North Vietnamese launched their largest attack of the war, the Tet Offensive of early 1968, involving a half-million communist troops. It was an inexplicable surprise. Military and intelligence leaders alternatively played or tried to avoid the blame game while soldiers, Marines, and airmen fought the monumental fight. American presidential hopefuls struggled with the escalation of fighting and casualties and more broadly with what to do (or at least say) about the costly and unpopular decade long war in Vietnam, all suggesting in one way or another that America's involvement in the war was drawing to a close.

For most soldiers and Marines, grunts in particular, the forecast meant nothing, not a damn thing. It was still humping and suffering in the bush, trying to stay alive and in one piece.

One such grunt was Specialist Isaac Jefferson, an M60 machine gunner with most of his tour behind him. In many ways, Jefferson could have been included in the stereotype of the typical black infantryman in Vietnam, steady in the field and solid in a fight, but a real pain in the ass back inside the wire. Jefferson knew that was so and took pride in it. The Army's remedy, it seemed to him, was to keep his black ass outside the wire, out in the bush. "*Fuck it, don't mean nuthin*" was the grunt's standard aphorism to such things and Jefferson's was no exception.

The standing joke was that everyone in the 1st Cavalry Division had his own helicopter. The joke was not funny to Isaac Jefferson. This time they had been out for days, humping during the day in the stifling heat, seeing nothing, and then warding off mosquitoes at night. The vaunted helicopter mobility just meant to them that they quickly could be moved somewhere else to hump and feed the mosquitoes and leeches — and to kill or be killed.

As it happens, and as it had happened to Jefferson too many times before, the drudgery of the day suddenly changed in a shocking instant. *Holy fuck*, thought Jefferson, hearing intense automatic rifle and machine gun fire up ahead continue unabated, now punctuated with explosions. *What the fuck have we gotten into this time?*

Jefferson took a knee, peered into the jungle growth for anything resembling a firing lane, for any movement. He heard crashing to his left and turned to see the lieutenant coming through the thick brush, gathering troops. The lieutenant did not slow when he reached him. A snapped command, "Jefferson, you're with me," and Isaac was on the move too.

The lieutenant led the group quickly and recklessly through the jungle, dropping off pairs of soldiers every ten yards or so, pausing each time only long enough to point out fields of fire and to whisper essential instructions. When they stopped, chests heaving and sweat pouring, Jefferson could make out light through the trees, suggesting open ground, most likely a rice paddy. The lieutenant caught his breath, faced the remaining men with him and told them, "The gooks are trying to flank us. We can't let them use the paddies."

Jefferson was alarmed, to say the least, to realize that the "we" amounted to no more than the lieutenant, his RTO, himself, and his assistant gunner. The entirety of the lieutenant's conveyed plan was, "Come on," as he took off running toward the paddy. Jefferson managed to choke out a "*fuck me*" before following.

The four men crashed through the brush toward the paddy, Jefferson's machine gun feeling like ten times its twenty-two pound weight as he tried to keep up with the less encumbered lieutenant while thorny vines tore at his clothing and exposed flesh. His a-gunner lagged behind, hampered not only by the weight of his gear, but by the belts of machine gun ammo snagging branches.

The lieutenant reached the paddy first and Jefferson could see him immediately raise his M16 to fire. Jefferson, unable to see what prompted the LT's action, spurred himself through the last few yards, his momentum carrying him out into the open paddy. What he saw instantly rendered his pain and fatigue insignificant.

Just inside the paddy along the opposing brushy dike were more than a platoon of NVA regulars running as fast as they could to clear the dangerous open. Without a conscious thought, Jefferson joined in the firing, sweeping a long burst from his machine gun through the enemy soldiers with deadly effect. The NVA survivors chose either to stop and return fire or to first crash over the dike and then fire.

Jefferson ignored the bullets striking around him or buzzing, zipping, snapping, or cracking past him. He continued to fire, his a-gunner clipping belt after belt of ammunition to the belt his machine gun was consuming at a rate of over 500 rounds per minute.

The assistant gunner went down with a grunt, the RTO with a short cry and the lieutenant silently. Jefferson, the last man standing, winced as a bullet burned through the ample flesh of his right shoulder. He dropped to his knees in the nasty paddy muck, his shoulder dripping blood from the entrance and exit wounds, his empty machine gun smoking, and its barrel glowing red. It was only then that he realized he was all alone and about to die.

Grabbing what remaining belted ammunition he could, Jefferson ducked and scooted back to the relative safety of the tree line as enemy fire sought him out. He rolled behind a felled tree to reload his already overheated weapon.

Jefferson ordinarily was meticulous about his ammunition, knowing that dirt caused jams and jams caused death. Now he had no time to be particular. He selected one belt only marginally less fouled then the others, loaded it, pushed the gun over the log, and ducked as he pulled the trigger. For the first time in many years, he sincerely gave thanks to the Lord that the gun did not jam or explode, taking off his hand or worse. And then it was back to the business of killing.

Clinching his jaw against the pain of the recoil to his bullet pierced shoulder, Jefferson resumed firing, this time with more measured bursts at the enemy now in the trees. He was barely conscious of men falling to his rounds, their deaths only prompting him seeking new targets.

The NVA wanted to kill him, needed to kill him, and tried their best to kill him. Dozens, scores, seemingly hundreds of rounds, missed Isaac Jefferson as he continued to fire. Bullets thudded and smacked into trees around him and into the log sheltering him. An RPG round rocked him. Still Jefferson fired and more NVA died.

An RPG finally found its mark. Designed as an anti-tank weapon capable of penetrating many inches of armor, Jefferson's log somehow managed to withstand the blast. The concussion, however, knocked Jefferson for a loop and into unconsciousness. The NVA easily could have come up and executed him, but they instead chose to capitalize on the respite and melt away, carrying their wounded. The dead were left, to be retrieved after the Americans counted and abandoned them.

The 1st Cav would continue to attack the NVA, first those trying to reinforce their dwindling forces that had seized the city of Hue, and then those driven out of the city by the U.S. Marines. Isaac Jefferson really did not care. He had awakened on a medevac helicopter and to the comprehension that he had not only survived, but he had just earned his second Purple Heart and thereby his coveted ticket out of the bush.

* * *

The Tet Offensive was a tremendous tactical victory for the American and South Vietnamese forces. Every communist gain had been swiftly reversed; whole NVA regiments, even divisions, had been decimated; and the Viet Cong was destroyed as an effective fighting force. One in five communist soldiers were doomed to become casualties, with over 40,000 of them killed. While that was roughly ten times that suffered by U.S. forces, the offensive was portrayed by the American press as a communist victory and the American public, weary of a war that seemed pointless and concerned about troubles at home, were willing to buy it.

It was in this aftermath that Tom Howard received his expected orders back to Vietnam. He was not upset other than the regret he felt for the impact on his mother and Katie. Tom Howard was not a political man, but he knew, he *knew*, that the cause was just, that America was the only hope for the South Vietnamese people otherwise doomed to slaughter and the survivors to deprivation.

Republican presidential candidate Richard Nixon's Vietnamization policy suggested that should he be elected, America's decade long involvement in the war would be ending. In that event, the country of South Vietnam's only hope to continue to exist was if U.S. forces held the North Vietnamese at bay while the ARVN, the Army of the Republic of Vietnam, expanded and transitioned to assume sole responsibility on the ground and eventually the air and sea as well.

While Colonel Kennedy was not a member of the Special Forces community, he was a highly regarded member of the Airborne community and had friends in high places. In the waning months of his long Army career, the esteemed colonel was willing to unabashedly tap his contacts and use his influence to keep tabs on his son and Tom. He for some time had been aware that Tom's orders were forthcoming. The colonel took it a step further.

Because of his fondness for Tom, Colonel Kennedy broke one of his once cardinal rules and used his influence to gain Tom a provisional slot with the Military Assistance Command, Vietnam, Studies and Observation Group, or MACV-SOG, the super-secret organization run by Special Forces that conducted surveillance and forbidden incursions into Laos and Cambodia. That the colonel knew of this raised no questions because the secrets surrounding SOG, like most Army secrets embodying hundreds of people, were at best secretive rather than secret.

While Colonel Kennedy knew that as ominous as the mission of MACV-SOG sounded (and surely was) and likely (correctly) that SOG casualty rates were atrocious, he also was aware that officers rarely led or even accompanied those dangerous missions. He therefore was satisfied that his intervention would benefit rather than harm Tom. It was enough for him that his son was over there, and, by choice, in the thick of it.

Tom Howard was ignorant of all this. He was given time to spend with family and to enjoy with Katie before he shipped out. He made the most of it.

Tom knew that Katie was in love with him. He also knew that he was in love with her. Tom once had heard advice given of "only marry a woman if you cannot stand to live without her." When he heard it, he dismissed it, not considering it to be sage advice. Now he reconsidered it. He had become cognizant of the fact that the thought of living his life without Katie was too painful to bear.

The next day, Tom managed to get Katie's father alone, awkward as it was. Without much of a preamble, Tom took a deep breath and all but blurted out, "Mr. Greer, I love Katie." When that statement produced nothing but a faint smile in return, Tom added, "I can't live without her." With still nothing but a faint smile in return, Tom took the plunge, "Mr. Greer, I want to ask her to marry me and I am asking for your blessing."

Bill Greer's smile broadened, he extended his hand and simply said, "You have it, son, her mother's too."

Tom's "Thank you, sir," was followed by an unconscious heavy sigh relieving the tension Tom had not realized he had been suffering. He excused himself and went straight to Katie. He led her to the front porch, took her hands in his, looked her in the eye, took a deep breath, and asked the question. If Katie was disappointed that Tom failed to make the proposal an elaborate romantic event, she did not show it. Instead, she gave him a simple answer to his simple question.

"Yes, Tom, I will marry you. All you have to do is not get killed in the next twelve months." The thought of it made her cry. Tom could think of no genuinely reassuring words, so he just took her into his arms and held her close.

***

Captain Tom Howard was pleasantly surprised upon landing in Saigon that his in-processing was relatively short. In fact, it ended abruptly when the admin sergeant looked up from his papers and said, "Oh, I see here, sir, that you're slated for MACV-SOG. That's above my pay grade." The sergeant then looked past the puzzled Green Beret captain and appeared to signal someone. Tom Howard turned and saw two Green Beret sergeants coming toward him.

"Captain Howard? Good. I'm Master Sergeant Riley, Jack Riley, if you please. If you'll come with me, please. This young stud will be happy to carry your bag." As he led the captain to a Huey slick with the rotor blades just starting to turn, all the sergeant would say was that he had orders to take him "out west to Indian country."

Tom Howard was perplexed. *Out west? I'm wearing khakis with low quarter shoes and I don't even have a weapon!*

As if the sergeant had read his mind, when they settled into the helicopter the sergeant hollered to him over the roaring turbine engine, "Sorry if we get your shiny shoes scuffed and your khakis mussed. At least I've got this for you," handing Tom a loaded CAR-15 carbine pointed down at the aircraft floor.

Captain Tom Howard had no idea that he was heading to regional MACV-SOG headquarters in Kontum for an in-depth evaluation for his still unknown provisional posting to the clandestine unit. In his short time in Special Forces, Tom had only heard vague references to

SOG as he had with other "spooky" things like the Phoenix Program. Real secret squirrel stuff, Tom was told. He had not paid them much attention. They had nothing to do with him. He was going to fulfill his dream of being a Green Beret A-team commander.

Now, however, back in-country, having heard the admin sergeant's remark about MACV-SOG and now on a mysterious flight to an unknown destination, he began to fear that his dream might be in jeopardy. He would learn that day that he was right, and he was wrong.

The flight was unremarkable. The countryside below appeared largely to be forested wilderness, except for a roadway of sorts the pilot was guiding on. The Kontum military installation was interesting, but not alarming. Tom was escorted to the headquarters that appeared ordinary, other than more extensive and elaborate security. There he met with a major who appeared to be at least ten years his senior.

"Welcome back to Vietnam, Captain. Let me get right to the point. I expect you know that things have changed over here since your last tour, a lot of it not good at all. However, if things go well for you today, you won't have to worry about that. We don't suffer the same shit the real Army does.

"You have been recommended to us by a credible source, we've checked you out and are inclined to think that we may be able to use you. That is, if you are willing.

"This is a volunteer outfit, so I am going to tell you in strict confidence who and what we are and what we have in mind for you. Then it'll be your call. If this isn't what you want, we'll send you on over to 5th Group [referring to the 5th Special Forces Group under which were all Green Berets in Vietnam]. Understood? Good.

"We are MACV-SOG, Military Assistance Command Vietnam, Studies and Observation Group. What's that mean? Well, certainly not what it says. That's a subterfuge, a very lame one I know, but one that supposedly offers politicians a level of deniability about what we really do. You see, we don't really work for MACV, at least not at our level. We're associated with the 5th SF Group, but we're not under their command. Be that as it may, you'll be able to wear the SF patch on your sleeves, left and right.

"'Studies and observation group' is a rather transparent misnomer for 'special operations group,' which is what we once were called and what we really are. Again, the deniability aspect. What we are is secret. What we do is secret. What I say now is secret. Clear? Good.

"Since 1964, we have been conducting, among other things you don't need to know about, forbidden cross-border ground operations for reconnaissance, intelligence, targeting, and an occasional rescue. We identify targets for Air Force destruction and otherwise disrupt the enemy's rear and cause him to invest thousands of troops there rather than here. With me so far? Good.

"We do it with recon teams, small teams comprised of SF, Navy SEAL, or Marine Force Recon, most often augmented with indigenous personnel, mostly Chinese Nung mercenaries, Montagnards or 'yards' from the hills, or Cambodians or 'bodes,' with support from the Air Force, 5th Group, and CIA. Just so you know, the Nungs, yards and bodes do not play well together and they all hate the Vietnamese, North and South, which feeling is mutual. It's just something we live with and adapt to.

"The teams are infiltrated and exfiltrated by helicopter and have fixed wing cover on and off with air support on call. Teams are led by sergeants. Officers rarely go out except with the ready reaction force, what we call a 'Mike Force' or a 'Hatchet Force.' Teams stay usually only a few days at a time as we've found that they lose their edge after that. That and that the longer they're out the more likely they are to be found. Still with me? Good.

"Our headquarters is in Saigon. Operational control is through three command and control centers. One is Command and Control North, or CCN, in Quang Tri/Phu Bai. They run teams, as many as sixty of them, in Laos and North Vietnam. Teams into Cambodia are run by

CCS, Command and Control South, out of Ban Me Thout. We here in Kontum are CCC, Command and Control Central. We were only added a year or two ago. We run an average of about thirty teams into the tri-border area of Vietnam, Laos and Cambodia. Unless they go in too deep, they are supported from SF camps just this side of the border.

"What we're looking at you for technically would be called a CCC Assistant S-4, but being a supply guy would only be part of the job. There are a lot of moving parts in what we do and it takes a lot of coordination. You would be seeing that the teams get what they need from conventional supply channels and the good stuff through 5th Group or the CIA. You also would help coordinate with the Air Force and CIA and on this side of the fence with the SF camps and LRRPs [pronounced 'lurps'], the long-range recon patrols of the conventional units, operating along the border.

"We had planned to send you down to the MACV Recondo school run by 5th Group over in Nha Trang, but we scrapped that idea because it's three weeks long and we need you before then. Instead, we, and now I'm talking CCC, are talking an orientation to include tagging along on two or three shakeout patrols and as many cover flights with maybe an exfil flight or two, just so you understand how important what you'll be doing really is."

The two men talked for a while longer with Tom eventually comprehending that it was he who was being evaluated. That Tom might decline was not really contemplated by senior SOG officers. Satisfied with what he saw and presupposing that the captain would volunteer, the major had him taken for a tour and then to "officers country" and chow in the mess hall. It was not until the next day that Captain Howard was told he had been accepted. He never really did volunteer. No matter.

Tom met his boss, another major, was briefed and again seriously warned that what they did was highly classified and of the dire consequences that would befall him should he ever divulge anything. He was taken to the supply shack, actually a fortified building of some size, where he would be working. There he was greeted by the same master sergeant who had met him on arrival. The two men exchanged brief histories.

Jack Riley had seventeen years in service, seven of them in Special Forces and he had been a recon team leader. He explained the nature of their business and it was evident that he could handle the job all by himself. The sergeant promised to hook Tom up soon with their contacts over at 5th Group and with the CIA where the "good stuff" came from.

The sergeant then gave his new boss a tour of the facility. Behind the front room where the two had their desks was a warehouse of goodies, weapons of all sorts, communications, munitions, and supplies of all kinds, all neatly stored in military fashion. Tom's interest was piqued by a large bin of foreign gear. The sergeant explained, "Yeah, years ago we went across the fence with foreign uniforms, weapons, and gear, but we eventually gave that up as too impractical, pointless really. It's still good for trading though. The CIA doesn't want it back."

The sergeant spent the rest of the morning further acquainting Tom with the job, explaining that he would be spending a lot of time in the air going "hither and yon" to assess needs, acquire what was needed, and sometimes accompanying the delivery. It was only then that Howard felt comfortable posing a question to the senior sergeant, "You wouldn't happen to know a captain by the name of Don Kennedy?"

The sergeant shrugged and said, "Sure. He's one of us. Top notch. Not SOG, but 5th Group. He's out near the border. Got him an A-team and a camp with a bunch of yards, Montagnards. Friend of yours?" When Tom answered in the affirmative, the sergeant said, "I will get word to him that you're here. You've got some things lined up for orientation and then I will see about getting you out there." He thought for a moment and then added, "Let me tell you, though, you don't want to stay there too long. That's Indian country for sure."

As was the custom in SOG, Tom chose his own gear. For his weapons, he chose the CAR-15 he had been loaned for the ride out. The rifle was the new carbine version of the M16A1 with a thirty-round magazine. For a sidearm, he chose over the .45 a Browning Hi-Power 9mm semi-automatic for which Riley tossed in a tanker's shoulder holster. Riley then took Tom out to a range to zero the rifle and play a bit with the pistol, a Swedish K submachine gun (the WWII vintage 9mm Carl Gustav m/45) and an AK-47.

The next day, Tom began his orientation missions, beginning with an introduction to the first team leader he would be with. The young team leader was a buck sergeant only recently elevated to the leadership position, but he had earned it through experience and merit. Tom met the other team members, attended a mission briefing, and then joined the four-man team for further briefing, preparation, and rehearsal.

They were to go out on a two-day shakedown patrol. While in-country and therefore relatively less dangerous than going across the border, it wasn't like there weren't any bad guys out there. It was a tremendous learning experience and Tom did well enough, in the words of the young sergeant "not too bad for an officer." Tom was cleared to accompany the team on an "across the fence" mission which, while scary, was uneventful.

Cleared for one more, a longer one, Tom accompanied the same team when it went back out after a few days of rest, briefings, and planning. The second night out the team detected headlights on a new branch of the Ho Chi Minh Trail. They called it in and were ordered to take a closer look.

The team spent the entire next day cautiously moving closer and were rewarded to observe a ZSU-23-4 parked under camouflaged netting, impossible to detect from the air. The ZSU was a seldomly seen Soviet tracked armored vehicle mounting radar guided quad 23mm autocannons, a serious threat to all but high-altitude aircraft.

The team eased away and reported their find. Predictably, anything worthy of being protected by such a weapon system was deemed a worthy target. The team was ordered to remain and observe. That night, after again spotting and reporting headlights near the site of the ZSU, the team spent hours of tense waiting before they received the alert of inbound aircraft and were richly rewarded with the rare opportunity to witness a B-52 bomber strike.

They were not able to survey the aftermath though. The NVA correctly surmised that a recon team was responsible and soon deployed specially trained hunter teams, forcing the team to withdraw and be extracted. A high-level reconnaissance aircraft though was able to detect secondary explosions and an image of what very well may have been a destroyed ZSU.

In between those missions, Captain Howard flew in aircraft, helicopters, or small fixed wing airplanes, to continue his education while assisting to monitor radio traffic of the deployed teams and to facilitate their extraction and supplying any essential needs they may have beforehand. The man in charge, however, most often was a sergeant, usually a team leader temporarily grounded for one reason or another or too short, too close to the end of his tour of duty, to go out on dangerous patrols. Those sergeants, without exception, were true professionals. Most of the flights were boring, but Tom Howard's last, after the ground mission with the B-52 strike, was quite the opposite.

* * *

It was an unusual cooperative assignment. Another branch of the Ho Chi Minh Trail had become of particular interest. CCC was rotating teams to recon the route across the border and the 4th Infantry Division was rotating LRRP teams (from the recently re-designated Company K of the 75th Ranger Regiment) to recon the route in-country. With other teams out elsewhere (the 4th ID hardly being idle), the LRRP's were stretched thin for air cover. CCC agreed to fly cover for their Team Viper and Tom Howard was to accompany one of those flights. He sat in on the briefings and took time to study the maps and aerial photographs of the area of operation.

They took off in a Huey C&C bird at first light on the second day of the LRRP team's patrol and were in position for the team's morning status call. The team confirmed their location and reported that they were proceeding according to plan. Tom Howard tried to make himself comfortable for what he expected to be a long, boring couple of hours flying over millions of trees that totally blocked any observation of the ground below. Not ten minutes later, however, the LRRP team made a chilling contact report.

"Covey Rider, this is Viper One Zero Romeo. Contact. I say again, contact. Over." That, of course, snapped those in the C&C bird out of their torpor. They acknowledged the report, passed it on to the LRRP CP and SOG TOC and all concerned nervously awaited a follow up radio call. The C&C pilot brought the ship closer to the team's NDP from which they could not have gone far.

That was it though. There was no follow up call. There were no return calls. Nothing. The risk of exposing the team on the ground having evaporated, the pilot flew even closer to try to catch any calls or failing that to look for smoke, mirror signals, troops in the open, something. Nothing. *Shit!*

Tom Howard had marked on his map the team's reported night position and compared it to the primary, secondary, and emergency extraction sites or "PZs" for pick-up zones he had marked during the briefing. He alternated between studying the map and what little he could discern below. *If they're on the run, which way would they go? Which way would I go?*

The map suggested toward the emergency PZ, but Tom's training and experience taught him that maps were not always reliable, that they did not take in to account many of the variables such as difficulty of physically moving through the terrain and enemy locations. Neither, of course, could maps tell you what in the hell was happening down there. Still, Tom's limited view of the ground did not conflict with his assessment. After several more minutes of negative contact or sightings, Tom made a fateful decision.

Howard spoke to the pilot on the intercom and, keeping his eyes glued on the SOG sergeant with a look that clearly meant *do not question or try to override,* he ordered the pilot to drop him at the primary emergency extraction site near the tree line to the north. When the pilot started to object, Tom quickly and firmly forestalled the opposition. While the pilot was the aircraft commander and the sergeant technically was the one empowered to make tactical decisions that could not wait to be relayed to higher at the TOC, Tom Howard was still a captain and neither the warrant officer pilot nor the SOG sergeant was inclined to buck him.

Ignoring the sergeant's look that could only be described as one of dismay, Tom directed him to make sure that the spare PRC-25 radio they carried on board was set to the aircraft's frequency and was operating. As the helicopter approached the PZ, Tom had the sergeant help him to get the radio on his back, grabbed several smoke grenades and checked his weapon. As the bird flared for landing, he, for no conscious reason, grabbed a cylindrical message container with brightly colored streamers and stuck it in a cargo pocket.

Tom Howard exited the bird as soon as it parted the waist high grass and raced to the tree line as the aircraft quickly departed. He crashed through the thicket at the field's northern border, cringing that he knew that he sounded like a herd of elephants. The trees and brush thinned as usual the farther he got from the greater sunlight afforded by the open field.

Tom halted at the base of a large tree. After catching his breath while listening for telltale signs that bad things were about to happen, he was about to key his microphone to report a safe infil (infiltration) when he heard small arms firing off to the northeast. He reported both events to the C&C pilot and SOG sergeant and said he was heading in that direction.

Tom moved about twenty yards and without really thinking, he stopped and hung the message container conspicuously on a branch. He began moving more stealthily, but still too quickly to by any means qualify as stealthy (*stupidly* was the word that came to Tom's mind), pausing every ten to twenty yards or so to listen and scan the area. The firing was sporadic and seemed to be approaching. He moved more quickly, again chiding himself for the recklessness, foolishness, of what he was doing as he nevertheless continued to do it.

After perhaps three hundred yards, something told Tom to slow it down and that he had better focus his senses. He found a good spot next to the base of an enormous tree that any other day he would have taken the time to admire. On this day though, his only thought of it was that it offered immediate cover and would be a good landmark for his return.

Tom strained his senses to the limit. More firing. Closer, he was sure. M16 and AK-47. Tom eased forward not more than ten yards when he caught movement. With his heart pounding, he eased down to a kneeling position and stared through the trees and brush, trying to identify the movement. It suddenly dawned on him that he was not wearing camouflage face paint (actually a waxy cream) and therefore he was not the invisible man he ought to be.

After a long thirty seconds, he again caught movement and then could focus on it. It was two NVA soldiers, one with an RPD machine gun, about forty yards ahead, directly between him and the sound of the firing. They appeared to be on a ridgeline, their backs to him.

Tom used his thumb and forefinger to carefully move the selector switch of his CAR-15 from safe to semiautomatic fire, thus avoiding a telltale and perhaps fatal audible click. He then slowly and with great deliberation slipped forward with his rifle at the ready, intent on the NVA who by then had set the machine gun up, facing away from him.

Tom paused behind a tree to scan both sides for a security element. Seeing none, he took a deep breath and resumed easing forward, planning and planting every step in full stealth mode, his heart pounding, barely able to breathe, eyes locked on the enemy.

Tom got to within ten yards of the NVA pair when he perceived that his presence had been detected or sensed. He brought his carbine to his shoulder and aligned his sights. As the heads started to turn, he fired three quick shots, a single and a double, into them. The 5.56mm bullet, while tiny (the equivalent of .223 caliber), was propelled by plenty of gunpowder and at close range the effects were ghastly. The enemy soldiers unquestionably were dead.

Tom Howard stood there for a minute, straining to detect if the distinctive pops of his rifle had alerted the NVA. He heard nothing. The firing in the distance had stopped though, not a good sign. Tom slowly closed the short gap to the dead machine gun crew and took up a position next to the bodies in order to see whatever it was they had set up to see, and to kill. He at first saw nothing other than the forest, but then distinguished natural routes up from the bottom and along the ridge.

He decided that he had to move. He went about twenty yards along the ridge in the direction he expected the LRRP team to be and eased down to one knee next to a tree just short of a small opening. Still nothing. "*Damn it,*" he thought, "*the team's got to be down there and has got to be close.*"

Ten seconds more of inaction was all he could tolerate. "*Fuck it,*" he resolved. Tom stood, stepped into the opening, fired three deliberate single shots and then outrageously yelled out, "TEAM VIPER, TEAM VIPER, COVEY RIDER DOWN, COVEY RIDER DOWN. COME TO ME. COME TO ME <u>NOW</u>!"

Tom waited no more than ten seconds and repeated the process. He was not surprised and certainly not thrilled that the reaction was a burst of AK fire. By the sound, the shooter was a hundred or more yards away and the bullets went high into the trees overhead, suggesting that the firing was at sound, not sight.

Tom did no more than drop to one knee and continue to scan with his eyes and ears the woods below and in the direction of the enemy fire to the east. He heard in the latter direction signal shots and Vietnamese voices. *The bastards are coming!* He forced himself to maintain his vigilance nonetheless.

Tom Howard's heart leapt as he spotted movement below, maybe seventy-five yards out. By reflex he brought the front blade of his rifle to bear while keeping both eyes open and his finger off the trigger. More movement, closer, materialized into a figure. It was a black man, *an American!* A second and then a third man appeared. Tom raised his rifle and fired three more rounds upward. The LRRP's responded by veering directly toward him. Now both they and he came under fire from multiple weapons, fortunately still ineffective.

As the LRRP trio hastened up the slope with the one in back covering their rear, Tom crab-walked to a fallen log and swapped out magazines, reminding himself that he only had five and had just burned through most of his second. He waved as the LRRPs neared and they piled over the log with him.

The apparent team leader, the black man Tom first saw, still struggling for air said, "*Goddamn,* but it's good to see you. We thought we were fuckin' dead men. Point traded shots with theirs and then all hell broke loose. RTO took an RPG through his radio. Blew both to shit. Tried to break contact and come up on the 90 [AN/PRC-90 survival radio used as a back-up], but it was inop. Murphy's fuckin' Law. No time to figure out why because they were on us like white on rice. Zapped a few, but there's a shitload more of 'em." Then, looking around, he asked, "Where're your guys?"

Tom Howard replied, "Sorry, friend, but I'm it." That got their attention! Before the question could be asked though, Tom shouted, "*Down!*" and fired a burst to their right. The three LRRP's shifted toward that direction and could see an NVA soldier writhing on the ground inside of fifty yards away. They then caught glimpses of others, many others, not far behind, skillfully advancing from tree to tree.

"Time to go," Howard said. "Follow me," he ordered. He took off running the way he had come, grabbing the RPD on the way. Each of the three LRRPs noted the dead NVA lying face down in their own gore and professionally noting their field of fire shuddered at the thought of what likely would have happened but for this crazy dude.

The four halted to catch their breath, but the sounds of approaching NVA spurred them on. They stopped after another fifty yards or so again to catch their breath while checking their rear; and then repeated the same twice more, Tom Howard regretting lugging along the heavy communist machine gun. Seeing through the trees the moving shapes of the enemy ever closer, the exhausted men once again took off.

They stopped when Tom could see through the trees the streamer of the container he had hung. He made sure that each of the other three could see it too. He explained its proximity to the PZ and then got on the radio while the LRRP's covered the rear.

"Covey, Hotel [Howard]."

"Go ahead Hotel."

"Covey, Hotel. Approaching papa zulu. In contact. Will come out same place I came in."

"Roger, Hotel. Cross through papa zulu to the farther field. Descending now. Snakes [Cobra attack helicopters] inbound."

"Roger, Covey. Look for three, then me."

"Roger, Hotel. Hustle."

Tom Howard turned to the LRRP's and said, "You heard it. On my command, light up the woods in sector fire and then haul boogie to the streamer and then through the hopefully obvious trail I made from the PZ. Reload there, catch your breath, and then run for all you're worth through that field to the next. Chopper ought to be down by then. I'll be right behind you. Good?" The three nodded and Tom told them to get ready. When in a moment they were, Tom commanded, "*Fire!*"

All four sprayed the area, knocking down at least two NVA not forty yards away, and the LRRP's took off running with Tom Howard providing a modicum of covering fire. The LRRP's were spurred on by AK rounds snapping past and whacking into trees around and beyond them. Tom reloaded, popped a half magazine single fire at the NVA and then still with the RPD he took off after the LRRP's. He stopped midway, faced the enemy and emptied his magazine as incoming fire tore up the woods around him.

Tom quickly ejected the magazine, inserted his last full one, jacked a round into the chamber and ran to the PZ. Like the LRRP's, he was impelled by incoming fire frightfully close. He halted one more time at the edge of the field to catch his breath and fire some rounds to hopefully slow the pursuers. He popped a smoke grenade for the cover the billowing smoke might provide and ran into and across the field, fully expecting the all too familiar punch of an AK round in his back.

Tom reached the thin tree line separating the two fields unscathed where he could see the extraction helicopter hovering just off the ground with the LRRP's on board. Tom turned back to the tree line he had just left, just in time to see an NVA soldier emerge through the thinning smoke of the grenade. He killed the man and after popping his other smoke grenade he took off toward his rescue, twice whirling to fire as he went.

Burdened with the heavy RPD, he had to fire his carbine one-hand-edly, what soldiers and Marines call "John Wayning it" after the famous actor John Wayne who often portrayed fighting men. Tom's chances of hitting anything in that fashion were zero, but just maybe the firing would slow the enemy and for a few more moments keep them from getting a clear shot at the hovering helicopter.

Tom then spun and ran flat out through the thigh high grass, rifle in one hand and machine gun in the other, straight at the awaiting helicopter. The LRRP team leader saw a broad smile on Tom Howard's face as he ran. He misinterpreted it and thought, *Crazy fucker!*

In actuality, what prompted Tom Howard to smile was seeing the snouts of a pair of AH-1 Cobra gunships appearing over the far tree line. The Cobra, a two-seater attack helicopter with the pilot and co-pilot/gunner seated in tandem such that the aircraft was only about three feet wide, offered virtually no target from the front. Facing outward from the front were fearsome armaments including 2.75 inch rockets mounted on either side of the fuselage and a minigun mounted in a chin turret (other variants instead mounted a 40mm automatic grenade launcher instead of each of the rocket pods or in the chin turret).

The sight of those awesome war machines coupled with the elation of impending escape are what caused Tom Howard to gleefully laugh out loud as he raced to join the LRRP's. Before Tom reached the extraction bird, the Cobras gunned down more NVA who had entered the first field and then tore up the tree line behind them with rockets and more minigun fire. Howard reached the chopper, handed up the RPD, and accepted the helping hands pulling him on board. The pilot was powering up and out before Howard even settled onto the floor.

Those on board could not see the hell the lead Cobra and his wingman continued to unleash and the deadly effects on the NVA pursuers. All were satisfied enough that they got away clean, a miracle in and of itself.

When the slick was safely away from the PZ, the LRRP team leader safed his weapon and extended his hand to the crazy dude and introduced himself. Howard replied, "Tom Howard," and then waved off the profuse thanks the rescued trio offered. The crew chief helped him to get the heavy radio off his back and then cleared the communist machine gun. Taking note of that, Tom sheepishly nodded his thanks and turned to look amid the jumble of bodies and gear to find his CAR-15 and likewise safe it. When he found it, he saw that the bolt was locked to the rear. Empty. *Shit!*

Howard squirmed to sit with his back against the rear wall, making himself as comfortable as possible on the hard metal floor. It was then that he started to shake as the events of the last hour began to sink in. He was not alone in that.

After a minute or two, Howard thought, *well, I can't just sit here and shake like a damn leaf,* and stumbled his way to the opening between the pilots. He found his headset and put it on so they could hear him over the noise. Howard praised and thanked them, told them that they never would have to buy a drink in a bar he was in and promised to write them up for medals. The pilot responded, "Bourbon, damn good bourbon, will do just fine, pardner, so long as there's plenty of it."

Howard gave them a broad smile as he said, "No prob, no problem at all," adding with a laugh, "I'm the supply guy." Howard then turned to settle back to the floor of the chopper and therefore missed the looks of astonishment exchanged between the pilots.

Meanwhile, when the noise of the departure of the American aircraft faded and the smoke from the rockets began to clear, the NVA had begun their business of hauling off their dead and wounded, more than two dozen all told. Their pitiful prizes were one American (that much they could tell) dead, but nothing of intelligence value and little otherwise of any value at all; and a strange empty cylinder with colorful streamers near where the Americans had escaped.

The helicopter landed minutes later and Tom Howard and the SOG sergeant hopped off. Howard left behind the RPD machine gun, knowing the bragging rights and trading value it would have for the brave airmen. He shook hands again with the LRRP's, thanked the crew chief, and then waved his thanks again to the pilot and co-pilot. Tom hastened out from under the whirling rotor blades and the pilot lifted off the tarmac, the nose of the Huey immediately dipping as the pilot powered the chopper to bring the LRRP's home and then head to the barn in search of alcohol and an audience for the newest story they had to tell.

For Tom Howard, the destination was his tent, even though it was not even noontime. Probably a medical consequence of adrenaline flow and ebb, Tom suddenly was beyond utter exhaustion. There was no rest for the weary though as a steady stream of well-wishers and the curious came by.

The CO, who had listened to the tail end of the radio transmissions and heard part of the sergeant's improbable tale of the events, came by too. He stood in the tent opening, motioned Tom Howard not to get up and after silently staring at him for a minute said to him, "I was just told that John Wayne had joined my command and I came by to get his autograph. Maybe you'll do though, son." After a thoughtful pause the CO shook his head and added, "Holy shit, son. That was fuckin' amazing, just pure fuckin' amazing," and then walked off, laughing as he went.

When he was finally alone, Howard made his way to the shower point to wash off the sweat and dirt. When he returned, he picked up his weapon to clean it and realized that someone had done it for him. That absolutely made his day, and he crashed onto his cot a happy man.

Tom slept through the rest of the afternoon, the evening, and the night. He awoke to daylight, quickly dressed and headed to the mess hall and then work. *Dealing with the beans and the bullets as a supply weenie might not be too damn bad, all things considered.*

8

MASTER SERGEANT JACK RILEY WAS TRUE TO HIS WORD. HE AR-
ranged for a Chinook to take Captain Tom Howard out to Captain
Don Kennedy's camp situated in the tri-border area of Vietnam, Laos,
and Cambodia so as to interdict enemy movements down the Ho Chi
Minh Trail and over to Kontum or down to Pleiku. The camp had an
official name, but Don referred to it as "Camp Ranger." He did not
do so as most presumed because of his Ranger background or because
what they did there was to run recon patrols along the border. Rather
it was because when one looked at a topographical map of the place the
center of the camp was marked by two elongated hills separated by a
narrow corridor giving the appearance of a mask like the one worn by
the Lone Ranger, the iconic namesake central character of the American
western TV series that had run from 1949-1957 with reruns on and off
for many years afterward.

The helicopter landed and the crew chief and door gunner helped
Tom offload a number of crates and wooden boxes (the men being quite
happy to get them off their aircraft) before the pilot wasted no time
lifting off and heading the bird back the way it had come. Clearly the
pilot had no desire to linger there, an ominous sign.

Don Kennedy appeared with the entirety of his ground mobility,
a jeep with trailer and a mule, the latter being an amazing contrivance
named an "M274 Truck, Platform, Utility, ½ ton, 4x4," or "Mechanical

Mule" or simply "mule." It basically was a motorized flatbed wagon nine feet long. Don had with him another Green Beret and a half dozen "yards" as the Montagnards usually were called. He beckoned Tom to him in the jeep, had the yards quickly load the vehicles, and both raced off the bald hill to the relative safety of the CP, the command post. Only upon reaching that cover did Don extend his hand to his friend and welcome him.

"Damn, it's good to see you, old friend," Tom said. "I come bearing gifts."

They headed into the CP. It was fashioned from two heavily sand-bagged conex shipping and storage containers over which and between them were stout logs covered with PSP sheets, perforated (or pierced) steel planking sections used to create temporary landing strips and sal-vaged or stolen with vigor; the PSP in turn layered with more sandbags. Angling off that set up were two other sandbagged conex containers with canvas tenting spanning the overhead space between them, and then a metal roofed, half-sandbagged plywood and screen "team house" to the south. All of that was ringed by a wall of sandbags waist to chest high, clearly designed for the CP to be the last stand if the camp was to be overrun.

Tom was anxious for Don to see what he had brought them. Some of it was easy, the crates of chickens and pigs for the Montagnards and the three wooden boxes that looked like what rifles came in. They were. Tom had brought in one box of six CAR-15's, another with old M1 carbines for the yards, and in the other he had jammed a partially disassembled M60 machine gun. It was like Christmas.

The rest was like Christmas morning, too. There were magazines for the carbines, two thousand link-belted rounds for the M60, bat-teries for the radios, some knives, and a box with the luxury items of cigarettes, coffee, sugar, salt, and Tabasco sauce. To top it off, there were two cases each of good beer and Coca-Cola (neither often getting past the REMF's), two bottles of bourbon and one of scotch, and, perhaps the best treat of all, two mermite insulated containers packed chock full with precious ice.

The Green Berets spent a long night of alcohol infused (as much as they dared out there in the hostile frontier) comradery. In the morning, after Don had gotten the day patrols out and inspected the bunker line, he and Tom shared coffee in the early morning sun outside of the CP. A sergeant snapped a picture of them, something both later would forever treasure.

The conversation turned to what the patrols were turning up (which was an alarming increase in enemy signs, spottings, and contacts) and defense of the camp.

"So, Tom, if you were Mister Gook, how would you hit this place?"

Tom thought about it long and hard and said, "Well, I'd start off pounding the shit out of it with artillery, rockets, and mortars; feign an attack on the west and hit you hard on the southeast. If you bolstered your defenses there, I'd be thinking of making the main attack on the north. Attacking the south would be suicidal and the west too obvious."

"Pretty much along my line of thinking. The only thing you probably couldn't glean is that it's awfully thick to the west, hard for command, control, and coordination. You're right about the east. Your M60 would help there, but I might need to put it on the jeep for the mobility. If I lose any of the M60's we'd be in a world of hurt." His points were not lost on Tom.

Two weeks later, Tom Howard was back at Camp Ranger, this time in a Huey accompanied by a Chinook with what once was an ACAV sling-loaded below it. The ACAV was a tracked armored cavalry assault vehicle, a variant of the M113 APC, armored personnel carrier. This one bore the markings of having come from the revered 11th Armored Cavalry Regiment, the Blackhorse.

Tom had found the ACAV on one of his foraging trips to Da Nang. He had been doing some old-fashioned horse trading with an old pro of a supply sergeant and spotted the thing in the adjacent scrap yard. The

ACAV had run over a mine which had blown off several road wheels and warped the body, rendering it a combat loss. The vehicle had been stripped of its tracks, road wheels, rear ramp, engine and drive train. About the only thing left besides the bare, gutted body inexplicably was the gun shield on top. The thing was so worthless to the sergeant that he did not even try to barter for it.

It was not so easy for Tom to acquire an M2 .50 caliber machine gun to mount on top. But, as the saying goes, where there's a will there's a way and, in this case, it was a pair of pristine SKS rifles, a cloth bag full of NVA belt buckles (fake, but convincing) and a case of scotch that enabled the weapon to disappear out the back door, so to speak, of another supply center.

Tom, with Don's concurrence, had the big helicopter put the ACAV down on the east side of Camp Ranger where the heavy machine gun could cover the entire east perimeter, close to a third of the southeast and almost that much of the northeast. Before Tom left the camp the next day, the ACAV was heavily sandbagged and soon would be surrounded by what from a distance would appear to be a hut or storage building. The .50 caliber Ma Deuce was mounted with a fabricated feed for connected belts of 500 rounds of ammunition with three more in easy reach. Don was able to shift the new M60 he had emplaced there (the idea of a mobile machine gun having been abandoned as impractical) to double the single one on the vulnerable north side. He was a happy man.

Don was even happier with the bonus Tom brought, crates full of mines. The mines employed by U.S. forces almost entirely were the M18 Claymore, a directional anti-personnel mine that was planted in the ground on attached metal stakes rather than buried. The Claymore's effectiveness was in that its C4 plastic explosive propelled 700 steel balls of about 1/8" diameter (about the same as a 5.56mm or .22 caliber bullet) in a 60° arc out to a lethal range of more than 50 yards. Claymores could be fired by a blasting cap attached by wire to a firing device called a "clacker" or rigged to be triggered by a trip wire. They could be connected to fire simultaneously in "daisy chain" fashion. They, in a word, were awesome, especially when augmented by Tom's smaller M14 "toe popper" mines, a few M16 "Bouncing Betty" mines, and a dozen old fashioned PMN land mines of Soviet design, Chinese manufacture and CIA stock, along with more M49 trip flares.

Unbeknownst to Tom Howard though, his friend Don Kennedy was not so deserving of his generosity. Don had stirred up trouble once again, although this time unintentionally. It was by letter, a letter he had sent when he heard about Tom's rescue of the LRRPs.

12 June 1970

Dear Mom & Dad,

Greetings again from the glorious tropical paradise of Vietnam, Republic of. Hope all is well with you. Sorry I've been slow to write, but things have been a bit hectic. Thanks for the care package. Keep 'em coming, please.

Things are mostly the same here. I've got about 200 yards (Montagnard tribesmen from the mountain regions) in camp, fierce little bastards (sorry, Mom), and it seems like as many family members, which is both bad and good (keeps them honest, I hope, but I could do without the livestock). I think you know that Tom Howard is with us, sort of, in Kontum. That's a hop, skip & jump from here, if you have a helicopter, that is. He says that he'll be over to see me soon. I will give him the grand tour of my magnificent little corner of the world.

I have to tell you that I'm probably again in hot water with Tom's Katie. I told her I'd watch out for him, but he's a hard dog to keep on a leash. I had to send a patrol out to recover a body a LRRP team had to leave behind. Booby trap city, but my guys are good and no probs. I later found out that our Tom, not two weeks back in country, went in <u>singlehandedly</u> and rescued the team. He has a way of doing that sort of stuff, doesn't he? He zapped a few dinks (NVA regulars) and got more probables from the air. He has a way of doing that too.

At least this time he didn't get shot in the process. Word is that he's up for his second Silver Star. (Should be a DSC, if not a CMH, in my humble opinion.)

Anyway, I expect they'll chain Tom to a desk over in supply. He'll hate it because I know he wants to be out here, but it works for me. Selfish of me, but I like the odds of him getting what we need from the "other guys," you know, and it'll save me a whole lot of grief from Katie when I get back.

Well, I know this is short, but we're westward bound at 0-dark-thirty.

Love,

Don

Colonel Kennedy, in a rare case of obliviousness, copied the letter and sent it to Tom's father Dan, thinking it would be nice to pass along the compliments. Similarly, unwittingly Dan sent it to Bill Greer and he, suffering the same malady, sent it on to Katie. With that, the proverbial shit hit the proverbial fan.

Dear Tom,

How are you? I am fine here in the Holy City. Hot, but I know you know all about that. My roommate, Mandy, is from Orangeburg up the road. Sweet girl. She thinks Citadel cadets are so-o-o cute. I hope that doesn't mean that I'll soon have to go home for the weekends to get some sleep. Daddy would like that!
Classes are fine and I love Charleston. I could live here. (Hint, hint.)

Now, my dearest, picture me batting my baby blue eyes and smiling sweetly when I innocently ask this: What's a LRRP?

A letter from Don to his folks made its way to me and I was able to decipher most of it, but not that. Now, Tom dearest, give me credit for going this far before I ask this: Why in the _hell_ didn't you tell me you were running around the jungle all by yourself, shooting people … and I imagine being shot at by people? You can't do that, Tom Howard. You can't shield me. I am a big girl and can handle it. I just can't take being shut out, okay?

Whew. It feels good to get that off my chest. Speaking of that (chest), I miss you terribly. Remember the weekend after jump school?

I can't wait for you to get out of that terrible place. I can't even watch the news anymore. I love you. Please, please, keep yourself safe until you can come back to me.

Love,

Katie xoxo

P.S. Daddy says to tell you that on second thought you really are a nut case. What's that mean?

Tom Howard leaned back in his chair and thought, *oh, shit!* He then spent the entire night crafting a reply that hopefully would make amends. He was distracted along the way with thoughts of payback with a certain fellow Green Beret captain.

Two weeks later, Tom was back at Camp Ranger with a load mirroring the first. By then the letters were funny and this time he got to walk through the village. He left with a Montagnard bracelet. Although crudely fashioned from spent brass casings, Tom would treasure it and for the rest of his life wear it as steadfastly as his wedding and Citadel rings.

Three weeks later, Don was medevacked, gravely wounded in a massive NVA assault on his camp.

* * *

Tom Howard took the news of Don Kennedy's wounding hard. He had learned of it via a courtesy call from a mutual friend at 5th Group.

175

Details were sketchy, but the wounds were serious and Don's condition was critical. The friend though was able to convey where in-country Don would be hospitalized, at least for a short while.

After more than a day more of inability to obtain details, it dawned on Tom that somehow Colonel Kennedy very well may have them. It then had been surprisingly easy to arrange a call to the colonel and Tom from him learned that Don indeed had been badly wounded, but stabilized at the evac hospital, flown to Japan, and where he was. Tom reminded the colonel that Don was tough as they come and asked him to call Katie.

Later in the day, Tom walked past the CO's office, saw that he was at his desk, and knocked on his door frame. When the colonel looked up, Tom asked, "Can I have a moment, sir?"

"Sure, Tom, come on in and take a load off. What can I do for you?"

"Sir, it's about Don Kennedy." By the colonel's look Tom could tell he knew him and knew about what happened to him, so Tom continued, "He's, well, he's my best friend."

Seeing that the young captain was struggling, the colonel cut him off with, "And you want to go see him. Japan?"

Taken aback at the colonel's intuition and the needlessness of the pitch he had crafted, Tom left it at, "Yes, sir."

The colonel raised his voice only slightly and asked, "Did you get that, Stan?"

Tom then heard from the adjoining office the voice of Major Stan Smith, the adjutant, acknowledging that he did. The colonel, his voice again lower, muttered, "Sneaky bastard!"

The adjutant retorted, "Got that too, Colonel," and then appeared in the doorway.

Speaking to both of his officers, the colonel then said, "Tom, get your shop in order, your khakis pressed and pack for a few days. Stan, concoct some bullshit orders for Tom and lay on a flight for tomorrow or the day after." Seeing Tom's stunned expression, the colonel added,

"What's the fun of being a Sneaky Pete if you can't make important shit happen now and then?"

Major Smith then suggested that maybe he ought to go with the captain, prompting the colonel to mock reply, "Maybe, and maybe while you're at it you instead should cut orders for yourself, somewhere good, like the delta," obviously referring to the Mekong Delta down south, a distinctly unpleasant area, "or up at Khe Sanh with the Marines," a most unpleasant place up near the DMZ.

Nonplussed, the major quipped back, "Sure thing, boss; you know I'd follow you anywhere," and disappeared around the corner. Tom knew a little of the history with these two officers. He knew that they had served together in the 173rd Airborne and had seen some nasty stuff. Tom also knew that this was the major's third tour, that he had ably led an A-team in his second and that the colonel had personally recruited him to SOG for this tour.

Still a bit rattled by what had just transpired, Tom Howard thanked the colonel and took his leave. Two days later, he was standing at the foot of Don's hospital bed in Japan.

Don opened his eyes, gave his friend a feeble smile, and acting unsurprised at seeing him there asked, "How goes it *dai uy* [Vietnamese for captain]?"

Tom, trying to match the nonchalance, feigned irritation and said, "Shitty fuckin' way to try to get out of my wedding."

Don laughed at that, coughed, collected himself and said, "It only hurts when I laugh. And, no, I'll be there with bells on. I'm told I'll have plenty of time on my hands. It seems that one-lunged Green Berets are not in particularly high demand these days."

The two settled down to talk. After some time, Don, staring off into space, said, "You know, for all the worrying you know I did about making the camp an impenetrable fortress, the little rice powered motherfuckers were looking like they were going to overrun the place. I thought maybe though I still could do something to thwart them and the next thing I knew is that there's one of 'em right next to me and before I could do anything he skewers the shit out of me with his bayonet. That really sucked."

Tom could not have been more astonished. *A bayonet! Jesus!* But that there was no foot pushing up the covers on Don's right side suggested that there was much more to the story. He would not get it from Don who appeared to know neither how it happened nor that it happened at all. In any event, when he looked back over at his friend he was back asleep. Tom sat there for a time wondering what he should do, how best should he handle this, but he was really lost for an answer.

After some time, Don's executive officer, First Lieutenant Matt Dixon, walked into the room. He was wearing hospital pajamas and a robe and he had a large dressing on his cheek and a swollen, black eye. If he was surprised to see Tom there he did not show it. He just gazed down at Don Kennedy with a look of heavy sadness.

Without prompting, Matt Dixon said, "As you know, Tom, we knew they were coming for us and we were as ready as we could be. They hit one of our ambushes. It didn't go well for our guys out there, but they gave us the time to get every swinging dick at his post. They hit us hard. Your fifty held them on the east. Rodriguez just kept blowing them apart until they blew him off the track and then a yard took over and then another when he was hit. The north side was even worse. Enough gooks made it through the arty, mines and small arms to breach the wire and take the trench there. Don led a counterattack and drove them out, and when he saw another wave coming, he told me to have one of the batteries adjust to fire on command 'danger close, Broken Arrow' [the coded designation for a ground unit in peril of being imminently overrun]. The crazy, heroic bastard, then ordered the remaining yards back and stayed out there alone. You know, Tom, I was on top of the CP and Don wasn't but thirty yards away at the north trench when the fuckin' gook came back to life and went at him with the bayonet. There wasn't a fucking thing I could do. Don blew the bastard away and then fell back, over a body, his foot sticking up over the body. I thought for sure he was dead, but then I heard him on the radio, ordering me to call in the adjusted fire; had me call the arty right on top of him! Then the rounds came in and I watched Don get blown up. The same shell that got him got me. The plastic surgeon says he needs to get the swelling down so he can close me up with a minimal scar. Anyway, the fire mission did the trick, blew the motherfuckers to pieces, scattered their shit to the wind, and stopped them cold. I went up to the line and Don, man, Jesus, his fucking leg was blown half off and he had both frothy red arterial and almost blue liver blood pouring out of his nose and mouth. *Fuck!*" And then Matt was quiet for a few moments before he added, "I'm sorry, Tom, but my wife is right when she says I'm a regular potty mouth when I get riled."

* * *

Tom Howard was able to come back for one other brief visit with Don Kennedy before he had to catch his flight back to Vietnam. It was a surreal visit. In contrast to the visit the day before, Don was oddly upbeat, explaining the mood as because the doctor told him that his "gut job" had gone well with no organs needing to be removed and no indication of any infection. Don at first said nothing about the leg, but then seemingly almost as an afterthought, he exposed it by pulling back the covers and said, "Shame about the leg though. It'll take some getting used to. I guess I'm going to have to get a real job now."

Both Tom and Katie kept in touch with Don who was released from the stateside hospital with a temporary prosthetic leg. He was staying with his parents at Fort Benning and making plans to go back to school, Georgia Tech in Atlanta he hoped. In one letter, Don offhandedly noted that he had gotten the Distinguished Service Cross and that his father had pinned it on him as one of his last official acts before retiring. That his friend had been awarded the nation's second highest medal for valor, subordinate only to the Medal of Honor, validated all Tom had heard and read about Don's incredible heroism that day.

As for Tom, with Don out of the picture he had little motivation to continue engaging in scrounging to the extent that he had. He instead became more involved in the operations side of SOG and its covert aspects with the CIA. He in fact became closer to a couple of his CIA contacts than he was with any of his fellow officers on SOG staff and he did not become close friends with anyone else out in the field.

Tom Howard's remaining months slowly went by without further excitement (other than receipt of the Silver Star Don Kennedy had predicted for the escapade with the LRRP team and a legendary celebration with the LRRP's and even a classified array of officers and senior NCO's from 4th ID HQ). With each passing day, he missed Katie more and longed to be with her. That would happen in due course, but what Tom Howard had no way of knowing was that events were transpiring that would further dramatically alter his life.

9

Strom Thurmond, the senior senator from the state of South Carolina, walked into the outer offices of his colleague, Senator Ernest F. "Fritz" Hollings, and giving curt nods to the staffers present walked right into the office of the junior senator from South Carolina (although quite senior in the Senate). What may have appeared to some a breach of protocol for anyone to do, particularly one from the other side of the aisle, was trivial to those present. While the two men were from opposing parties, they were loyal representatives of the Great State of South Carolina and had been formidable bastions of the state for many years.

"Mornin', Fritz. A few minutes of your time?" Of course, ample time already had been allotted.

"Certainly, Strom. What can I do for you?"

Strom Thurmond launched into it with the vigor of a man half his age. "You know as well as I do that the American people are tired of this war [pronouncing it "wo-wuh" with his famous southern drawl] and one way or another we're gonna be out of there soon enough. I hate to give in to the commies, but ..." and he let the sentiment remain unspoken. He continued, "We'll be out of there and the people are gonna be clamoring to downsize the active military to save on taxes. Sure, we'll keep troops over in Germany to stare down the Ruskies and keep our nukes handy, but otherwise we'll cut the military 'til it hurts." None of that, of course, was news to Fritz Hollings and he did not disagree with the senior senator's reasoning.

Senator Thurmond continued, "Special Forces, even though we're gonna need them to deal with all these third world countries always stirring up trouble and those crazy Muslims, are gonna get cut to the bone. A lot of top notch, expensively trained fighters are gonna be shown the door. What a waste of money and talent!"

Fritz Hollings knew and agreed with that as well, but continued to sit politely while the elder statesman vented and laid the groundwork for what was really on his mind. He smiled, showing his famous teeth, when Strom Thurmond got to the point. "Let me cut to the chase. I see an opportunity here for the State of South Carolina."

Thurmond proceeded to lay out his idea for a reserve unit comprised of reservists and/or national guardsmen from several states, foremost being South Carolina, recruited from the best in or from the active military. His idea was for the federal government to acquire 50,000 acres in the Jasper County pinelands and establish there a post housing an elite unit that not only could be available in times of crisis, but could help with the training of their fellow guardsmen and reservists, those of surrounding states, and even the active military. The land, he said, could be gotten cheap if they allowed the sellers, mainly timber companies, to retain timber rights; and the state and community would profit from the development of the post and in many other ways.

Seeing that the younger senator was receptive, he continued, "What we need though is someone, *our* someone, to devise what the unit will be and what they'll need; and ultimately build it from the ground up after he helps us sell the idea down home and here in Washington."

Senator Hollings thought for a minute, remembered a conversation he recently had and decided that there really was no point in playing it cagey. "I have a friend from down Beaufort way, a banker, whose daughter's fiancé, also from there, and a Citadel grad I might add [as was the senator], right now is a Green Beret captain in Vietnam and supposedly is considering getting out when he gets back."

Thurmond mulled that over and then mused, "A captain would be a might younger than I was thinking, but we could provide the horsepower from elsewhere. We'd probably do that in any event. I tell you what, why don't you talk with the boy when he's back and if you like him get him on board?" Hollings agreed to do it.

"One more thing," Thurmond added, "can you get Westy on board if he beats Watson?" Thurmond was referring to Democratic South Carolina Lieutenant Governor and gubernatorial candidate John C. West, who also had been Hollings's classmate at The Citadel. Hollings responded that he would see what he could do when the time was right. Satisfied that he had accomplished as much as he could at this point, Strom Thurmond took his leave.

The plans artfully took shape in a short time. Fritz Hollings confided some of them to Bill Greer, including their interest in Tom Howard, and enlisted his friend's help in postponing any career change by the young man. Although somewhat ashamed with himself, Bill Greer accomplished that through Katie while concealing the ulterior motives. Tom Howard cooperated by surviving his second Vietnam tour intact and unwittingly accepting an assignment back at Fort Bragg.

* * *

Tom's homecoming was better than the first time. For one thing, he was not banged up. For another, there was Katie. Tom's flight in was early enough in the day for the two to break away from the family for a brief, but vigorous private reunion. The family homecoming party afterward filled the Howard home to the point of bursting. There were the Howards, the Greers, family friends and, the big surprise, Don Kennedy and his parents.

Don looked perfectly fit and showed no sign of being bitter that his Army career had ended. He even seemed genuinely satisfied that with his West Point ring and combat record he could land a USAR (U.S. Army Reserve) slot with the safety net of the assured medical retirement pay regardless, which, coupled with his VA benefits ought to enable him to afford finishing his master's degree at Georgia Tech. Colonel Kennedy, having retired after twenty-eight years in the Army, spent much of the time talking with the Howards and Bill Greer about the prospect of moving to the Carolina coast.

After feasting on low country boil, the gathering soon broke up, ultimately leaving Tom, his father, and uncle on the back porch with bourbon and cigars. It ended as before with the two older Howards chuckling at a soundly sleeping Tom.

The next day, Tom was introduced to the frenzy of activity involved with the final plans and preparations for his upcoming wedding. But for the time he got to spend with his Dad and the wonderful stolen hours with Katie, after a couple of weeks of being an unimportant cog in the wedding prep machine it almost was a relief when he had to drive up to report in at Fort Bragg.

The first person Captain Tom Howard met at the John F. Kennedy Special Warfare Center was a sergeant major by the name of Hector Ramirez, the embodiment of a Green Beret warrior. Tom took an immediate liking to the man and he to him. Sergeant Major Ramirez, who seemed to know an awful lot about him, including his upcoming leave, explained that the smartest thing would be to put to use his combined experiences at the Fort Benning School for Wayward Boys and from across the pond. That basically amounted to the two of them bouncing around from one training event to another, seemingly at the senior sergeant's whim.

The two men quickly became friends on a first name basis. Tom learned that Hector had made a combat jump in Korea with the 187th Airborne Regimental Combat Team; had served with the 82nd Airborne in the Dominican Republic in 1965 and a year later his first of three tours as a Green Beret in Vietnam; and that he now was back at Fort Bragg for his sunset assignment. Tom felt comfortable enough to confide to Hector that he most likely would be getting out too.

Tom soon met Hector's wife, Linh, a wonderful Vietnamese lady of boundless energy. Tom got to know her quite well after Hector insisted that he move in with them since both of their boys were off at school, the oldest over at Davidson College just north of Charlotte, and the youngest up at West Point. Tom's asking if his moving in might ruffle some "Swick" feathers (referring to SWCS, the U.S. Army John F. Kennedy Special Warfare Center and School), prompted Hector to laughingly ask, "You mean flagrantly fraternizing with a lower enlisted dog?" and to employ the popular Army adage, "fuck 'em if they can't take a joke."

Before long though, it was time for Tom to face the music, quite literally, and he headed back down to South Carolina. There was a bachelor party he would not discuss, a bachelorette party Katie would not discuss, the rehearsal dinner, and finally the main event.

Gathered with his groomsmen and Katie's father in the courtyard of the majestic antebellum Beaufort church, Tom commented to his best man, Don Kennedy, that he under the circumstances felt surprisingly calm. Without skipping a beat, Don in characteristic fashion replied, "Life becomes easier when one gives up all hope," prompting a chorus of similar additions from the others, likening his calmness to that of a man on the gallows after the noose is tightened, a man facing a firing squad after the blindfold is in place, even the thief on the cross. Tom looked to Katie's father for relief, but Bill Greer too was enjoying the banter. Tom was about to express feigned outrage when his soon to be father-in-law was summoned to the narthex and with that summons Tom's calmness completely evaporated in a flash.

The butterflies vanished though as Tom entered the sanctuary. Perhaps it was the magnificence of the richly adorned church or maybe it just was that Tom simply was ready. Tom scanned the people filling the pews on both sides of the center aisle, smiling at those with whom he made eye contact.

His gaze then fell upon his best man and groomsmen, the servicemen like him, sharp in their dress blue uniforms, complete with medals and badges; Captain Don Kennedy with his Distinguished Service Cross prominent above his many other awards, Tom's former Citadel roommate Captain Pete Swanson with the many medals Air Force pilots always seem to have, and Sergeant Major Hector Ramirez with his most impressive array of medals and badges; and then to the two others, both handsome young men in their fine navy blue suits. They were Tom's cousin Tim (Uncle Bob's son) and Katie's little brother Trey (for William Greer III), a year younger than she and a rising junior at Furman University. As the processional music began, Tom's attention turned to the back of the church and the bridesmaids commencing their march down the aisle.

There are memorable moments within momentous events and Tom should have foreseen that Don Kennedy would provide yet another one. As Katie's maid of honor, a thoroughly alluring young lady, neared, Don leaned close to Tom and whispered, "What do you think, use my considerable charm or go with the wounded warrior approach? That seemed to work okay for you."

And then there was Katie. Heavenly was the only befitting way to describe her and when her veil was lifted, Tom felt as though his heart would burst from his chest. Tom somehow managed to correctly say his vows.

The reception was a blur. While Tom grumbled about the southern tradition of the newlyweds departing early, it was the only thing that saved their wedding night for the planned hours of lovemaking were soon cut off by mutual exhaustion.

Don Kennedy was not yet through with them. Upon their arrival at the honeymoon resort, an amused bell captain handed Tom a telegram. Opening and seeing it was from Don, Tom had to laugh as he read, "Hope we both got lucky last night." Handing it to Katie as they followed the bellhop to their suite, Katie read it and when the meaning registered she frowned and said, "That rascal!"

Tom leaned close to her and speaking so that the bellhop could not hear, said, "Yet another innocent victim dragged off kicking and screaming by my band of rogues."

In like fashion, Katie whispered back, "Get rid of this guy and I'll show you kicking and screaming!"

After a marvelous week, Captain and Mrs. Howard were in married housing at Fort Bragg. Katie had gone there with no small amount of trepidation, fully expecting to spend many lonely hours while Tom was working. She, however, was delighted to learn that the unconventional warfare specialty of Special Forces drew in unconventionally uproariously fun people and it was not long before her parents complained that she did not drive down to see them often enough. For Tom and Katie it was to be a productive, as in reproductive, time, but only for a short time.

* * *

A capable aide to Senator Hollings learned that Tom Howard's Citadel roommate, Pete Swanson, an Air Force captain whose Vietnam experience included some months as a FAC, forward air controller, with the Army's 1st Cavalry Division, now was a tactical officer at The Citadel. He gave the captain a call and, divulging little, got him to invite the Howards down to Charleston for among other pretextual things the weekly Friday parade at the school. A dinner was arranged at the historic and splendid Francis Marion Hotel on the Battery with Captain Tom Howard and Katie, Captain Swanson and his wife; the surprise of Tom and Katie's parents; and, the ultimate surprise, Senator Hollings and his wife. The fine setting, fine food, fine wine, fine company, and exceptionally fine preparations all worked to the senator's advantage.

At the close of the meal, a senatorial aide appeared and escorted the group to a well-appointed conference room with the table and chairs replaced by comfortable leather chairs and side tables, the exact number needed. After everyone helped themselves to the bar offering coffee, soft drinks, and more fine wine, the senator decided the time was right to ease into his pitch.

He and Senator Thurmond had the idea to take advantage of the wealth of military experience soon to be going to waste by the unavoidable consequence of downsizing as the Vietnam war drew to a close. The idea was to create a new Army unit at a new military reservation in Jasper County, an undisclosed 50,000 acre location being considered, and suggested that sister units elsewhere may be an option.

Senator Hollings smiled his famous smile when he stated that federal and state funding was not expected to be an obstacle he and the senior senator could not overcome. The senator's aide took his cue to pass around impressively prepared informational packets designed more than anything to demonstrate that the idea was not just a lark. Interest certainly was piqued, although the same thought lingered in everyone's mind, "*But what does that have to do with any of us?*"

As if reading their minds, the senator said, "We'd like local input from prominent citizens." Pausing only long enough for Dan Howard and Bill Greer to appreciate the intended connotations of that, the senator turned to Tom Howard and said, "Tom, we know and respect your background and we'd like you to get on board this train; in fact, to design it, build it, and then drive it, if that's the right word. We can arrange for you to be TDY to a temporary site at the provisional location," everyone understanding that to mean that deals already were being cut, "on paper as a consultant to a senate subcommittee," again the famous smile, "with contacts to my staff and Strom's." No thought was given to that Tom might decline, and he didn't.

It was agreed that they would reconnect in a month's time after the materials had been digested and everyone's personal considerations had been taken into account. The materials furnished provided a vague concept, which Tom was expected to develop; preliminary plans, which Tom was expected to develop; expectations, which Tom was expected to develop; and contacts, which Tom was expected to rely heavily upon.

A month later, armed with only keys to a gate and some doors, a provided government vehicle and a road map with his destination marked by a red dot near the town of Ridgeland and a smaller place called Switzerland, of all things, Tom drove out there. The gate key worked, a good first sign. Tom found himself in a fenced enclosure with a cluster of commercial trailers and an OD pickup truck with military markings. The trailers had electricity and Tom tentatively set up shop in the obviously intended one set up with a couple of desks and chairs, a table with chairs, a file cabinet, and a working telephone.

There were maps tacked on the wall, respectively from the state department of agriculture, the state department of transportation, the county tax assessor, the forest service, the timber company, and a military topographical map. Wondering why the military would even have a map of private property in the middle of nowhere, Tom unpinned the topo map because he was more familiar with them and studied it for a while. He decided to drive around and look at the place. Fifty thousand acres was a lot of land to cover so he settled on eyeing enough of it to get a feel for it.

Driving back to the renovated old home place where he and Katie were temporarily staying, Tom thought, "The place doesn't even have a name. It needs a name." He pondered that notion as he drove and came up with "Camp Marion," after the famous South Carolina Revolutionary War general and celebrated guerilla fighter, Francis Marion, the "Swamp Fox." He started referring to the place by that name and the name stuck.

Two days later, Tom had a staff of two, Sergeant Major Hector Ramirez (also TDY from Fort Bragg) and Margaret Ayers, "Miss Margaret," an extraordinary secretary loaned to them by Bill Greer. They started with a "to do" list, a daunting task in and of itself. The list was topped by "Get help" and Tom's first test of what kind of help they could count on from his primary contact with Senator Thurmond's staff. He was rewarded with immediate authorization to bring on two more officers and a couple more support staff.

Howard's first call was to Don Kennedy who was over in Atlanta, close to earning his master's degree in civil engineering at Georgia Tech. Without divulging his motive, Tom invited him down for the weekend and Don accepted.

Promptly after dinner the first night, Tom, with Hector covering his flank and Katie in reserve, made his pitch for Don to come on board as a reserve captain wearing several hats, operations and training officer, recruiter and construction superintendent. Don showed interest, but remarked that he had reservations because he was eyeing an envious position with a civil engineering firm in Charlotte.

Hector jumped in, scoffing at that and saying, "You don't want none of that shit. You know you don't. You want to spend your life worrying how best to lay sewer pipes? Hell, no! You're a *warrior*, by God. Come back and do good things with good men, for good men." When Don then expressed concerns as to his physical abilities, Hector snapped back with, "Hell, we don't need you to jump out of any damn planes. You've been there, done that. Now it's time to put all you've learned to good use with the youngsters who just may need it to survive."

Don Kennedy went back to Atlanta and procrastinated for only a day before calling to say that he would do it. He admitted that it in fact was the perfect impetus (as in "the right kick in the ass") to get going and wrap up what he had left to do to get his degree. He could be there within a few weeks. He then turned around and extended his new-found enthusiasm to convincing his parents to go ahead and buy the majestic house next to Dan and Bea's on the river outside Beaufort they had been eyeing, agreeably offering to take up residence in an apartment over the three-car garage there and to help them out with things.

Don still technically was in the reserves and it was a simple thing to get him activated so he could get paid. That he technically outranked Tom was not an issue, not in the least.

The three soldiers and Miss Margaret (now fully relinquished to the cause), worked tirelessly to formulate a concept of the unit they were tasked to create and to devise a provisional organization and its mission. Knowing that the goal was to capture special operators and highly skilled technical people, they decided to boldly recommend an entirely new animal, a composite special operations unit initially head-quartered at Camp Marion; with one of three operational companies there (Company A) collocated with Group Headquarters and with supporting attachments and installation support personnel; and two mostly independent sister companies, one to be out in the desert (Company B) and the other in the mountains (Company C). Each of the three special ops companies would be comprised of a company headquarters, a Green Beret ODA, a reinforced Ranger platoon, and support detachments.

They needed a name for it and settled on "15th [an arbitrary number] Special Operations Group (Airborne), or "15th SOG (Abn)" for short. They then crafted the proposed unit's mission and set the standards for the desired personnel:

"**Mission:** To train for and provide a dynamic special operations asset capable of providing in a broad spectrum of terrain and climates long range reconnaissance, target acquisition, target destruction via artillery and air (fixed and rotary wing aircraft) [and years later missiles via drones] and/or organic weapons; and to provide training to active, reserve, and national guard units on all aspects of the same.

"**Recruiting Standards:** All operational personnel to be Airborne, Ranger, and Air Assault qualified, members of the Special Forces component duly qualified; willing to commit to activation for a full year, followed by annual periodic activations (including training at and with the sister companies and specialized training and deployments (possibly to hostile zones)) totaling three months or more; with preference given to combat veterans, proven leaders, experienced instructors, those possessing special skills (e.g., target acquisition, communications, weaponry (including snipers), language, and otherwise as needed)."

They then agonized for several days devising a rudimentary TO&E (table of organization and equipment) and sent their work product up the chain. Both the name and the concept were surprisingly in short order approved, at least preliminarily. The TO&E, with its budgetary limitations, was chewed on for considerably longer.

In the meantime, the meager 15th SOG staff set out to conceive the physical development of the installation and reservation, something they knew would take considerable time to come to fruition and something they surely would need before they had many more boots on the ground. Capitalizing on Don's engineering knowledge and working off topographical maps, aerial photographs, and county maps, together with invaluable insights and input not only from their "handlers" (as they had taken to calling the assigned government staffers), but also from the Howard elders and Bill Greer, they conceptualized the structure of Camp Marion.

Starting with a modest post proper, initial plans called for a headquarters building fronted by a four acre pond and flanked by the two enormous live oak trees there; a common building for the quadruple usage as a mess hall, a training facility, an infirmary, and for recreation; a row of barracks buildings also capable of serving other purposes; secure, climate controlled buildings for communications, an armory, and an ammunition bunker; maintenance and storage buildings, including for the parachutes and sundry equipment; and a guard shack at the front gate. For security purposes, the post proper would be cordoned off with chain link fencing topped by barbed wire and the access from the county roads bordering the reservation would be barred by barbed wire topped hog wire fencing. Utilities were roughed in, but they would have to wait for the experts to finalize.

They then turned their attention to the reservation. Working off maps and personal observation (occasionally aided by helicopters flown by pilots needing stick time), conferring with an array of experts and with more invaluable insights and input from the Howard elders and Bill Greer, they steadfastly conceptualized Camp Marion "outside the wire," beyond the post proper.

The plan was to create an airstrip long enough to handle C-130 aircraft; to be flanked on one side by a rifle range extending nearly its entire length with staggered berms at 50, 100, 200, 300, 500 and 1,000 yards; and flanked on the other by a drop zone of approximately 100 acres; a borrow pit of 20 acres or more would be dug on the north side and the dirt used to improve the existing network of logging roads. Over time, more land either would be clear-cut or thinned depending upon training area desires and input or direction from the logging company retaining the rights to the timber and various environmental agencies. Trees would be harvested as they were at Fort Stewart, Georgia; that is, bulldozed rather than cut so that no stumps remained to hinder training.

The daunting challenges of building Camp Marion and Alpha Company were compounded by the need to not only recruit personnel, but also to get teams recruited and working on similarly building the sister companies (hampered by their locations were still being wrangled at the political level) and then unifying them; learning and complying with staggering and often conflicting requirements imposed by the Army, Army Reserve, and National Guard, as well as other governmental agencies at federal, state, and local levels (including the mind boggling paperwork so central and precious to all governmental entities, something Miss Margaret saved the men by handling almost exclusively); trying to assess and stay within the bounds of the moving target of budgetary concerns; and giving thought to logistics and operations down the road.

Faced with those challenges, the SOG staff decided to send up the chain their physical and structural concepts to at least get the ball rolling. Again, they in due time were pleasantly surprised. Although it first seemed like every person in the bureaucratic chain felt compelled to change something, the plans were provisionally approved, architects and engineers were brought on board, funds were allocated, and contractors were hired. Some of them, of course, were hired on the basis of connections, but they all soon learned to bow to the oversight by Don Kennedy and, much more fearfully, Hector Ramirez.

Long before those latter phases transpired, the SOG staff had turned their focus to getting players on the field, so to speak. The enormity of the task was compounded by that while the proposed personnel list largely was approved, the slots were divided between the Army Reserve and the South Carolina Army National Guard (SCARNG) (as presumably would be done with the sister companies in other states) and that not all were approved for full time service.

As both a blessing and a curse, the word somehow was out in the Special Forces and special operations communities of opportunities available at Camp Marion and with 15th SOG; and with the war in Vietnam grinding to a halt and military cutbacks all but certain, the meager SOG staff became inundated with calls, letters, and resumes, many quite impressive. More than a few of the applicants were willing to take demotions, including officers to warrant or even noncommissioned ranks.

But even with this pool to choose from, Tom Howard was not inclined to waste the golden opportunity of the ability to recruit his own people.

"Hector," he asked, "how hard is it to track down vets?"

"Not so hard, if you know the right people."

"Do you?"

"I could make some calls."

An hour later, Hector had from Tom a list. He made some calls. The next day Tom had the list back with the names on it annotated with addresses of homes of record and a few with telephone numbers. Tom enlisted the aid of Miss Margaret to track down a few more of them while he started making calls to the numbers he had. Two of them hit pay dirt.

The first call was answered on the fifth ring, the "hello" sounding like "h'lo" encouraging.

"Hello. I'm looking for Dwayne Mitchell."

"Found'm. Who's this?"

"Does 'Corndog' mean anything to you?"

There was a pause before the reply, "Maybe. Who *is* this?"

"Corndog, this is Tom Howard. You did some tracking for me in the delta."

A longer pause suggested that the man was searching his memory. Tom helped him out. "I was the Alpha CO for a day, took over after Coach."

That made the memory links click. "Oh, sure ['shore'], I ['ah'] remember. Curious why you're calling me after all these years."

"I'm looking for a tracker, more specifically someone to train people to track; long term, as in years long term. It would involve getting back in uniform with a couple of bumps in pay grade, a move to the South Carolina coast, and trips to the mountains and desert. Might you have interest in that?"

"Might. Can't say my feet are firmly rooted here. Tell me more."

Tom proceeded to explain and could tell by the questions asked that he had piqued the man's interest. He ended by inviting him to come down, travel expenses reimbursed (he'd have to figure out how), details to be worked out. Corndog said he would think on it and Tom knew that he had taken the bait.

Tom was not so devious as to set the hook and reel the man in though. Instead (and pressing the fishing analogy one last step further) he graciously allowed some slack in the line and the opportunity to escape the hook.

"I don't want to mislead you. There's a catch here."

"Oh?"

"You oughta know that we're an Airborne Ranger LRRP outfit and you'd have to go to jump school and Ranger school."

Tom waited for the "thanks, but no thanks," reply. After probably a full minute, Corndog's voice came back on the line after an audible sigh.

"Well, can't say I'm wild about that idea, but won't say it's a deal breaker either. You are talking full time E-6, right?"

Tom knew then that he had him and the time was right to set the hook. "That's right, staff sergeant. One year full time guaranteed, extendable by agreement. Jump pay, too."

To make a long story short, in not too many weeks Don Kennedy had a tracker trainer on his staff who disappeared for months after a few weeks alternating between learning the wilds of Camp Marion and intensive physical training in preparation of Airborne School, Ranger School, and the NCO Academy. When Staff Sergeant Dwayne "Corndog" Mitchell returned to Camp Marion, he was one capable, confident and motivated individual eager to assume the dual roles of a squad leader in the Ranger platoon and trainer on tracking and patrolling skills.

After SSG Mitchell developed his training course with the Alpha Green Berets, Ranger leaders, and then the enlisted operators, he was off to train the sister 15th SOG companies. When he returned to Camp Marion, he was fully ready to begin what would become a "gotta have it" course for special operators nationwide and beyond.

Before all that transpired, Tom Howard's other major success had solidified Alpha's core. Captain Craig Clark's benefit as commander of the Ranger Platoon was immeasurable. Securing him for that position had taken the teamwork of Tom, Don, Hector, Miss Margaret, and even Katie.

Miss Margaret had tracked Clark down to Macon, Georgia, where he was in his third year of the Walter F. George School of Law of Mercer University. Timing had been perfect. Tom's call caught him at the time studies took a back seat to interviewing for jobs, the time in law school that preceded all but ignoring class work while preparing for the Bar examination. Tom's call had been answered by Clark's girlfriend.

"May I speak to Craig Clark, please?"

"Can I ask who's calling?"

"Uh, just tell him an old reliable." Tom smiled as he imagined the scene of a pretty girl with a perplexed look on her face as she handed the telephone to Clark with that odd identification.

In no time, Craig Clark got on the line. Tom identified himself sufficiently for Craig to recognize him and then explained the nature of his call. Tom's proposition triggered a whirlwind of thoughts compounded by a myriad of factors Tom had no way of knowing or even suspecting.

While Craig's top 10% class standing and otherwise impressive resume afforded him the prospects of a lucrative position with one of the Atlanta mega-firms or the prestige of serving for a year as a law clerk to a federal judge, that was not why he went to law school. Craig instead envisioned himself as a prosecutor, the vow of poverty it entailed notwithstanding. It would be difficult, if not impossible, to do that and play army at the same time.

Craig nevertheless agreed to meet with Tom the next weekend on "neutral ground" in Savannah. Craig brought along his girlfriend (whom Tom correctly surmised fit centrally into the equation) and Tom brought both Don Kennedy and Katie, Don to "knock rings" with the fellow West Pointer and to trade stories relating to their horrid leg wounds and Katie to chum with the girlfriend and to serve as designated driver on the way home in the likely event that alcohol was involved. (That their destination was the famed River Street rendered the likelihood a virtual certainty.) It was to prove to be a delightful and productive evening.

It was weeks later though before Tom heard back from Craig. After inquiring whether the job was still open and being told that it was, Craig explained that he had been given an offer to join the Office of the United States Attorney for the Southern District of Georgia in Savannah and that the U.S. Attorney assured him that he could within reason accommodate reserve training. The provisional "within reason" needed to be hammered out.

It took several rounds of negotiations to achieve a fair compromise, ultimately a testament to Craig Clark's perceived value to both parties. Craig would be exempted from the mandated first year of full time service and excused from some of the training while the U.S. Attorney would delay his start time to allow him to complete IOAC (failure to do so would eliminate any chance of promotion beyond captain) and could live with him being gone for six one-week periods each year. It was one of those rare deals where everyone concerned afterward justifiably patted themselves on the back.

Recruiting continued. Probably the most difficult was to select their bosses, the company, group, and installation commanders. For Group Commander, they selected a retiring lieutenant colonel with considerable experience in airborne units, including the 75th Ranger Regiment and Special Forces.

Tom and Don were dismayed when a South Carolina Army National Guard lieutenant colonel was imposed on them to nominally command the installation as a part-timer. He had no combat experience and while he was both Airborne and Ranger qualified, he had done nothing with either of those skills afterward. He was received with trepidation, but he quickly allayed all fears by assuring everyone that he perceived his role as another head to bounce ideas off, a dispute arbiter, a buffer against SCARNG and USAR headquarters and other governmental pains in the ass. In all these things, he performed superbly. As an added bonus, he and his wife became fast friends of Don's parents.

Tom and Don recruited commanders for Bravo and Charlie Companies, each a Vietnam veteran with combat command experience and an impressive record. Those two commanders in turn and in time followed Tom's lead in building their respective commands. Tom and Don were still working on Alpha's commander when word came down that no, Tom was to be it, like it or not.

That posed a problem. Tom had planned to be the Green Beret A-team commander and now he had to recruit someone else. That too proved to be easy though. In fact, the entire A-team quickly took shape and it was a "dream team" in anyone's book.

Recruiting for Alpha otherwise continued to be productive and before long the recruited officers, warrant officers, and NCO's began trickling in. On them fell the burden of having to deal with arriving shipments of all manner of things, from office equipment and supplies to bunks, mattresses, and lockers; from parachutes and other gear to weapons, ammunition, and sensitive items; and from generators and other very heavy things to hundreds of boxes of little things, all of which had to be off-loaded, inventoried, stored, and secured. Getting the balance of enlisted men promptly on board therefore became a hot priority.

It would take months of hard work to get Camp Marion to be a functioning post and to get Alpha Company operational. It happened nonetheless. Things began to impressively take shape.

In recognition of their stellar performance and responsibilities, both Tom and Don were promoted to major. An epic party ensued, precipitating a lamentable session of PT (physical training) the next morning with Tom and Don (who by then was up to running with an experimental prosthetic designed for that purpose) later trying to convince themselves that the bonding effects with the new officers, warrants, and NCO's made it worthwhile. Hector retired from the Army one day and the next he was a SCARNG Command Sergeant Major able to "double dip" his pay. That celebration was more culinary, but the effects of the savory but spicy cuisine prompted Tom to cancel PT the next morning. (He blamed it on the rain, an excuse all concerned were quite willing to accept.)

$$10$$

ALPHA COMPANY HAD ITS GREEN BERET A-TEAM (LATER TO BE DES-
ignated as an "ODA," Operational Detachment Alpha) and Ranger
platoon. Each man was armed with his choice of an M16A2 or CAR-15
(XM177 Colt Commando, a carbine version of the M16 series), both
automatic rifles firing the 5.56mm (.223 cal.) (later to be replaced by
the M4, basically a CAR-15 upgrade, which ultimately became the
standard issue rifle for the military); and some also with the M1911A1
Colt .45 caliber semi-automatic pistol (later the choice between the
M9 (Beretta Model 92 9mm), which would replace the M1911A1) or
various non-issue pistols, e.g., Glock, Sig Sauer, etc.). Each man also
familiarized himself with the AK-47 and its variants, of which Alpha
was allotted a dozen from CIA stores.

The snipers (Alpha started with three two-man teams, later doubling
it) worked with variants of the Remington Model 700 bolt action rifle
(firing a .308 cal. round, essentially the same as the 7.62mm); or the
M21 (firing 7.62mm), an adaptation of the old M14 semi-automatic;
but would "play" with others and ultimately settle on customized Model
700s (as did the military at large, designating the weapon the M24).
Years later, the awesome Barrett .50 caliber rifle (M82 series) would be
added to the mix, giving the snipers killing power out to a mile (at a
whopping cost of well over $5,000 a copy). The snipers experimented
with a vast array of optics for day and night shooting. For night shooting,

there was initially the Starlight scope that greatly magnified available light, then infrared scopes, and ultimately thermal scopes.

For supporting weapons, Alpha was allotted two M60 machine guns, later to be augmented by an M249 SAW (squad automatic weapon firing the 5.56mm standard rifle round from drum magazines) for the ODA and each Ranger squad; a pair of old M2 (later the improved M224) 60mm mortars; and for anti-tank or bunker busting weapons the M72 LAW (light anti-tank weapon) (later the AT-4).

Specialists were critical to the spec ops unit. Signals, intelligence, technicians, parachute riggers, an armorer, supply, cooks and others were recruited or sent to school to expertly fill those roles. Radio communications would be vital to Alpha's fulfillment of its mission and its life blood in the field and the 15th SOG founders were particularly particular in recruiting soldiers in that field and in trying to get the most advanced equipment available to spec ops units.

* * *

One thing overlooked in the process were signs. They were neither conceptualized nor budgeted. No one seemed concerned about them, which Tom Howard and Don Kennedy took as authorization to do as they pleased. The problem was compounded by that the unit's crest was still on a drawing board somewhere, but neither Tom nor Don were willing to let that defeat them.

For placement at the guard shack at the entrance they got the state road department to create for them a generic sign, "Welcome to Camp Marion, Home of Alpha Company, 15th Special Operations Group (Airborne), USAR/SCARNG." Ho-hum.

Don Kennedy, however, had secret ("trust me") plans for another, to be placed where the entrance road leading to the planned headquarters building began its curl around the planned pond. The two were painfully aware that regulations over signs, shoulder patches, and unit crests were taken very seriously by those high above lording over such things. The SOG men avoided (in fact ignored) proper procedure with the sign they wanted because of the "bureaucratic bullshit" they had faced regarding the unit's insignia and that the proposed unit crest remained "under consideration." Instead they employed the "better to beg for forgiveness than ask for permission" approach, a Special Forces forte.

All Tom Howard knew about it was that he was to arrange with his father or uncle to have three massive heart pine squared posts milled and delivered. He was not to be disappointed.

The sign when unveiled was impressive:

Standing there admiring the sign, Tom asked Don, "So what do we do when some panty waste bureaucrat tells us to replace this magnificent artwork with some regulation piece of shit?"

Don retorted, "Feed the sonofabitch to Hector, of course."

* * *

With the insignia, the shoulder patch, however, they could not dance around proper procedure. Tom, Don, and Hector had fretted over it way too long. They initially agreed that since most of the 15th SOG members were required to be Ranger school qualified and therefore entitled to wear the yellow on black "Ranger" tab over their shoulder patch [Green Berets would not be authorized until 1983 to wear "Special Forces" tabs], they really did not need anything other than an "Airborne" tab over the patch; and they wanted an inverse "LRRP" tab underneath the patch. The patch itself was a struggle.

The three men had agreed early in the discussion upon a round tricolor patch with the bottom third being tan, signifying desert sand and Bravo Company; the top third gray, signifying mountains and Charlie Company; and the middle third green, signifying woodlands and Alpha Company. The patch would be heavily bordered in black, signifying night operations.

Each man, however, favored his own design for the center. Hector's was a black dagger pointing down with a diagonal lightning bolt superimposed over the blade. Not bad, but not very original. Don's was a snarling tiger with black on yellow cat's eyes. Cool, but not really suited to an official shoulder patch. Tom won the insignia contest with a simple centered duplex crosshair reticle in bold white and his explanation that it reflected what 15th SOG fundamentally would do, target people. That agreed upon, the three readily agreed that the "Airborne" tab ought to be a complementary white on black. The design and annotation also won the contest with the bureaucrats and was approved.

Don's idea was not trashed. Instead it was the design they chose to submit for the unit crest accompanied by the motto, "Semper Deinceps," Latin for "always forward." (A damned Military Intelligence unit already had secured "Always out front.") That too in due time was approved, as was the cost of a large rendition of it to adorn the wall of the conference room in the headquarters building.

Miss Margaret reminded Don that they were required to post certain things. Always mindful of "duty first," Don saw to them first (albeit in Don Kennedy fashion).

The first one arguably was more or less technically compliant:

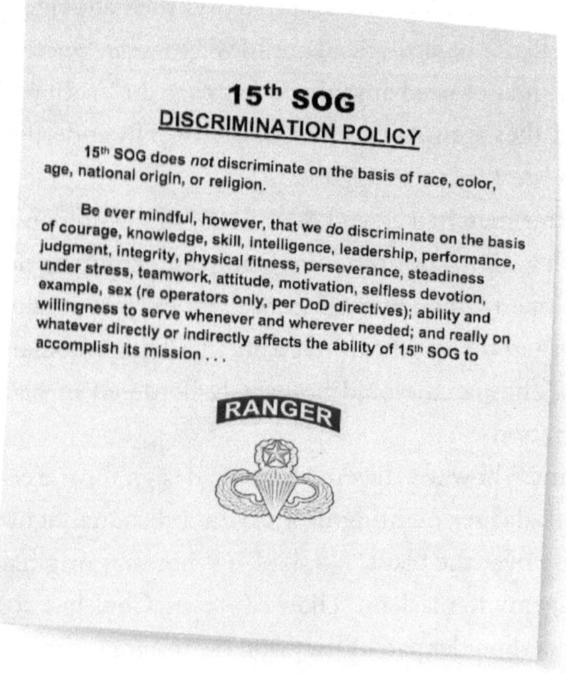

The next one, however, while making its point would take a darn good lawyer on a good day to argue conformity:

15th SOG SAFETY RULES

The feds (OSHA, etc.) and the state require that safety rules be posted. These are them. Read them. Know them. *Follow them.*

Rule No. 1 – *Always* remember that this is a hazardous occupation – we work with sharp instruments and things that go boom, not to mention jumping out of freakin' aircraft.

Rule No. 2 – Don't be stoopid. Keep your head out of your ass.

Rule No. 3 – Think safety. Live to fight another day and in the process don't kill anybody you're not supposed to.

Rule No. 4 – Remember that "negligent" or "careless" are not words you really want to see on your evaluation reports.

Rule No. 5 – Safety rules are not posted or briefed for kicks and giggles. Take them seriously and abide by them.

Don decided to finish his artistic roll before returning to more mundane tasks with a couple more posters, one motivational and the other inspirational, the first being:

And his coup de grâce in true Don Kennedy fashion:

* * *

Aside from the direct benefits of the military skills the recruited operators and specialists brought to 15th SOG, there were collateral benefits as well. Many if not most of the personnel coming to the unit brought with them side skills, such as mechanical, carpentry, even farming, and others that were valuable to the unit, the post, and the community at large (as well the various Howard family enterprises because they always had on the payroll a number of the SOG men whom they compensated well and accommodated their competing military duties). For instance, Sergeant Lewis, the armorer, began a side custom firearm business that was to become internationally renowned among gun enthusiasts; another NCO bred from American Kennel Club champion lines Labrador Retrievers, Brittany Spaniels, and American Foxhounds; and there were several reliable construction and painting crews.

Other collateral benefits came in the form of wives and extended families brought along. Hector's Vietnamese wife introduced and made successful a nail and pedicure salon in nearby Ridgeland and the two of them a "Mexasian" restaurant there that became so popular that they opened a "competing" one off Interstate Highway 95; a Korean wife teamed up with a Chinese wife to open a successful Chinese restaurant in Beaufort and Hispanic wives teamed with companions from Texas and New Mexico to open a Tex-Mex restaurant there too; several of the men joined together to build and with their wives operate a barbeque and fresh seafood place in neighboring Switzerland in the proverbial middle of nowhere, before then not much more than a curious sign on the side of a country road, with the locals soon learning that hours of operation depended on military duties and to call ahead to Miss Margaret before venturing out there; a German wife, a seamstress, opened a shop that soon expanded beyond alterations to embroidery and even custom clothing; and the list went on.

High among the collateral benefits came in the form of a government-imposed ecologist. Tom, Hector, and Don (the latter of whom ultimately would eat his words) complained bitterly about it and when the ecologist arrived, the simmering opposition almost turned into near revolt, for the scientist was not only young, but female. She in turn had more than a little concern with having to work with not only military types, but "snake eaters" as Green Berets often were referred to.

The fears of both sides soon were allayed, however, when it became apparent that they shared common goals and completely put to rest when she asked for a rifle and to be trained in its use in what was to be her personal war against wild hogs, coyotes, armadillos, and poisonous snakes (explaining the latter in that nonpoisonous snakes naturally would reproduce to fill the minimal biological gap). She would become of tremendous help not only in coordinating the locations of roads and adapting training areas, but also in the planting of food plots for both the benefit of wildlife and incorporation into training scenarios (the latter somewhat pretextually as the maturity of the plants happened to coincide with deer season). She also was fun to be around, a big plus. Her name was Eve.

* * *

Another family factored centrally into Camp Marion and environs becoming a thriving community, the Jeffersons.

In 1975, Major Tom Howard was sent to Fort Irwin in California, one of the prospective venues for the tentative first training exercise with the combined 15th SOG. He had favored Fort Stewart, Georgia, seconded by Fort Carson, Colorado, but with rumors abound that Fort Irwin was to be designated the National Training Center, it was worth a look see. Howard flew commercially, coach class, and with the anti-military sentiments having subsided he wore his uniform, complete with badges but not ribbons.

Before the airplane had even left the ground, however, a flight attendant approached him and quietly asked him to gather his things and follow her. She took him to the first-class cabin, invited him to take a seat and quietly told him, "Captain's compliments, sir. He said to tell you that he flew F105's in Vietnam." Howard in turn asked her to convey his appreciation and settled into the much more comfortable seat.

During a brief stop in Denver, the flight attendant again approached Tom. He, expecting to be bumped back to coach, was pleased to hear that another officer would be boarding and that the captain had directed that he too be afforded a vacant first-class seat, the one next to him.

Two minutes later, the other officer boarded the plane. With the practiced eye of a military man, Tom took in the essentials before the man even reached his seat: He was Army, a captain, combat with the 1st Cav, CIB, Bronze Star with "V", Purple Heart with oak leaf cluster, Good Conduct Medal (signifying prior enlisted service), now assigned to the 4th Infantry Division at Fort Carson, Colorado (nice!). It, however, was not until the two shook hands and greeted that Tom noticed the silver crosses of a Chaplain on his lapels. Tom's surprise was too obvious and the captain chuckled and said, "I know, I know, Whiskey, Tango, Foxtrot?" Yet another surprise.

The captain, who likewise had surveyed Howard's uniform and knew he was greeting a Green Beret major, reverted to more proper protocol. He took his seat, extended his right hand and said, "Isaac Jefferson, sir."

Tom Howard took the proffered hand and replied, "Call me Tom, Chaplain."

"Isaac for me, if it pleases the major. I'm not much for 'Ike.'"

"Isaac it is."

They struck up a conversation and the long flight, with cocktails, afforded them plenty of opportunity to not only get acquainted, but plenty of time for each of them to decide that they liked the other.

Jefferson gave an abbreviated account of the action for which he had been decorated (a version Tom correctly surmised was way too modest) and then gave a better account of what had followed.

They had bumped into a larger NVA unit and he, an M60 gunner, had fired them up and helped drive them off. As a parting salute though, the NVA sent an RPG round his way, which sent him sprawling. His wounds were not serious, but he was kept in the Army hospital in Vietnam a few days until the ringing in his ears caused by the RPG blast subsided.

He looked up the second morning and was shocked to see two sergeants major, one he recognized from his battalion and the other an imposing black man and not only a sergeant major, but a Command Sergeant Major from no less than the Pentagon named Davis. Jefferson was more willing to give a good recounting of that encounter.

"So, there I was, a lowly E-4, facing two E-9's for no apparent reason. It was tense, I must say. The black CSM got right down to business. 'Specialist,' he said, 'your Sergeant Major here tells me that you are not interested in promotion to sergeant.' He stared right through me and then said, 'That's bullshit, son. Bullshit. You are a hero and your superiors have confidence in your abilities to lead. The men of your unit need and deserve brave, good leaders. Your people, and now I am talking about black people, need and deserve black men being recognized for their bravery and they also need and deserve to see black leaders put in leadership positions. Your opposition is just selfish, plain selfish. Take the earned stripes and wear them with pride.'"

Jefferson continued, "The man was not taking 'no, thanks' for an answer. I was close enough to my DEROS that I was sent home, still with time on my enlistment. I hadn't been home long, Detroit, not enthused about my prospects, when orders came in the mail along with a handwritten note from the CSM. Presupposing I'd reenlist, I was to be promoted to sergeant, assigned to the ROTC department at Colorado Christian University and there afforded the opportunity to take college courses not conflicting with my duties." I figured, 'oh, why the hell not,' and agreed.

"I then heard from no less than the CO there, who told me to sign up for nine hours of core classes, that they'd work around it. I was amazed!

Then, under the general heading of 'the Lord moves in mysterious ways,' I met my Sarah. She led me to Biblical Studies and the CO was fine with that. Amazing! I even was able to reenlist for the same assignment and finish both my bachelor's and my master's! I'm working on my doctorate. Of course, the Army being the Army, there was a catch: I owed them four years in the Chaplain Corps. Even then I was blessed to be assigned to the 4th ID. I'm a blessed man, sir, er, Tom. I'm now on my way to some boondoggle in San Diego. Frankly it's a waste of the taxpayers' money since Sarah and I are planning on a change."

"What sort of change?"

"Out. Finish my doctorate, find a place to teach or preach, wherever the Lord calls us, I guess."

Listening to this heartwarming story and finding himself drawn to the man, Howard had an epiphany as the plane approached its destination. He said to the captain, "Isaac, you should think about South Carolina. I am stationed with a bunch of rogues at a small post not far inland from the coast." Boldly he continued on a roll, "We can find you a good place to live, build you a church, provide you sinners, maybe get you a Guard or Reserve chaplain's slot for some income on the side, and retirement security. Seriously, think about coming down. Bring Sarah. Check us out. In the meantime, I could see if I can put flesh on the bones of what I said."

The two officers exchanged information and parted in the terminal. Tom gave the matter a lot of thought the next few days, talked about it with Katie, his father, and Bill Greer, and even checked on the feasibility of a chaplain's slot. When a week later Isaac called to accept the invitation, Tom was able to assure him that he was not just blowing smoke.

The Jeffersons came a few weeks later. By then Tom had obtained provisional and conditional commitments: Bill Greer would provide four acres close to the front gate of Fort Marion for a church on some sort of favorable lease/purchase plan and would finance the cost of materials; the Howard family and 15th SOG would provide much of the land clearing and construction labor; the Howards would spruce up the old home place for the Jeffersons to stay in; and SCARNG would seriously consider Jefferson to fill a vacant Chaplain's slot that possibly could be expanded to cover Camp Marion and possibly help fund the church (always though a sticky issue with notions of separation of church and state) in lieu of building a chapel on post (something Tom felt remiss in not having provided).

Tom and Katie, often accompanied by Don Kennedy, gave Isaac and Sarah the grand tour of Camp Marion, Beaufort, and surrounds on up to Charleston and down to Hilton Head, allowing a good while to show off the old home place. The five became fast friends. The Jeffersons, Howards, Greers, and Kennedys discussed every aspect they could think of and before the visit was over all concerned were inclined to make it happen. In due time, it happened.

When the Jeffersons made their move, the old home place was ready for them and they had plenty of help moving in. Isaac immediately commenced his ministry, using the training room for Sunday services. Each week drew more in attendance. Construction of a church morphed from Tom's promise to a priority and then an urgency as the Camp Marion facilities soon grew woefully inadequate. Plans were made, funds were secured, and the construction process commenced.

There, however, was a slight glitch. One day Don Kennedy, ever the devil's helper, presented Isaac with orders he had procured for him for jump school. Reveling in Isaac's grim reaction, Don matter-of-factly expressed, "What the hell would it say about us if we had a chaplain without the faith to jump?" Isaac could not fault his reasoning. (Well, he could have, but…)

So Isaac launched into a painful but productive regimen of running, push-ups, and pull-ups and then headed off to Fort Benning for the three-week course. When Isaac proudly returned with his paratrooper wings, Don followed his congratulations with the evil suggestion that he ought to next go to Ranger school. Isaac drew the line by emphatically responding, "Oh, hell no!"

Instead Isaac eagerly pitched in on the construction of the church and used that as a ministry opportunity, showing the volunteers that being a Christian did not require being fault free or stuffy. In less than three months, the church buildings were completed. First was the annex, a project by which Tom's Uncle Bob, never a churchgoer, surprised many by volunteering to direct. He tagged one of his builder friends to be the general contractor. When the builder complained that the contract offered scant profit, Uncle Bob snapped at him, "Think of your goddamn soul, man!" (Sometimes you just had to shake your head with Uncle Bob.)

The annex had a pastor's study (furnishings a gift from Tom and Katie Howard) with windows facing a serene stand of woods in the back (soon to be enhanced with dogwood and redbud trees and azaleas and camellias, Eve's contribution); rooms for Sunday school classes, administration, and storage; a large, modern kitchen with appliances and fixtures salvaged by Bob Howard from a failed restaurant; an assembly hall opening to a covered outside area with long rows of tables and a barbecue pit constructed by Camp Marion soldiers (under the *very* close supervision of Bob), which also would serve as a covered walkway to the chapel.

When that building was dried in, construction of the chapel itself began, led by Dan Howard and Don Kennedy. To naturally deter termites, serious threats to structures in the south, the building sat on heart pine blocks and was framed in cyprus. The wood was provided by Carl Howard. While he had a rigid policy that he would not cut cyprus, live oak, or mature oaks of any kind, he knew where nature had taken down such trees. He took Jake's crew out and personally supervised the reclaiming of just the right fallen timber and then personally supervised its milling and curing.

The chapel was entered through a pair of massive arched oak doors

Don Kennedy had found in an architectural reclamation business in Atlanta, was sided with board and batten and topped with a tin roof. The sanctuary, with seating for over a hundred, had antebellum pews and an incredible altar acquired from a church that had "modernized" and stuck them in storage (a gift of the Kennedys), and stained glass windows (paid for by the many of the families, with Hector Ramirez insisting that he pay for the one behind the pulpit he himself had crafted from select oak).

It was a beautiful little church in a beautiful setting and cause for celebration by many, which indeed they did as they witnessed the finishing touches: A massive, roughly hewn cross flanked by two slightly smaller ones (gifts of Carl and Bea Howard) affixed to the front of the chapel, in front of which a sign (a gift from the Greers) was unveiled that said it all:

MARION CHAPEL
Sharing the Good News with All God's Children
Rev. Isaac Jefferson

The congregation of Marion Chapel grew quickly. For many folks just hearing Isaac Jefferson preach one time was enough. The congregation began with Camp Marion people and then their families and friends, young and old. Uncle Bob and his family soon joined as well, Uncle Bob explaining that he was tired of the preacher at First Baptist telling him he was going to hell. When the black community learned that there was a powerful and loving new black preacher in their midst, they came to see and many joined. Before long the pews were filled every Sunday and soon services were brightened by a choir that sang marvelously, accompanied by the music played on a fine piano donated by the Greers. (An organ would follow.)

It was a thriving, vibrant church. It became the focal point of the Camp Marion community. With white, black, Hispanic, and Asian parishioners, it was an unusual (some would say eclectic, others aberrant) congregation for the rural south, but not unusual for military communities. It was a microcosm, indeed a model, of America and it was strong because it had at its core warriors, women attracted to warriors, and children that came from their union.

And they had not only Isaac and Sarah Jefferson, but before long a baby to cherish. Settled and with a bright future, the Jeffersons decided to start having children. Little Emily Jefferson came along and became like a little sister to the Howard children (an affinity that never ended), the relationship soon extending to the entire Howard family and the Camp Marion family and before long to the community and beyond.

I I

WHILE THE MISSION OF 15TH SOG INCLUDED READINESS FOR combat operations, its primary mission was training, first themselves, then National Guard and Reserve NCO's and junior officers, and later small units. It would grow well beyond that, but first they had to grow into it.

The 15th SOG special operators, to a man, came there motivated, trained, experienced, and proficient, but to gel as a team always took time, practice, communication, and hard work. Accordingly, Alpha Company spent a lot of time in the field, more often than not to practice land navigation and patrolling skills; so much so that the operators were only half joking when they groused that their leaders (mainly Howard and Kennedy and for a few years Ramirez and Clark) were bound and determined that every man step foot on each of Camp Marion's 50,000 acres, especially those under water.

Don Kennedy's favorite game was the adult version of "capture the flag," made exponentially more challenging with daunting time constraints, active patrols with soldiers equipped with the MILES system (the "Multiple Integrated Laser Engagement System" where each soldier had a laser affixed to his firearm and laser sensors to detect hits), ambushes, booby traps with simulator explosives, and sometimes even hostile aircraft; not to mention leaders routinely being "killed" or mates purposefully being "wounded" and needing to be dealt with, and all manner of things Don's devious mind could come up with if anyone appeared to be getting too cocky.

They also spent a great deal of time at the range honing their marksmanship at the set targets and going through various courses devised to be as realistic as possible. They also cross-trained on every weapon organic to the unit as well as foreign weapons like the AK-47, British L85 and SA80 assault rifles and the novel Austrian Steyr AUG's. The designated snipers spent even more time there mastering their deadly art.

Being an airborne unit, they jumped often and all who already did not have it, soon wore the star above their wings, designating senior status (30+ jumps (half with combat gear) and graduation from the Jumpmaster Course) and most (including Don Kennedy and Isaac Jefferson) acquired the wreath about the star signifying master parachutist status (65 jumps, 25 with combat gear, and 36 months in jump status). At any given time, more than half of the Green Berets also wore the Military Freefall Parachutist Badge or "Halo" (high altitude, low opening) badge.

Being by definition also an air assault unit, Alpha with the benefit of pilots from Hunter Army Airfield down in nearby Savannah constantly seeking flight time, regularly practiced air assault techniques. The 15th SOG operators also sought and got training from active special ops units, individually went to a variety of schools, and annually they collectively trained with their sister companies respectively for desert and mountain warfare, who in turn would come to Camp Marion for refresher training in that environment.

15th SOG lived by the adage that there is nothing like doing to learn and nothing like being a teacher to learn. For 15th SOG, training as trainers began with schools, augmented by classes by the schooled and more experienced, then doing, over and over, day and night, whatever the weather. As trainers, they began with small groups of SCARNG NCO's and junior officers and later small units. One of the cornerstones of Special Forces is to train indigenous forces and, frankly, the state and motivation of many of the guardsmen fit the bill all too well. Alpha Company nonetheless succeeded. Word began to spread, first in state and then in the special ops world, that Camp Marion and 15th SOG afforded good training opportunities. Camp Marion became a desired training venue and Alpha Company became respected and desired as trainers, such that before long there was a waiting list for training.

As word spread farther, training expanded to an array of others. A captain by the name of David Petraeus came up from Fort Stewart, the Army post below Savannah that housed the 24th (later redesignated the 3rd) Infantry Division, and asked the 15th SOG to lay on training and serve as OPFOR (opposing forces) for small units from the Second Brigade. That expanded to the First Brigade and then to the 1st Battalion of the 75th Ranger Regiment stationed at Hunter Army Airfield in Savannah and on to special operators stationed in the southeast United States, as well as to groups of Citadel cadets.

What, however, really made them the most renowned was that the training they offered not only was challenging and effective, but it was much more fun than that offered by the more rigid active Army. The Camp Marion sniper training not only was excellent, but also was capped with a wild hog hunt that served to not only control the numbers of wild hogs, but also enabled Alpha to often conclude training weeks with an awesome barbecue. For that they became legendary in the special ops world.

While Alpha Company had wanted to appropriately dub themselves the "Swamp Foxes" for their namesake, they found out to their chagrin that the South Carolina Air National Guard already had incongruously adopted the name. Nobody could agree on a fearsome stealthy predator to adopt for their logo and it was not until Alpha Company began to be called the "Swamp Hogs" that they had a moniker that stuck. Soon a sign appeared front and center on the wall of the common room:

ALPHA, 15TH SOG

SWAMP HOGS

The ultimate grunts
"Go ahead, punk, make my day…"

They even had t-shirts and challenge coins made (by a local enterprise of their own) with that logo, which special operators and enthusiasts near and far were happy to trade for or buy. When asked if Hollywood might object to their incorporating for the bottom line the immortal words of Clint Eastwood's "Dirty Harry" Callahan in the iconic 1971 blockbuster of the same name, Don Kennedy expressed confidence that their "legal consultant," Hector Ramirez, could handle it.

Alpha trained hard to earn their place in the spec ops world. It was no small feat to become respected in that exclusive world and Alpha worked hard to gain that respect. Year after year, 15th SOG operators placed high in the premier Best Ranger Competition and in the International Sniper Competition. Alpha Company also regularly distinguished itself in annual unofficial competitions with instructors from the Special Warfare Center and School at Fort Bragg and from the U.S. Army Sniper School at Fort Benning, as well as with the Regimental Reconnaissance Company of the Special Troops Battalion of the 75th Ranger Regiment also at Fort Benning. Don Kennedy made the Army Times by placing well in the tough 10K Charleston Cooper River Bridge Run, the accompanying photo reflecting not only his prosthesis, but also his t-shirt emblazoned with the "Swamp Hogs" logo.

As a whole, each of the three 15th SOG companies became sought after for tough opposing forces (OPFOR) in training exercises and their training curriculum (particularly in long range reconnaissance patrol (LRRP) skills) was acclaimed and in high demand for units ranging from the National Guard to the full sphere of spec ops, including the vaunted Tier One units (the Army's Delta Force and Ranger Regiment), Navy SEAL DEVGRU (also known as SEAL Team Six), and the Army and Air Force special aviation units (and in later years MARSOC, the U.S. Marine Corps Special Operations Command formed in 2005)). Off the books, 15th SOG even worked with operators from the equally secretive SAD/SOG, the Special Activities Division/Special Operations Group, the CIA's paramilitary unit. In time, they also trained with elite spec ops units from foreign countries, including the British SAS (touted (although hardly undisputed) as the best of the best), Canada, Israel, France, South Korea, Thailand, and others.

In addition to training, the 15th SOG operators and technicians did field testing of weapons, ammunition, experimental communications equipment, and equipment of all kinds. For many, that was the most fun part. Glock, the pistol manufacturer wanting a bigger piece of the Army pie, brought them cases of pistols and pallets of ammunition and asked them to abuse them as much as they could to prove the quality of the weapons. They did not ask for returns. The 15th SOG operators fell in love with the Glock handguns and other splendid weapons such as the Heckler & Koch MP5 submachine gun.

The assortment of other things tested included such things as rappelling ropes and gloves, boots, hydration packs to replace canteens, insect repellent, and more. But it certainly is arguable that the greatest evolution in the modern military was in the development of night vision devices and individual night vision goggles rendering the American military unsurpassed in the ability to "see" and fight at night or in other low visibility conditions and 15th SOG played a significant role in field testing experimental versions of each and later in training in and training on each version adopted by the Army.

The concept and organization of 15th SOG was evaluated and endorsed at highest levels. Although neither the organization nor concept was approved for the active Army, in a few short years the value of 15th SOG became undisputed as a special arrow in the spec ops quiver. While the 15th SOG "arrow" was not pulled from the quiver for actual combat or black operations for many years (few of the charter members of 15th SOG would again see combat), the 15th SOG archers, so to speak, were in high demand to hone the skills of the special operators (and in later years conventional warriors) called upon to conduct real world operations around the globe.

As goes the saying, "Success breeds success" (attributed almost certainly incorrectly to soccer legend Mia Hamm), 15th SOG's reputation enabled it to easily recruit members when the need arose.

* * *

While people naturally came and went over the years, for Alpha Company a core group remained and life was good. For Tom Howard, it was an idyllic life. He had his professional life, good friends, and a wonderful, close-knit family. Katie was a wonderful wife and she gave him three marvelous children. Jonathan, the oldest, and the youngest, Bradley Oliver (known as "Bo"), grew up on Camp Marion and in roaming with their father, grandfather, and sometimes even their great-grandfather, the accumulated acreage of the Howard family. As the boys aged, their different personalities emerged, with Bo gravitating toward the Camp Marion soldiers and weaponry and Jon their families and fascinating array of foreign languages and cultures. The middle child, Margaret, called

Maggie, a bright, precocious girl, was commonly predicted to become the family's first doctor (the Jeffersons' Emily to be the first lawyer).

The highest points of life, however, all too often are set in stark contrast by the lowest of lows. For Tom Howard, a low point was the death of his grandmother, Miss Faith, whom he dearly loved. She was laid in what was to become the Howard family plot on the grounds of Marion Chapel after a tender service officiated by Reverend Isaac Jefferson. The lowest point for Tom was the death of his grandfather not quite six months later.

After reading the usual reassuring scriptures, Reverend Isaac Jefferson delivered a stirring eulogy:

"My friends," he began, "we gather here together in the Lord's house to celebrate the life of Carl Howard. Well, I say that, but many of you are outside the Lord's house," alluding to that the sanctuary was packed, standing room only, and there were as many people clustered in the annex and in folding chairs out in front of the chapel. When the polite laughter subsided, he more solemnly continued:

"All of us are deeply saddened by this great loss and many of you mourn, and rightly so. Mister Carl's passing was, and will continue to be for some time, a great loss indeed to family and friends and to the community. It is okay to cry. You, too, Bob Howard, let it go. I cry too. But we can and we must take comfort in one certainty: There is no doubt, *no doubt*, friends, that Mister Carl is with Jesus and his beloved Faith.

"We all know that Mister Carl had a great heart and by his actions that he was a man of faith. Here I speak of spiritual faith. I bear witness to that his faith was deep and passionate. Mister Carl befriended me when the Lord first led me here, unsurprisingly to those of you who best knew the man, and I will cherish for the rest of my days here on Earth the many, many times he and I wrestled with scriptures and matters of faith.

"Friends, I have been saved many times in my life. My parents guided me well through my youth and teen years, turbulent years here in America. The Lord spared my life in Vietnam when I must confess I was not of His flock. There was a man, a stranger, who saw hope in me and led me to my Sarah, who saved me even before Jesus. And then there was Mister Carl.

"Few of you think of preachers ever struggling with faith, but we do. We, too, see the evil in the world. We get immersed in baffling scriptures. The Lord does not answer our prayers quickly or clearly enough to our liking. We doubt. We fail. We need someone to turn to. Now, don't get me wrong, I am truly blessed to have Sarah at my side, but it was Mister Carl who the Lord sent to take my other hand and guide me. No, that's not right. Tom Howard has that other hand. Mister Carl instead was behind me, whispering in my ear and now and then giving me a good shove in the right direction, sometimes even a needed kick in the butt.

"But Mister Carl was put on this Earth for more than mere me, so much more. He started out here as a swamp logger, as he liked to call it. Now that was in the old days before they had all those fearsome machines Dan and Bob like to block traffic with. Axes and saws, muscles and sweat, chains and mules. He was tough then. He was tough to the end.

"Mister Carl went off to the First World War, the War to End All Wars, and came home a sergeant with scars to bear witness to what he suffered and overcame over there. He was cited for conspicuous valor, an act of amazing bravery that saved the lives of a score of men.

"Overcoming challenges was what Carl Howard did. Look at his successful businesses. Look at his wonderful family. He was a cornerstone of this church, yet another understatement. He was a Mason too, godly men of character. Many of his proud Masonic brothers are here to pay tribute to him.

"Friends, I could go on and on, but all I'm really doing is reminding you of what you already know. So, I will close. First, a prayer. Please bow your heads. 'Lord, please help me each and every day to be more like Mister Carl Howard. Amen.' And now a closing hymn. I will confide to you that Mister Carl forbade 'Amazing Grace' from this service. He said it was 'too Baptist,' no offense intended, and I am confident none taken. Instead, friends, let your hearts be lightened by the hymn Mister Carl chose." At that the Marion Chapel choir commenced the heartfelt singing of "In the Sweet By-and-By" and its apt words: "There's a land that is fairer than day, and by faith we can see it afar; for the Father waits over the way to prepare us a dwelling place there … In the sweet in the sweet by and by, we shall meet on that beautiful shore …

"Please rise for the benediction. 'May the Lord bless you and keep you; may the Lord shine His face upon you, be gracious to you and give you peace. Amen.'"

Carl Howard's body was laid to rest next to Faith's, first with a few more words from Reverend Jefferson and the Lord's Prayer; then full military honors, impeccably performed by Camp Marion soldiers; and finally with a solemn, impressive Masonic funeral service ending with the Master displaying a sprig and reverently saying, "This evergreen is an emblem of our faith in the immortality of the soul. By it, we are reminded of our high and glorious destiny beyond the 'world of shadows' and that there dwells within our tabernacle of clay an imperishable, immortal spirit, over which the grave has no dominion, and death not power."

Isaac Jefferson concluded the graveside service with, "And now, friends, the ladies of the church and our very own Uncle Bob are pleased to send you off with delightfully full bellies, the kind of thing we do here every Sunday. Come back and see us."

The family had been directed to remain afterward. The Jeffersons were asked to join as well. Dan Howard faced the family and said, "Thanks for sticking around. It's getting harder and harder to get y'all together and Bob and I figured we might as well do the reading of the will today."

Dan did not actually read the will so artfully crafted by the lawyers. Instead he summarized the disposition of Carl Howard's formidable estate. The Howard businesses would go to the sons, he and Bob; each also with bequests of properties, Dan's being the house out on Edisto Island and Bob's the old home place and acreage, roughly of equivalent monetary value. Carl's island, which many thought to have been a foolish investment, and the vacant lot adjacent to the Edisto house were put into a trust, along with a sizeable amount of money. A separate trust was established for younger Howard generations, including a considerable amount of money and a number of parcels and tracts of land. That Emily Jefferson was included was met with mild surprise, but without complaint. The same was true when Dan announced that Marion Chapel was to be generously endowed, including a stipend effectively for at least ten years doubling Isaac Jefferson's theretofore modest remuneration.

When it was all said and done, not a soul left dissatisfied.

* * *

Elsewhere on the globe, the 1980's were unstable and increasingly violent. Tom Howard, promoted to lieutenant colonel and made Group Commander, took due notice and pressed 15th SOG to remain vigilant.

It therefore was accepted with trepidation when Jonathan Howard graduated from high school in 1989 he eschewed college and instead enlisted in the Army for flight school. The feeling was greatly exacerbated when he was bumped from the program after flunking a color vision test, the same test he had passed multiple times in his youth and even in his prescreening. Instead of the cockpit of a helicopter in Alabama, Jon found himself in the turret of an Abrams tank in Germany.

On August 2, 1990, the irrational Iraqi dictator, Saddam Hussein, citing transparently pretextual cause, invaded, conquered, and annexed neighboring Kuwait. In response, the United States and coalition forces launched Operation Desert Shield and Tom and Katie's fears were realized when Jon was among the many deployed to the region.

Tom Howard also was called up. Kicking himself that he had not retired when he said he would when he had run the gamut of 15th SOG and was reassigned to SCARNG headquarters in Columbia, Tom read the orders to report to the staff of the U.S. Special Operations Command staff at MacDill Air Force Base outside of Tampa, Florida. Though unhappy about it, Tom was not about to seek a way out.

The special ops headquarters boasted a formidable assemblage of tier one warriors. To be sure, it would be difficult to conceive of a greater collection of A-type personalities. That is not to say that every one of them was the real deal. While they all bore the array of badges one would expect of elite special operators, and they all had impressive service records, many had not been tested in actual combat. They also could be catty, like old women.

So it was that when at his first staff meeting Lieutenant Colonel Howard was introduced to the legendary commander, General Carl Stiner, and reference was made to his coming from the South Carolina Army National Guard there were some subtle (and soon to be regrettable) snickers from the side seats.

Standing in the doorway immediately behind them was a Command Master Chief Petty Officer whose uniform was adorned with the trident of a Navy SEAL. Calling the man "imposing" would have been comparable to referring to a Great White shark as a big fish. The Command Master Chief respectfully cleared his throat, catching the general's attention.

"Might I butt in for a moment, sir?"

"Certainly, Master Chief."

"Sir. Now I may be mistaken, but it seemed to me that when you introduced the colonel, there were some little girl snickers from some straphangers in the cheap seats. Of course, I could be wrong. Probably so. I am just an old frogman. Hard to imagine from such an elite group of warriors such disrespect. Or stupidity, my humble pardons to anyone due." If the Master Chief had not at first had the full attention of everyone in the room, he did now, with most thinking, "*this is going to be good*," and more than a few thinking more aptly the exact opposite.

"You see, sir, being the highly-trained special operators we are, with extraordinary observation skills, I expect everyone noticed that the colonel is an Airborne Ranger Green Beret. Perhaps some missed his CIB, his combat infantryman's badge, and not every one of our Army colleagues has one of those, I don't believe. Perhaps some missed that the colonel's got the SF patch on his right shoulder, signifying of course, a combat tour with a Special Forces unit, and not every one of our Army colleagues here has one of those either, I don't believe. Hmmm, what was that? Oh, yeah, some little outfit called MACV-SOG." A collective "*oh, shit*" feeling engulfed the guilty parties while the innocent enjoyed the show.

"While Colonel Howard may not be a tier one SEAL or Delta operator, let me tell you that he was the founding father and ultimately commander of the 15th Special Operations Group, composite Green Berets and Rangers. It started at Camp Marion, South Carolina. Some of you may be lucky enough to be familiar with them, the 'Swamp Hogs.' I am. Been there, got the t-shirt." It then dawned on Tom Howard who the speaker was, but the thought was interrupted as the man continued:

"It soon expanded to mountain and desert units, later an amazing urban warfare center, then a godawful swamp warfare site, and then my beloved Navy got on board with a reserve SEAL unit. Rumor has it that an air wing is in the making too, rotary and fixed. The colonel here figured centrally in all that.

"But that's not all. I did a little homework on the colonel," and after pausing for effect, while making eye contact with a couple of the naysayers, "as I do for everyone who joins our gang. It seems that the colonel has picked up a decoration or two along the way." Pretending to read off a sheet of paper, the Master Chief continued, "Let's see, hmmm, an ARCOM with "V" device, a Bronze Star with "V" device; the Silver Star times two; and, oh yes, the Purple Heart times three.

"Now, I know that there're one or two in this illustrious group who can match or top those honors, but I also made a phone call to an old army friend and you know what he told me? The second Silver Star was for singlehandedly, *singlehandedly*, rescuing a LRRP team trapped behind enemy lines."

The silence in the room was palpable. The general appeared amused while two or three of the attendees appeared to be on the verge of puking. Satisfied, the Master Chief smiled and closed with, "My pardons, General. By your leave, I will go about my business."

Later that day, when Tom looked up the Master Chief to thank him for what he had done, he found him in no lesser company than that of General Stiner. When the Master Chief spied Tom, his eyes lit up and turning back to the general he asked, "Time for a war story, sir? I even brought a corroborating witness." The general nodded, the three entered his office and the Master Chief launched into his story:

"Sir, about ten years ago when I was still spry enough to be on a team, we went to Camp Marion for a different place to train. They gave us an objective, three days and three nights to take it and about ten thousand acres to play with, allowing us to infiltrate wherever we wanted. Being SEALs, we chose to come in through the most evil swamp we could find. They shoulda figured that."

Tom Howard chimed in. "Sir, for two full days and nights they, in our own damn back yard mind you, evaded our hunters, a home team of SF and Rangers, and then shocked the guys manning the objective by taking them before they knew it. The most humbling part was that they then got clean away! We first saw them when they showed up with the OPFOR flag at base camp, asking where the beer was.

"The best part, though, was after the debrief. Our Sergeant Major, Hector Ramirez," the general indicating with a smile his familiarity with the man, "called in the entire OPFOR, locked their heels, and gave them a royal blessing out, calling them, as I distinctly recall, 'short bus special operators.' It was, as they say, 'a learning experience,' in a most humbling way."

The Master Chief chimed back in, "That's what training is all about, fuckin' up by the numbers so it doesn't happen when a real mission and lives are on the line; but, sir, I gotta say that the Swamp Hogs didn't let wounded pride interfere with one helluva a party afterward."

Tom chuckled and said, "I'll drink to that."

The general, deciding that it was as good a time as any, broke out a bottle of Wild Turkey and the three old warriors spent the evening in war story mode, some of them even true.

A few days later, Tom Howard found himself back at the door of the general's office. He knocked on the door frame and General Stiner, on the telephone, signaled him to come in, close the door, and have a seat. The general wrapped up the call and turned his full attention to his new subordinate.

"Tom, I've been thinking, thinking and talking on the phone, that's what I do. Between us girls, Tom, there's some unhealthy friction over there in the Gulf. As you may know, General Schwarzkopf is not one of our biggest fans. What I'd like you to do is go over there ASAP, talk with Kraus and his people in 5th Group, get a good feel for things, and then gain an audience with the general. Use my name, the Chief's if necessary. I want you to persuade him that our guys can be a real asset to him.

"Once you get Stormin' Norman on board, I want you to go back out to the field and spend a few days to monitor the hopefully favorable changes, find out what we can do for them, and come back and report to me. Orders for you are being cut, and I'll see that the necessary calls are made to grease the skids."

Tom Howard was ushered before General Schwarzkopf seven days later, feeling like he was being tossed into the den of the bear. Stormin' Norman was notorious for his violent temper and for chewing up lieutenant colonels and spitting them out. For Tom though it was nothing of the kind. The general was almost affable. He started the conversation with, "So, I've ruffled some feathers in the special ops world and you've been sent here as the lamb to slaughter?"

Tom replied, "Well, sir, I don't doubt my expendability, but it's really nothing of the sort. My mission is to explain to you that 'our guys can be a real asset' to you," holding up his fingers simulating quotation marks, "something I believe I can do in ten minutes' time and be on my way back to Florida, and soon thereafter South Carolina."

"Ten minutes, huh?" The general looked at his watch and said, "Make it eight. Go."

Tom pulled out a map and from it showed the general in the allotted time how dozens of teams could and would covertly infiltrate the battle area days before the attack and provide operative intelligence on the terrain, conditions, Iraqi forces or lack thereof, and other factors he, as commander, would want to know, need to know, that satellites and aircraft simply could not be totally relied upon to do. He stressed that the teams could and would stay ahead and to the west of the attacking forces, well beyond the prudent range of his own scouts, and continue to provide such intel. He assured the general that the Special Forces teams fully understood that mission and would succeed or die trying.

The general sat back in his chair, looked at his watch, actually smiled and said, "Good enough. Tell 'your guys' and General Stiner that this command welcomes and has full confidence in and appreciation of the value of the Special Forces contribution to our accomplishment of the mission." After some moments of thought, he added, "You also could suggest to the good general that I would be pleased by your being assigned here as liaison officer."

And so Tom Howard became a veteran of Operations Desert Shield and Desert Storm. When the dust settled afterward, General Schwarzkopf publicly commented that the Special Forces had been his "eyes and ears" and the "glue that held the coalition together." Tom headed back to MacDill where a grateful General Stiner pinned one more medal on his chest before sending him home.

While Tom had planned to then resign, he was enticed to stay on by a promotion to full colonel with the amorphous position as a senior advisor and more so by both the commanding general and governor confiding to him their fear of a repeat of the embarrassment neighboring Georgia had suffered when its 48th Brigade failed to be certified as combat ready for deployment to the Persian Gulf.

I 2

JONATHAN HOWARD'S EXPERIENCES IN DESERT SHIELD AND DESERT
Storm were far more gritty, literally, than his father's. Deployed to the
Gulf with the 3rd Armored Division (3AD), the "Spearhead" division
of World War Two fame where it spearheaded the First Army through
Normandy, fought in the Hürtgen Forest and then the Battle of the
Bulge, crossed the Siegfried line into Germany, and fought its way
deep into the country, Jonathan was a crew member in one of the 1,800
M1A1 Abrams main battle tanks in theatre. It was to be the first test of
combat for the new tank and first taste of combat for all but a few of the
tankers. Jon, a Spec 4, had earned his advancement from loader to driver
to gunner and intensive training had readied him for the task at hand.

The 3AD crossed the berm into Iraq on Day One with 1AD on its
left and the 2nd Armored Cavalry Regiment (2ACR) on its right. That
day they blew through shocked Iraqi blocking positions and advanced
18 miles into the country. Jon saw no enemy tanks. Instead he fired the
main gun at bunkers and gunned down stubborn enemy infantry with
his coax, the M240 machine gun mounted coaxially with the main gun,
while the TC (tank commander) did the same with his big .50 cal up top.

Day Two was more of the same, advancing another 35 miles, the
Iraqis in their way killed, captured, or caused to flee. Jon was credited
with three tank kills that day. The first was an impressive hit on a T72 at
well over 2,500 meters that blew the turret off with a spectacular fireball.

The other two, also beyond the enemy's effective range, probably had been abandoned by panicked crews, but counted nonetheless.

The division met its first serious resistance on Day Three when they bumped into the Iraqi Republican Guard. Scouts in Bradley fighting vehicles first detected the enemy in the early morning darkness and with their superior thermal and night vision systems were able to creep undetected up to within two kilometers of their front lines. There they patiently awaited the arrival of tanks to augment the already awesome destructive power of their 25mm chain guns and TOW (tube-launched, optically tracked, wire-guided) missiles.

Jon's tank was one of the first to arrive. They eased up to a slight rise so that only the turret peeked over it.

"Driver, stop," the TC commanded over the intercom, "gunner scan sector for targets." The TC then, through his night vision goggles, scanned either side of the tank to insure that they had not blundered upon an LP that in his mind should have been there and to decide where to reposition the tank after each shot or two.

Jon reported, "Got a line of dug in tanks 2K out and something interesting behind them. I'm thinking command track."

The TC dropped back down and got on his oriented magnified sights. "I'm on it, but I don't identify a track." Just then there was a flash and then glow at the target a mile away. "Identified, I think, but whiskey tango foxtrot?"

Jon replied, "That's a dumbass sentry lighting a damn cigarette. That's the rear hatch behind him. Kill spot ought to be right about here," as he eased the point of aim over a tad.

"HEAT in the tube, right?" The TC was referring to the M830 high explosive anti-tank round. The loader confirmed it. "Loader, stand by with sabot for before or after." He was referring to the M829A1 armor-piercing fin-stabilized discarding-sabot round, essentially a non-explosive dart of depleted uranium capable of penetrating at maximum range the armor of the T-62 and T-72 Russian tanks they were facing and destroying and killing via the overpressure and molten steel resulting from the kinetic energy penetration.

"LT may want to take out the tanks first."

"Better to cut off the head of the snake," Jon offered.

"I'll check with him."

After the platoon tanks reported in and the platoon leader concurred with their choices of targets, he alerted the company commander who had joined the line that they were ready to engage. The other platoon on line did the same. The CO radioed back, "Stand by. Fire at my command and then fire at will."

The TC relayed the command to the crew. Jon confirmed his point of aim. The CO came back on the radio and betrayed his nervousness by repeating, "Stand by to fire, stand by to fire."

Although he knew through his own sights that the gun was still laid on target, the TC went through the prescribed drill. "Target?"

"Identified," Jon responded followed by an "up" from the loader signifying that the gun was loaded and the safety was off.

"*Fire!*" the captain unnecessarily yelled into the boom microphone affixed to his CVC (combat vehicle crewman's) helmet.

"*Fire!*" relayed the TC, also too loudly.

"*On the w-a-y,*" announced Jon as he squeezed the trigger on his controls.

BOOM! The 120mm smoothbore cannon fired and the sixty-ton tank rocked back with the recoil. The muzzle blast and sand kicked up temporarily blinded the TC and gunner, but the range was far enough that it cleared in time to see the round's tracer and then the flash of impact. There, however, quite disappointingly was no secondary explosion and it was Jon's turn to come over the intercom with a "whiskey tango?" No sooner had the words left his lips than the vehicle flared and began burning.

"Sabot loaded," the loader reported.

Jon made sure that the computer was set for the faster round and then tracked to his preplanned second target. "Tank identified."

"Up."

"Fire," ordered the TC and Jon again instantly squeezed the trigger after his "on the way." Again, the cannon roared and the tank rocked back with the recoil. An instant later, Jon and the TC were rewarded with the sight of a flash and fireworks display of sparks, telltale of a sabot hit on armor. The TC barked, "Driver, back up!" Before the behemoth even could move, the turret of the enemy tank was spinning off the chassis as stored ammunition exploded.

The TC directed the tank to a position about twenty yards away and from that new vantage point he and Jon scanned for more targets. There were none. The combined firepower of eleven Abrams tanks and three Bradleys had made short work of the Iraqi line of tanks. They were well beyond the effective range of any infantry weapons, so Jon scanned out farther. The suspected command track now was burning brightly. There were no more targets.

The TC ordered, "Cease fire. Safe all weapons." Switching to the platoon net, he radioed that the sector was cleared with two kills. He then told Jon to continue scanning. Soon though, the order came down to cease fire and secure weapons. They were to overwatch as the infantry came up and were led to the enemy position by mine clearing engineers. Once the engineers got the infantry to the Iraqi front line, they reversed course to clear and mark lanes for the tracked vehicles to follow. In the meantime, the TC allowed Jon to come out of the turret and watch the show as the Air Force mercilessly hunted down the fleeing Iraqi vehicles and methodically destroyed them with missiles, 20mm cannons, or 30mm Gatling guns.

It was the loader who first realized and excitedly said over the intercom, "Hey, guys, that's five for us. We're aces!"

Cleared to advance, Jon's TC directed the driver through the closest cleared lane, past the T72 they had killed and up to Jon's first target. It indeed was a command vehicle, but wheeled rather than tracked. It was smoking, but no longer burning.

The TC had the tank stop and hopped down to check it out and one of the bodies that looked interesting. He returned to the tank, plugged in his CVC and radioed his find to the platoon leader. He then handed Jon a slightly scorched beret with a garish metal crest, quietly keeping the dead colonel's pistol for himself.

Jon's unit joined in the pursuit of the decimated Iraqi unit. He saw dozens of destroyed vehicles and scores of Iraqis waiting for the chance to surrender, but the Americans met only scattered, token resistance. The next day, Day Four, was much of the same. It was "TC" day though, Jon's tank commander blowing up an Iraqi fuel tanker with his .50 cal and later pulling the trigger on a probably abandoned tank, just to be able to say he did, and just in case "ace" status turned out to require that the kills all be armored vehicles.

On the fifth day, however, the Iraqis put up stiff resistance, paying dearly for it with the loss of some three hundred vehicles and countless men. Jon's platoon nearly met disaster when they were fired upon by a platoon of enemy tanks. The Iraqi commander had learned the hard way the deadly effectiveness of American thermal sights and ordered his remaining tanks to lay in wait hull down with the engines off. That and camouflage allowed them to avoid detection until the Americans were in range.

A volley of fire destroyed a Bradley and a round glanced off the turret of Jon's tank with a loud, sobering clang. The American return fire was more effective, Jon scoring another kill before the Air Force was called in to finish off the Iraqi unit.

3AD continued to advance and was poised to attack the remnants of a Republican Guard tank brigade when a cease fire was ordered. It was over. One hundred hours of ground combat and it was done. Kuwait had been liberated and, in the minds of coalition leaders, Saddam Hussein had been adequately punished.

Third Armored was ordered to Kuwait where they were stuck for weeks as the victim country began its recovery. Then it was back to

Germany where the tankers proudly displayed their 3AD patches on their right shoulders as well as their left. Jon and his TC were awarded Bronze Stars and the other two crewmembers lesser ARCOMs, but all with the "V" device for valor.

Jon Howard, nearing the end of his enlistment, found himself beset by the industrious reenlistment NCO.

****

Jon was in the motor pool when the reenlistment NCO approached. The crew driver spotted him first and called out, "Run for your lives, boys, the bounty hunter approaches."

The sergeant responded with, "Careful troop. I might forge your signature to a re-up contract for ten years in Louisiana without a bonus." He approached Jon, read his name tag, introduced himself, and handed the tanker a business card. "Be at my office at 0800. I've already cleared it with your first sergeant. I think you'll like what I have to say."

The next morning, a leery Specialist Jon Howard reported as directed. The sergeant did not allay his concerns by opening with, "Come right in, Jon, if I can call you that, grab you some coffee and fixins, donuts too, and have a seat." Jon did so and the sergeant continued, "Jon, have you seen the scores on your foreign language aptitude test?" Jon shook his head no. "Anyone as far as you know?" Again, Jon shook his head no. The sergeant in mock disgust exclaimed, "Amazing, just freakin' amazing. It's a wonder that people in this Army can manage to get their boots on the correct feet!"

He turned serious and said, "Listen, Jon, they're off the charts. Do you speak any foreign languages?"

Jon replied, "Yeah, a few. I can get by in a few. Spanish, Vietnamese, Korean, German," adding after a pause, "southern." The first four raised eyebrows and the last produced the intended chuckle. Jon then added, "Oh, and a smidgen of Arabic."

"Listen, son, I'm gonna confide to you what I've done with you, some trade secrets. When I saw those test results I went over to a buddy in S-2, showed them to him, and told him if he sent a copy up the intel chain I was going to collect a bounty on you from the CIA or NSA. He's nobody's fool and neither is the S-2, and they did. A warrant officer is flying in to interview you, should be here in an hour or so. In the meantime, let me tell you what options I can offer you, all pretty darn good, so you can compare whatever he might put on the table. Help yourself to more coffee."

The intelligence warrant officer arrived not much later than expected and the sergeant surrendered to him his office, saying on the way out, "I'll be across the hall on the phone, sir. Holler when you want me. Don't forget that I want credit."

The warrant officer got right down to business, first giving a nutshell summary of Army Military Intelligence ("MI") and then more or less repeating the sergeant's colloquy about test scores and language skills. He then said, "I expect you have some idea what you want to do when your enlistment expires and the good sergeant has offered you an attractive reenlistment option or two. Trust me when I say that I am authorized to offer you something better, much better."

Seeing that he had piqued the specialist's interest, the warrant officer continued, "First off, you get the promotion to E-5 and whatever bonus is on the table. The Army will send you to college, any approved school offering good foreign language programs and an ROTC program. From where you're from, I suggest you consider UGA, the University of Georgia, maybe a major in Linguistics and a minor in an approved language, maybe Arabic. You'll be in a reserve unit, MI if available, but we'll want you to stay in school year-round with the goal of graduating in three years. Presuming you do well, of which I have no doubt, you'll make E-6 along the way, be commissioned as a second lieutenant on graduation, and sent to MIOBC, the MI Officers Basic Course at Fort Huachuca, Arizona. Presuming you do well there, too, figure a year at the Defense Language Institute in Monterey, California, to learn a language we particularly need at the time, after which you'll be off and running. Lots of options.

"I am open for questions, but I'll be leaving you a packet of info and my contact info. No rush, but we'd like to get you in school this fall and that does not happen overnight."

After consultation with his father, Jon agreed. He applied to and was accepted at UGA, got in with a reserve unit with the 513th Military Intelligence Brigade at nearby Fort Gordon, graduated with honors in three years, got his commission, did exceptionally well at MIOBC and thereafter was sent to Monterey. There he got more than he bargained for.

One of the language instructors was an attractive lady about Jon's age, of what he suspected to be Thai or of Thai descent. Jon saw her a number of times before screwing up his courage to approach her in the cafeteria where she, for once, was seated alone at a table, eating her lunch while reading a book. He asked her if he could join her and got an okay for a response.

They introduced themselves and he thereby learned that her name was Arinya (aptly meaning beautiful, which she most certainly was; and smart, which he was quickly learning also was appropriate) Sarathoon (meaning tiger, prompting in Jon a lascivious thought he managed to subdue, hopefully before she sensed it), that she went by "Arie," that he had correctly pegged her as Thai, that she was multilingual, and that she was at the army intelligence center as a DoD (Department of Defense) civilian.

They had a pleasant conversation and Jon was more than pleased when she agreed to continue it over dinner. The ice having been broken, so to speak, the dinner conversation was lively and fun, delving too. At one point, it turned very interesting.

Arie started it. "I know that 'Howard' is not an uncommon name, but you wouldn't happen to know a Tom Howard? He'd be old enough to be your father, I suppose."

"Well, I have a Tom Howard who happens to be my father."

"He wouldn't happen to have been a soldier in Vietnam and later a Green Beret?"

"Yes, he was. Uh, where are we going with this?"

"Well, my father was in Special Forces too, only of the Royal Thai Army. Before that he served in Vietnam as part of the Queen's Cobras, which would have been in 1967, I believe, and there met an American lieutenant named Tom Howard. They again met some years later at Fort Bragg. My father, whose given name, by the way, is Kaapo, spoke of him fondly."

Jon replied, "I'll check and let you know," thrilled with an excuse to see her again.

A telephone call that night confirmed that his father indeed had met the man in Vietnam on a joint operation, that they had gotten friendly during their short time together, and that the two bumped into each other years later at Bragg. There they had a raucous evening of alcohol and mostly amusing (some to the side-splitting, "beer out the nose" extent) war stories, what his father classified as "epic, a classic example of fostering international relations."

To make a long story short, Jon and Arie began to date, which led to trips together to southern California where the Sarathoon family had emigrated (or immigrated, depending on one's point of view), Washington, D.C., and to South Carolina; which led to a proposal, an acceptance, and what was Isaac Jefferson's first Howard wedding and a reunion for Tom and Kaapo. Jon and Arie would become a team, in more ways than one.

Jon's first duty assignment was back to the 513th MI Brigade at Fort Gordon, this time as an active duty first lieutenant, where Arie also found work as a civilian contractor. Jon did well and was duly promoted to captain at the two-year mark, and got in his company command in which he performed admirably. Before Captain and Mrs. Jon Howard left there, they both realized they had made career choices and commitments they hoped and prayed would coincide.

Jon was sent TDY to Fort Meade, Maryland, then to Washington, D.C., assignments so vague that everyone assumed (correctly) that they were "spooky." During the latter, Jon was joined by Arie who was there for some related "DoD training" and the couple stayed with Tom and Katie. A simple mathematical computation would have put the conception of Jon and Arie's first child during that time.

Then Jon and Arie were off to Hawaii where Jon was stationed with the 500th Military Intelligence Brigade at Schofield Barracks and Arie had another vague job with a DoD agency. As one might expect, it was a glorious time. There their first daughter was born and their son was conceived.

***

Years before this, life had dramatically changed for Tom and Katie Howard. For Tom Howard, one of the advantages of working for your father who, at 72, was willing to start slowing down and that both your uncle and best friend were happy to be hard at work was to regularly start the morning by going over to Dad's house to enjoy a couple leisurely cups of coffee and either discuss things or simply chat.

One particular morning started as a quiet one, and ended as a monumental one. Dan was content to gaze out over the dunes and beach to the ocean while Tom perused the newspaper. Reading one article he growled, prompting his father to look over and ask, "What?"

Tom replied, "This congressional race. The Republican doesn't have our interests to heart and the Democrat is an empty shirt. Either way we lose. What we need is an old fashioned conservative Democrat with a brain, a backbone, and some moral fiber."

That struck a chord with the elder Howard, a successful businessman, a Christian, and a Mason. It also annoyed him a bit. So, with a little bite in his voice he responded, "Well, why don't you do something about it?"

Tom looked over at his father and asked, "How would I know who else to back?" Seeing that his father was even more annoyed and surmising the true meaning behind the question, he amended his question to, "You mean run?"

Truly perturbed, Dan shot back, "And why the hell not?"

"What do I know about Congress, about politics, about any of that stuff?"

"Damn, son. There are books. I expect old Dave Hadaway could give you all you needed. You could read 'em in a week. What you really need to do, though, is jump on in and get out there talking to people, finding out what they need, what they want, what they don't; and showing them Tom Howard."

"You're serious?"

"Only if you are."

"I don't know. The power's up there in Columbia. Hell, I could take most of the district and still lose it there."

"Well, then take most of the district and what you need in Columbia. Maybe a third? I don't know. I don't know politics or numbers."

"Hell, Dad, if you knew numbers you'd be working for a guy named Daniel Howard, wondering how he got so freakin' rich."

Dan Howard smiled and he and his son talked on, exploring the possibility, feasibility, desirability, and all aspects of a congressional run that came to mind. Dan expressed his first thoughts as, "First thing, after of course, some very hard soul searching and praying to the Almighty for guidance, you'd have to see where Katie stands. The idea'd be dead in the water without her on board all the way. Then we'd need to talk to men with political ties and experience, the Greers and maybe you can get to Senator Hollings. I expect Mayor Joe Riley up in Charleston would be willing to talk with you. He's a good politician. As I recall, he's a Citadel grad too, right?"

"Yes, sir. He was a couple of years behind me. Knew him, but it wasn't like we were drinking buddies or anything."

Dan Howard resumed explaining his train of thought. "Worth a shot. Maybe get some pointers and connections to somebody with the Democratic party. See if they'd back you or at least not stand in your way. You'd need to get pointed to a good, experienced campaign manager and somebody who knows how to beat the bushes for money. You'd have to have at least some idea of where you stand on the big things and begin learning about whatever it is you ought to know."

"Geez, Dad, you've about got me talked out of it. *Whew!* Let me get over to the office and get some work done, chew on this, and think about bringing the idea up with Katie."

Katie's reaction was as expected, intrigued, but cautiously so. She warmed to the idea over the next several days and then gave it her blessing. The three living generations of Greers (the elder, whom Tom referred to as "Dad's Bill;" Tom's father-in-law, William, Jr.; and Katie's brother, William, III, called "Trey," a lawyer) were mulling it over.

Tom had made a phone call to the Senator Hollings aide who had most helped him with 15th SOG and Camp Marion, and a couple of days later he conveyed that the Senator's first comment was "big jump for a first timer," but that he'd be supportive depending upon how successful Tom otherwise was. The aide then confided that he had been tasked to back channel him some pointers and other assistance.

Tom took that as a good enough sign and, through a connected classmate sworn to secrecy, made an appointment with Joe Riley. That was encouragingly fruitful.

Tom decided to proceed, albeit quietly. His first major surprise came with a covert telephone call from an aide to Senator Strom Thurmond, a Republican. In clandestine fashion, the man said, "Tom, do you know who this is?" Tom recalled the voice from the earliest Camp Marion days and acknowledged that he did know who it was. The man continued, "Good. This did not come from us, you understand," and proceeded to give a name and private telephone number. "He's expecting your call. Good luck." Tom soon had his campaign manager, a campaign finance chairman, a volunteers' coordinator, political consultants, and a host of other players on the field.

Tom's candidacy was announced and formalized; his campaign committee took shape, and volunteers began to fill the ranks; and money came in, first in dribbles and then as an encouraging flow. Like a train, the campaign slowly left the station and then gathered speed. Tom worked tirelessly, as did a gratifying number of others, and support began to grow. The news media declared Tom a plausible candidate.

The slogan of Tom's campaign was "Responsible Government" (including drastically curbing expenditures in most areas other than veterans' affairs) and the cornerstones of the campaign were his prudent and sensible ideas of what a second district congressman should be and do: his Citadel and military background, always strong in South Carolina; his character and dynamic personality; and that his opponent had none of those things.

Tom began to be considered a viable candidate, his status improving with indorsements from Fritz Hollings and Joe Riley; coupled with that Strom Thurmond's indorsement of his opponent was rather lackluster. Tom had the Democrats, more than his fair share of swing voters, and he pulled a fair number of veterans from the right. And it certainly was a big plus that Katie had become the darling on the campaign trail.

Tom made some mistakes along the way, but his experienced opponent surprised them by making more. The man's fatal mistake was to agree to a public debate.

The Republican was allowed to make the opening remarks. He deployed his campaign rhetoric that he was the conservative, experienced candidate while Tom Howard was the converse. Knowing that Tom's military service and his lack thereof was a thorny issue, he tried to deflect it with, "I am not saying that my opponent is a bad person. To the contrary, he's a fine Christian man, a war hero like his Daddy,

Grandad and even his son, but he's aligned himself with the liberal, wasteful, socialist Democrats and that's not what the good people in the South Carolina second need or want."

Tom countered reasonably well and then was the first to field a question from the panel. Tom expected the leading panelist, a strong right-winger, to be unfriendly, but if he was surprised that the man went for the throat right off the bat he did not show it.

"Candidate Howard, you're a Vietnam veteran and Gulf War veteran. Was either war a mistake?"

Tom pondered the question only a few moments before smiling and answering, "The Gulf War clearly was not. A tyrant invaded a weaker neighbor for no reason other than greed and power. Kuwait sought our aid and as we always must stand ready to do, we provided it, judiciously and successfully.

"As for Vietnam, good question, Mr. Latimore. I have asked myself the very same question many times. It's actually an umbrella for many questions. Was it a mistake to back the weak, corrupt South Vietnamese government? Probably. Was it a mistake to show the world that we would fight communist aggression? Certainly not. Was the cost too high? Certainly for those who had loved ones killed, maimed, or otherwise scarred. But for the country as a whole? No, I don't think so.

"History has shown that America has a bad habit of following wars with years of lethargy in the face of serious threats to our welfare, our very survival. That's how we were post-Korea. John F. Kennedy started the revival, but he was taken from us. Vietnam kicked us into action and we then had an invaluable new generation of combat veterans, advanced weaponry, experienced leaders, and a hostile world knowing, *knowing*, that we *will* fight back. Forget not that it was Republican President Richard Nixon who lacked the fortitude to end the war honorably."

The Republican danced around the question, was thrilled to be able to capitalize on a friendly question, and then disappointed that Tom Howard neutralized it in his response. The debate continued like two cautious boxers jabbing each other and trading points. Finally, Tom got the question he was looking for. Picking up prepared charts, he responded:

"Why me? Well, for one thing I learned at home, in church, at The Citadel, and throughout life that honor is a man's most precious commodity. I will faithfully and honorably serve you as your congressman. Your values are my values.

"Our priorities for our federal government in Washington should first and foremost be national security, because if we're not safe, we're dead. Second is health, because if we don't have our health, we're dead. Third is our children's education, because if they can't compete we have no future. Fourth is our welfare, our prosperity here at home, because that is the American dream. An integral part of each is our humanity, because we really are good people and it's plainly the right thing to do here in the United States of America, God bless her.

"The other reason to elect me is that all this talk about parties is plain hogwash. Let me show you on these bell charts. Y'all remember them from high school, don't you? This first one shows the people of this district, liberals to the left and conservatives to the right. See how the peak is almost centered? That's why for more than a century we voted mostly for conservative Democrats. This one shows the Republican party. See how the peak is way to the right of where most of us are? They aren't changing. They want *you* to change. This one shows the Democrats. See how in the last twenty years the Democratic party lost much of its base by becoming more liberal than the majority of the people?

"That's why I am running as a conservative democrat, a moderate, a representative of my constituents, on the left side of center only to be faithful to the principles of our great Constitution rather than to the big business donors my opponent is so beholding to."

The Republican candidate lost ground there, first without a sensible response and thereafter, his confidence totally shaken, simply unable to artfully dodge questions and lamely falling back on his campaign rhetoric.

The adverse panelist tried another trap. "You have brought God into several of your answers, but what about separation of church and state?"

Tom seized on the question. "I'd like to think, sir, that I bring God into everything I say and do. The founders of this great country and framers of our great Constitution, knowing full well that history had irrefutably established that bad things happen when the institution of the church, any church of any faith, meddles too strongly in the affairs of government, mandated that there be a separation of state and church.

"Need I remind you that the greatest threats to America, to our very survival, now are religious fanatics who intentionally misinterpret their holy books to further their own ends and in exerting a stranglehold on their governments cause or allow one atrocity after another? But separation of church and state is a far cry from separation of state and God. Any government separating itself from God is doomed, and rightly so."

The panelist again should have quit there, but instead tried to regain momentum. "You talk about God, but you've killed people."

Tom cut off the question, if one was forthcoming, by saying, "I'm not going to talk about killing people."

The panelist pressed too hard. "Because you're ashamed?"

Tom replied, "Regretful, but not ashamed."

The debate wound down. The newspapers gave the win to Tom and were not kind to his opponent. Neither were the voters on election day. Tom Howard won by better than a three-point margin.

13

1996 WAS AN EVENTFUL YEAR. CAMP MARION AND 15TH SOG thrived, as did those associated with it directly and indirectly. Jon Howard was making a name for himself at his first duty assignment and Maggie Howard was doing superbly in medical school, as was Emily Jefferson at the College of Charleston. Don Kennedy had decided to hang up his spurs, so to speak, and take a senior management role with the Howard family enterprises and he, much to everyone's surprise and delight, had become an item with Eve.

After spending years working as an ecologist at Camp Marion, Eve had gone back to school to earn both her master's degree and then a PhD. She had gone to work on research projects on barrier islands along the Georgia coast, earning her considerable acclaim. She was awarded a senior managerial position that encompassed the South Carolina low country as well. It was at a reunion with old friends at Camp Marion that she found herself looking at Don Kennedy, still a bachelor, with a different eye.

Never one to be timid, she had suggested to him that he take her out to dinner in Charleston to celebrate. After that, they would have dinner whenever she was in the area, but not something that could be considered dating. Not satisfied with the platonic relationship, one evening she again took matters into her own hands, bolding asking Don, "Am I so repulsive that you won't kiss me?"

"Hell," he replied, "I thought you were gay."

"Gay, my ass. Take me upstairs and I'll show you what a damn fool you've been all these years."

Don still lived in the suite above the garage, his mother still residing in the house after his father passed away. The bed offered a beautiful view of the river through a set of French doors and floor to ceiling windows. That night it offered much more. Afterward, Eve broke the contented silence with a question. "Do you think we're compatible?"

Don pondered the question for a few moments, wondering as to its connotations and deflected whatever they were by responding, "I don't know, what's the proper way to eat an Oreo?"

Eve raised up on an elbow, exposing a lovely breast and stared at her new lover, incredulous over his ridiculous response. Then she laughed and said, "You're right. Time enough for the checklist later. Right now, take me back to the stars, stud muffin." A month later, Eve moved in and Don Kennedy's bachelor pad was transformed, as was he.

* * *

For Tom Howard, it was with enormous pride that his son Bo was graduating from his alma mater, The Citadel, albeit that Bo was going into the Marines when global conflicts were escalating. There had been Somalia in 1993, continued trouble with Saddam Hussein, and increasing violent terrorist attacks with one wealthy terrorist leader named Osama bin Laden becoming more outspoken and bold.

Bo had entered The Citadel with every intention of following in his father's footsteps, even to joining 15th SOG at Camp Marion after his active duty commitment, but events at the school conspired to cause him to instead follow in the footsteps of his grandfather and great-uncle. (Or maybe it was Divine providence.)

Bo did not know much of his grandfather's exploits as a Marine, other than he had enlisted when WWII was looming, had fought at

Guadalcanal, and wounds suffered at Peleliu ended his war as a gunnery sergeant. Bo mentioned those things to one of the USMC tactical officers at The Citadel, Major Church, and some weeks later Bo was called into the major's office. Major Church loved the Marine Corps and read everything about it he could put his hands on. As most career Marines were, he was enamored with the legendary Marine Lewis "Chesty" Puller.

Puller was the iconic Marine's Marine. He had left VMI, the Virginia Military Institute, to enlist in the Marines to fight in World War One. He was too late, though, and saw no action. He gained a commission through OCS, lost it in a bout of downsizing, but then regained it in time to fight with distinction in the "banana wars" in Haiti and Nicaragua; he then heroically commanded the 1st Battalion of the 7th Marines at Guadalcanal and the regiment at Peleliu; he went on to further valor in Korea; and ultimately he achieved three star rank. What made Puller so famous though was that he was the only Marine to have earned five Navy Crosses, second only to the Medal of Honor, plus the Army's equivalent Distinguished Service Cross. He also had a chest full of "lesser" decorations, including the Silver Star, Bronze Star and Purple Heart.

Cadet Howard's remarks intrigued Major Church and sent him back to his books. He called the cadet in to share with him a photograph he had found in an obscure book. Bo Howard viewed the grainy black and white photograph, obviously from the Pacific in World War Two, depicting a tough looking man, who he took to be an officer, talking with apparent pleasure and pride to a younger, ragged Marine with a bandaged head and splinted leg. Howard was about to shrug it off when he read the caption. Dated 1944 and placed at Peleliu, the standing man indeed was a Marine officer, Chesty Puller no less; and the wounded Marine was one of Puller's men, one Sergeant Daniel Howard. *Holy shit!*

That prompted Bo to tell the Marine major that he believed that his great uncle (referring to Bob Howard) also had served under Puller in the Korean War. Major Church explained the "Frozen Chosin" to Cadet Howard. The conversation led to other Marine Corps exploits, including Iraq and Afghanistan where the major had distinguished himself and about which he had plenty of good stories to tell.

One thing led to another and the major was suitably impressed with the cadet to loyally suggest to him that he consider switching over to Naval ROTC and pursue a commission in the Marine Corps. Bo, at first completely opposed it, thought it over, and warmed to the idea.

The turning point, however, was when his grandfather's friend from Florida had stopped by one weekend when Bo was home. The man, Stu Markowitz, was darkly tanned, driving a big Cadillac and was a real character. He regaled Bo and his father with stories from World War II, and much to the chagrin of Dan Howard, only somewhat embellished accounts of Dan's heroics. Markowitz insisted that Dan drag out of storage the relics of the war he, Stu, had brought back, including Dan's Ka-Bar, a .45 pistol, and some "Jap stuff," Stu's recounting of how he accomplished that, yet another cause for laughter.

Bo relayed to Major Church what he had learned from the veteran, the major realizing in the prideful telling that he had accomplished his mission of recruiting the cadet. Bo consulted his father and older brother and listened to their input, but all concerned knew that he had, for all intents and purposes, already made up his mind.

And so it was in the United States Marine Corps that Bo was commissioned early in the morning before commencement ceremonies, his proud father and grandfather at his side. Major Church presented each of them framed prints he somehow had gotten made of the photograph he had first shown Bo.

Bo had asked his father to wear his uniform one last time to graduation. Tom did not think it wise, being technically unauthorized and he being a member of Congress and all, but he compromised by relenting to wearing the uniform at the early morning commissioning ceremony, after which he would change into a coat and tie for graduation.

Tom pleased Bo by impressing his classmates and instructors with his rank, his ribbons and badges, his green beret, and his Special Forces combat patch. Most notable to many was the Purple Heart ribbon with two oak leaf clusters. In a setting where bemedaled and otherwise adorned military men were common, there were few who could so starkly demonstrate a history of close combat.

Unfortunately, as Tom Howard posed with Bo for photos, their image also was captured by an early bird Charleston News and Courier photographer. When publication of that photograph fortunately did not produce the feared fallout, Tom proudly displayed it in his Washington office next to a rather grainy photo of him in jungle fatigues standing next to his friend Don Kennedy in tiger stripe fatigues and the grainy photo of his father Major Church had kindly given him. Years later there was to be one other photograph centrally displayed.

* * *

Sadly, not long after Bo's graduation Daniel Howard, the family patriarch, died at the age of 75. As he had done with Dan's father, Reverend Issac Jefferson delivered a fitting eulogy:

"My friends," he began, "we gather here together in the Lord's house to celebrate the life of Dan Howard. Well, I say that, but many of you are outside the Lord's house," alluding to that the sanctuary was packed, standing room only, and there were as many people clustered in the annex and in folding chairs out in front of the chapel. When the polite laughter subsided, he continued:

"Those of you who were here for Carl Howard's funeral some years back may recall that is how I started the eulogy then. Those of you with great memories will remember more of what's coming. Am I that lazy? No, not really, it's just, just so fitting.

"Dan Howard was Mister Carl's son. There is a lot of meaning in those words. So, yes, I pulled out my notes from Mister Carl's service and decided it would be entirely appropriate to track them. I pray you don't mind, Miss Bea."

As he had done with Carl's, Isaac began with the comforting scriptures all needed to be reminded of at such a time of great loss and then he began the eulogy that had taken far more time to compose than he had suggested in his opening. Preachers were not immune to the crushing emotion of the loss of a loved one.

"All of us are deeply saddened by this great loss and many of you mourn, and rightly so. Dan's passing was and will continue to be for some time a great loss to Miss Bea, Bob, Tom, family and friends. It is okay to cry. You, too, Bob Howard, let it go. He was your older brother, business partner, and best friend. To all I say this: Take comfort in that there is no doubt, *no doubt*, friends, that Dan is with Jesus.

"Now, friends, we all know John 3:16, the so-called gateway Bible verse. Oh, if it only could be that easy." That certainly got the congregation sitting up straight in the pews and chairs as did the next seemingly incongruous sentence, "Dan, like his father before him, befriended me when the Lord first led me here and was and forever will be a cornerstone of this church. His gifts to the community are renowned."

Isaac let the people sit perplexed for a half minute before continuing with, "I say that not to brag on the man, but to remind you that, by his actions Dan Howard demonstrated that he truly was a man of faith; and to bear witness to that Dan Howard humbly did as the Bible teaches us over and over, in James, Luke, Colossions, Peter, and even John, to do. In just two short verses after verse sixteen John goes on to tell us, 'Little children, let us not love in word or talk but in deed and in truth.' So the Bible tells us that deeds, not words, reflect faith. Lay the life of Dan Howard before you and be comforted by knowing he left this world right with God.

"Yes, it is right to lay Dan's life before us. We are here not only for reassurance, for comfort, but to celebrate the life of this most honorable man. I've already reminded you of his charitable generosity. Where did that come from? I will remind you of that too.

"Dan was molded after his father. Dan grew up here. He started out as a swamp logger, not because he had to, but because Mister Carl figured he ought to. Like his father, Dan went off to war where he, like his father, was decorated for truly astonishing valor and he too was seriously wounded. Dan Howard, in hellacious battles in the forbidding jungles of Guadalcanal and the blasted barren landscape of Peleliu, time and again put his life on the line to save the lives of his fellow Marines. What more of a measure of a man?

"I will tell you what more: The love that prompted such selfless valor, the love for and devotion to Miss Bea and his family, the love for this church and this community. The Bible teaches us that it is grace to be blessed, but the true test of faith is to be a blessing to others. Dan Howard indeed was a blessing to each and every one of us and so many more.

"Miss Bea, Bob, Tom, kids, I say this from the bottom of my heart as God is my witness: I pray that someday I can be half the man Dan Howard was. Thank you, dear Lord, for letting me stand in his shadow. Amen.

"Now, friends, I close with the benediction and as you head out to the graveside and the ceremonies there, please think of Dan Howard as a duet from our wonderful choir offers the hymn Dan chose for you." With that the pair began a truly gripping rendition of *"Holy, Holy, Holy! Lord God Almighty."*

Tom Howard lingered at the graveside after the ceremonies, the military and Masonic honors masterfully done, and Isaac's closing. He stayed because his sense of loss suddenly had become so overwhelming that he simply could not do anything else. Katie in turn sensed her husband's emotion and need to be alone and steered family and friends away.

Tom cried in shoulder shaking, chest heaving sobs. He tried to think of words to say, but his mind just kept going back to Isaac's closing words. He decided that he need not pray for his father and instead silently said, "*Lord, thank you for blessing me with Dad and Grandad, with Katie, our children, and with so many others I am sure in your favor. Let me be no less.*"

Tom composed himself and went to where Katie was waiting. She gave him the loving hug he needed and they went hand in hand to join the others.

* * *

As also had been done with Carl Howard, afterward the family gathered for the reading of the will. This time though, the group was not only augmented by the Jeffersons, but also by the Greers and Don Kennedy. There curiously was one other, an elderly black man.

Bob Howard deferred to Tom Howard to officiate. Miss Bea was set for life. Bob would have the majority interest in the Howard family enterprises, Tom a large minority interest and Bea enough of an interest to maintain a voice. Tom was to get the house at Edisto Beach and some designated properties. The Marion Chapel endowment fund would be considerably fortified. The grandchildren (again including as such Emily Jefferson) would each get a fair amount of money and property and for the great-grandchildren and ensuing generations the family trust was handsomely bolstered.

However, as also was done with the reading of Carl Howard's will, a surprise awaited until the end. This one was regarding Carl's island, the one many had considered a foolish investment. It had been placed in a family trust and Dan, the trustee, had now given directions that it, now worth millions, be developed into a family retreat (with "family" defined to include the Greers, Jeffersons, and Don Kennedy), fully funded to provide a spacious clubhouse on the larger fresh water lake, a row of beach front condominiums for use by the family, a ferry with docks on the island and on the land side, and other amenities. The rest of the island would remain wild, that is, except for the surprise within the surprise.

Though few in the family even knew they existed, and only Dan and Tom actually had communicated with, there were squatters on the island; offspring of the emancipated slaves who originally settled there following the Civil War. There on the lee side of the island they had carved out homesteads and ever since eked out a modest living through fishing and limited farming, while respecting the rest of the island. Carl Howard had let them stay and even had electricity run out to them and water and waste treatment facilities provided, conditional only on that they continue to respect the land and run trespassers off.

To them, represented by the elder present, was to be deeded the property they were using and then some, including the smaller fresh water pond and utilities, the deeds providing right of first refusal restrictions on re-conveying the property and other covenants to which the grateful grantees already had agreed. In exchange, they for modest remuneration (and an 18-foot Carolina Skiff, a Jeep, a pickup truck, and a tractor) would care for the buildings and grounds and provide fresh food and cooking for the family guests.

As with the reading of Carl Howard's will, not a soul left dissatisfied. They went their separate ways with one common thought, "*Carlisle*," the name Tom and Uncle Bob had come up with for the family island, "*how very appropriate!*"

* * *

It was at the funeral that Bo's fiancé had truly realized the magnitude of the family she was marrying into. Bethany had grown up accustomed to exclusive Charleston society, but had rebuffed her family's snobbish concern over her relationship with an outsider. While she was not thrilled at the prospect of going off to be a Marine Corps wife, she believed Bo when he told her that his goal was to command a company and to then give it up, to then settle down to take a place in the family business. She was not sure what that meant, but the Howards certainly appeared to be both respected and prosperous. Besides, she truly loved Bo.

But young men can be so foolish. Bo was torn between having the wedding at the Citadel Chapel or Marion Chapel. When Bo expressed this dilemma to Bethany, it was, in military parlance, a "lesson learned block of instruction," the concept he soon was to become familiar with at the Platoon Leaders Course at Quantico. Bo got into the dilemma maybe ten words before Bethany, smiling and cuddling next to him, said, "No, sweetie. The wedding will be at First Baptist and the reception will be at the marina. Here, let me show you the invitations Momma sent me." Bo Howard smiled back at his bride to be, concealing the realization that he no longer had any control over his life whatsoever.

The wedding was beautiful, the reception wonderful, and the honeymoon delightful. Bethany found that Quantico was not all that bad and actually was excited when they were to be sent to their first posting in California.

* * *

Tom Howard was beginning to outshine his fellow first term congressmen and congresswomen. Although first termers rarely find themselves appointed to a committee involving direction of vast amounts of money, Tom attained junior positions on the House Intelligence Committee and the Veterans' Affairs committee and soon became a valuable asset of each. Tom's constituents began seeing his face in the press and more and more were pleased with help gotten from Tom's home office in Columbia and satellite office in Beaufort, the latter of which Emily Jefferson admirably first ran, even while distinguishing herself at college up in Charleston.

Tom learned early on that to stay in office required that every single day he be personally involved in campaigning and fund raising. Tom

Howard was respected, but he still was a Democrat and the Republican party was gaining strength in South Carolina, a red tide Tom Howard feared would sweep him away each time he ran. He so feared not out of pride or ambition, but out of a strong desire to accomplish things he truly believed were for the betterment of his constituents, his state, veterans, the country and ultimately the world.

Tom held his seat, although disconcertingly each time by a narrower margin. Each victory gave him more respect, more visibility, and more seniority, all leading to better committee appointments and those to continuation of the cycle.

* * *

Much, too, had transpired with the family in the decade. Jon Howard received a below zone promotion to major and he and Arie went back to Fort Huachuca and then Fort Leavenworth. Maggie Howard completed her residency at Scottish Rite Hospital in Atlanta and was recruited to join a highly respected pediatrics group in Charleston. She too married at Marion Chapel and surprised everyone and no one by wasting no time in starting a family. "Little sister" Emily Jefferson graduated with honors from law school and went to work in Charleston on the legal team of Mayor Joe Riley who was in his historic seventh term of office. (He would go on to serve an even more amazing ten). She too married, of course at Marion Chapel, and also quickly started a family.

Bo Howard completed his assignment in California and both he and Bethany were pleased with his new assignment to Camp Lejeune, North Carolina, where he was promoted to captain, given the company command he so desired, and where his first son was born. Bethany reluctantly agreed with Bo's plea for her to acquiesce to his recanting his pledge to her that he would leave the Marine Corps after he had commanded a company, knowing full well that in a world at turmoil it was what he had to do.

For Tom and Katie, the flurry of grandchildren (including, *de facto*, Emily's) both was a blessing and a curse, the former far outweighing the latter.

Don and Eve rocked along, as did 15th SOG.

The decade, however, ended with another great loss in the Howard family. Uncle Bob died of a heart attack at the age of 68. True to his nature, stories of his death abounded. Bob's favorite would have been (or perhaps even was?) the one untruthfully but delightfully claiming that he had died in his boat with an eight-pound bass on the line. Bob was memorialized in many ways.

One was at the local dirt race track where a bronze plaque adorned the main entrance proclaiming:

IN MEMORY OF BOB (ROBERT CARL) HOWARD (1932-1999)

Beaufort County born and bred, Korean War veteran (USMC), prominent local businessman, Mason, co-founder and co-owner of this track, winner of the Cup four times (and his teams another four)… and by all accounts one helluva guy who is sorely missed.

Bob's son Tim similarly memorialized him by displaying his father's awesome '55 Chevy race car in the showroom of the dealership. Bob's wife, Jean, honored his memory by never remarrying (although by her own account she "catted around some").

But what many would remember would be Isaac Jefferson's eulogy:

"My friends," he began, "we gather here together in and about the Lord's house to celebrate the life of Bob Howard, 'Uncle Bob' to most of us. It saddens me to say that this is my third Howard funeral service, but it again gladdens me to see that Marion Chapel once again is bursting at its seams with you good people who came to honor the wonderful man.

"Those of you who were here for Dan's funeral only a few years ago may recall that I then felt it appropriate, fitting, to use Carl's as a rule and guide. It would be a disservice to Uncle Bob though to again do so today. Uncle Bob was, well, he was Uncle Bob. I am told that when I first met him some twenty odd years ago it was past his heyday, but I honestly can't imagine his earlier life being that much more of the celebration of life he made it every day since we first met.

"I will say that I admonished Bob at both his father's and brother's funeral that it was okay to mourn, okay to cry. I say the same to you. Bob Howard touched all our lives and we are saddened that he is gone from us.

"Now, there may be some who wonder if Bob is with the Lord or the devil took him first. Well, friends, I know, I *know* it is the former and not the latter. It's not the latter because I am confident that Bob's soul was too tough for the devil to deal with. I know it is the former because I knew Bob Howard. He was a founding member of this church and if he was not some snob's view of a pillar of the community, he no doubt was and always will be a cornerstone of this church along with his father and brother.

"Marion Chapel owes its existence to many and, if we were to list them, Uncle Bob would be near the top. Surprised? If so, that would be as intended. Matthew 6 teaches us that charity is a demonstration of faith, and discreet charity is favored by God. Rejoice when I say to you that Bob Howard's faith was strong, that he served the Lord well, and that he is with the Lord. But I don't want to get too 'churchy' here today. Uncle Bob wouldn't have it.

"He, like Mister Carl and Mister Dan, started out as a swamp logger. He, like Mister Carl and Dan went to war, his being Korea, and as they did, nearly died in heroically doing his duty. He came home and went to work in and continued to build the family businesses. He married Jean, another camouflaged angel; raised a fine son, Tim; and was a mentor to Dan's son Tom. If there was an event in Beaufort or Jasper counties, Uncle Bob was a sponsor. If a football team needed helmets, a quiet donation from Uncle Bob produced them. If people were in need,

Uncle Bob was there. If anyone stood up for what was right, Bob had his or her back. On the other hand, if someone didn't do right, they'd have Bob on their back, sometimes quite literally.

"Who Bob Howard was is best reflected in the faces here today. Bob's family, of course, is here because they loved him and loved his love of life. His fellow parishioners are here because they loved him and loved his selfless love of God. His fellow veterans are here because he is deserving of their honor. His Masonic brothers are here because they know he was a good man. We are all here because we knew and loved him and because we loved to laugh with him. God, my friends, is here because He knew Bob Howard, He loved him, and He knew that Bob knew Him and loved Him.

"Blessed be the Lord and blessed be the memory of Bob Howard. Amen.

"And now friends, as you head out to the graveside, let your hearts be lightened by the hymn Uncle Bob chose." At that a celebrated Irish tenor took his place in front of the Marion Chapel choir and the people quickly overcame their surprise and cheered to the music and lyrics of the modern, upbeat hymn, "*Lord of the Dance.*"

* * *

As the 20th century closed and the 21st century began, by all accounts life was good with the extended Howard family.

On September 11, 2001, however, Islamic fundamentalist and terrorist Osama bin Laden changed the world, in a most violent way. He orchestrated the hijacking of two passenger airliners to crash into and take down the twin towers of the World Trade Center in New York, accompanied by a similar attack against the Pentagon in Washington and another hijacked plane forced by brave passengers to crash in rural Pennsylvania. Nearly 3,000 innocent people died. And the War on Terror began.

The world was let in on that the United States was going after bin

Laden and his al-Qaeda terrorists and Taliban allies in Afghanistan. Jon Howard, gone for long periods of time, was correctly assumed to already be over there. Bo predictably would be deployed there as well in what was beginning to be called the War in Afghanistan, Operation Enduring Freedom.

Bethany Howard kept to herself her regret that she had not held her husband to his pledge. Versed from five years of experience as a Marine Corps wife, she took some comfort in surmising that if and when Bo was deployed, because he had already commanded a company others would be given the opportunity to get their "ticket punched" instead of him, while Bo more safely would have a staff job.

She was correct in that. Bo was not in command when his unit predictably received orders to deploy. She, however, was not correct in equating Bo's complaint in an e-mail that he was not much more than "glorified airport security" at Camp Rhino with assurance that he was out of danger.

While as the daily news informed the world that the U.S. Air Force was pounding suspected terrorist training camps and that Northern Alliance fighters supported by U.S. Special Forces were doing well in wresting control of the country from the radical Islamists, Camp Rhino, south of Kandahar, was surrounded by hostile forces who were anything but idle. Bo was subjected to incoming fires, rockets, mortars, snipers, and an occasional probe. When he led convoys, something he often did, roadside bombs added to the list. Bo witnessed Marines maimed and killed. He was involved in firefights and twice had put his M16 to good use. Bethany would only realize her error when, after his return, Bo was awarded a Bronze Star for valor.

* * *

In 2003, President George W. Bush, despite straining military commitments to Afghanistan and elsewhere around the globe, decided that

Iraq's dictator Saddam Hussein had to go. The plan to depose him and his ruling Baath Party proceeded despite cautionary advice from respected, knowledgeable military and political leaders, including Congressman Tom Howard. Tom Howard was unabashedly vocal about his prescient opinion that while Saddam and his cronies needed to be eliminated as a threat to the region, it would be a grave mistake to afterward get too involved in a conquer and occupation scenario.

Tom was subjected to harsh criticism, but in the eyes of many he was proven to be correct. While the coalition forces indeed quickly crushed the Iraqi military, seized Baghdad, and forced Saddam and his central leadership into hiding, a bloody war of insurgency ensued as the United States stumbled and bumbled through the rebuilding process at a dismayingly increasing cost in dollars and blood, with dubious success on the horizon.

2004 found both of Tom's sons there, Jon in Baghdad and Bo some forty miles to the west in Fallujah.

* * *

Captain Bo Howard was living his dream. He was commanding a Marine rifle company in combat. It had not been an easy thing to achieve. Bo had been chafing in a staff position as his battalion readied itself for deployment. The proper protocol would have been to float the idea to his boss, the S-3 operations officer, secure his permission to take it up to the XO, the battalion executive officer, and then secure his permission to take it directly or indirectly to the CO, the battalion commander. Bo was torn between not liking his chances of success in that fashion and risking being labeled as one of those loathed opportunist officers if he circumvented the prescribed process.

Bo was still procrastinating when one day an opportunity presented itself and Bo impetuously (providently?) decided to seize it. What he later declared as his driving thought was "fortune favors the bold," a translation of an ancient Latin proverb favored in the military, it actually was "*Fuck this shit. All they can say is no.*"

That day the CO and XO lingered after a staff meeting. He lingered too, in earshot outside the door. When he heard the two men wrapping things up, he stepped back into the doorway and asked, "Pardon me, sirs, but may I have a few moments of your time?"

"All right. Come on in."

"Sirs, I confess and apologize for not taking this up the chain, but I would like to sell you on giving me a company." It was bold on many levels. Not only was Bo doing it wrong, but there were no command openings. The only prospective one was Bravo. The captain there had commanded the company for his allotted time and Bo correctly surmised that the CO was struggling with whether to extend him for the deployment, his performance having been rather lackluster.

Both senior officers scowled and Bo's heart sank. "*Dead in the fuckin' water,*" he painfully thought. However, a glimmer of hope appeared when the CO opted to explore the notion.

"Why? Why would you want a company? You've already had one, you've been down range in Afghanistan, and now you're on the major's list. Your sights ought to be ahead."

"Sir, trust me when I say to you that I'm not asking for this to enhance my career. Either way I've promised Bethany that this deployment will be it for me in the Corps. No, sir, it's because we are going to war, a real shooting war where the stakes are as high as they can be. The missions will be tough and the lives of a lot of Marines will be at stake. Maybe it's just my overinflated ego, but I truly believe that I could best ready the men and then lead them in combat."

The XO continued to frown, whether from adversity to the idea or still being miffed at the breach of protocol, Bo could not discern. In either event, it would not be his call though. The CO's poker face was more troublesome. "*Well,*" thought Bo, "*my record stands for itself and at least I made my pitch.*"

The CO stared at Bo for a long time, what had to be a couple of minutes, his face and eyes still not revealing a thing. Bo noted a subtle change in the man's eyes. *Here it comes.*

"Bo, I was thinking of giving you the 'I'll think about it' dodge, but then I said to myself, *'No, you're a goddamned commanding officer and a good commander makes decisions.'* I have been kicking myself for failing in that regard for some weeks now. I am concerned that Bravo is not up to par. You go down there and whip them into shape. Do that in thirty days and you can have the company over in the sandbox. Fail to do that, to my utmost satisfaction, and I'll knock your dick in the dirt and park your ass back here where you can read about us in the papers. Am I clear, Captain?"

"Crystal clear, sir." Bo refrained from adding a lame "you can count on me" assurance.

Bo's do-or-die period did not begin until after the change of command ceremony. He used the few weeks preceding it to his advantage. While his Assistant S-3 duties kept him busy, particularly since the S-3 was in no mood to cut him the least bit of slack, Bo used all his spare time to prepare, first to ready himself physically and proficiently, second to devise a plan, and third to surreptitiously meet independently with the Bravo Company first sergeant and gunnery sergeant to get the real pulse of the company and to float his ideas.

The battalion commander's assessment of Bo Howard's first address to his assembled company at first was shaded toward negative, but he later came to the conclusion that it was spot on.

"Men, Bravo Company does not enjoy the reputation of being the best in the battalion. Frankly, I don't give a shit about that. I really don't care if we're first, second, or even third. What I do care about is you being Marines in all that revered name means. That is the definitive. We're not about the stateside competitive bullshit of whose dick is biggest. We're going to war, men. Some of you are going to die and it's about time you let that reality sink in.

"If you can't shoot, you're dead. If you can't move, you're dead. If you can't think, you're dead. But if you can shoot, can move, can think; and you do shoot, move, and think, then a lot of virgins in paradise will be tasked out to the martyrs, the many motherfuckers we, Bravo Company, will send there.

"First though, we've got thirty days, no more, to get our shit together. Let me tell you this here and now, we will use every minute of those thirty days to do it and we will not fail. Are we clear?"

The company of Marines responded with, "Oorah!"

"What was that, ladies?"

"Oorah!!!"

"That's better. Now I know the first sergeant got you all spiffed up for the ceremony and anticipated inspection by me. I have other plans. Company, ten-hut!" The Marines sharply came to attention.

"First Sergeant, have the men fall out and change into running gear. Assemble in three zero mikes. Platoon commanders, on me."

When Bo and his lieutenants were left alone, Bo said to them, "You won't be running today. The gunny intends to run them into the ground and I can't afford to embarrass any of you in front of them. If you're not up to a long, hard run while maintaining your officerly dignity, get that way in a hurry. As for training, that will be mostly an NCO affair. I will tell them that we will be going back to the basics, physical training and individual combat skills, for the rest of this week. I expect you to recognize your weaknesses in individual combat skills and in whatever spare time I give you this week have your platoon sergeants work with you on the side to strengthen them.

"We, that's you and I, in the meantime will focus on you in a combined arms urban environment. The men will work up to training next week as fire teams and then squads. You will observe, assist, learn, and note any deficiencies not corrected by your NCO's and have them fixed.

"The week after that, that's in two weeks' time, we, the company, will be up to platoon level training for a week and you then will be at the forefront. The final week will be company level training, range time, and evaluations. At the end of that week, gentlemen, we'll either be across the board combat ready or you can join me handing out towels at the gym."

14

The arrival of an army scout helicopter at a U.S. Marine company field headquarters was unusual. That when the helicopter shut down the crew chief stood by it with an MP5 submachine gun in hand to rather emphatically ward off the curious certainly was more so. What prompted action by the company first sergeant though was that the passenger strode through the Iraqi dust straight toward the company CP like he owned the place. "*What the fuck*," he thought as he marched out to confront him and to demand, respectfully of course, his business there.

The visitor saw the senior sergeant on an intercept course and slowed as he pulled his laminated identification, suspended on a beaded chain around his neck. The two met, professionally greeted one another, and after one look at the credentials abruptly cut off further inquiry by the sergeant, the visitor, Major Jon Howard, followed the sergeant inside.

"Skipper," the sergeant started to say, but got no further because his captain already was on his feet. Instead of saluting the army major, Captain Bo Howard unabashedly, and quite unmilitarily, warmly embraced him.

Bo turned toward his Marines present and said, "As you were. My brother." Leading the major outside to some place that might offer a bit of privacy, the captain added over his shoulder, "Make sure the boys don't steal his ride."

269

Recalling the serious man with the submachine gun, the first sergeant replied, "Not a problem, sir."

The two brothers talked for as long as either of them could spare. Jon left his brother with, of all things, a cell phone and accessories (functioning cellular service being one of the many incongruities in devastated and dilapidated Iraq), cautioning him not to lose it or use it for anything other than communication between the two of them. As the two rounded the CP, the pilot took notice and started the blades turning. Jon and Bo again hugged.

It was Jon who said the parting words, "Watch your ass in there, Bo. It's going to be a shit storm." He then boarded the helicopter. The pilot lifted off and, giving Fallujah wide berth, headed back to the relative safety of the Green Zone.

Fallujah not only was a large city with a population more or less of 100,000, but also decidedly not a friendly place. Hundreds of insurgents had been recruited, impressed, or imported for the sole purpose of killing Americans. They had the advantage of being on the defensive with countless fighting positions, prepositioned stocks of weapons and ammunition, no hindrance of rules of engagement, and either belief that they were engaging in a holy war, a jihad, or considerable remuneration. Rumor had it that the courage of many was bolstered with narcotics.

For the Marines who had the advantages of training, communications, and firepower, Fallujah would supremely test their mettle. Fighting would be slogging house to house, block to block, hampered by that there were more than two hundred mosques requiring high level clearance to engage or even access. The enemy was fully aware of those restraints and had no qualms about using the mosques for their combative purposes. They also cared little about collateral damage and death resulting from their actions.

As for the availability of fire support, Bo Howard sardonically commented to his sympathetic, equally perturbed JTAC (a "Joint Terminal Attack Controller" trained to direct combat aircraft in close air support

(CAS) operations), "When seconds count, fire support is just minutes away. Nothing is too good for the U.S. Marines and that's what we get, nothing."

It indeed was to be a shit storm.

Captain Howard led his company of Marines right into it, often up front with the lead platoon, prompting his gunnery sergeant to proclaim, "Dammit, Skipper, you shouldn't be up front like that. You ain't no expendable platoon commander. You keep this up and one of these times you're gonna get your shit scattered to the wind."

"My, aren't you little Miss Suzy Fucking Sunshine," Howard replied.

"Just sayin', sir, just sayin'."

"Besides, if I get my ass blown away, you can get a CO who knows what he's doing."

"Shit, sir, probably get some delegator who'll send my sorry ass out while he eats ice cream back at the rear."

"They have ice cream back there?"

"Sure, but only for the pogues."

"With ice cream, I could be a pogue."

"No, sir, I don't really think you could."

Sudden firing up ahead with Dwight Dervis's second platoon ended the banter. The team of Captain Howard, the JTAC and the FO with their respective RTO's, the gunny and the senior corpsman slipped forward to the sound of M240's and M249's ripping off bursts and M4's popping out rounds with intermixed grenade explosions. Howard already had cleared the attached sniper teams, one Marine and the other SEAL, to overwatch positions. Ricochets of incoming rounds whizzed by. They passed bloodied Marines being helped or carried back. *Shit!*

Reaching the platoon commander, Bo Howard asked, "Whatcha got, D?"

The second lieutenant, young but steady, replied, "Same ol' shit, sir, hajis in that corner building with AK's, RPG's, and at least one RPK.

Probably the ones we pushed out of the last corner. I've taken four casualties already, two of them needing evac."

"Saw them. Keep your heads down while I see what sort of CAS we can get. Still a no go on artillery and I already know the Cobra teams are working to the west."

Listening, both the JTAC and FO gave the captain an "on it."

The lieutenant spoke up. "Sir, if we can get a tank up here, right here or maybe forward a bit, he probably could take out that corner of the building and with any luck collapse it or at least distract them long enough for us to get across the street to it."

Bo hazarded another look at the target building and ducked back down. "Yeah, Dwight, I'll buy that." Turning to his trusted RTO, he told him to call in the request for a tank and then, turning back to his platoon commander, told him to begin maneuvering his men to be ready to follow through if and when they either got air support or a tank. With nothing more at the moment to accomplish at the exposed position, Bo told the lieutenant that he and his folks were moving back, pointing to the location.

In the shelter of a doorway, Bo Howard studied both his map and aerial photo while awaiting word on the CAS and tank. A few minutes later he got the typical bad news/good news report, negative on the CAS and the Cobras were off station to rearm and refuel, but a tank was heading their way, ETA ten minutes.

That made his decision for him. Bo told his equally sharp RTO on the company net, "Push third platoon to get up on line to the right. Tell first platoon I want one squad to move up and cover second's left, another to join us here, and to leave the other one back with the XO. I want the snipers back down here, too. Make sure the XO and battalion know what's happening."

Bo then sprinted up to where the second platoon commander had moved, meagerly sheltered by a thoroughly riddled car. A quick peak told him that the new position would offer the tank gunner a smidgen more of a target. Bo quickly told the lieutenant that, as expected, they would have to do it "the good old fashioned way" and explained his ordered maneuver, unnecessarily adding, "D, it'll be hairy. As soon as the tank fires, have your guys haul ass for all they're worth. I'll get you as much covering fire as we can put out."

Bo was encouraged when his young lieutenant smiled back and said, "That's why we get the big bucks, sir."

"Yeah, right. Hold tight until the tank arrives and third herd gets on line and set. Three sixty security. We've bypassed a lot of buildings and alleys, too many for comfort. I'm going back to my little cubby and when first's squad gets here I'm going to clear this building on the right and set up the CP upstairs." The lieutenant nodded his understanding. Howard clapped him on the shoulder and headed back to his doorway sanctuary.

Bo was pleased to see the second platoon Marines who had removed the wounded were hustling by, back to the fight. The two sniper teams and the first platoon squad soon arrived. Bo gathered in the alley his reinforced CP group and explained what he wanted to do. They understood.

Howard followed them to the building and watched them expertly breach the door and storm inside. After he heard them announce the ground floor clear, he skirted the posted security, entered the dark confines of the building, and then followed the lead element up a set of stairs leading to a hallway with doors to windowed rooms facing the target building. As the squad continued to clear rooms left and right and the snipers began to set up in the room at the head of the stairs, Bo pondered whether to set the CP up there or back downstairs. He decided to stay upstairs.

The tank rumbled up and was directed to move up to the riddled car. Lieutenant Dervis radioed his readiness and Bo got everyone else prepared to fire as soon as the tank did.

The tank's 120mm cannon boomed and a millisecond later a blast took out the corner of the target building. The Marines let loose with everything they had at the doorway and windows and then just as quickly checked their fire. Bricks were still raining down when the second platoon squad rushed across the street. Bo Howard was not surprised to see Dervis with them. The Marines below flattened themselves against the front wall of the building and the Marines above resumed firing at the upper windows to keep the insurgents back.

Bo watched Dervis give a thumbs up to someone on the near side of the street, presumably the leader of his supporting squad, and follow his men into the building. There was firing inside. A tense few minutes passed before Bo was able to breathe a sigh of relief as Dervis reported that the building was clear, that the enemy had fled out the back, leaving a couple of dead behind.

Bo was pleased to watch the second squad sprint across the street and enter the building as the third squad followed and split to take up security positions at the front right corner of the building and what had been its front left corner. He was reminded that the tank was still there when its .50 caliber machine gun opened up. A minute later, the report was relayed that apparently thinking they had safely gone far enough up the street, a couple of insurgents had crossed the street and the tank was able to fire up the following pair, neither of which made it to the other side.

Dervis radioed that the building offered a disappointing view to the north, so Bo decided to stay put for the time being. He radioed his progress and status to battalion. A temporary lull followed as the battalion commander realigned his companies accordingly.

Enemy fire erupted from a building to the northeast, of which Bo and the Marines with him could only see its roof line, a half a dozen top floor windows, and a few windows of the floor below. Bo could see an occasional muzzle flash and impacting rounds from second platoon's return fire. Bo's snipers were firing as well, but reported no kills. Bo heard the SEAL sniper telling the Marine sniper, "Slow down your rate of fire, pard,' or you'll be shootin' machine gun ammo before the day's out." (The sniper rifles and M240's were chambered for the same ammunition, but the sniper rounds were of considerably higher quality.)

The firing back and forth continued with more than a few enemy guns targeting the CP's building. Bo Howard heedlessly alternated talking over the radio, scanning with his binoculars, and studying his map and aerial photo. He determined that the tank would be of little use for two long blocks, a long day's work the way things were going, so he released it back to battalion control.

Soon second platoon reported two more casualties, one a KIA. *Godammit!*

Bo, cautiously standing in the shadow a few feet back from the window, studied the building through his binoculars and kept going back to one particular window that seemed to be ideal from the enemy's point of view, but from which muzzle flashes appeared only sporadically and they were not the typical long flame of an automatic weapon. Bo's snipers concurred with his assessment that it likely was a sniper's hide.

"Gunny, get me a rocket team up here."

"Aye, aye, sir," and he was gone.

The Marines were equipped with the AT-4 anti-tank weapon. It was a portable, single-shot disposable weapon manufactured by Saab Bofors Dynamics of Sweden that fired 84mm rockets. Although generally ineffective against main battle tanks, it was useful against fortifications and buildings, especially the HEDP (high explosive dual purpose) round.

Before long, the rocketeer appeared. Bo Howard recognized him. Good man. Borrowing the FO's binoculars, he handed them to the Marine and led him to the adjacent room. He cleared the room and took up the same standing position away from the window opening. After confirming that the room offered a good vantage to the target, he talked the rocket man to the target, telling him to aim so the rocket struck below the window frame. He did not want it to impact an interior wall such that the main effect of the blast would be wasted deeper inside. The Marine understood. Satisfied, Bo issued final instructions and went back out into the hallway, knowing that the back blast from the rocket in the enclosed space would be tremendous.

The rocket man took the time to arrange a couple of chairs to steady his aim, readied the weapon, adjusted his goggles, and yelled his readiness. He yelled, "Rocket out" and triggered the weapon. The rocket whooshed to the target and struck true. While it was disappointing not to see the results of the blast inside, Bo was satisfied he had done all he could and released the rocketeer-now-rifleman back to his squad. Bo rejoined his CP team and the snipers in the adjacent room.

Firing continued from the building, but not from the smoking room the AT-4 had hit. Bo was informed that there still was no CAS available and that the use of artillery still was not permitted. The good news was that a pair of Cobras would soon be heading back, fully loaded. That coincided with a radio report from Lieutenant Dervis that he had sent a squad forward to reconnoiter and who had reported back a covered route to the new target building. Bo responded by telling him to have the squad stand by a safe distance from the building to allow for Cobra gun runs.

Bo Howard's time was not idle as he awaited the aircraft. His attention was drawn to the snipers talking between themselves excitedly. He walked over and asked, "Whatcha got?"

The SEAL sniper responded without taking his eyes off his scope, "Nothing much on the target building, but got some activity at the mosque up and over to the right. Got a Mercedes at a side door. Looks like they're passing munitions. Yep, there's an armload of RPG's, too."

Bo got the scene in his binoculars and agreed with the sniper's assessment. He had the RTO radio Third Platoon for what they could see. The platoon commander radioed back that he could see the mosque, the car, and figures moving, but could not discern much more. Bo took the handset and told the lieutenant to have his men ready to engage on order. He then said to the SEAL sniper, "Okay, take 'em. My call. I'll take the heat."

"On it."

It was an easy shot for a skilled sniper and moments later his rifle boomed and the man at the trunk almost instantly crumpled dead with a bullet through his spine at the base of his neck. An insurgent in a black track suit stepped out and sprayed a burst from his AK-47. The Marine sniper killed him with a round in the chest, the man dropping like a marionette with its strings cut. The sniper boasted, "Call the taxidermist!"

The SEAL smiled at the bravado and said, "Good shot, Marine, but watch this, boys." He put a round through the car's license tag and another through the bumper. He then lowered and slowly and methodically reloaded his weapon.

The Marine sniper quipped, "Well, that was pretty fucking exciting."

The SEAL looked at him and just smiled. He got back on his scope, confirmed the intended puddle of gasoline beginning to form on the concrete under the car, smiled again, and casually put a round into the puddle.

The gasoline vapor was instantly ignited by the red-hot bullet and spark of its impact; fire and smoke became visible to the naked eye. A cheer went up in the room as the car erupted in flames. Moments later the car exploded, and moments after that, the explosives stacked inside the door of the mosque did the same. Smoke billowed out of the building and panicked, choking men burst out of the front door.

Bo Howard brought the radio handset still in his hand to his mouth and knowing that the third platoon commander was glued to his at the other end simply said, "Kill them." Three heartbeats later, Third Platoon gunned the insurgents down.

The Marines, their hearts pounding and adrenaline flowing, surveilled the suddenly quieted scene as they reloaded their weapons. The mosque smoked and there was some muffled crackling as small arms ammunition inside cooked off, but there was no movement. Even the target building was momentarily silent.

Resumption of firing from the target building coincided with a radio call from the Cobra leader that he was coming on station. Bo radioed Lieutenant Dervis to have the building marked with a Willy Pete, a white phosphorous smoke grenade from an M203. He did, the Cobra pilot radioed that he observed it and Bo radioed back, "You are clear to fire, guns only. I say again, guns only. I have friendlies too close for rockets." The pilot radioed back his understanding and the pair of attack helicopters commenced their gun runs.

Through his binoculars, Bo could see the Cobra fire chewing up the building. The Cobras broke off and Bo knew that the Second Platoon squad would be moving to assault the building. He did not know that Lieutenant Dervis had reinforced them with himself, his RTO, a SAW gunner, and several riflemen.

Suddenly, Bo Howard was alarmed by firing. "*That was fucking close!*" he thought and instantly headed to the room doorway. Turning to his left, he saw figures emerging through the exterior door at the far end of the hallway, one that led to an outside set of steps. The Marine assigned to guard that doorway lay sprawled on the landing. A Marine peeked out of a doorway halfway down the hall and was driven back by a burst of AK fire.

Bo instinctively brought his M4 to bear and fired as soon as a black clad enemy exposed himself in the doorway. The man crumpled on top of the Marine. A second insurgent thrust his rifle around the opening, fired a burst, and then charged in. Howard fired back and the man spun and fell, only to expose another behind him.

Bo was firing at that man when an AK round struck him in the right hip, causing him to fall back against the door frame. He brought the carbine back to bear and resumed firing. He was still firing when more AK rounds hammered him.

The first of these rounds caught him squarely in the center of the chest. Although the ballistic plate of his body armor deflected the round, the impact of it still was a sledgehammer blow, a stunningly painful shock instantly followed by yet another round that snapped the collar bone on his left side. The combined effect of the bullet impacts caused Bo's knees to buckle even as his body began an involuntary, ungainly pirouette. He landed painfully hard on the dirty floor, both his rifle and helmet skittering away.

As an RTO leaned out of the doorway, firing short bursts down the hall, the gunny reached out, grabbed the loop on the back of the captain's body armor, and dragged him out of the line of fire and back into the room. There he unceremoniously dumped his commanding officer and joined the fight. The corpsman and an RTO converged on the wounded captain as the firefight raged just outside.

The cacophony of gunfire quickly ended, soon followed by shouts of "clear." By then, Bo Howard was propped against the wall with his gear removed and uniform cut and torn to expose his injuries. Bo, gritting his teeth against the pain while trying to be manly about it, and trying to will his head from spinning, looked up to see the gunny with a smoking M16 in his hands. All Bo could think to say was, "Don't say it."

The corpsman announced to no one in particular, "Through and through, right hip and left clavicle; moderate bleeding; emerging contusion, sternum; conscious and alert. I'll patch him up, but need a litter to get him to the CCP. Probable priority evac, but not my call." The corpsman skillfully attended the CO and then asked him, "How's the pain? Want some morphine?"

Instead of answering the question, Bo asked, "How bad is it?"

"Well, sir, for some officers a bullet in the ass would result in traumatic brain damage, but I'd say you'll be okay."

"Well, I'll take that as a compliment and so I'll ignore the insult to my brothers in the officer corps. Tell me though, am I out of the fight?"

"Yeah, I'd say so."

Bo was suddenly pissed. *Out of the fight! Leaving my company behind!* He articulated those emotions succinctly as, "Well, fuck me to tears."

They were interrupted by the gunnery sergeant. "Skipper, Dervis just called in. They cleared the building, but the hajis chose to put up a fight this time. They killed a few, but took three casualties, none KIA or urgents though. Dervis wanted you to know that in the room you rocketed they found two very dead bad guys, one a red-headed white dude, and recovered a Dragunov."

Bo knew that the Dragunov was a Soviet semi-automatic scoped sniper rifle. He replied, "Good to get that thing out of circulation. Call it in to battalion. The S-2 might want to take a look at the dude, maybe take his picture." It then dawned on him. "You said 'they.' Dervis was with them?"

"Yeah, apparently so. Reckless. Sorta like a chip off the old block, I'd say."

Bo had to smile up at the sergeant. "Yeah, maybe so. Maybe so. Listen, don't let it get lost in the shuffle that Dervis needs to be written up for a medal. The snipers too. You too, by the way. Okay?"

It was their turn to be interrupted. The corpsman chimed in, "Sorry to interrupt, gents, but the litter team's here. Sir, how 'bout that morphine now?"

Looking up to gunny and seeing him nod his head affirmatively Bo Howard turned back to the corpsman and said, "Okay, why the hell not." After the corpsman administered the shot and duly noted it, he got the captain on the stretcher. Bo looked over at his RTO's and gave his final command, "Call the XO up. Inform the platoon commanders and battalion."

As he on his stretcher was being lifted, Bo looked back over to the gunny. He started to issue final orders, but stopped himself, knowing the man knew exactly what to do. Instead it was the gunny who spoke:

"Just so you know, sir, you dropped three of the motherfuckers and our guys got another three. Third herd just reported that three more ran into them and are KIA. Second got their wounded out and feel secure enough with their little outpost up there. We're good now. Trust us, sir, you trained us well and we'll carry on and make you proud."

Bo choked out a reply, "I'm already as proud as I can be, Gunny." Notwithstanding the sincerity, he instantly regretted the remark, whether the sentimentality or banality of it, he was not sure.

The gunny followed them down the steps and outside. There he could not stand to refrain anymore. Kneeling next to the CO he admired and making eye contact, he said, "Damn it all, sir, I told you so; *I fuckin' told you so!*"

And then Bo Howard was gone, on his way to the CCP. He passed the XO on the way, but by then the morphine obviously had begun to take effect. Bo was only vaguely cognizant of the passing encounter and a few minutes later what was going on at the CCP where there were wounded on stretchers or leaning against the wall and people milling about; and there were people talking, on the radio, to each other, to him. He really did not follow whatever was being said to him or asked of him. A medevac helicopter came and went with a load of more seriously wounded Marines.

A corpsman checked on the captain and said, "Hang in there, sir. We'll get you out on the next bird. It'll be a few before it's here."

Bo laid uncomfortably and tried to take stock of his situation. He was conscious that the right leg of his trousers had been cut to the waist and his privates were barely covered. Running his hand over his intact right front pocket he felt a lump. Only after fumbling to remove it did he realize it was the cell phone his brother Jon had given him. Betraying that the narcotic buzz was a first for him he drew the attention to himself by laughing out loud.

Somewhat comprehending that he had an audience, he drunkenly announced much to their amusement that he was going to call his brother on his "spiffy, spooky cell phone." They then were treated to one side of a rather bizarre conversation.

"Hey bro, whatcha up to?" An apparent reply and then, "How 'bout we meet for lunch?" Bo called out to a nearby corpsman while failing to unkey the phone, "Where'm I going?" He was answered and resumed his conversation with his brother, "How 'bout the 31st CSH. Half hour or so?" The medic shrugged a likely yes and Bo continued, "Yeah, half hour or so. Gotta go. See ya." Bo fumbled to disconnect the phone. It did not matter to him whether his fellow Marines and Navy corpsmen were laughing with him or at him. He just closed his eyes and dreamily awaited the medevac.

* * *

Major Jon Howard was at the evac hospital helipad before Bo. While Jon's life was spent playing connect the dots, he desperately hoped that the picture he framed connecting these dots was wrong. He gravitated toward the group of hospital orderlies standing with gurneys next to the helipad. Seeing his rank, none hazarded to question him.

Soon a medevac Blackhawk helicopter thwapped into view, flared, and set down. The cargo of wounded was quickly unloaded and the men hurried into the emergency room. Jon's hopes were buoyed when Bo was not among the wounded. That hope, however, soon was dashed when the orderlies quickly returned to the sound of another approaching medevac bird. It landed and there was Bo, near naked but for bandages.

Jon hurried to his brother, but the only reaction he got from him as he accompanied the gurney and held his hand was a weak smile. Jon was halted at the door, the orderly there unimpressed with his rank. Denied access, Jon Howard could do nothing but stand there, lost in thought.

As Jon stood there, a civilian, intrigued by the odd sight of an Army officer unnecessarily and inexplicably rushing to help a wounded Marine and getting bloody in the process, approached him and asked, "Know the guy?"

Not thinking, Jon answered the man's seemingly innocuous question, with, "Yeah, my brother."

The man gave Jon a polite, sympathetic reply and, with his heart suddenly pounding, he abruptly walked off after taking in the officer's name and rank on his uniform tabs. As soon as the man rounded a corner, he scrolled through the series of pictures he had just rapidly snapped on his digital camera. A broad smile reflected his thoughts, *"Paydirt. Pay-fucking-dirt!"*

Jon was too impatient to wait outside. After putting in a call to his section, he walked inside, flashed his credentials, and asked to be directed to Captain Howard's bay. Bo was wheeled in from x-ray and from having his wounds closed and rebandaged. A nurse looked him over, asked if he needed to be there, and decided to accept his curt "yes" in reply. Jon was still there when Bo awoke some hours later.

A week later, the cover of Time magazine sported a photo of a bloody, bandaged, but clearly smiling Marine being hurried from a helicopter emblazoned with a red cross by serious hospital orderlies along with a soldier who appeared out of place and more concerned. The caption, stolen from the 1969 hit song by The Hollies and soon thereafter by Neil Diamond, was "He ain't heavy, he's my brother." The reporter had done his job and the caption went on to state in smaller print, "Shown here, Marine Captain Bradley Howard, evacuated from fierce fighting in Fallujah, is accompanied to the 31st Combat Support Hospital by none other than his brother, Jonathan, an Army major stationed in Baghdad." The accompanying article further identified the brothers as from South Carolina and then morphed into a report of the Fallujah battle, the destruction and the host of American casualties flooding Baghdad military hospitals from the fierce fighting.

The image and caption, and sometimes with the article, promptly went viral on the internet, the military not excepted, and the Howard brothers became, depending on one's point of view, famous or notorious. Both were aghast, Bo afraid of the impact on Bethany and his mom; with Jon sharing similar fears, but also coupled with concerns as to the reaction by his superiors. It was entirely too conspicuous for someone in the clandestine world of intelligence.

Major Howard was summoned to go see his boss a couple of days later, the summons Jon had been dreading. "Jon," the colonel said, "the general saw the Time cover and told me to tell you, and I quote, 'This ain't Hollywood. Get back to your cave.' To put it in context, that's about the mildest rebuke I ever heard from the man. He also told me to tell you, and I quote, 'Tell him that his brother is doing fine in Germany and he'll be going back to Lejeune soon. One bullet glanced off his hip and did no more than put another hole in his ass. A second broke his collar bone, but that'll mend in time. Another one hit him dead center in the chest, but his ballistic plate saved him with nothing more than a big bruise.' You might want to let his wife and your folks know."

A relieved and grateful Jon Howard went back to his cave. There were no adverse consequences to the unwanted publicity. In fact, it had no effect on Jon's being selected for assignment back to Fort Leavenworth and the SAMS course, the School of Advanced Military Studies. Jon was to become a Jedi Knight, as graduates of that exclusive course were called, a first-class ticket to a below zone promotion to lieutenant colonel.

Bo was given convalescent leave, which he tried as much as he could to spend alone with Bethany and the kids at Carlisle. The children most of the time were absolutely delightful, but as each day drew to a close, Tom and Bethany longed for them to surrender to sleep. All in all it was one of the best times of Bo's life.

Bo returned to Camp Lejeune on light duty. After his unit returned home, he was included in the awards ceremony where he not only received his Purple Heart, but a Bronze Star for valor, the latter of which would be relegated to a 5/16 inch star on the ribbon of the first one from Afghanistan. Letter orders apprised him of the "I was there" awards he also was authorized to wear.

Later his CO presented him with a curiously heavy package. Opening it, he found a dented body armor ballistic plate with a handwritten note from none other than Major General James Mattis, saying: "A trophy for a proven warrior and a daily reminder to thank the Good Lord in heaven every day for His good graces." That trophy would be framed and find itself prominently on Bo Howard's office wall.

This time, Bo fulfilled his promise to Bethany and formally requested that he revert to reserve status. His CO called him in and said, "I got your request, Bo. I hate to see it because you are a fine officer and a damn good Marine, but I understand. This 'War on Terror' is going to be hell for service families for the next ten years. But I am going to delay your request. I had the adjutant check and your promotion date will be in just over ninety days. You ought to stick around until that happens. I have told the XO and neither of us will object to you taking all the leave you're allotted in the meantime."

* * *

It was about the same time that Congressman Tom Howard went in confidence to fellow South Carolina Congressman Jim Clyburn who had first been elected to Congress in the neighboring 6th District the same year Tom was in the 2nd. It was a courtesy call. The two were allies and friends. Tom confided to Congressman Clyburn that he was seriously considering not seeking reelection. The two men discussed it at length and Congressman Clyburn asked Tom to keep it under wraps until he could run it past some people and get back to him. The response some weeks later, to say the least, was unexpected.

15

TOM HOWARD MET COVERTLY WITH SOUTH CAROLINA CONGRESS-man Jim Clyburn and Georgia Congressman John Lewis, Senior Chief Deputy Whip of the House of Representatives. Tom was not surprised that Jim Clyburn had taken his secret to John Lewis. The two were powerful in the Congressional Black Caucus and otherwise.

After some polite pleasantries, Congressman Lewis warmed with the question, "So, tell me, Tom, how is Isaac Jefferson doing? Sarah? Emily?"

Tom was surprised at the question, not knowing of the acquaintance. He smiled and replied, "Wonderfully. I talk with Isaac often. Marion Chapel is thriving. Emily is still with Joe Riley. She and hers stay close to mine."

Congressman Lewis, pleased, smiled and continued, "And your older son Jonathan, still in the intelligence world?"

Tom was equally surprised at that knowledge, but hid it as he replied, "Yes, he is. He's soon to be a lieutenant colonel, although I'm afraid back again to Afghanistan. At least this time I'll know he's there."

"And your son Bo?"

Tom was no longer surprised. He replied, "Fine, just fine. He left the Marine Corps and is back home working himself into the family business."

The senior congressman used that as his springboard. "Well, he of all people would appreciate the conversation we're about to have." Tom thought that odd, but the senior congressman gave him no time to consider it. "Tom, I was both saddened and elated to hear of your wanting to leave Congress." *Elated?* "You have been an important ally, a vital one, on many important issues. What I am about to propose accepts your leaving Congress, but not public service." *Huh?* Tom did not have to wait long for the other shoe to drop, so to speak.

"How well do you know Senator Barack Obama?"

Tom, even more perplexed, cautiously responded, "Well, we've met, talked briefly, nothing of great substance."

"If I were to prophesize that he is to be the Democratic candidate for President in 2008 and speculate that John McCain will emerge as the Republican candidate, what would you say?"

Tom pondered the notion and gave a measured response. "Well, I don't have either the experience or a crystal ball to see that, but I expect you do. I have great respect for Senator McCain as a man of strong character and intellect. I would put him to the right of center about the same as I am to the left, but equally as willing to apply reason. On the other hand, he's stuck with the party line and sources of money. My impression of Senator Obama is that he is a very smart man. I have to assume that you and his other key backers have the race issue covered. He'd still have to avoid the appearance of being too liberal. I for one would like to know where he stands on the military and veterans. If you are asking me who I would vote for, I would stick with the party."

Both Congressmen Lewis and Clyburn smiled, appreciating the characteristic candor and anticipating Tom Howard's reaction to what was about to come.

"Well, Tom, you missed the mark there. That was not the implied question. Pardon me, please, for being obtuse. That question is whether you'd be willing to run for the presidential nomination."

Tom, absolutely incredulous, blurted out, "What? No! That would be insane. I would get my ass kicked, pardon my French, and the harm to the party could be bad, certainly not good."

Congressman Lewis smiled again and continued. "Well, let me explain. We want you to run for the nomination. You won't get it, of course; in fact, you'll be out of it well before the convention, but we need you nominally in the fray. We want Obama to get the nomination and go on to be our next president. I am confident that we can show you why and we are confident that you will agree.

"Barack will start off surrounded by a pack of wolves; no, more like a school of piranha. He's going to need some cover, somebody to be his umbrella in the storm, his lineman in the game, however you'd want to put it; someone in the limelight to facilitate his election. Hillary can't or won't do it. She wants the nomination.

"In a nutshell, what we are looking for is a viable candidate to all outward appearances who surreptitiously is actually running a carefully crafted campaign to thin the Democratic crowd so that Barack emerges in front while inflicting as much damage as he can along the way to the Republican opposition. In sum, what we're looking for is a candidate like you. No, not like you, *you*."

It was not like a light bulb flashed in Tom's head. It was more like a light on a dimmer switch being slowly turned up. Words and phrases came to mind, drowning out the congressman, "*sacrificial lamb*," "*expendable*," "*hung out to dry*," "*take one for the team*," "*take a bullet*," and so forth until Tom managed to refocus his attention on what the man was saying.

"We'll help, behind the scenes, of course. You'll get money and top drawer staffers. We'll feed you information. You'll run your own campaign, although we'll nudge you now and then. And when you've accomplished the mission, we'll help you gracefully and advantageously bow out.

"Tom, do not take me wrong in this because I am not suggesting that you would ever agree to do this for any selfish reasons, in fact I am certain you would not, but there would be collateral benefits. What if we were to show you that it would be a win-win proposition times two?"

Reading the confusion on Tom's face, Congressman Clyburn jumped in to explain: "Barack Obama, you, Bo, and the country; not in that order. Barack obviously, the country for reasons again we're confident we can establish, you because you'll get to live the dream of speaking out nationally without dreading the political fallout, and Bo because we honestly cannot think of a better man to follow in your footsteps in Congress and we'd like to help make that happen. That's not a bribe, Tom. Trust me. I would not so insult you. We say Bo's the right man in all sincerity. We'll support him if he chooses to run, whether or not you choose to join us."

Tom looked at his two colleagues and simply said, "Sell me on Obama."

* * *

Bo Howard was satisfied that his brief brush with fame was over and that his life was settling. Bethany and he bought (in a manner of speaking, the mortgage being a frightful albatross around their necks (the abiding doom saying from the 1798 poem from *The Rime of the Ancient Mariner*) even with Bill Greer structuring the payment schedule most favorably) the house on the Coosaw River next to Miss Bea's, spent some money, and put in a lot of effort to renovate it and make it theirs, and Bo believed that he was becoming more of an asset to the family business. He could see down the path of his life and he liked what he saw.

Bo, therefore, was wholly unprepared for when his father, his "little sister" Emily Jefferson, and a vaguely familiar black man came to see him—with the sole purpose of fucking it all up.

Despite that his internal radar was sounding alarms, Bo gave Emily an affectionate hug, confirming to Congressman Jim Clyburn what he had been told. His father then introduced the Congressman to Bo and the two politely shook hands. The four sat and Tom ceded the floor to his colleague.

"Bo, this is strictly confidential. I am going to get right to the point. What I say may be shocking, but hear me out, please. Your father is stepping down to run for the presidency. I will leave him to explain that much. We, and forgive me if I don't define that term right now, but we want you to run for his seat. His leaving creates a void we need to fill.

"You're a Beaufort man of substance, a Citadel man, and a Marine and a celebrated wounded warrior; you handled your celebrity status well; you're smart and a good looking young man, and you've got good family connections; you've got good political connections too, more than you know; and, trusting that your politics are like your father's, the nation needs you to take his place, fill his shoes. I guarantee you full party support."

As predicted, Bo indeed was shocked. He gave his father a questioning look and then out of curiosity, but more so as a diversion, he turned to Emily and asked, "And what, dear lady, is your part in this grand conspiracy?"

"No part," she replied, "it's just that I am being groomed to run for city council and they thought we could go to politics school together and help each other out."

"City council where?"

"Charleston. We bought a house on Limehouse Street, maybe the worst house in the Battery, but it's still the Battery. Robert seems to think that he's seen enough TV to do most of the renovations himself."

Bo rolled his eyes at her and said, "Don't I know it. *HGTV* [Home & Garden Television] and *This Old House* [another vastly popular home improvement show] will be the death of me, that is unless I have to watch one more time *Barney & Friends* [the children's TV show with a purple dinosaur adored by kids and abhorred by adults] or *Happy Feet* [the kid's movie featuring penguins and songs delightful only so many times]. Tell Robert that if he needs help with demo to call Bethany. She just gutted the kitchen mostly all by herself."

Bo then returned his attention to the men. "Well, forgive me if I haven't a clue what to say. I need to talk with Dad, although his co-conspirator status tells me where he stands. If it makes sense, then I'll need to chew on it and talk it over with Bethany. We're just now getting settled into the house here and after the moves the Corps put us through, that may be a deal breaker."

His father was no surprise. He articulated the pros and cons and explained clearly how the pros won out. Later, Bethany was the surprise. When Bo explained the matter to her she demonstrated that she was no longer the Charlestonian society girl requiring family blessing before acting. She was all for it and said so.

Within two weeks, Tom's announcement to step down was made, immediately followed by Bo's statement of candidacy, and it was big news. While Tom appeared to temporarily melt into the background, Bo leaped into the forefront of South Carolina political news with a campaign strategy and rhetoric largely mimicking that of his father's in his first election. Bo was unabashedly riding the still strong patriotism of the country (the Time cover appearing over and over) while aptly portraying himself as the sensible middle of the road candidate. There were powerful indorsements, not the least being from retired Senator Hollings and Congressman Clyburn, as well as influential veterans and the ever-strong voting block of teachers and business leaders. As Katie had been for Tom, Bethany Howard, now huge in her third pregnancy, was a big hit with the voters and the press.

Bo Howard rocked along well enough in the early months of the campaign and managed to win the Democratic primary without a run-off. He proceeded to steadily close the gap in the polls and did quite well in his first major televised public debate. In it he used his father's bell chart idea, now polished and enhanced in the age of computer graphics and PowerPoint, something with which his opposition blundered by failing to recall. It played as well for Bo as it had for Tom.

Evincing that he was "a chip off the old block," as the saying goes, Bo adroitly fielded a question about the problem of Islamic terrorists. "Candidate Howard," the panelist asked, "we have been at war with the Muslim world now for over a decade. You yourself fought them, killed them. Tell us how we rid ourselves of this menace."

"Well, sir, first of all I do not agree with your premise. We have not 'been at war with the Muslim world.' Islam is the world's second largest religion with nearly two billion followers, about one fourth of the world's total population. Compare and contrast that with Christianity, the world's largest religion with followers making up a third of the world's population, with Islam distantly trailed by Hinduism and Buddhism.

"While indeed many Muslims hate us, some love us, and most don't care about us one way or the other. Of those who hate us, maybe a few hundred thousand across the globe are willing to do violence to us. To put that in further perspective, that roughly is the equivalent of the number of violent criminals in prison here in the United States and not much larger than the MS-13 criminal street gang.

"So, what is the solution to the real problem? The solution is to identify, locate, isolate, and kill or neutralize the terrorists and combatants in such a way as to not drive others to their cause while at the same time showing the world that, regardless of the hate message radical imams may preach, we Americans pose no threat to the Muslim world as a whole.

"One thing we need to do is to stop the hypocrisy of spending billions of dollars to fight terrorists while funding their cause by spending that much and more buying middle eastern and South American oil where we know, *we know*, the governments laughingly turn around and funnel tremendous profits to those terrorists. We should commerce with our friends and not our enemies, and that goes far beyond just oil.

We do that and we will thrive and they will either amend their violent aspirations or wither on the vine.

"Mostly though, what we need are smart people in Washington who have the courage to stand up and do the right thing, the right thing for America, the right thing for the world. I don't profess to be the smartest guy on the planet, but I'm smart enough and I vow to you and to all that I, as your Congressman, will follow my father's lead and work hard to do what is best for my constituents, our state, our veterans, and our country without doing harm to those elsewhere who would do us no harm."

The message resonated well. Other things went Bo Howard's way too, with even a dicey issue resonating well. When asked about harsh criticism from the Christian Right that he was too liberal, Bo tossed it back by saying, "You know, I've read the New Testament too and for the life of me I can't understand how true Christians could be so selfish and loveless." And, very much like his father's, so went Bo's campaign.

It was a toss-up as to which candidate carried the debates. In the end though, it did not matter. What ultimately carried Bo Howard to victory was his opponent. Some rather sinister dealings came to light, as did allegations of sexual misconduct. The man's vehement denials did not ring true and people began to distance themselves from him; not a stampede, but enough that Bo Howard's victory was not a tremendous surprise.

Tom knew polls and numbers well enough to see it coming. Before Christmas he and Katie had vacated their suburban Washington house, taking nothing but clothing and personal items, and Bo, Bethany, and the kids moved up. Tom and Katie made their home at the beach house while Tom studied and prepared for his upcoming pseudo-campaign and the points he wanted to make in the process.

* * *

It was more than two full years before the presidential election and more than a year before the primaries when Tom commenced his campaign for President. He decided on a campaign slogan of:

America: Strong. United. Free.
Strong in might, strong in principle.
United States, united people.
Free, the envy of the world.
Vote Tom Howard for President,
a proven sensible leader.

Tom refused to be a "sound bite" candidate, one hiding behind amorphous rhetoric. He told his handlers that he was going to come out strong.

His handlers urged prudence, one saying, "You know, many a boxer has come out of the corner swinging, only to end up on the mat in the first round. You're no good to anybody knocked out."

Tom heeded the advice and launched his campaign on his moderate democratic values and his congressional and military records. He advocated a strong military and better care for veterans (the latter seeming to many as again being his mantra) while otherwise urging that federal spending be curbed. He allied himself with those like-minded.

One of those allies was Lieutenant General Claude M. Kicklighter, U.S. Army, retired. Tom had met the tall, distinguished man who was quick to introduce himself as "Mickey" Kicklighter when the man was a colonel, the division artillery commander of the 24th Infantry Division at Fort Stewart, Georgia, just south of Savannah and not far from Camp Marion. Colonel Kicklighter was one of the senior officers Tom had briefed when 15th SOG was in its infancy. The two men had politely chatted after the briefing and Tom learned that he was born and raised in the small Georgia town of Glennville at the western edge of the same military reservation, that he had married a girl with South Carolina roots, and who had considerable family property along the Savannah River just outside of the city of Savannah. The talk of the two military men segued to logging, solid common ground.

Kicklighter's career had skyrocketed after that, enviously including residence in the general's quarters at Schofield Barracks in Hawaii when he commanded the 25th Infantry Division and where he returned after a brief stint at the Pentagon with a third star and command of all Army forces in the Pacific. When the general retired from the Army, he stayed in government service, including being Assistant Secretary of Policy and Planning, Department of Veterans Affairs, and Chief of Staff of the department. A career soldier, veteran of the vaunted 101st Airborne in Vietnam, years later the Director of the Department of Defense's Iraq Transition Team, and ultimately the Inspector General for the Department of Defense, he was a strong ally indeed.

General Kicklighter was not Tom's only powerful ally in the fight for veterans. Tom gained allies in the federal department and his state's counterpart department; he found them in Congress and otherwise in government; he found them in advocacy and lobbying groups such as NOVA (the National Organization of Veterans' Advocates), NVLSP (the National Veterans Legal Services Program), the American Legion, and the Veterans of Foreign Wars (VFW); he found them in wounded warrior groups and in corporations; and he found them as individuals.

As strongly as Tom felt about the issue and the need for it to be front and center, he could not afford to be myopic. He brought back out the bell chart that had served him so well in his first campaign, and his son as well, now much more sophisticated but the message was the same. It again resonated well with the media and polled national voters alike.

To the reporters and analysts taking note, Tom Howard was an interesting study in contrasts. He was perceived at his core a product of his upbringing, a southern boy ("American by birth, southern by the grace of God") from the South Carolina low country who by no means was racist. He was a Christian. He had grown up in the company of warriors, including his grandfather, father and uncle; Green Berets with the motto, "*de oppresso liber*," to free the oppressed; and Army Rangers with the motto, "Rangers lead the way;" he was tempered by the Citadel Honor Code ("A cadet does not lie, cheat or steal, nor tolerate those who do"); and he had not only served his country in uniform, but had killed for her.

At the same time, Tom was perceived as gravitating toward being an antiwar candidate. In one speech that gained worldwide attention, he said:

"Am I antiwar? Certainly. No rational person who has personally seen the face of war would be otherwise. War, by definition, is horrific. Wars cost billions, trillions, of dollars better spent elsewhere; and the butcher's bill is horrendous.

"Is there ever need for war? Sadly, but certainly, yes; but only after every, and I do mean *every*, other means has been exhausted. But while we must avoid war if we possibly can, we cannot be passive. We must be vigilant in identifying threats to the United States and threats to our friends and we must be ever ready and fully prepared to eliminate those threats by whatever means necessary.

"On the eve of the Iraq War, General James Mattis gave a famous speech to his Marines, in it telling them that there is 'no better friend, no worse enemy' than a U.S. Marine. Indeed. That should apply not only to our Marines, but to the United States of America as a whole.

"While we, as the greatest and most powerful nation on Earth, have obligations in the global community, we are not called to use our wealth and power to impose our will on others and we are not the world's policemen. Teddy Roosevelt is said to have said, 'Walk softly and carry a big stick.' Well, whoever made that adaptation had it right. That is exactly what we must do. We should be altruistic rather than sanctimonious. We must be benevolent, not arrogant. Do not forget that we can find in our own short history much of which we now decry around the globe."

The media cut through the rhetoric like a hot knife through butter and zeroed in on eliminating threats "by whatever means necessary" and tried to nail Tom Howard down on the meaning, pointedly concerning nuclear weapons. Tom refused, instead saying, "The words 'eliminate' and 'necessary' each have but one definition; the former constrained by the latter, emphatically but not timidly." The intended obfuscation was unsettling at home and abroad.

And so it went for months. As before, but now on a national, indeed international stage, Tom Howard's Congressional record was scoured, lauded, and derided; he was quoted and he was brushed off; praised and criticized; lionized and denounced. The one constant was that Katie Howard was adored.

Tom evaded few of the issues and with most he triggered the intended lively debate. For instance, asked to comment on an opponent's promise of tax cuts, he, as the media and the public had learned to expect, used it as a springboard. Tom said, "Well, it's nonsense, utter nonsense. It, of course, sounds good and plays well, but it's illusory. The fundamental problem is not taxes. Taxes fuel the machine, the government. The problem is that the machine has grown grotesquely, obscenely. The government, and I am talking about the federal government here, has lost sight of its function and *that* is the root of the problem.

"The function of the federal government is fourfold, and fourfold only: First and foremost, national defense, for without security we have nothing. Second, keeping the states united. Third, handling those things that the individual states either cannot do or cannot effectively do, such as international relations, interstate commerce and relations, the environment, education. And, finally, those few other things the Constitution expressly limits to the federal government.

"Taxes are necessary to enable those functions. Taxes are too high because the federal government wants the money for things way beyond actual governmental functions. Taxes are not rightly for the government to spend on things they want to, only for things they *need* to. To quote the famous Republican senator from Illinois, Everett Dirkson, 'A billion here, a billion there, pretty soon it adds up to real money.' Indeed!

"It would be good to cut taxes, but first we must rein the federal government in. Why is it that we Americans bitterly complain about government waste and then blithely keep in office the very representatives who either waste the money or allow it to be wasted? I call on watchdog groups to be more vigilant, bold, more vocal as to those in government not being good stewards of the taxpayers' dollars and I call upon the voters to heed what they report. Throw the bums out and be more careful with whom you send in their stead."

And so it went, with Tom Howard boldly speaking out and all the while taking every opportunity to advocate for veterans. He made a decent showing in the Iowa caucus, won by Obama, and the New Hampshire primary, won by Hillary Clinton, enough to keep him afloat while others were sunk. He turned his attention to the next primary, the one in his home state of South Carolina.

Tom was proud of and grateful for his support, but he had to admit to himself that his prospects of winning his own state were slim; "*hell, slim and none and Slim just left town,*" he reckoned. He also had to admit to himself that the more likely result was he would be in a distant third, fourth or even worse, a most embarrassing scenario, as well as unproductive. The media would drop him like a bad habit once the outcome became evident. He resigned himself to the fact that it was time for him to start steering his supporters and as many other voters as he could to Barack Obama and withdraw from the race before the primary. He confided all that to Katie and she concurred.

Tom made the call to his handlers, who also concurred, and they strategized how to best do it, a respectable, graceful out. Tom, however, was not satisfied with graceful.

He did have one more bit of fun in the aftermath. He was a guest on a talk show with a none too favorable host. Playing to his audience, the host thought he would score big by trapping the candidate. Silly him.

"Candidate Howard, what do you think about the NRA supporting your opponents?"

"Well, they should support me instead."

"Why? Because you're an NRA supporter?"

"No, because I'm rational."

"So, you don't support the NRA?"

"I didn't say that. I do like guns though."

The host sensed a set up there and therefore ignored the gratuitous remark. He could not help pressing the issue and decided to circle back for the kill.

"So, are you saying then that your opponents, the Republican candidates, are not rational?"

"No. I'm not saying that."

"Are you not saying that because it's not true or because you just don't care to say it?"

"Yes."

At that point, the host committed the cardinal sin of losing his cool.

"Are you just fucking with me?"

"Yes."

A competing media outlet picked up the discourse and ran it midday just for the fun of it. It generated sufficient consumer interest and reaction to throw in as a filler piece with the evening news with a "You gotta see this" lead. A technician masterfully bleeped the profanity with both the "f" and the "ing" audible. By morning, the video had gone viral, prompting even more coverage and air time for Tom Howard.

Tom relented to one interview about it. After a bit of similar banter, Tom disappointed the interviewer while making points with voters by cutting it off with, "Listen. This has been fun, but I really have to get back to work now."

* * *

It was not long after Barack Obama's victory when Tom Howard was invited to go see him at the transition team headquarters. The President-elect was most gracious and grateful. He asked, "Tom, what can I do for you, I mean seriously and sincerely?" Tom declined anything, saying that it had been his honor and privilege to have served the country, but he was ready to go back home and tend to the family businesses, but mostly to be a grandfather. Before leaving though, he did look the President-elect in the eye and say, "I ask only one thing of you, Mister President, that is to be faithful to the men and women in uniform who will remain faithful to this great country, regardless of the cost."

Before completely parting ways with Washington, however, Tom and Katie would be invited to the Commander-in-Chief's Ball, where the President publicly praised Tom for his service to the country and sacrifices for her. It was not a perfunctory event. The President had taken the time to learn and now chronicle Tom's Vietnam tours and awards for valor and wounds sustained; that he was a Green Beret, founder of an elite special operations unit, and a decorated veteran of Desert Storm before serving in Congress for more than a decade; and finally "a most worthy candidate for this office I am blessed to now hold," concluding with, "Ladies and gentlemen, please join me in proudly honoring this true American hero!"

16

WHILE BO HOWARD AND TOM HOWARD WERE ENMESHED IN THEIR political battles, 15th SOG was ordered to prepare to deploy a company at a time to relieve elements of the 173rd Airborne Brigade Combat Team at Combat Outpost (COP) Sierra in the Korengal Valley in the Kunar Province of eastern Afghanistan, an area of high, rugged mountains, richly forested at lower altitudes and lush in the valley floors. It had been a hotbed of activity for years and remained untamed.

On paper, each company in turn of the 15th SOG would be deployed for six months. In reality, personnel shortages due to members in non-deployable status for one reason or another caused each company to have to be augmented by soldiers from the other two, but never from without. Alpha Company, slated to go first, worked feverishly to prepare, both logistically and tactically.

The 173rd had seen plenty of combat there and suffered more than a few casualties. The same was true in the neighboring Pech Valley where elements of the Ranger Regiment were posted. The 15th SOG command and staff studied reports, maps, and aerial photographs and even made calls to the veterans of the region. They decided to go with the venerable military maxim that offense is the best defense and accordingly while they would be vigilant in the static defense of the COP, the Rangers would conduct aggressive patrolling and ambushes and the Green Berets would augment the same, regularly work with local villagers and soon train and fight with selected troops from the Afghan National Army ("ANA"), forerunners to the ANA Commando Corps and ANA Special Forces.

The nightmare truly was the logistics: What, how, when to pack; what to requisition or buy on the open market with allotted funds; aircraft requirements from Camp Marion to boots on the ground in Afghanistan, each with a precise loading plan; and a million details, each having the potential of creating utter chaos. Not a single soul doubted that Murphy's Law was in full force and effect.

That is not to say that the soldiers did nothing but plan, work, and worry. Time was taken for some frivolity too. The outpost needed a personal, unofficial name. By luck of the draw, Bravo Company got to first propose the name. They squandered it. Days of thought and plenty of discussion, sometimes heated discussion, produced nothing more than the unimaginative name of "The Alamo."

Charlie Company went next and offered the name "Beau Geste" after the classic 1966 Foreign Legion movie. It did not take a research whiz to discover that Beau Geste was a character in the movie, that the fort actually was named "Fort Zinderneuf." Charlie suffered no small amount for their blunder.

When Alpha took its turn, they promptly bowed out of the competition, stating emphatically that while they were there the outpost would have a far better name, *their* name. They even already had made a handsomely painted sign adapting the "Swamp Hogs" sign that had graced their training room for three decades with "Swamp Hogs" supplanted by "Hog Heaven." (Nobody had considered that the ANA troops who would be sharing the compound with the Americans might be offended by the reference to the unclean animal, which fortunately they did not, or at least did not express or show it.)

The outpost would continue to be reinforced with both material and personnel as it had been for the unit from the 173rd Airborne they were replacing, only moreso. The outpost's defenses were bolstered by a mortar tube and crew; a tripod mounted Mark 19 (Mk 19) automatic 40mm grenade launcher; a tripod mounted .50 caliber machine gun; and a tripod mounted M240 machine gun. There was sophisticated communications equipment with a pair of operators; sophisticated tactical surveillance equipment, including night vision and thermal scopes, maintained by a specialist; sophisticated targeting equipment, including a counter-battery radar team capable of detecting the source of incoming fires, and team; and there were two UAV (unmanned aerial vehicle; also called RPA's (remotely piloted aircraft) and drones) teams greatly extending the unit's range for surveillance and targeting. Even a mechanic was attached for the maintenance of the generators, refrigerator, heaters, and fans. There also was an Afghan interpreter familiar with the local dialects. Finally, on and off there would be OGA's, people from "other governmental agencies" (i.e., the CIA). All told, the outpost's defenses were formidable indeed.

Unbeknownst to 15th SOG, they had one more asset: Lieutenant Colonel Jonathan Howard.

* * *

Early on in their deployment, Alpha Company, as reinforced, faced the predicted frequent, but fortunately inaccurate, mortar and rocket fire, but the "eye in the sky" drones and counter-battery fires and air strikes were effective to eliminate or deter those threats. Enemy sniper fire continued to plague them, though. However, the Alpha snipers (and occasionally Navy SEAL or Delta Force operators who came out for the sport), again with the help of the drones, soon all but ended that annoyance as well. Armed with M24A1 Remington sniper rifles firing match grade .308 rounds and another firing the heftier .300 Winchester Magnum ammunition, all with superb optics, the American snipers systematically killed many of the enemy snipers who ventured within a quarter mile of the outpost and scored a few confirmed kills at twice that distance.

One sniper on the M82A1 .50 caliber Barrett, an incredible weapon costing nearly $9,000 each plus optics, took out an insurgent beyond the 1,800-meter tracer burnout range. Still the enemy kept coming, as evidenced by frequent contacts by the patrols and ambush teams.

Lieutenant Colonel Jon Howard was well aware of the situation. When he first was made privy to that 15th SOG was being deployed and where, he reviewed the reports of their predecessors there. While Jon knew that Korengal was a very bad place, he had not realized how much of the enemy effort was directed at COP Sierra. While the enemy hit the other COPs and FOB Blessing sporadically, they were relentless in their harassment of COP Sierra. That prompted the question in Jon's mind, *"Where are all these fuckers coming from?"* He resolved to find the answer.

He got on the intercom, "Mister Henderson, got a minute?" While waiting for the Chief Warrant Officer third grade to join him, Jon reviewed in his mind the man's credentials, *one of Bill Gates' braniacs at Microsoft; joined the intelligence branch of the army reserve for "excitement;" was earmarked early as a genius in his specialty, imagery analysis; and in a world of geeks was known as a "geek with a capital g."*

When CW3 Clifton Henderson appeared in his doorway, Jon's first thought was, *"He certainly fits the bill."* After directing the man to sit, Jon asked, "How much more time do you have with us, Cliff?"

"About four months, sir, unless I get extended."

"Outstanding. I have a project for you." Pulling out a map and some aerial imagery he explained: "This is Combat Outpost Sierra in the Korangal Valley of eastern Afghanistan. The unit taking it over is the 15th Special Operations Group, specifically Alpha Company thereof from South Carolina. Just so you know, my father founded that unit and I grew up with them, a few of them still with them and here now. That COP is subjected to steady enemy attacks.

"I want to find out who the bad guys are and, where you come in, where they're coming from. Use all the reports and imagery I have gathered. I am getting more. Questions?"

"By when?"

"Yesterday."

"Got it, sir. I'm on it."

True to his reputation, in amazingly short order Cliff Henderson devoured and digested everything they had, made specific requests for more information, and then gobbled that up too. He exhausted everything the Army and Air Force could provide and then everything the OGA's could/would provide. He created digital files and subfiles. He organized, collated, stored, reviewed, and started all over again. He, however, simply was not able to answer the question, to solve the puzzle.

The break came when a mixed team of Alpha Green Berets and Rangers managed to capture a prisoner after a firefight, a rare occurrence, but even more rare in that they did so in a fashion that his comrades were unaware and probably unsuspecting. The Taliban fighter had been blown off his rocky perch by a well-placed M203 round, had fallen down a steep rocky slope into the river below, and had been swept away. His surviving comrades had fled in the other direction. Hours later and more than a mile downstream, the fighter had been spotted clinging to a rock by the pilot of an OH-58 Kiowa scout helicopter. The Taliban was in no condition to offer any resistance when the Alpha patrol descended upon him and plucked him from the frigid water.

Jon Howard had anticipated the possibility of such an occurrence and had persuaded his boss, a brigadier general, to issue an order directing that any such enemy prisoner of war (EPW) be immediately isolated from any others and "taken directly and without delay" to a designated secure site and there "completely isolated;" that "this headquarters alone be notified without delay" and that further direction would follow. The order was complied with and the "further direction" came in the form of Lieutenant Colonel Jonathan Howard personally.

The notification had been immediately passed along to Jon and he literally dropped what he was doing and hastened to the site. There he met with the interrogation team and told them, "Gentlemen, thank you. This guy might be a golden nugget. For reasons you don't have the need to know, I need to know who he was with and, most importantly, where they came from. Promise him the moon, whatever it takes, but I want him singing that tune. Anything more would be icing on the cake. How much time do you need to prep?"

The team leader looked at his team and then back at the colonel and said, "We're good to go, sir. It's what we do."

"Outstanding. I want to sit in. Paint me as a new staff guy wanting to observe."

"Roger that, sir."

The team, joined by an interpreter and followed by LTC Howard, entered the interrogation room where the EPW sat on a hard chair huddled under a blanket and facing a bare table with three chairs. The two interrogators and the interpreter quietly took the seats at the table while LTC Howard took a lone seat in the corner behind them. The hidden audio/video camera had been recording for some time, as were the backup systems.

The EPW was absolutely terrified. He had grown up hearing stories of the horrors mujahideen and even innocent civilians faced in Soviet hands, lived with reports that Afghan puppets were as bad, and he feared that the American infidels might be worse, probably so if they were CIA.

The lead investigator read the man's fear and chose his approach. To the interpreter he commanded, "Tell this piece of shit that the guy in the corner is an observer, but I am in charge." The interpreter did and the EPW's glance over at Howard confirmed his understanding.

"Now tell him that he is going to tell me his name, where he's from, his commander, and where he came from. Tell him he can cooperate now or he can cooperate later, but in either event he is going to cooperate. Tell him we will let him go after he cooperates."

The interpreter spoke for a time. The EPW said nothing. The interpreter spoke even more animatedly. The EPW still said nothing. The interpreter turned to the interrogator and shrugged his shoulders.

The interrogator looked back at LTC Howard, who subtly signaled termination of the interview.

The interrogator stared menacingly at the EPW and then abruptly stood and left the room, followed by the other Americans and the interpreter. The EPW was left for the time being, the hidden recorders running. The interpreter was dismissed for the day and the Americans returned to the team room. There LTC Howard commanded the lead investigator, "I need you two, your immediate boss, and your CO."

Calls were made and the men sat silently until a captain and a major appeared. LTC Howard wasted no time. "I trust you know who I am and who I work for." As soon as the two officers nodded affirmatively, Jon dropped the bomb. "Your interpreter is a mole."

He gave the men in the room a few moments to digest that awful fact. "He just told our EPW not to say anything about two named guys. I need to follow up on them. In the meantime, put the EPW back in complete isolation and put your terp on a short leash, but he must not suspect that his cover is blown. Clear?"

Following a chorus of clears, LTC Howard left them to ponder the consequences of allowing a mole to penetrate their organization and what damage he already had caused.

Jon Howard stormed into the intel office, grabbing his startled deputy along the way and without a hint of explanation slammed the door of his office, parked his now dumbfounded deputy in a chair, and immediately got on a secure telephone. After the audible signal confirmed the secure status, the deputy listened to one side of the conversation:

"Dave, you clear to talk? Good. Listen, I need to know pronto everything there is to know about two characters, one, Ismail Askar Kunar, and the other, Abdul Hassan Khalil. What? You're freakin' amazing! Tell me." What the deputy could not hear was the reply:

"Ismail is a war chief. Whereabouts unknown. He's operated in both Nuristan and Kunar. Unconfirmed reports attribute attacks in the Pech District to him. Again unconfirmed, but he is believed to be able to field a couple hundred fighters, making him a bigger fish than Ahmad Shah."

Jon knew that name. In 2005, he had gotten tangentially involved in Operation Red Wings targeting that man and his band of fighters not too far from COP Sierra. Jon had adamantly counseled using airborne surveillance platforms, only to be rebuffed, the spec ops command instead opting for insertion of a four-man SEAL recon team despite spotty communications at best. It was a catastrophe. The recon team's mission was soon compromised and they were attacked by Shah and dozens of his men. The SEALs fought back admirably, but three of the four were killed. A rescue team, again without the benefit of surveillance aircraft, responded, only to be blown out of the sky. A forty-million dollar MH-47 helicopter was destroyed and sixteen more special operators were killed. Ahmad Shah and his surviving men escaped to Pakistan where they were believed to still be.

The CIA agent continued, "Khalil is chief of a village about midway between FOB Blessing and COP Sierra. He's figured to be working both sides. Again though, unconfirmed. I have heard his name and Ismail's together, but I'd have to check on that."

Jon asked, "Thanks, buddy. Can you do some homework on those two ASAP? 'Unconfirmed' won't get me to where I want to go."

"Can do, Jon. I'll call you quick as I can."

Jon turned toward his deputy and said, "Sorry for the secret squirrel stuff. To bring you up to speed, I have been trying to track the fighters harassing COP Sierra. That's what I've had Henderson working on. I just got some potentially eye opening info. Assuming that to be correct, I'll want to quickly assemble a team to put on it, work up through briefing prep. Right now, I want to feed this info to Henderson and see what, if anything, he can make of it and then I need to brief the general."

CW3 Henderson's eyes lit up when he heard the name of the village. "Excellent,' he exclaimed, "now I can narrow my focus. It sure would help if we could get the Air Force to share *all* the surveillance feeds for a circumference around there with the radius being the distance to Sierra."

Jon briefed the general who was sufficiently intrigued to immediately call his counterpart in the Air Force for the desired intel, which before long was forthcoming, and to persuade him to be the intermediary to get orbiting surveillance aircraft to routinely scan the target area and provide results of the same.

So much intel began flooding in that Jon saw the necessity of giving Henderson another imagery analyst, then another, and then a third. Before long, Henderson and his sub-team were able to map out likely enemy in, around, and through "Midway," as they had taken to call Khalil's village, and collate it with known enemy action and activity around COP Sierra. Jon then brought on a signals intel analyst to analyze provided signals intercepts likewise collated, which Jon, with his linguistic abilities, personally involved himself.

Satisfied that they were on the right track, Jon knew that it was not really actionable intelligence unless he could predict when the enemy would be there. He agonized over that until he realized that he was looking at it too narrowly. The better alternative would be to entice the enemy to be there at a time of their choosing. Jon switched his focus to what to recommend in that regard.

Jon again briefed the general and the general was sufficiently satisfied to call the spec ops command with the suggestion that they send over a field commander and staffers for an actionable intel briefing that could be quite fruitful. He made calls to the Air Force, Marines, and OGAs as well. Showing the respect they had for the general, all agreed. The general directed Jon to contact the 15th SOG commander at COP Sierra and have him and two others at the briefing.

Jon then holed himself up with Henderson to devise a briefing and brought in one more member to his little task force, the "go to guy" for creating a masterful PowerPoint demonstration as all but required in any military briefing, presentation, or class.

* * *

"Good morning, gentlemen, and thank you for coming over here," Jon began the briefing, "my name is Jon Howard. I am an intel guy. I am not a gunslinger. I have not pulled a trigger on a bad guy since 1991. I am not an ops guy. I am an intel guy, one with a vested interest in what I am about to dangle before you. With me is Chief Warrant Officer Henderson. Yes, he is a geek, but you will soon learn one very, very smart geek. Also with me is Lieutenant Colonel Bill Stanford, my Air Force counterpart; Major Gus Addison, our tier one liaison; and Dave, well, just Dave. They each can validate certain points that may be called into question.

"You, I am sure, are all well acquainted with Kunar Province," a map of which appeared on the screen, "and the Korangal Valley," a map of which then appeared on the screen with FOB Blessing and the COPs depicted, followed by another of the same in satellite photo format. "The part we are interested in is here," his laser pointer dancing about the sector between and including FOB Blessing and COP Sierra. The next slide zoomed in on the COP.

"I said I have a vested interest in this and I do. You see, COP Sierra, code named here "Miss Piggy" for reasons soon to be apparent, is currently manned by 15th SOG, the 15th Special Operations Group, a reserve slash guard spec ops unit comprised of Special Forces and Rangers and the unit my father, Tom Howard, yes, the congressman and recent presidential hopeful, conceived of, formed, and commanded. I grew up with 15th SOG's Alpha Company, the 'Swamp Hogs' at Camp Marion, South Carolina.

"So, when I learned the Swamp Hogs were deploying to Miss Piggy, the name I chose because they dubbed COP Sierra 'Hog Heaven,' I endeavored to find out who the bad guys in their AO were, where they were coming from, and how they could be killed. Enter Mister Henderson, Dave, and a host of others from the Army, the Air Force, and OGA's.

"We ascertained that the main bad guy is one we will call 'the Joker,' your typical warrior/smuggler/bandit, but one with a couple hundred fighters at his beck and call." Beginning there, PowerPoint slides were projected for each talking point Jon Howard made. "We then determined that the Joker hangs out somewhere southeast of Wanat and likes to come down by various routes, cross the Pech at various points between FOB Blessing and COP Michigan, and head up the Korangal Valley, again by various routes, all too frequently aimed at Miss Piggy. The one constant we established is that he uses this village we will call 'Midway' as a way station, staging area, and field headquarters. The village chief there is a guy we will call 'Two Face.'"

"There, unfortunately, is no way of predicting when the Joker will be there with an attractive force. I reiterate that I am not an ops guy, but I have a rough plan to propose and it involves forming a joint task force, baiting the Joker down to Midway and wiping them out with an air strike followed by ground forces, spec ops and conventional. Here's how I envision it.

"First, would be forming a joint task force, but for discussion purposes that'd best be left for last. Second, 15th SOG (from here on I'll just refer to them as 'Alpha') will increase their patrols out to Midway, sucking up more to Two Face each time and introducing him to a Civil Affairs team who will offer him an enticing aid package. We will employ SIGINT assets to ascertain what calls that produces. At the same time, the Air Force will target the Joker's supply lines from Pakistan with the goal of interdicting them and making him hungry and concerned about his ability to keep his force intact and maintain a presence in Kunar.

"Third, we actually will deliver the aid, far more than Two Face's village can use and much of it perishable, stored in containers we will position outside the village, except, that is, for the included herd of goats. Again, SIGINT comes in to play along with satellite and high altitude aerial surveillance to see if Two Face contacts the Joker and the Joker bites and begins making a move toward the loot. There will be so much that he'd need more than half his men to tote and guard it.

Fourth, once we know that the Joker is in Korangal Valley and headed toward Midway, that last leg we expect to be at night, ground units will infil to staging areas from where they can move to cut off squirters from Midway and covert surveillance will intensify over what we expect to be several columns of the Joker's troops and Midway and approaches to it. I believe we can have live feed of that to the JTF TOC. When the Joker is confirmed to be nearing Midway, attack aircraft will stand by to strike and the staged ground units will begin to move to their designated interdiction positions.

"Fifth, when satisfied that the Joker is at the aid site with his joined forces, again expecting it to be dark then, the Air Force will bomb it in a manner calculated to be devastating to the hostile forces while minimizing collateral damage to the village itself. Again, live feed scenario.

"Sixth, the ground force (and here I am supposing conventional forces), covered by attack aircraft, fixed wing and Apache, will air assault to sweep the target while the spec ops ambush teams, supported by an AC-130, take out the squirters.

"Seventh, intel teams will chopper in, sweep through, photographing, tallying and collecting. That will include Two Face, whom we intend to relocate to Cuba along with another guy who surfaced along the way. I reiterate that the KIA score could well be in the two hundred range.

"Finally, my team will collect info from all the sources involved directly and indirectly, analyze it, and submit our product as segments of the after-action report. We also hope to be able to trace the enemy routes and hopefully track them back to the Joker's base and maybe beyond into Pakistan. That info will be passed along to the appropriate headquarters.

"Gentlemen, that's what we have other than the supporting evidence available to you. My opinion is that this is actionable intel. That concludes my briefing. Questions?"

And the grilling session began. It started off hot. A Ranger colonel who looked like he could chew nails spoke out as if he had been. "Colonel, you opined that this is good stuff. Maybe, maybe not. You intel guys have no qualms in sending shooters out on nothing more than a guess. It's easy for you to say, they're not your guys."

Jon nearly exploded. *Motherfucker!* He told himself to calm himself before responding, but his mind screamed back, "*Fuck it!*" Taking a breath and looking the Ranger dead in the eyes, he said in a measured tone that did nothing to hide his rage, he said, "Colonel, yes, that *is* my opinion. I stand on it. It is an opinion based upon the facts as presented and my analysis based upon training and experience, with a lot of help I might add. You're not the only one who has been here before and you're not the only one who has met the enemy based upon flimsy, even faulty intelligence. This is neither flimsy nor faulty intelligence.

"And, lastly, Colonel, they *are* my guys. Those 15th SOG guys and their families are *my* friends and neighbors, my entire family's. But it's your call, sir. That's why you have the green tab. You decide whether this is a reasonable opportunity on a worthwhile target or to kick it to the curb." Snubbing any reply, Jon turned to the group as a whole and said, "Gentlemen, your questions, please."

The Q&A resumed. Most of the questions were insightful while some, a very few, could only be labeled as boneheaded. Jon fielded them all well, often referring back to the slide show and turning to the others at the front as appropriate. It was altogether positive. However, after a while the law of diminishing returns kicked in. Jon sensed it.

"Gentlemen, we've been at this for some time. We all can keep at it, but I propose instead that we intel types leave you all alone while you chew on it over the lunch we can bring in shortly. Afterward, we'll come back and we can discuss it further, including what of what you've seen you'd like to take with you."

The afternoon session did not last as long, but Jon thought it was equally positive, if not moreso. The group cordially left to take the matter to their respective superiors.

Jon Howard was in for nearly a week of apprehension. He knew his idea was being considered because a designated point man, the Special Forces colonel Jon noted had said little while clearly absorbing much, called a number of times with specific questions and requests, including for daily intel updates, which Jon was pleased to oblige. Jon was elated when the colonel's final call was to invite him to the first planning session of JTF Midway for Operation Dark Knight.

There Jon realized that he was the junior man at the table (but he at least was at the table). He resigned himself that the ops guys were in control, but was pleased that his concept of the operation was largely adopted. He was delighted that the Air Force Space Command had stepped up in a big way with tasking surveillance satellites to the target area and sharing both information gathered and analysis thereof by their own experts. He was even more thrilled to learn that a B-1B bomber was to be tasked with it being likely that the munition of choice would be a 2,000-pound Mark 84 JDAM smart bomb and that an AC-130 Spectre gunship would be on station promptly after the bomb drop.

Plans were made, proposed, discussed, changed, detailed, refined, finalized, and put into play. Both Two Face and the Joker unwittingly cooperated. The loot there for the taking simply was just too great of a temptation.

As the operation was set into motion, Jon Howard, Cliff Henderson, and Dave found themselves temporarily without active roles. They instead watched the show in the JTF operations center and during relatively idle times Jon was amused by Dave's obvious efforts to recruit Cliff.

The scene in the ops center intensified as the Joker's men entered the target box and the ambush teams were ordered to infil to the designated staging areas. The excitement then ebbed as they began to wait the estimated two hours before the Joker and his men closed on Midway. The intensity grew when that occurred and peaked when the JTF commander cleared the B-1 to commence its run and ordered Chinooks carrying the ground force to head to the target.

The B-1 bomber dropped not one but two JDAMs, one at the congregation of enemy fighters around the aid pods and another at a structure at the edge of the village where the consensus was that the Joker and his command group had located. The results, observed via live feeds from surveillance aircraft, were truly astonishing.

The first bomb struck one of the pods, vaporized a dozen enemy fighters, and by its concussion and fragmentation killed or incapacitated as many more. The second bomb missed the target building, but it was "close enough." The superheated concussion wave from the huge explosion crushed the two guards against the front wall and incinerated them a microsecond before it blew in the wall and caused the roof to collapse. Only a couple emerged from the rubble and they collapsed within yards.

Before the Chinooks entered the zone, two DShK heavy machine gun positions were detected and obliterated respectively by an AC-130 and an F-15. A third had avoided detection, but exposed itself by firing at one of the lead Chinooks. Lacking the sophisticated night vision capabilities the Americans enjoyed, it fortunately missed and was quickly destroyed by a pair of Hellfire missiles launched by an Apache, followed by a generous hosing of 30mm rounds for good measure. (When asked later why he expended so much ordnance at such a small target, the gunner's reply was, "They don't pay me extra to bring that shit back.")

The Chinooks landed with scant opposition that was quickly eliminated or driven off, the bulk of the leaderless fighters surviving the JDAM's instead fleeing as anticipated. Three of the four ambush teams made kills. Alpha's caught a group of ten, killed six of them and wounded and captured the other four. One group of about a dozen enemy fighters evaded the ambushers, but could not evade the incredible sensors and fire control systems of the orbiting AC-130 which in spectacular fashion slaughtered them. It and a host of other aircraft continued to voraciously hunt down and kill fleeing fighters.

The butcher's bill initially was 65 confirmed kills, upped to 73 after

Alpha Company patrols reached the destroyed DShK positions, upped again to 84 after analysis of the video of the first bomb strike allowed counting of 11 vaporized or splattered enemy, with an estimate of half as many more dead or mortally wounded scattered across the area. A body suspected to be the Joker, Ismail Askar Kunar, was pulled from the rubble, which was confirmed by reliable intelligence before completion of the after-action report. CW3 Henderson and his other imagery analysts spent the better part of a day reviewing surveillance recordings to come to the conclusion that less than 50 of the Joker's men escaped.

American casualties were easier to calculate: Zero.

Abdul Hassan Khalil, Two Face, shocked by the air strike and again when the alien-like assault troops with their NVG's in place kicked in his door and briskly flex-cuffed him and covered his head with a hood was stupefied by being roughly taken to an awaiting helicopter. He was taken to an unknown place and there he spent days in disorienting and frightening isolation. For days after that, the only break in his isolation was prolonged and intense interrogation sessions. The final blow came when his interrogators concluded that he was of no more intelligence value and had the thoroughly bewildered man summarily sent to Gitmo (the familiar name for GTMO, the Guantanamo Bay detention camp located in the Guantanamo Naval Base in Guantanamo Bay, Cuba), there to face detention for an indefinite period of time.

The mole interpreter Jon Howard had revealed reportedly was killed while resisting arrest.

CW4 Henderson left Afghanistan a few weeks later, promoted to that rank and awarded a Bronze Star (both expedited as only generals can do). It had been the excitement of his life and there was no going back to Microsoft. His superiors and co-workers there just shook their heads when he informed them that he was going to work for "the government."

Jon Howard was surprised when the Ranger colonel he had butted heads with appeared one day. He shook Jon's hand and in token of his appreciation and respect handed him a special 75th Ranger Regiment challenge coin and a copy of a glowing official Letter of Commendation.

***

Alpha Company's remaining time at Hog Heaven was relatively quiet, almost boring. They came home proud of their performance and accomplishments and proud that in their time there they had suffered not a single killed and few wounded, none disabling. Bravo Company's role changed to train and ultimately transition the COP to an ANA Commando post. Charlie Company's role was minimized to its ODA and a single squad of Rangers and then only for half its planned deployment.

In April, 2008, more than 1,600 soldiers of the 218th MEB (Maneuver Enhancement Brigade) were deployed to Afghanistan, the largest deployment of the South Carolina Army National Guard since World War Two, to take over Combined Joint Task Force Phoenix. Their ranks were augmented and their capabilities enhanced by a dozen of Alpha Company's operators volunteering to join them.

Before then, Jon Howard returned to the United States with his third Bronze Star medal and a recommendation for a below zone promotion to colonel. He mused to himself, "*Well, Jon boy, no guarantees there, but it beats the shit out of being damned by faint praise.*" Even more gratifying was that he was bound for the Pentagon and the coveted assignment to the Intelligence Directorate (J2) of the Joint Chiefs of Staff (JSOC). He would gain that promotion in due time and later would go on to serve the president directly as deputy to the National Security Advisor, a posting that would lead to a brigadier general's star. The pivotal event leading him there was nothing atypical for Jon.

It was a full meeting of JSOC. Jon, a mere lieutenant colonel in a sea of stars, did not rate a seat at the table. As the current speaker briefed an issue via an omnipresent PowerPoint demonstration based upon a summary of the voluminous report Jon had been handed and held in his lap, a comment led to discussion. Jon scanned the report as he listened to the discussion.

One of the deputies, a brigadier general, one Jon privately considered alternatively an arrogant asshole and an insufferable prick, his ambition for a second star indiscreet and his lust for another and even a fourth transparent, was advocating his position to the point of it becoming a harangue. The comment had prompted Jon to review the relevant part of the report, the bio of the key informant, a transcript of his statement, and a translation of the same. It took him but a minute to discern an error, a material one.

While it was unusual, in fact strongly discouraged, for a staffer to do more than pass a note to or more rarely whisper in the ear of his superior at the table, Jon felt compelled to speak out.

"Pardon the interruption, General, but I suggest that there may be another way to look at this."

The general was clearly miffed and he narrowed his eyes menacingly at Jon. Jon's immediate reaction was the thought, "*Geez, I'd like to play poker with this guy.*"

The general responded by saying rather venomously, "Intel, as you know, *colonel*, is always subject to interpretation."

Jon Howard, not one to be cowed, replied, "It's not a question of interpretation, *sir*, but a matter of translation."

The chairman, a four-star general, knowing full well Lieutenant Colonel Howard's extraordinary language abilities, was interested. He interjected, "You got my attention, Colonel. Please explain."

"Very well, sir. Looking at the detailed report I have before me, sir, I see that the source principally relied upon is from an Afghan region along the Pakistani border, up near Tajikstan, an area with which I am familiar. It is a region where local dialect corrupts Pashto and Dari with both Tajik and Nuristani. The translation upon which we are relying puts the threat west of the Khyber Pass, in or near Jalalabad, Afghanistan. However, I believe it is much more likely that, assuming the transcription of the statement in the report to be correct, a more correct translation places it on the *east* side of the pass, vicinity of Peshawar, Pakistan; the import being taking the military, at least the conventional military, out of the equation. Having said that, may I be so bold as to suggest that our friends in the CIA take another look at it, put another ear to it, and consider reconsidering?"

The chairman rocked back in his chair, his face betraying nothing. Not a man to procrastinate, he turned to the CIA representative in attendance and asked, "Given the gravity of the situation, how long would it take Langley to do that?"

The CIA rep was quick to respond, "Coming from you, sir, I would say not long, not very long at all. May I be excused to make a phone call?"

"By all means." The CIA rep got up to leave, passing Jon Howard on the way. As he passed, Jon helpfully whispered to him, "Page 212, second paragraph, and page 230 near the bottom."

When the CIA rep had cleared he room, the chairman added to the entire audience, "May I suggest [it, of course, being no suggestion at all] that we table this discussion while the CIA squirms and agonizes or maybe loads up to shoot Colonel Howard down in flames and in the meantime, we take up the newest Korean issue?"

The appointed briefer on that topic took the cue and headed to the podium while the technician seamlessly switched to the pertinent PowerPoint demonstration. The topic was about covered when the CIA rep returned and took his seat. The briefer wrapped up her part and took her seat. The chairman looked at the CIA rep and raised his eyebrows as a signal to report.

The CIA rep actually smiled, prompting a moment of panic for Jon Howard, relieved only by the words that followed, "Please don't kill the messenger, sir, but the consensus among the pertinent linguists at Langley is that Colonel Howard is right on the money. The Director humbly begs your pardon, sir."

The chairman laughed and said, "It seems that we have yet another translation issue. I cannot imagine the Director begging for anything." Readdressing the entire assemblage, he said, "All right, let's pick up where we left off in light of this development."

The subject briefer did not return to the podium. Instead he sheepishly said, "Sir, in light of the development, I recommend we table it for the day, pending, uh, pending review and reconsideration."

The chairman did not hesitate. "Agreed. Done. Lunch. Reassemble at 1330, no, make it 1400."

Jon Howard dutifully waited for the senior officers and staffers to leave the room, trying his best to in the meantime be invisible. As he exited, an aide to the chairman discreetly pulled him aside and quietly said, "The chief told me to pass on to you 'a hearty well done,' and to tell you in strictest confidence that it made his day to see the 'good general' taken down a notch or two."

Later that day, Jon got a call from the Director of the CIA. "Jon, do you recognize my voice?" Jon acknowledged that he did. "Good. If we were to slip you reports a day or two early, could we avoid getting publicly spanked by you?" Jon assured him that was likely. "Excellent. You know if this Army thing doesn't work out you've got a golden parachute over here." Jon thanked him, quite pleased that he had not inadvertently burned a bridge.

***

Bo Howard remained in Congress, an increasingly difficult feat because South Carolina, having been carried by the Republicans in 2004 and then 2008, had become a red state. Still, with a great deal of help, he persevered and began making a greater name for himself in Washington and a greater positive impact for his constituents.

Tom Howard had long since returned home. While he did whatever he could to help Bo and found time for some political commentaries and occasional speaking engagements (his preference being veterans' affairs), his time was largely consumed by assuming the chief role in the family enterprises. Tom also devoted more to his responsibility as trustee of the family trust.

In that regard, in reviewing the books of the trust, Tom discovered a perplexing entry. He could not trace a significant amount of the funds used to develop Carlisle. He put the books away, let them simmer for a couple of days and then returned to them. He found no explanation. Tom decided to call his brother-in-law, the trusted family lawyer for years.

"Trey, start the clock running, I have a legal question, dealing with funding in the family trust."

Trey cut him off. "Tom, I suspect I know what it's about. I don't have time to answer it right now. Why don't you and Katie come up for dinner tomorrow night? There's a new fancy restaurant I've been wanting someone to take me and my bride to. I am told they have the best wine list in town. That'll be my fee. Come early and plan to stay over and enjoy the Holy City a bit."

The next afternoon was spent in Charleston chatting under a massive live oak tree in Trey's back yard. Alcohol was involved. Even after Tom was ready to go out to dinner, he feared getting in a car with any of them at the wheel. He expressed his concerns to Trey who replied that he had planned for that. Trey freshened their drinks, poured them into cheap, touristy plastic cups and beckoned, "Come, ladies, your carriage awaits." When the four of them came out the front door, there before them indeed was a carriage, and a horse drawn carriage at that. Before the men took their seats, Trey whispered to Tom, "Don't worry, my frugal friend. This part's on me."

It was a wonderful ride through the historic district to the restaurant that had once been a mansion. The four were welcomed like royalty and led through the well-appointed interior to their table in a cozy, private alcove. The waiter was an expert at respecting their privacy while somehow sensing the need to serve them in some way, promptly doing it and again seemingly disappearing, repeating the cycle time and again during the multi-course meal. Tom wondered at the cost and whether he would have been a better steward of the trust's funds if he instead had gone to Trey's office and paid his worthy although painful hourly rate. His concerns, however, were unjustified. When the coffee was served and a different bottle of wine was ceremoniously inspected, opened, tasted, approved, and served and the waiter had again done his disappearing act, Trey did not disappoint.

"Well, Tom, Katie, thank you for a most marvelous meal, fine wine, and splendid company. Now, I suppose, it's time to get down to business. So, Tom, the trust books don't add up. I am surprised that your father went to his grave without telling you. I have known the answers for, what, twenty-five years or more?

"It was back when I was a mere associate in the firm, on the partnership track, but with no guarantees. I met your Dad after you and Katie tied the knot and he took pity on my plight by tossing me some business. I suppose I handled the things well enough because we, the firm, got more and more. It wasn't long before your family became a client of note and then a top-drawer client, so much so that the firm not only made me a partner, but waived the buy-in fee. But I get ahead of myself.

"Before I spoil my little story by getting to the point, let me say this. Most men have their follies. I suppose some, but fewer by far, women do too. It might be a boat, a motorcycle, a condo at the beach, or other such nonsense. For your Granddad, everyone said it was his pool. They were wrong about that. It wasn't folly and it wasn't the only time that he engaged in what naysayers would have called folly.

"The same went for your Dad. The two of them, as rough as they liked to portray themselves, had brains. Pardon me, ladies, but they had balls too. Balls in war and balls in business. I could say the same about you, Tom Howard, adding of course politics to the mix. In fact, I am saying the same about you. Pardon me for not saying this out loud before, but I am proud to be related to you, if only in law.

"Anyway, one day Dan called and asked to meet with me and the corporate and tax lawyers on the team, to clear the whole afternoon. That, of course, was music to our ears. He brought with him a friend from the war, Stu Markowitz. I trust you've met him?"

Tom and Katie each nodded with smiles, reflecting that they knew the man and knew he was a character. Trey continued, "I confess that at first I was quite taken aback by the man. He was so, so, let's say stereotypical. He had about sold Dan on an investment scheme, but Dan was too prudent to act without consulting us. The idea itself did not sway me from my first impression of Stu, but as he laid it out, I came to the conclusion that it was brilliant.

"By that time, the Disney corporation had gobbled up huge tracts of land around Orlando for Disney World. Others followed suit to capitalize on the success and the so-called smart money said that land values there had peaked. Stu thought differently and he knew that there were individuals and corporations anxious to cash in too soon.

"I remember balking at the outrageous price for the land, even the swamps, but Stu said, and I remember this to this day, 'Don't begrudge them getting rich. We'll be the ones later laughing all the way to the bank.'

"To make a long story short, we, the firm, not only blessed the idea, but were able to structure it most favorably. I had some money in rather disappointing investments and asked to throw in. Our Dad got in on it, too. Even Isaac Jefferson was in on it, although Dan fronted the money and never let him know until we sold.

"Coinciding nicely with kids in college with scholarships not covering nearly enough; that would be Maggie, Bo, and Emily; Stu told us that the time was right, that the land was reaching its peak and he had interested buyers. To put it mildly, he sold the land for a bundle, a very, very big bundle. Again, I will toot my own horn by saying that we, the firm, structured it most advantageously. Dan put his considerable share into the trust."

Trey pulled out his business card holder and on a card from it wrote a number with a lot of zeroes and passed the card over to Tom. "Look familiar?" Seeing from the look on Tom's face that it indeed did, he said, "End of story. More wine?"

On the way back to Trey's house, again in a horse drawn carriage, although this time under the stars, Tom asked Katie, "So what was my folly?" Her response was classic.

"Well, duh, there was that second tour in Vietnam, all that Camp Marion and SOG business, Desert Shield and Desert Storm, politics and, oh, the list goes on. Maybe I'm on it too."

In a rare occurrence of not to be outdone with his wife of so many years, Tom smiled and said, "No, no, no, maybe, maybe, and hell no."

Tom went back to his endeavors with a lighter heart. Mostly though he was enjoying an idyllic life with Katie and the grandchildren, as well as with his two best friends, Don Kennedy and Isaac Jefferson.

17

FOR TOM HOWARD, THANKSGIVING IN 2011 WAS GOING TO BE MON-
umental for the family and the extended family; the "old timers" from
Camp Marion and their families; and the returning heroes from Alpha
Company and their families. It would be celebrated at Carlisle. His
invitations were tantamount to patriarchal edicts and were treated as
such by all. Tom included the island's permanent residents and made
sure they profited nicely from providing the caterers the low country fare
that would accompany the prime ribs and acclaimed cobbler desserts.

Planning for it had commenced months earlier with the vigor and
detail of a man with entirely too much time on his hands, money to
burn, and the determination that the event would be a memorable one
indeed. Tom had a massive tent erected with a wooden floor and seating for more than two hundred, surrounded by large fans in case the
ocean breeze failed them (with space heaters standing by in case the
thermometer did). A sound system and six gigantic flat screens were
installed for the PowerPoint presentation he and Emily Jefferson were
conspiring, with strictest secrecy, to create. Katie and Maggie, of course,
were included, but even from them Tom withheld the final product. Tom
arranged for entertainment, a bagpiper to set things off and for after
dinner an Irish balladeer and comedian from Savannah's River Street.
He rented a second ferry boat to facilitate getting everyone on and off
the island without undue delay, and another just for the caterers and

vendors. He sought perfection. Above all, he prayed daily to the good Lord above to grant him fine, warm weather.

And it all came together.

Now, after a joyous afternoon of glorious coastal Carolina fall weather; fellowship of family and friends, old and new; and the insurmountable thrill of watching and listening to children and grandchildren having a wonderful time, the group assembled under the tent at their designated places at the tables. Flanking Tom on the dais were his wife Katie, looking fine as ever and clearly enjoying the event as much as he; his mother, now known to all (even him) as "Gramm'um," the matriarch of the family and at 85 still a force, albeit benevolent, to be reckoned with; and his two best friends, Don Kennedy and Isaac Jefferson.

In addition to seats for those on the dais, the large table front center was occupied by Sarah Jefferson, Eve Kennedy (finally!), and Tom's Aunt Jean, always a hoot (and a dangerous confederate with Eve, particularly with alcohol involved). That table was flanked on one side by one with Tom and Katie's Jonathan, Maggie and Bo with their spouses, Isaac and Sarah's Emily and her husband, and the current Alpha Company commander and his wife. The growing families of each were in tables behind them. On the other side of the front center table was a table with Bill Greer and his wife, Trey Greer and his, the current commander of Camp Marion and his wife, Craig Clark and his, and the elder of the Carlisle families and his wife.

Tom walked to the podium, its front adorned with the crest of 15th SOG and a family crest no one could identify, settled the crowd, and welcomed and thanked them for being there. At his direction, the assemblage stood as one and remained standing for the Pledge of Allegiance to an enormous flag spanning the end wall of the tent behind the dais and then joined in singing the national anthem, wondrously led by a Marion Chapel choir member. Only some of the children needed to refer to the lyrics as they appeared on the large screens. Isaac Jefferson followed with a perfect prayer.

Taking their seats, each person found on his or her plate three bronze challenge coins, those of 15th SOG, Alpha Company's with the fierce wild boar logo, and a new one crafted to memorialize their contributions to and their combat deployments in the War on Terror. As the caterers flocked to serve the food and beverages, Tom paused a few moments before taking his seat at the table to once again behold and marvel at the happy congregation arrayed before him and gave his own silent prayer of thanks to God.

The crowd again quieted as they launched into the appetizer of fresh shrimp cocktail and/or chilled fresh oysters, then salad, and then the main course of prime rib along with the choice of fried shrimp, steamed oysters and/or crab (or for the children the necessary chicken tenders). As plates were being cleared to make room for the cobbler and ice cream dessert, the screens came to life and displayed a series of Thanksgiving wishes from dignitaries, some video-recorded and others e-mailed with the text and their photographs, names and titles (some, like the President and the First Lady, the Governor, former Senator Ernest "Fritz" Hollings, Beaufort Mayor Billy Keyserling and Charleston Mayor Joe Riley needing no identification). As the cobbler dessert disappeared, the screens switched to images of and relating to Camp Marion and people one way or another associated with it, orchestrated to not only entertain, some uproariously, but to set the stage for what was to be the culmination.

And then it was time.

On cue, "the girls," as Tom could not refrain from calling them, Maggie, Emily, Bethany and Arie, had the younger children ushered out by the bagpiper with squeals of delight to play under the watchful eyes of two young ladies from church. On surreptitious cue, Don Kennedy then stepped up to the podium and called the people to order, telling them that Tom Howard had "a few" words (holding up and wiggling the fore and middle fingers of each hand to playfully mock the word "few") and suggested that they govern themselves accordingly by fortifying themselves with filled glasses, with reinforcements standing by. Tom joined in the laughter Don predictably brought on and allowed his glass to be filled as well.

Few were surprised that Tom would speak. This, after all, was his affair and there was no doubt that he had spent a fortune on it. Also, few of his secret machinations had remained secret. The gathering quieted in anticipation. Even the remaining older children complied, sensing that this may be an historic occasion in their young lives.

Tom squeezed Katie's hand, stood and stepped up to replace Don at the podium. He slowly made eye contact with each and every person assembled there. Then he began.

"We gather here today on this dedicated day of thanksgiving to give thanks to the Almighty for His many blessings, as do millions of our fellow Americans. However, we here at this place have more cause to do so than many of them because the Lord has bestowed upon us, each and every one of us, more blessings than most.

"The good reverend has already thanked the Lord for all of us for the second safe return of Alpha Company from Afghanistan." Raising his glass, Tom called for a toast to them for their service and sacrifice. When the people had settled back into their seats, Tom resumed.

"Thanksgiving, as we all know, is said to have originated in the early 1600's in Plymouth, Massachusetts, with the Pilgrims. The Pilgrims, of course, were immigrants. A century ago, my grandfather was an immigrant. So, a little trip down memory lane, if y'all don't mind.

"My grandfather, Carl Howard, Mister Carl, came to this country as a young teenager. Actually, he was sent here, alone, at that tender age. Why, I do not know. Oddly enough, that question was never, to my knowledge, asked. Oh, I have my suppositions and trust me when I say that I could bore you to tears, sleep, or flight with them and the ultimately pointless philosophical and theological thoughts stemming from them, but give thanks that I only impose on my dear friends Don Kennedy and Isaac Jefferson to humor such foolishness.

"My grandfather was sent to this foreign land alone with the name and address of a relative in New York who would take him in for a time. It was not long before he made his way to Charleston and then down here to Beaufort. I can't tell you why or how it came to be, but for whatever the reason and means, I am eternally grateful.

"A little side trip here, a bit of trivia. 'Beaufort' obviously means 'beautiful fort,' but the settlement here was not as many suppose, given its name from a beautiful fort here. I expect there was something of a fort as the native Indians were not at all happy with the intrusion, but the name 'Beaufort' bears its name for no apparent reason from English nobleman Henry Somerset of the House of Beaufort.

"Anyway, back to where I was. Carl Howard came here and he labored as a 'swamp logger,' as the older of you may remember he was fond to call himself. Few of you may know this, but back and before then, Irish immigrants were not held in high regard. The story goes that back before the Civil War the swamps around here teemed with malarial mosquitos and rather than risking the lives of valuable slaves, wealthy landowners used Irish contract workers. It was with an Irish gang of swamp loggers, probably descendants of those men, with whom my grandfather signed on under a helluva man named Jimbo Thompson, with whom my father and even I worked later in life as well."

"After but a few years, Carl Howard went off to war, World War One, the War to End All Wars. Few of us know, however, that in reality he was not just over there, but he was *back* over there." That certainly piqued interest.

"You see, he had come to America not as 'Carl with a 'c' Howard,' but as 'Karl' with a 'k' *Hughard*' [pronouncing it as "hyoo-yard"]. The image of the family crest that adorned the podium now appeared on the screens. "'Hughard' is an ancient, noble German name. It literally means 'brave heart.'

"Why, when, and how my grandfather became 'Carl Howard' is forever lost, but presumably it was to better fit in here across the ocean.

Interestingly, some say that the common English name 'Howard' originated from 'Hughard;' others say that its roots instead are the Anglo-Scandinavian 'Haward,' meaning 'high guardian.'

"Be that as it may, a brave heart my grandfather had indeed and he also was a guardian. He volunteered to serve in the Army during World War One." An aged, grainy photograph of the young man in doughboy uniform appeared on the screens. "He was trained as a mechanic, but found himself in combat nevertheless. He was brave and he was a hero." An image of the newspaper article Bill Greer had shown Carl so many years before, skillfully redacted and highlighted by Emily, appeared on the screens, followed by the image of Carl's Victory Medal with silver star affixed.

"He survived his wounds suffered at Meuse-Argonne and returned to Beaufort where he met, courted and married Faith, an Irish girl, a fierce Irish girl as I am told." An aged wedding photograph appeared on the screens, followed by photographs from their 50th anniversary.

"With the help of Bill Greer (that's the elder Bill Greer, Katie's grandfather), they moved into what we call the 'old homeplace' and started the mechanic business and started a family." Photographs of young Dan and Bob Howard appeared. "Then and through the Great Depression, when people could hardly pay, Carl offset the shortfalls in cash by working relentlessly. And with trades of stuff, including land. By the late 1940's, Carl and his son, my father Daniel, had amassed holdings of hundreds of low country acres. But again, I get ahead of myself.

"In 1939, with Germany and Japan seeking and acting to conquer their neighbors and more, a war involving the United States was obviously imminent, although our leaders chose to bury their heads in the sand and most Americans followed suit. My father was not one of them.

"Dan Howard enlisted. He chose the Marine Corps and was a corporal by the time he and his fellow Marines landed on Guadalcanal under the command of the legendary Chesty Puller." The screens now showed young Dan Howard, robust and proud in the dress blues he likely had borrowed or rented for the photograph, followed by another picture of him, this time rail thin and darkly tanned on an island beach.

"My father spoke little of that time, but we know he fought bravely, heroically, there and later on, at Peleliu, where he was seriously wounded, rendered unfit for further combat duty." The photograph that Major Church's research had produced appeared on the screens. "That's my Dad on the ground with the bandages and leg splint. The guy with the pipe is Chesty Puller.

"Dad stayed in the Corps as gunnery sergeant range instructor at Parris Island, for which he was quite renowned, until the end of the war. Not long afterward, he married Miss Bea, Gramm'um, who had been his nurse." The wedding photo appearing on the screens showed the handsome veteran, his eyes glued on Bea, a beauty if there ever was one.

"Dad then went into Grandad's logging business, for a short while, with his little brother, Bob." That brought chuckles to some, those who knew that "Uncle Bob" was a head taller than his brother and years later outweighed him by eighty pounds or more. The screens showed a picture of the three of them standing in front of a truck parked on a logging road in a swamp and holding formidable looking chainsaws.

"I say 'short time' because after just a few short years it was Uncle Bob's turn to take a break from the family business. Some of you perhaps don't know this, but before Uncle Bob made his fortune from the family farm equipment business and car dealership, he fought as a Marine in Korea." That brought chuckles from everyone who had known Bob Howard, because his patent pride in having been a Marine was unremitting. Tom resumed, "He coincidentally served under Chesty Puller, until frozen toes did him in. You see, Uncle Bob was one of the "Frozen Chosin." Tom opted to ignore that some of the younger people sadly did not even know what that meant.

"He jumped right back into the family business and worked hard alongside his father and brother," the screens showing a photo of Uncle Bob proudly standing next to an enormous John Deere feller-buncher logging machine, "although he did take some time to play too." The screens showed Bob leaning out of the driver's window of his "pride and joy," the awe-inspiring '55 Chevy race car which to the day still adorned the showroom floor of the car dealership.

"Then it was my turn. Vietnam." Although he had carefully scripted with Emily the PowerPoint, taking pains to minimize himself, she went "off the reservation" at this point by flashing pictures of Tom in his Citadel cadet uniform, he as a second lieutenant in full battle gear knee deep in a rice paddy, Tom's favored photo of he and Don Kennedy at Don's Special Forces camp, and then he in his green beret with Katie lovely in a sun dress. Tom frowned until the last two and had to smile when mischievous smiles on the faces of Katie, Maggie, and Emily revealed that they were proud parties to the crime.

"Afterward," Tom continued, "somehow I was tagged to help bring to fruition Senator Strom Thurmond's idea of preserving the skills hard learned over there. Senator Fritz Hollings was instrumental in it too. That was what led to Camp Marion and 15th SOG. It may have started out with me as the only 'boots on the ground,' but it was saved from probable foundering by some truly amazing people.

"There can never be Camp Marion tributes without first spotlighting Miss Margaret, bless her soul." Several photographs of the wonderful lady over the years appeared on the screens. "She in fact was first after me, a gift from heaven and Bill Greer, and she was the glue that held us together and made some sense out of what we were stumbling and bumbling about. It is certainly no overstatement to say that Camp Marion would never have happened without her.

"When I say 'we,' my little band of rogues at what were to be 15th SOG and Camp Marion started with Command Sergeant Major Hector Ramirez, God rest his soul." Hector's photo appeared on the screen, his uniform displaying an incredible array of ribbons, awards, and badges. "He, as you can see, was a bear of a man, the absolute epitome of a Green Beret, and just a fine, fine fellow. I cajoled him to join me. No, that's not right. He *jumped* at the opportunity for that's what Green Berets fundamentally do, create formidable fighting forces. 15th SOG never would have happened but for him either.

"Don Kennedy here was the second man I recruited for 15th SOG. As many of you know, I met Don when I was working for his father, a colonel with three wars to his credit, a chest full of medals, and a combat jump star on his parachutist wings. Colonel Kennedy was more than that though. He was the last of the great gentleman colonels of days sadly gone by.

"Don was the one who got me into this business, deviously so, I might add. He was, and still is, a 'sneaky Pete' in more ways than one. I was a leg during my first Vietnam tour. For the one person in this room who may not happen to know what a 'leg' is, it is what we paratrooper types call people too smart to willingly, some indeed joyfully, jump out of operational aircraft. Anyway, my being a leg embarrassed Don, so he conspired with his father to have me go through jump school and then Ranger school. I later followed in his footsteps as a green beanie and we were back in Vietnam at the same time." The photo of the two of them at Don's camp again appeared, followed by one of Don towering over his Montagnard mercenaries, and then one from his Distinguished Service Cross award ceremony.

Don frowned over at Eve, knowing she had dug all but the first out of a box buried in a closet, to which she responded by sticking her tongue out at him. Her timing was poor because as she was doing that, Tom drew everyone's eyes to Don and her by adding, "Don Kennedy, ladies and gentlemen, stands on level with my father and grandfather as the bravest men I ever met." The screens then displayed the last photo zoomed in to focus on Don's ribbons, the top row of which with the DSC added, would be entirely awards for valor. Don flushed and groaned and Tom let him off the hook.

"Y'all may not know this, but Eve was with us from nearly the beginning too." Her photo came up on the screens, depicting her looking fine in a t-shirt and jeans in one of her many planted fields on Camp Marion. Another equally flattering one appeared with her dressed for an occasion. Tom continued, "How Don waited so many years before hooking up with her just boggles my mind." He playfully let Eve suffer during the crowd's embarrassing concurrence and then let her off the hook too.

"Anyway, with Hector and Don on board, we were able to draw in more impressive, remarkable warriors, both for the A-team and the Ranger platoon. One was Craig Clark here and another, 'Corndog,' who I am sure you old-timers will recall, both with whom I am proud to have served in the delta. Don did a splendid job and deserves the primary credit for the renown the Swamp Hogs earned and the foundation upon which their later, and current, fine reputation was built." The people began to clap for Don and then they stood and cheered him, even while most silently recognized Tom's self-effacement.

"And last, but certainly not least, the Reverend Doctor Isaac Jefferson. Before the Lord sent Sarah to save him and lead him to be a soldier of Christ, the good reverend was a warrior of a different sort." The screens showed a young black man with a bit of an afro, love beads, a Jimi Hendrix red bandana, and incongruously an M60 machine gun. That stirred the viewers. Isaac groaned out loud, started to glare at Sarah, the responsible party, but could not do it. Instead he merely smiled over at her.

"He was the guy you didn't want to be seen associating with in the rear, but wanted at your side when the bullets were flying. He was the iconic machine gunner courageously, selflessly, and heroically saving his friends.

"Here is a man who expected to return to Detroit, of all damned places, likely to be defeated by all the ugliness of the era, who instead was steered by an angel named Sarah and ordained as a minister destined to be to this day *our* minister." The screens displayed a photograph of a happy and proud Reverend Jefferson taken at the blessing of Marion Chapel. The words, images, and personal memories of virtually all present, many of whom were his parishioners, prompted another standing ovation.

"These men served our country admirably and went on to serve her and us laudably at Camp Marion." Tom paused as a series of photographs flashed on the screens depicting those and other men at the camp over the first ten years of 15th SOG's existence.

Tom resumed. "As I was saying though, my grandfather fought in the First World War, my father fought in the second, my Uncle Bob in Korea, and my friends and I in Vietnam. I don't believe it's too bold to say that we made the world safer for democracy. But we could not make the world *safe* for democracy. There remained many who despised and continue to despise Americans for what we have, who and what we are, what we stand for.

"Jonathan, my oldest, was next to go. He grew up on Camp Marion and around Camp Marion families. By the time he finished high school, he was fluent in Spanish and Vietnamese and could get by in Korean and German." Photographs appeared on the screens showing Jon with Hector's Mex-Viet children and Jon working in the Mexasian restaurant Hector's wife ran. "He should have capitalized on that linguistic aptitude at college, but he chose not to. Instead he chose to enlist." Pausing for effect, Tom added, "He and I had a chat about that."

When the appreciative laughter died out, Tom continued. "His timing was awful. He was a tanker in the 3rd Armored Division..." (the screens displaying a great photo of Jon on the turret roof of an Abrams tank at a tank range in Grafenwöhr, Germany)... "and he deployed with them for Desert Shield and Desert Storm." A photo of Jon and his fellow crewmembers standing before a dustier tank in the desert came up. "Unlike me safely ensconced in the rear, he was enmeshed with the first major tank warfare since World War Two, and he came back a decorated hero.

"Someone finally tripped across his 201 file though and learned that he had more to offer the Army. The Army offered to send him to college and let him choose the University of Georgia." After the expected catcalls from loyal South Carolinians, Tom went on: "At least they're Bulldogs and win a lot more football games than my Bulldogs do.

"Jon graduated with a degree in foreign languages and pursued a career path in Military Intelligence. He deployed to Afghanistan a number of times and then was back in Iraq, this time at the same time as my younger son, Bo. You may have seen their picture in the news?" The famous Time magazine cover page appeared on the screens, to the delight of all. "Both my boys came back as heroes." That triggered a standing ovation and cheers.

"For those of you who may not know, Jon, back in Afghanistan, was the mastermind behind your kicking such serious ass in Joint Task Force Midway and Operation Dark Knight." Tom could not just pause there. With those words and a displayed photograph of the Hog Heaven sign standing before battered sandbags launched the members of 15th SOG to their feet with wild, prideful cheers.

"Jon, as many of you, still serves today. He went on to the JCS, Joint Chiefs of Staff, and as you earlier heard from President Obama, served him well as a deputy National Security Advisor." On the screens appeared a photo of Jon and the President in the Oval Office. It was not the typical posed Oval Office shot (one of which Jon had), but instead caught the two of them obviously poring over documents or images (the same having been blurred before the photograph was released) with the CIA director and an admiral looking over their shoulders. It was with transparent pride that Tom added, "I may be gone from Washington, but I still have friends there and the word is that Jon's impending star is expected to be only his first." More applause.

"Bo's feats, on the other hand, were somewhat less clandestine." A photo of Bo in full "battle rattle" appeared, followed by that Tom and Emily could not help but to again show the famous Time picture. As it was then followed by one of Bo with the Capitol in the background, Tom continued, "As you know, he followed me in Congress and I am proud to confess that by all credible accounts he is doing a much better job. And as for him, let me just borrow another cliché and toss out another idiom by saying, 'Stay tuned, sports fans.'" Tom once again paused until applause quieted down.

"Now, let us rightfully focus on you." For many minutes, Tom individually called the 15th SOG veterans to their feet with specific accolades for each, culminating with the heartwarming and inspirational iconic Lee Greenwood rendition of *God Bless the U.S.A.* while the screens displayed the image of an American flag fluttering in the breeze,

Tom then allowed a few necessary moments for everyone to compose themselves before continuing: "So, why this history lesson, this trip down memory lane?" He left the question hanging before answering it. "Because that is who we are, what we are. Proud warriors one and all." He paused yet again for effect, his eyes slowly and deliberately sweeping the assemblage. "But, my friends, it is not all we are.

"We Howards all married well; very, very well. Katie, the love of my life who I thank God for every day, *every* day." Another splendid photo of Katie graced the screens with Tom beckoning her to stand, followed by photographs of all the Howards with their wives with Tom naming each and having them stand as well.

"So did you, Isaac." And Isaac Jefferson smiled broadly because he knew it was true. Sarah reluctantly stood as several photos of her flicked on the screens. "And you, Don," a sunrise photo of Eve and him on the Edisto dunes appearing. "And so did *all* you men." A series of photographs danced across the screens of the 15th SOG men and their wives, to the absolute delight of all.

"And see what we produced. My immediate family, my sons, and my daughter Maggie, Doctor Maggie, the beloved Charleston pediatrician; and 'little sister' Emily Jefferson, who we claimed as family when she was a child and who predictably has gone on from being a trusted advisor to Mayor Joe Riley to a mover and shaker herself," each with respective photos. "And their better halves," with photos of Bethany, Arie and Maggie and Emily's husbands appearing. "And just look at these darlings," as wonderful photos of the many Howard grandchildren joyously cascaded and then uproariously morphed into dozens of the children of Alpha Company members.

And then it was time to settle down. The video culmination was a slowly revolving video camera suspended from the center of the grand tent with a live feed to the screens. Tom Howard silently and patiently allowed for a full revolution and then the screens fading to the video of a sunrise over the Carolina beach before concluding, his face solemn.

"My friends, why did I, why did I on this day of thanksgiving, this day of celebration, feel the need to remind you of the warriors among us? Why indeed?" Tom paused as he once again made eye contact with all and he satisfied himself that he had their full attention.

"To pose to you this ultimate question: What did we warriors achieve from our legacy of devotion to duty, our sacrifices, our valor?" Pausing one last time, Tom took a deep breath and closed.

"Let me share with you the answer, what I am confident to be the undeniably correct answer that has taken me a lifetime to realize. Here it is:

"Look around you one more time. Please, look at one another. See each other. We gathered here are all family. We here are one family. We here are a proud family. We here are a blessed family. We are happy. We are loved. We are secure. And we are free. Those things, those invaluable, inviolate, invincible things, my dear brave hearts, are our triumph."

Poor is the country that has no heroes, but beggared is that people who, having them, forgets.

—Unknown, taken from *Mike Force*
by Lt. Col. L.H. "Bucky" Burruss

SUGGESTED READING

Dear Reader: If you are an avid reader, as am I, of works that chronicle and celebrate those brave men and women who faced the ultimate test of fortitude and from them are a lesson to us all, I truly hope that you in particular found this work satisfying. To you I offer these better works in case you somehow missed them. I heartily recommend each one. ("f" denotes fiction.)

— Ray Mayer

AUTHOR'S ALL TIME FAVORITES
Once an Eagle (f), Anton Myrer.
We Were Soldiers Once… And Young, Harold Moore and Joe Galloway.

CAN'T GO WRONG AUTHORS
Ambrose, Stephen
Atkinson, Rick
Bond, Larry (f)
Bowden, Mark
Clancy, Tom (f +)
Coyle, Harold (f)
Griffin, W.E.B. (f)
Lester, Rick (Richard A.), if he ever blesses us with his book of stories
Nolan, Keith William

340

Pressfield, Steven
Shaara, Jeff and Michael
West, Bing

WORLD WAR TWO
Ambrose, Hugh, *The Pacific*
Camp, *Last Man Standing*
Sledge, *With the Old Breed*

KOREA
Brady, *The Marines of Autumn*
Drury and Clavin, *The Last Stand of Fox Company*

VIETNAM
Brokhausen, *We Few*
Bunch and Cole, *A Reckoning for Kings (f)*
Caputo, *A Rumor of War*
Del Vecchio, *The 13th Valley (f)*
Gwin, *Baptism*
Marlantes, *Matterhorn (f)*
Roth, *Sand in the Wind (f)*
Webb, *Fields of Fire* (f)

WAR ON TERROR
Bellavia, *House to House, a Soldier's Memoir* (the quote in Chapter Four is from this book, the end of the Prologue)
Luttrell, *Lone Survivor*
Naylor, *Not a Good Day to Die*
Scahill, *Dirty Wars*
Tapper, *The Outpost*
Zucchino, *Thunder Run*

… and last, but certainly not least, I highly recommend you go to my publisher's web site — www.deedspublishing.com — for military books they have published before mine:

WORLD WAR ONE
Bach/Hall, *The 4th Division in the World War*

WORLD WAR TWO
Babcock, *War Stories: Utah Beach to the Liberation of Paris*
Babcock, *War Stories: Paris to VE Day*
Beichl, *Reported Killed in Action*
Denton, *World War II WAC*
DeVos, *Family of Warriors (f)*
Speranza, *Nuts!*
Williams, *Dear Dad*

KOREA
Clark, *Massacre at Hill 303*

VIETNAM
Babcock, *War Stories: Vietnam 1966–1970*
Babcock, *What Now, Lieutenant?*
Childs, *The Battle for Chu Moor Mountain*
Eisenbrandt, *Vietnam Nurse*
Jimison, *Dear Mark*
Lawrence, *Reflections on LZ Albany*

WAR ON TERROR
Babcock, *Operation Iraqi Freedom I: A Year in the Sunni Triangle*

SPECIAL THANKS

NO BOOK, ESPECIALLY NOT THIS ONE, BECOMES ONE WITHOUT EX-traordinary, essential help. I first want to thank my wife, Julie, for bearing with me the many, many hours devoted to this work and for her editorial assistance (she, being a most avid reader, quick to spot overlooked errors). Next, thanks go to my son, Wes, a University of Georgia Grady School of Journalism grad whose input also was invaluable. And then there is Rick Lester, a Charlie model gunship pilot in Vietnam, my CO in A-5/32 Armor in the 24th Infantry Division and a career Army officer, whom I am proud to call my friend and even more proud that he calls me one. He opened the door to me at Deeds Publishing. And, last but not least, the folks at Deeds. Bob Babcock made the publishing process pure joy, something I am confident few authors can say of their publishers, and I thank and praise him, as I do Mark Babcock for the layout and magnificent cover design.

—Ray Mayer

. . . AND A FINAL REQUEST TO YOU, THE READER:

Please be so kind as to take the time to post a review of *From Valor, Triumph* on Amazon and wherever else you may care to, the importance of which cannot be overstated. *Thank you.*

ABOUT THE AUTHOR

Ray Mayer is a Citadel graduate, was an Army officer (a tanker, M60A1's) and then before retirement was a lawyer in Georgia, a career prosecutor. He and his wife Julie enjoy the magnificent life of the northeast Georgia mountains.